That Summer at the Seahorse Hotel

Adrienne Vaughan

The PARIS PRESS

First published in 2018 by The Paris Press

ISBN: 978-0-9955689-2-1

Copyright © Adrienne Vaughan 2018

The right of Adrienne Vaughan to be identified as the author of this work has been asserted by her in accordance with the Copyright Design and Patents Act 1998.

All rights reserved. No part of this publication may be reproduced, stored in a retrieval system or transmitted in any form or by any means without the prior written permission of the publisher.

Cover based on an original photograph © Shevtsovy

Cover design: Trevor Stocks www.stocksdesign.co.uk

Author photograph: Peter Alvey Photography
www.alveyandtowers.com

ABOUT THE AUTHOR

Adrienne Vaughan has been making up stories since she could speak; initially to entertain her sister Reta, who never allowed a plot or character to be repeated – *tough audience*. As soon as she could pick up a pen she started writing them down.

It was no surprise that Adrienne grew up to be a journalist, diving headfirst into her career after studying at the Dublin College of Journalism. These days she is recognised as a talented author and poet, having published several highly-acclaimed novels and an award-winning collection of short stories and poetry. *That Summer at the Seahorse Hotel* is her fourth novel.

Adrienne lives in rural Leicestershire with her husband, two cocker spaniels and a rescue cat called Agatha Christie. She still harbours a burning ambition to be a 'Bond girl'.

www.adriennevaughan.com

For rights enquiries: lisa.eveleigh@richfordbecklow.co.uk

DEDICATION

For Marion,
my amazing, wonderful and inspirational mother,
with love forever. X

CONTENTS

Acknowledgements
That Summer…
Prologue
The Vampire Set
Sending Signals
Station to Station
Lazarus
A Long Lunch
Smoke and Mirrors
Her Maiden Voyage
Total Recall
Suffering Sabotage
Case Closed
The Kiss of Judas
Something Borrowed
Nothing to Wear
Memory Making
Well, Well, Well.
The Pirate
Archie's Favourite
Food for Thought
Undressed Rehearsal
Sending the Girls In
Honesty is the Best Policy
Trixie's Plan
Needs Must
Treasure Island
The Coffin Dodger
Skullduggery, No Less
Sea Change
To the Bat Caves
The Legacy
Family Affairs
The Understudy

The City that Never Sleeps
Scare Tactics
Not on the Guest List
Champions Await
Stairway to Heaven
The Red Kimono
Showtime
Finale

References
Glossary of Terms & Quotations
Praise for Adrienne Vaughan

This book is a work of fiction. The characters and incidents are either fictitious or are used fictitiously. Any resemblance to any real person or incident is entirely coincidental and not intended by the author.

ACKNOWLEDGEMENTS

Seahorse was inspired by a story I read as a teenager, about a girl inheriting a large estate from a movie star she had never even heard of, so I've always wondered ...

Addicted to theatre and film from an early age, I blame my grandmother Alice Houlihan, who loved 'fil-ums', had a deep affection for Ronald Coleman and herself resembled Mae West.

And her daughter, my mother Marion Wrafter, whose movie knowledge is encyclopaedic, being able to name actors, their spouses and children at a glance – or so it seems. So, to both these wonderful women; thank you for passing on the passion, I'll keep working towards the BAFTA!

I'd like to say a huge thanks to Rebecca Waite, costumier extraordinaire, who has worked with some of the biggest names in the business and on many of today's most successful movies and TV shows, for taking the time to impart in depth details of her fascinating career, so warmly and generously shared; I'm truly grateful.

Also invaluable as 'back stage research' my time on the BBC *Poldark* set as guest of writer Debbie Horsfield and producer Margaret Mitchell of Mammoth Screen Ltd – with special thanks to Aidan Turner and all the cast, I would never have known about the hot water bottles without you!

There at the beginning, my mentor and earth angel, June Tate; copy editor, Julia Gibbs and beta reader/hawk eye, Natalie Keene – who all loved *Seahorse* from the start. My bestest writing buddy, Lizzie Lamb and the New Romantics Press, June Kearns and Mags Cullingford, and all my wonderful friends in the Romantic Novelists' Association – a huge and priceless support.

Massive thanks to one of my favourite authors and pals,

Adele Parks, who finally nailed the title over a glass of wine in The Betjeman Arms. For snippets of detail via my brilliant Facebook team: Martin Stanley, Deirdre Cotter Daly, Aine Daly, Grainne O'Brien, Carol Lanigan, Tawna Wickenden, Katrina Creighton Wrafter, Martin Phillips, Catherine McEvoy, Marie Teresa MacBride Kearney, Jeanie Nic Fhionnlaigh and Isabella Tartaruga.

Special thanks for always believing – my close family and friends – especially Marion, my sister Reta Wrafter, brother-in-law John Reddy and 'one's aunts'.

Added to this, a fond farewell to my dear friend and staunch supporter, the incomparable and hugely missed Madeline Poole. Rest assured the 'Peaker Park' team – Jane, Debs, Vanessa, Carole and Jilly will keep the flag flying, Mads.

At this point, I would like to introduce my fabulous agent Lisa Eveleigh, who is a new and dazzling character in the latest chapter of this author's story. Thanks for taking the leap of faith, Lisa.

And as these final credits roll, to my real-life leading man, Jonathan – thank you for being the star that you are!

PS. One final thank you. I like nothing more than a long-haul flight to pen a few thousand words of my latest tome. Chatting to a charming lady about movies and books on a flight to New York I was convinced my notebook was in my bag until I arrived at my hotel and realised it was missing. Panic set in, hours of work and thousands of words gone – *Seahorse* was sunk!

I called the tour operator, the airport, the airline; I was awake all night – not a word. Anxious hours passed. Then a call; a member of the United Airlines team – a real-life knight in shining armour called Al Balparda – had searched the plane and found the notebook, promising to keep it safe until I could collect it and get on with finishing the story.

And so a happy ending. I sincerely hope you enjoy this book; thank you.

That Summer ...

Through seaweed hair and slitted eyes,
We woke to watch the Sun God rise,
Laid nestled in our sunken dune,
Where swooning, we had bathed in moon.
But night had left us high and dry,
The dawn flashed waves, mid seabirds cry,
And silken sand, now smooth and damp
Gave telling of our lovers' camp.
So fingers touching, side by side,
We stood to face the rising tide,
For soon we would be crying too,
Sweet sea salt tears, soft as the dew
That glistened on the sandy gorse,
Dark, prickly leaves to draw remorse.
Yet solid, in your calm embrace,
We're unashamed, there's no disgrace,
We gave our love, all ours to give
And while I breathe and while I live
My heart is sealed, I'll never tell,
Your secret's safe ... *Seahorse Hotel*

"It is not in the stars to hold our destiny, but in ourselves ..."

William Shakespeare

PROLOGUE

*O*nly minutes before the sun had been shining, the sand warm underfoot as they ran laughing over the dunes, searching for a secret place, somewhere to hide from the world and make love. A love so fresh, so startling, it filled every daylight minute with glittering promises and the long black night with agony; the cruel and constant ache of separation. For their love was forbidden, their love was wrong, their love meant hellfire and eternal damnation and they could not care less, or care more.

The rain was sudden, torrential and hot, the hottest rain she had ever felt. Caught in the downpour they were skittish as puppies, running back to the house. He had taken off his tee-shirt, wrapping it round his precious guitar, desperate to spare it. He tiptoed behind her, upstairs where she found towels and dry socks. There was a shirt stuffed in his duffle bag, a striped one, cool. She put it on, it suited her. She twirled for him, curls flying as she danced, looking under her fringe, eyes alight.

He caught her as she spun and pulling her to him, breathed her in.

"I want that back, it's the only good shirt I have," he said.

"No, I want to keep it."

She stepped away. He lunged at her and she skipped off, breaking into a run along the galleried landing. They were barely clothed as they raced laughing, tripping with giddiness, *to the secret staircase leading to the library. She was half-wearing his shirt, he had pulled on jeans. He was carrying the red kimono, trying to persuade her to swap it for his shirt. She turned quickly to escape him and slipping on silk fell into his arms as they reached the last step. The door, disguised as a bookcase, flew open and they tumbled into the room.*

The first thing she noticed was the silence. Someone had been playing the piano earlier, Elton John, her favourite, Tiny Dancer. *The music had stopped. The grandfather clock chimed the quarter hour.*

A cultured voice cut through the quietude.

"So, The Seahorse Hotel continues to provide its legendary services."

He made a sound, a gasp, all air let out of him. Then pulling her to him, wrapped her in the flash of crimson, hiding her in his embrace. She wriggled free. The room seemed full of people.

Fenella jolted awake, her heart beating hard at the base of her throat. It was the same dream, always the same, as vivid as the actual day yet played out slowly, languidly until it neared the end, the race along the landing, falling into his arms, the rush of excitement, happiness, ecstasy turned so suddenly to fear. Why did the dream never end? She had been there, it had surely been real – the love, the passion. She could feel it still, burning in her chest, whenever and wherever she awoke, London, Hollywood, Paris, she was always in the same place, clawing through the mist, the panic still raw. And then it would melt away, like mist on glass blown by lips, a farewell kiss and she could not remember what had happened next and why she felt so lost, so lonely and abandoned, every time she dreamt that same dream.

Now, in another place and time – and no longer a girl – the dream had come again, ending abruptly as she woke, the room full of people evaporating into the dawn as the trill of the phone nagged her to wakefulness.

"Long distance, Miss Flanagan, Ireland, shall I put it through?"

She knew immediately who it would be, still using a landline, dialling reception. But she was wrong, it was not Archie and when asked if she were sitting down, she pulled the sleep mask from her eyes and sat back, propped on pillows, the call was unprecedented and so was the news.

Barely able to say goodbye, Fenella replaced the receiver. The caller had been calm, imparting the information in an almost business-like fashion and whether Fenella chose to believe it or not, she was to be in no doubt that in the very near future she would lose someone very special indeed. Someone who had shared her dreams, dispelled her nightmares and made her feel, above all else, loved; her greatest ally, at times her deadliest enemy but always her dearest, most precious friend. The kind of friend who knew secrets, secrets hidden in the deepest, darkest corners of her soul and whose vow of silence had helped her survive that terrible day and every day since.

Suddenly desperate to return, she cut short the promotional tour – the film company was piqued – and giving only a vague explanation, packed hurriedly to sit waiting in a daze for the car to the airport, a flight to London and home.

Once back at the Lodge, anxious and weary, she went straight to her room. Trembling, she found herself flicking through pages, an old album, faded photographs; the early days in black and white, then vivid as the seventies and eighties flashed by. Images of the house, the beach, the parties. She stopped.

'The Fabulous Five', he had named them and they were indeed fabulous. Humphrey tall and broad, arms folded across his tanned chest; Archie grinning, tight jeans, hair tamed with a red bandana and the Dark One, chin tilted, sardonic smile, wearing his favourite shirt and the love beads she had made. She touched the image with a finger; caught in his embrace he was tickling her and she was scowling, scowling yet beautiful.

Bernice, the fifth member of the crew, had taken the picture; she had taken hundreds that summer, her new Polaroid camera constantly pointing.

It was Bernice who had made the call, knowing the news would pierce her heart, as indeed her own was pierced. Pain was something they had shared over the years. Pain and passion.

Fenella sank into a chair and closing her eyes allowed herself to go back, back one more time to that day, the day the picture was taken. She must have drifted off, for when she woke her face was wet with tears and the album had been flung across the room, pages ripped from its ageing spine, screwed up and scattered on the floor.

Rubbing at a paper cut, she looked down, her hands stained with print. Had she done this? Desperate yet again, to wipe the memory of the past or worse, frantic to find the memories she had lost, the ones that would not come at all.

As she rose to gather up the shreds scattered about the room, she spied the empty bottle behind the chair. Still no recollection. She gave herself a shake, straightening her shoulders. A change was coming, she knew that. Maybe the time was here at last, time to face the past and look those dark secrets in the eye, whatever devastation the truth might wreak.

She dropped the bottle in the bin, along with the remains of the album. An uncertain future beckoned – and not for the first time.

THE VAMPIRE SET

The stage was set for seduction. Its centre piece a beautiful four-poster bed scattered with cushions, velvet coverlet drawn back revealing crisp white linen, a ribbon of silk on a pillow, sensual, suggestive …

"I could just climb into that and crash," Lol whispered. Mia pulled her colleague out of earshot to where the crew sat huddled on the stairs.

"And action!"

Amelia stood at the window, the carved balustrade before her. She was waiting. Lifting a hand to her hair, she pushed strands loosened by the breeze – wind machine – off her pale face and removing a turquoise glove to secure the comb in her hair, noticed her hand was trembling.

Please don't get make-up on that glove, Mia thought.

The wind was building.

"That wig looks ready to collapse," Lol said.

"Quiet on set!"

They watched as she waited, chewing her lip, drawing the white fur stole over her shoulders.

Or dirty that stole. Mia was anxious.

The dolly bearing the camera slid across the set.

The male lead appeared, cape swirling – dramatic effect. He locked the door.

"What on earth?" Amelia said, aghast. Lol was pleased, the costume worked; he looked threatening and sexy at the same time.

"Tonight, with or without your consent." He moved his

mouth at her lips.

"Really, sir?" she joked; his scent was odd. She tried to relax. He kissed her. She drew back. The camera still rolling. She could smell whiskey.

He whipped off his mask. "You!" She dragged herself back to the script.

"Who else?"

That's not the line they rehearsed, Mia thought.

"How dare you?" She pushed past him, he wobbled, regained his balance.

"Sir, if you think I will acquiesce, you are much mistaken," she said.

His line now. "It's you making, er ... the mistake." *Oh dear.*

"I will *not* submit."

He flung himself at her, missing his mark, they scrabbled about.

"Still rolling," called the director.

Lol pulled a face at Mia; that would have to be cut. The camera swung back, the boom operator sidestepping the action.

The male actor said something too quietly, the soundman fiddled with a control.

He took a dagger from its sheath and – camera moving in – held it against her throat. He kissed her again, biting her lip. Close-up on the blood. Close-up on eyes flaring.

Lol shook her head.

Amelia was over-acting.

"It's supposed to be a parody," Mia whispered.

"Tragedy more like." Lol hissed in reply.

The actor pushed the blade at her mouth, sliding the metal from her lip, splitting the skin – good special effects. It oozed bright blood. He took the knife to the bodice of her gown. Camera pulling back. Boom in.

"I will devour every inch of you, your mouth, your breasts, your heart, you will be mine,"

"I will not be a victim," she said haughtily.

Mia caught Lol's eye, Amelia did haughty very well.

"No, not a victim," he said in his rich, deep voice. "But my wife, I will take you and you will take me."

He pushed her against the wall. The camera rolled in. Holding her tightly, he placed the dagger at the fabric stretched across her breasts.

"I will drink of you and you of me."

He took the knife to the cloth. It jagged.

He tried again. It snagged.

He looked at her, she at him. She used unseen fingers to pull at the fabric. He tried again.

"CUT!" someone yelled. "For Christ's sake, *wardrobe!* Shouldn't it just come apart?"

"Bugger," the vampire said, disappointed he had not witnessed Amelia's bosom spilling out; this part had to have some perks. "That's the first time we got that dialogue right all morning."

"First time *you* got it right, you mean." She twisted free.

"Dresser, is there a dresser on set?" one of the assistant directors called. Mia passed an armful of hot water bottles to Lol.

"Not your shout," Lol dropped the bottles on the stair. "Let's grab some grub before the hordes descend." It was nearly noon.

"Someone has to go." Mia replied, ignoring the offer of an early lunch.

"It's Poppy's job and she's busy with her own *leading man*, not our problem." Lol said. Mia handed over the clipboard and wrapping extravagant locks in a high ponytail scurried away, tiptoeing over cables as she raced towards the puce-faced assistant director.

"They nearly got it right that time," he growled.

"Not my actor," she said quickly. "But I can sort it."

"How long?"

"Ten minutes, max." She ferreted in her kit bag, clear plastic, so she could see quickly what was needed.

A loud groan, the sound of wood splintering, masonry cracking and then a gasp as the balustrade gave way, the vampire had been leaning on it, swigging from a hipflask. He disappeared. People started shouting, running in every direction. The vampire sat in the midst of the rubble, brushing brick dust from his cloak.

"Let's call it a day," the director announced.

The second assistant sighed. "Will we ever finish this bloody shoot? Every time we need to be outside it rains. Every time we're on set, something falls apart."

Mia peered out through the gaping hole in the backdrop, bits of balcony strewn across the lawn. Beyond the set she could see a forest of trees sweeping up the mountain, a glint of sea and there like a halo, a new rainbow, bright, fresh and feisty. The view was so vivid, so beautiful it took her breath away. *Oh, what she would not give to be out there.* She looked down at the rubble.

The vampire slid into view, a flurry of first aiders checking him out.

"I'm fine, honestly," he lisped through dislodged fangs.

"Is he drunk?" the second assistant asked, wide-eyed. Mia ignored the question, picking up discarded clothing. She liked the vampire, one of her mother's former paramours. There had always been a long line of suitors where her mother was concerned, most of them merged and mingled, always friendly, always kind, yet none of them really interested in the actress's only child. The girl with no father, not one that had ever been named, officially anyway.

One did stand out, quite spectacularly of course, the one and only Aloysius Fermoy Fitzgerald, known by his stage name Archie Fitz. Dear Archie, the most remarkable of her mother's friends, if not always for the most wholesome of reasons. She looked at the vampire. He and Archie had fallen out, some long ago argument they could not remember but would never forgive. The vampire placed the classic brogues before her.

"Be a darling and make these more comfortable, can you?" he begged, fangs now pocketed. "They're rubbing my heels, no skin left." She gazed into his dark, bloodshot eyes. He looked worn out, every century etched on his pale, blood-sucking face. Shoes were outside her area, footwear a professional cobbler's job, they would have to be sent away, more delay.

"No problem, James." Mia took the shoes. "When do you need them for?"

"How do I bloody know?" he called back, painfully picking his way across the floor to the sanctuary of his dressing room and a good stiff whiskey.

Lol had retreated to the wardrobe truck.

"Don't do his shoes for him," she said, blowing smoke through her nostrils.

"If you get caught …" Mia warned, eyeing the roll-up. Lol shrugged.

"Old soak. If he wasn't half-cut all the time we'd be finished by now. Good job he didn't break his bleedin' neck, they'd have to find a stand in, even more hanging around. Should just can the whole thing."

Mia was only half-listening, she was checking costumes, pinning on names of actors, notes about alterations, repairs.

"Poppy's always missing, skeleton staff that's what we are." Lol was lighting another cigarette. "Who's our union rep? We get paid little enough, friggin' slave labour."

"Go away if you're going to smoke, out of the truck!" Mia was firm.

Lol extinguished the cigarette, waving to disperse the smoke.

Mia's phone trilled. She pulled it out of her pocket.

A text.

How's it going? When will you be back? R x

Lol watched Mia's face soften.

"Lover boy?" she asked, something indefinable in her tone. "Missing you, is he?"

Mia caught her breath, suddenly elated; her man, her lovely man, wanted her home. His timing was perfect, how she missed him, longed for him. Ignoring Lol she tried to text back, fingers full of pins. She hit call. Straight to voicemail. Despite being high in the Wicklow Mountains there was hardly any signal.

"No reply?" Lol craned her neck to look at Mia's phone.

Mia did not comment. Lol was a good friend but an incorrigible gossip. Ten years Mia's senior, Lol had been 'back stage' all her life. Sneeringly cynical about affairs of the heart, Lol had been single for as long as Mia had known her and little wonder. Lol was permanently annoyed, snarling and spitting her way through the day, drinking and smoking her way through the night; though just caffeine and tobacco, these days.

Sometimes Mia wished Lol would consider an alternative career. A dresser was a young person's job; tiring, relentless, often unappreciated and at times desperately lonely. Filled with warm camaraderie while on location but suddenly sad when a movie wrapped, the party over and no one home to welcome you back to a semblance of normality. "A professional vagrant." Her mother called her. Mia was determined not to end up like Lol. The very thought filled her with dread. She would have a profession and a personal life, whatever it cost. She twisted the makeshift ring on her finger.

"A cup of tea?" she asked her colleague. "Nah, let's knock off, I'm knackered."

Mia gestured at the costumes filling the truck, the third assistant director had just delivered the call sheet for the next day. "There's work to do."

"Leave you to it, then." Lol grabbed her bag. The door opened onto the courtyard, it was already dusk, the navy blue sky bubbling with black clouds. "It's nearly dark, we can make an early start tomorrow."

"Just another hour or so," Mia said. "I'll see you later." She closed the door, relieved. Maybe she could get ahead, nail some of the trickier tasks. The costumes for the grand finalé were complex, many pieces needed bringing together to create the perfect ensemble for each character attending a fabulous, eighteenth century masked ball. Besides, Mia liked to work alone, do things her way.

She always had.

SENDING SIGNALS

"Are you *still* on location?" The distinctive, classically-trained voice sounded exasperated.

"Yes, for another week or so, why?" Mia was surprised. Her mother rarely called and never used the mobile; Fenella considered communication her daughter's duty. Besides, the actress was incredibly busy, always in demand and Mia could ring Trixie, Fenella's personal assistant, if it was urgent, no need to bother her mother with anything trivial, no need at all. Fenella took a deep breath wishing she had persuaded Trixie to make the call.

"Darling, I've terribly sad news. Are you in the middle of something?" Fenella was desperate for a way out.

Mia had just finished for the day and was in no mood for her mother. She always felt she had to stand to attention when she spoke to the 'great actress', ensure every word uttered assured her parent everything was just so, nothing to worry or even think about. All was well in Mia's world, always. She glanced around the dank caravan, dishes in the sink, duvets dumped in piles. All she wanted to do was kick off her shoes, pour a glass of wine and telephone Rupert, her relatively new and rather fabulous fiancé, indulging in a long, amorous call, full of lust, longing and desire.

"No, nothing in particular." Mia was nonplussed. Her mother's idea of terribly sad and her own were aeons apart. Perhaps a favourite plant had wilted, a treasured gown torn, a precious book lost.

"Are you sitting down?"

"Yes," Mia lied.

"Prepare yourself … it's Archie."

Mia stopped twirling a strand of conker-coloured hair. "Sorry?"

"Uncle Archie, darling. I'm afraid he's worsened." Fenella's voice faded.

"But, he was getting better, his treatment …" Mia blurted.

"The cancer's spread, more tumours ... he won't be with us much longer."

"How long?"

"I'm not sure." Fenella had no idea, Bernice had been vague or perhaps Fenella had just not taken it in.

"But, I need to see him, I must …" Mia looked out of the small window, the glass splattered with watery tears. The moon was trying to break free as grey mist clung to the mountain.

Fenella swallowed. Trixie was listening.

"Yes, of course, darling. He's asking for us, you in particular. So, if you can, be there … I mean." Quiet again. "But if you can't, he'll totally understand, we all will. Remember him as he was, the last time you saw him. When was that?"

"What?" Mia gave her head a shake.

"The last time you saw Archie, darling?" Fenella could see Trixie glaring.

"Florence, I think. Yes. I was working."

"We had that lovely day together, the three of us," Fenella confirmed. "A concert in the Boboli Gardens, then lunch."

"Four of us," Trixie piped up, slamming a desk drawer. "I hope she can make it."

"Is that Trixie, what did she say?" Mia was anxious, she wished Trixie had phoned instead.

Fenella's perfect jaw clenched. "She hopes you can make it."

"Of course I'll make it," Mia replied, sounding stronger. "Which hospital?"

"Well, that's it, darling, he isn't in hospital. He's at home."

"In Chelsea?" Mia could not picture him there.

"No, in Ireland. He's gone home to Galty."

Mia felt her heart lift. "But *I'm* here. I'm in Ireland."

"Are you? Why?" Fenella felt flustered.

"I'm on location."

"I didn't know you were in Ireland." Fenella's turn to glare at Trixie. Trixie shrugged, not her job to keep the actress informed of her daughter's whereabouts. Fenella was pacing the floor. She had to get to Archie before Mia. She must see him first.

"I'll leave right away," Mia said.

"But your work?" Fenella tried.

"Doesn't matter, it's Archie ... I'll leave immediately."

"No!" Fenella snapped. Trixie dropped the diary to the floor. Fenella calmed. "No, darling. Not without me. Too much of a shock. Wait till I get there, we'll go together. Far better for all concerned."

Mia was deflated. She wanted to see Archie alone, to say goodbye with no one else there; no stage, no audience, no final speech.

"Trixie will organise my flight. Meet me in Dublin, we'll travel down together."

Fenella was sharp now, any hint of emotion sucked away.

"But I'm in Wicklow," Mia told her, hoping she would understand, she was closer to where Archie lay dying.

"Meet me in Dublin, I *want* us to go together." Fenella was firm. "Trixie will text details, you know I can't do that text thing, gives me a headache. You *will* be there?"

"Yes, yes of course." As the news took hold Mia was in no mood to argue.

"You're worried about taking time off, I can tell. Who's directing? Do you want me to call, clear it for you?"

Mia stifled a sigh. "No, don't do that. See you in Dublin." The line went dead.

"Poor Archie ..." Mia said to herself.

Fenella handed the mobile to Trixie. "Is it switched off?" Trixie nodded. "Don't you ever do that to me again, do you hear? You put me right on the spot!"

Trixie looked her in the eye. "You put yourself on the spot. Archie specifically asked for Mia. He said you can come if you want but Mia *must* come. He must see her."

Fenella paced the floor, they were in the parlour of the home they shared, the room they used as an office.

"See her why? Why does he specifically want to see *my* daughter, that's what I want to know?" She was at the window, fiddling with the shutters.

"Who knows?" Trixie watched Fenella stressing, she did even that stylishly.

"That's precisely the point." She turned on her friend. "Who knows? Who bloody well *does* know?"

Trixie was unfazed. "Interesting dilemma, dichotomy, whatever?"

Fenella was staring at her hands. She ran to the mirror, pulling at the collar of her immaculate linen shirt. "God! Blotches, I'm covered in blotches."

"Take deep breaths, it's only stress," Trixie told her.

"Stress? I've an audition tomorrow, I can't go looking like this."

"More deep breaths, it's calming. Now, would you like vodka or a pearly pink pill?"

"Which do you think?" Fenella asked, wide-eyed.

"Both," Trixie gave the blotches a cursory glance. "That *is* a double-whammy blotch fest!"

Fenella was distraught. "Christ, who are you mixing with? I don't even know what you're saying half the time!"

"Well, let's hope Archie's not terribly coherent either, goodness know what he *has* to say to your daughter," Trixie threw back, heading for the bathroom.

Fenella picked up the phone. She was going to ring Archie, find out for herself why he wanted to see Mia. But it was Bernice who had called; Bernice knew they had quarrelled, saying it was best Fenella came and made her peace face to face. Trixie reappeared with the medicine. Fenella took the pill and drank the vodka neat.

Mia was suddenly, soul-achingly sad. Letting the phone slide onto the crumb-spattered work surface, she hauled open the fridge and dragged out a half-empty bottle of rosé. Casting about for a clean glass, she poured a measure into the nearest mug and holding it to her chest, stood at the door sipping the cold, sweet wine.

A storm grumbled in the distance, black shards of angry cloud slit across the orange sky, as the last dregs of sun slipped beneath the peaks. Oddly the view seemed to ease her. At least she was here, in Ireland and Archie could well be witnessing this same night fall, there was some comfort in that. And as she watched the storm build she felt close to him, hearing his unmistakable voice, crystal clear in her head.

"Our revels now are ended. These our actors, as I foretold you, were all spirits, and are melted into air, into thin air."

A slow handclap. She must have said the words out loud. Embarrassed, she took a gulp of wine.

"Who's there?" she called.

"Only me." Courtney Watts, the assistant director emerged from the shadows, hair blowing wildly. "Prospero I think, *The Tempest.*" He held his jacket across his chest. "May I come in?" He raised his voice above the wind. *Oh, God,* she thought, *what's wrong now?*

"Of course."

She stood back as all six feet two of him filled her lonely caravan. A shortfall of accommodation trucks meant only a couple of aged caravans were available by the time she and Lol had arrived; it was supposed to be a temporary arrangement, maybe Courtney had found them an alternative. *Maybe not, he looked so serious.*

"Awful night," he confirmed. Mia grew worried. It had not been a good day on set. "No one else here?" There could have been a couple of bodies buried beneath the bedclothes. He was avoiding her eyes.

"Lol went to the pub with the others."

She guessed he was making sure the coast was clear to let her know her services were no longer required, she was let go, leave it at that. *Christ, this business could be so fickle.*

"Am I in trouble?"

"No, no, nothing like that. May I sit?" He looked for a chair. Mia dragged debris off the bench beneath the window. Courtney sat, long legs folded up in the small space.

"A drink?"

"Thanks. Whatever you're having."

Mia tipped the remainder of the wine into another mug.

"We've had a call. Hard to get a signal here, I thought I'd come and tell you." He kept his gaze fixed on the mug.

Mia leaned against the sink, relief swept through her, she was not being sacked.

"Do you mean Archie? Archie Fitz?"

Courtney pressed his lips together in a sad smile.

"My mother phoned, I … I know," Mia told him.

"Great," Courtney finally looked at her. "No, sorry, not great, I didn't mean …"

"I know, good I got the call, just before the storm, must have had a signal briefly." She indicated the discarded phone.

"I met him you know." He stood, bending to avoid the roof. The wind howled, the caravan shifted. She gave him a smile, they had been so close, once.

"Of course you did, a party at Galty House." She looked up into his face. "His birthday."

"Yes, one hell of a night. Worked with him a couple of times since, too. He was amazing," Courtney said. "Kind, warm, generous."

"Crazy, bad tempered, lazy too," Mia added ruefully. No canonisation, not for Archie, he would despise that.

"To Archie, he was one of the greats." Courtney raised his mug.

"Not dead yet." Mia was solemn. "Let's just drink to him."

"Archie," they said together. The phone beeped, Mia grabbed it.

"A text, my fiancé, he must have heard."

Courtney made to leave. Mia had a fiancé, he had a wife, they had moved on.

"Thanks," she called after him. "Thanks for coming." It was a terrible night out there.

The text read:

'**What's happening? Will you be home at the weekend or what? R x**'

Despite her sadness the message lifted her; her man was longing to see her and she was aching to see him too. She could not wait to bury herself in his warm, forever there embrace. She pressed 'call'. Straight to answerphone. No signal.

She sighed, weary and worried, and finished the wine. Closing her eyes she tried to remember the very first time she had met Archie, her mother's oldest friend. But she could not picture it, that first encounter. Probably because she had been too young to remember, probably because Archie had always been there, right from the very beginning; even before the beginning, if truth were told.

The storm rattled on, yet despite it Mia slept soundly, warmed through with wine and reminders of Archie's love, a love she had never, ever had cause to doubt. And somewhere deep in her dreams Mia Flanagan knew that whatever happened she was going to miss Aloysius Fermoy Fitzgerald OBE, very much indeed. It would be just like losing a father. The very same.

STATION TO STATION

T2 Dublin Airport was familiar territory for Fenella Flanagan, she danced up the escalator, blowing a kiss at the portrait of Pierce Brosnan at the top, as she glided past the gallery of quintessential Irish faces, heading to passport control.

Fellow travellers looked left and right, questioning if it really was the famous actress or just someone who looked like her. A classical beauty even now in her fifties – Fenella was a beauty with brains, guile and talent – and was totally aware that being an 'icon' was a full-time job, twenty-four-seven.

"Miss Flanagan, welcome home," the immigration officer gave her his best smile. She checked his badge.

"Sean, good to see you, great to be back." She had never seen him before in her life.

"We guessed you'd be home," he leaned in to whisper. "When the newspapers said Fitz was in a bad way."

"Sometimes, you just need your friends around you." She was aware of the agitated queue growing behind her. She would not comment on Archie's condition, besides she had only spoken to Bernice and her version of things, even the weather, could vary wildly from her own.

"Will you go straight to Wexford or stop over in Dublin tonight?" the officer asked, oblivious to the unrest his conversation was causing.

"Stop over. My daughter's on location in Wicklow, we'll go together in the morning."

"Young Mia is here?" He was clearly a fan.

"Working on that new vampire film near Aughrim."

"I read that. Your man, James Quinn, is giving them hell!"

Fenella smiled, removing her shades. "Surely not!"

A man behind coughed. The officer ignored him.

"Well, be sure and tell Fitz, we love him. See if he can't pull himself round and make a bit of a comeback. There's no one like him, none of the new fellas can act their way out of a paper bag."

Fenella tightened the knot of her Hermes scarf.

"All in order?"

She tried to move on, people might think she expected differential treatment, they would be on Twitter or Facebook instantly, saying she was arrogant, then her agent or worse, her PR, would be begging she 'get with the programme' and 'keep a handle on things'. Times had changed, she knew the score.

"Indeed, Miss Flanagan, away you go," the officer pronounced, and despite the bundle of fury which took her place, continued to gaze after her, until she disappeared into the Arrivals Hall.

The traffic was nose to tail. She could not remember Dublin being this busy but it was rush hour and she had not been in her homeland for … how long was it? Nearly five years.

She was pleased to see her usual driver waiting.

"Where is it, Miss Flanagan, The Shelbourne?" He took her bag.

"No, Thomas, not this time. Connolly Street, just a stopover before I take the train to Wexford tomorrow." She took in the grey landscape of the Drumcondra Road. It had started to rain.

"Sure, I could take you down to Wexford, no problem," the driver reassured her via the rear-view mirror. With so many taxis licensed for the city, good fares were hard to come by.

"Thank you, Thomas, but myself and my daughter will take the train together, a sentimental journey, you know how it is."

"Of course." He tapped his fingers against the steering wheel as they waited at lights. "It's a lovely journey alright, all along the coast, sure you're on the beach half the time." He turned the wipers on full.

Fenella adored and abhorred the beach in equal measure but was desperate to see Archie, and the train was the quickest and easiest route, beach or no beach. She was hardly able to keep her eyes open as they crawled through the murky streets, people and buildings turned taupe with misty rain, even in June.

"At last!" he said when she answered the phone.

"At last? I've been calling for days, goes to voicemail every time." Mia stopped herself sounding frustrated, she did not want a tetchy conversation, it was ages since they had seen each other.

"Yeah, sorry about that, lost it."

"You *lost* it?" She was immediately concerned.

"Misplaced it, I mean,"

"Oh, I see, where was it?"

"In the airing cupboard."

"Airing cupboard?"

Mia was surprised he knew they even had an airing cupboard.

"The tank was …er… making noises, I went to investigate, must have fallen out of my pocket."

Mia was impressed, Rupert developing an interest in DIY? He was hardly the most domesticated of creatures. Was this a good thing, was he happy because rehearsals were going well or home looking for things to do because they were not. Had he been sacked … again?

"Everything okay?" he asked, quietly.

Suddenly she wished she was there, close enough to fling herself into his arms.

"You haven't heard?"

"Something awful, I can tell."

There he was, her gorgeous man, the one who understood every nuance in her voice. "It's Archie, he's gravely ill, asking to see me." The words caught in her throat.

"Hey, steady-up." His tone instantly soft, caring, everything she adored about him. "Think about it, ill as he is, he's able to send for you, his favourite girl."

"You're right and I have to be strong for him and for mother too, you know …"

The phone was pressed so hard against her face it would leave a mark when she hung up. She could hear music in the background, one of their favourite songs. He was playing the soundtrack to *All for One!* They had met on the set of a woeful remake of *The Three Musketeers*. Some bright spark had decided the classic tale ought to be turned into a musical. How they had laughed, lived and loved, despite the awfulness of everything that gruelling, grinding three months in a derelict Tuscan castle had thrown at them.

"How's it going? All the other stuff?"

Kind, lovely guy, she thought, *trying to change the subject, cheer me up.* "Bloody mayhem, as usual. James dropping his fangs and smashing the set to pieces. Amelia shrieking and wailing like a banshee over every tiny thing. Rain stops play every five minutes *and* we had a major prop issue, sent the director into a tailspin and everyone else to the pub!"

He gave a low chuckle. "Just another day at the coalface, then?"

Mia slumped on the bench, gazed at the pewter sky.

"How long do you think you'll be away?" he asked.

"No … idea." The sob came in her voice again.

"Sweet thing, try not to worry so much. See how things are

with Archie, do whatever you have to, finish filming and get home when you can. I'll take care of things here till your return, I promise."

Exquisitely English; looks, voice, charm, Rupert was incredibly laidback. An attitude Mia often tried to imitate, always failing hopelessly.

"He's going to die, Rupert," she said.

"We're all going to die, my love," Rupert replied helpfully. Silence. Someone who had been a father figure all her life was seriously ill. Mia was a worrier. She would be stressing big time. "I'm sorry." More silence.

"How're things with you?" Mia asked finally.

Rupert chose to be selfless, declining to mention his sorry state of affairs, rehearsals were not going well; he was teetering on the edge of unemployment yet again.

"Absolutely fine but tell me your plans?"

"Mother wants to meet in Dublin, travel together. I'll get back to the shoot as soon as I can." Mia had been fretting about how much extra work her leave of absence would create, she needed to get ahead of herself. She was already dragging bits of script out of the filing cabinet in her brain, wondering which scenes they were filming next, what costumes would be needed.

"Will the movie finish on schedule?"

"I doubt it," Mia replied, head back on track. "It's tricky, no one likes the costume designer, two of the principals were married once and seem to be revisiting past issues between takes and then this set malarkey with James."

"Same old, same old." Rupert gave a laugh.

"I just wish I was home but ... I need to see Archie." She was trying not to cry.

"Come on, Mia, chin up," he said soothingly, then. "Sorry, the door. Christ, I'm late."

"Oh."

"Be strong, now." The phone died.

Mia had never seen her mother look so tiny. The vastness of Connolly Street Station dwarfed her. She was suddenly moved, protective of the diminutive creature in the long, linen coat, ebony hair pushed into a straw trilby, huge dark glasses covering her face. She was buying a magazine, Mia hoped it was *Hello,* her mother's take on the celebrity stories were far more fascinating than anything the magazine could deliver. At least it would distract them, give them something other than the bald reality of Archie's impending demise to talk about, a more amenable common ground.

"Darling!" Fenella gave her only child a brief hug. "I've managed to buy tickets, why is it so difficult? No staff. Just a hole in the wall, a desperate state of affairs." She steered Mia towards a row of carriages. "Is there even first class? No one to ask." She scanned the train for signage. Mia indicated a coach.

"This one, it'll be fine." She lifted her mother's Aspinal leather holdall onto the luggage rack. It was surprisingly light. Mia slung her backpack on top. Fenella slipped into a seat, pulling her collar about her ears.

"Are you cold?" Yesterday's dampness had morphed into a beautiful June morning.

"Perished," Fenella replied, shoving her hands in her pockets. "I'll need a hot whiskey once the bar opens."

"Probably isn't a bar. Maybe a trolley." Mia offered.

"No bar and I'm to be served from a trolley?" Fenella leaned her head against the window. "True is it that we have seen better days," she quoted, from something Mia did not recognise. Mia sometimes wondered if her mother ever made up her own sentences, having spent most of her life using words created by others, characteristics and emotions too, it would seem. *Stop it, she told herself, be patient, be nice.*

Mia placed her phone on the table, sure Rupert would call wanting to know how the trip was progressing, he knew how upset she was and how spending time with her mother could be fraught, never mind the gravity of the current situation. Fenella had not even opened her magazine. Mia offered some water. Fenella shook her head.

"What *is* this obsession with taking water everywhere? Are these islands, probably the wettest on the planet, suddenly to become an arid desert? Could this travesty happen so quickly that one could die of thirst between Connolly Station and Greystones?" She pushed her sunglasses onto her head, pressing at her eyelids with her fingers.

"You might be glad of it when the trolley comes and there's no mixer for your whiskey." Mia poked her gently with the bottle. Fenella gave a tight smile.

"You look tired, darling, is the shoot very wearing?"

"No more than any other," Mia said.

"How's James?" Fenella and James had once been close.

"Cranky," Mia told her.

"And Amelia?" Another friend of Fenella's.

"Crankier."

Fenella laughed. "They probably know it's going to bomb. I mean, aren't vampires on the wane?"

"By the time they release this one, they'll be back in vogue," Mia looked at her properly for the first time, she had a touch of vampire about her today, waxen beneath the expertly applied make-up.

"You look weary too. No sleep?"

"My own fault. The hotel had a live band, kept me awake all

night." Although staying awake all night was sometimes better than dreaming, Fenella often considered.

Mia was surprised; her mother either stayed in one of the five-star haunts of the rich and famous or with equally smart friends.

"No one's around." She read Mia's thoughts. "And besides, with Archie so ill I don't feel like partying." Fenella pulled her glasses down over her face, people were boarding, filling the carriage; closing her eyes, the movie star shrank back into the cream coat.

The train rolled out of the station, starting a journey Mia had always adored. The elevated line snaked through the city as she peered into offices of state, elegant courtyards, taking in the playing fields of Dublin's legendary seats of learning and the sweeping grandeur of its squares; she settled back to enjoy the view as they trundled on.

"Which whiskey when the trolley comes?" Mia would have tea and shortbread, a tradition she and Archie had established long ago. No reply; Fenella was already asleep.

A little girl with long fair hair appeared in the carriage, checking seats, eyes red-rimmed from crying. Mia put her hand out as she passed.

"What's wrong?"

The girl shook her head. "I might have made a mistake but I think I've lost someone." She had an American accent and blushed at such an admission.

"I hope not," Mia replied. "Do you think they got off the train?"

"I'm not sure. It's too early for Rosshaven Harbour, isn't it?" she said, fighting back tears.

"Much too early. Is that where you're going?"

The little girl nodded.

"Good, so am I. Why don't you sit with my mother and I'll try to find who you're looking for, okay?"

About to burst into tears again, the youngster climbed into the seat Mia vacated. Fenella was sleeping behind her glasses.

"Stay here, I'll go check the other carriages and the loos."

She nodded.

"Who *am* I looking for?"

"My uncle, Ross."

"What does he look like?"

"A boy," the girl said.

"Another clue?"

"He shouts on his cell-phone. A *lot*," she confirmed.

"I'll be right back," Mia gave a smile and headed off. Two carriages forward she came across a group of teenagers.

"Excuse me, did you see a little girl with a man earlier?" The boys said no, but one of the girls looked up.

"Yeah, they were over there." She pointed at a table. "Then she was on her own, asleep I think. Have you lost them?"

"Someone's in the toilet. Been in there for hours," said one of the boys. "I had to use another one, miles away."

"Thanks." Mia was already on her way to the lavatory. She tried the door, locked. She knocked, politely. It might not be the girl's uncle in there at all. Mia was praying it was. She listened, trying to hear if there was someone inside. It was difficult, the carriage was noisy, the train rattled over the tracks.

"That's why I'm calling you, it has to be done."

She heard this quite distinctly because it was said very loudly indeed.

"We have no choice." Again loudly. The second American accent she had heard that day.

"This *is* our last chance." Shouting now. It had to be him.

Mia took a breath and rapped on the door. "Go away, this cubicle is engaged!"

"Is there a little girl with you?" she shouted back.

The door opened a crack.

"I beg your pardon?" a man hissed.

"Is there a little girl with you?"

"Are you *crazy*?" he snapped, flinging the door open. "I'm in the bathroom!"

The carriage fell silent, everyone looked at the young woman, the one with the wild red hair accusing a man of being in the toilet with a little girl.

"I meant travelling with you, is there a child travelling with you?"

"Christ!" A tall, dark bundle of frenzy whipped out and pushed passed her. "She was asleep. Where is she?" He was charging down the carriage. "Pearl!...Pearl!... he called. Mia followed him.

"Is there a child lost?" A woman got up from her seat.

"It's okay." Mia stopped to reassure her. "She's with my mother. She woke up and her uncle was gone, it's fine, he was in the loo."

"At last," said the man beside her, heading off to use the facilities. "No consideration some of these tourists, think the whole of Ireland is a theme park for their fecking convenience." He stomped away.

"Don't mind him." The woman opened a packet of Silver Mints. "He's always giving out, should be glad of the tourists, we'd be four and a half million euro poorer without them." She offered Mia a mint. "I hope the child is alright. Men! I wouldn't leave a goldfish with my fella."

By the time Mia reached the carriage Fenella was wide awake, whiskey in one hand, business card in the other. The little girl and the shouting stress-head nowhere to be seen.

"What happened?" Mia plonked down in her seat.

"Pearl's uncle, a most charming man, arrived to collect her just as the drinks trolley appeared. He paid for my drink and gave me his card, invited us to dinner, a thank you for child-minding, I suppose." She gave Mia a smile. "Lovely little girl. They'd been to the zoo, she wanted to meet an octopus. We were chatting away while you were gone."

"Must have recognised you." Mia's mother received all sorts of invitations.

"People often think they know me, because they've seen me before, you know that."

Mia looked at the card. Smartly embossed.

Ross Power, Chief Executive, Harbour Spa Hotel, Rosshaven, County Wexford, Ireland.

"Wouldn't fancy dinner with him, jeez, he charged past me like a madman. Poor kid."

"Really?" Fenella sipped her drink. "I thought he was delightful. They're Americans, bought the old hotel in the harbour. Spent a fortune on it by all accounts. Imagine, five-star luxury in our little fishing village."

"You're up to speed." Mia handed the card back. The Harbour Spa Hotel did not appeal to her one bit.

"Pearl told me everything, proper little chatterbox, a bit like you at that age."

"I thought I was quiet," Mia said. *When had she stopped talking, asking questions, she wondered for the thousandth time?*

"Not when you were little." Fenella finished her drink. "Are we nearly there yet?" she teased sitting back, smiling; her encounter with the Americans had cheered her up no end.

Mia watched the glorious east coast glide past, the only sound the reassuring rumble of the tracks. The view, drenched in sunshine, had never looked lovelier, the landscape changing as the railway sliced through coastal towns melding into holiday villages with bunting fluttering in the breeze. She loved being perched on the very edge of the land as it fell suddenly away, watching mesmerised as the deep, dark sea filled every view to the horizon and beyond. She leaned against the window, drinking it in.

Nearing their destination, Mia looked at her mother, eyes open at last.

"I love this journey, I could never tire of it," she told her.

Fenella gave a small smile, the curve of coastline soothing her.

"Seductive," she replied. "I grant you that." As the carriage slowed, they gathered their belongings. "I hope he's still with us, it would be too cruel if …"

Mia touched her mother's hand. "He'll be there, he'd never go without saying goodbye."

They waited as the other passengers disembarked.

"Rosshaven Harbour," called the guard. "Anyone else for Rosshaven?"

The two women alighted onto the sandy stretch of platform, the scent of sea wrapping quickly around them. They each took a long breath, neither realising that something deep inside had said 'home', as surely as if the breeze had whispered the very word.

LAZARUS

Bernice opened the door and peering into the gloom held her breath, fearing the worst. There was a huddle in the middle of the bed, no movement, no sign of life. The time had come and he was gone. She was suddenly weak with sorrow and disappointment, Fenella and Mia were only hours away; whatever their differences, she wanted Archie to see them and they him, before the end. Their relationship was precious, they should have their goodbye.

"Aargh!" A shriek. Bernice clasped her breast in fright. A couple of thuds, a bang. "Fecking rats, feck off, feck off will ye!" A clatter, something flew through the air and landed at her feet. It wriggled. She screamed. A head poked into the room.

"I thought you were dead!" She indicated the body-shaped bedclothes.

"Good job you chose art over medicine," Archie replied. "Never felt better in my life." He stepped into the room. The rat looked at the man, twitched its nose and scurried away. "Everyone's a critic!" Archie slipped his sister a smile, he had given her a fright. "And that cat needs drowning, useless thing."

Bernice tutted. Archie was trying to amuse, there was no cat. He had been a delicate child and fearing allergies or worse, pets had been banned, even goldfish. Or was that because Archie had swallowed the one they won at the fair, she could never remember.

"Ready to greet your audience?" She pulled at the bedclothes.

"The Flanagans? No need to stand on ceremony there, can't

wait to see them." Archie went to the window, drawing back the curtains. Sun streamed into the room, dust dancing in shafts of light. He blinked sore eyes, searching past lawns, hoping to spot a taxi rolling along the lane but it was too early, his visitors were still an hour away. Bernice said Fenella was vague about which train and would not hear of a car being sent. Archie declared that was typical, she was sulking. They had argued the last time they had talked, some old not yet forgotten grievance they were picking over like a scab. It would be forgiven the instant they were in each other's arms, it was always the same.

"Come and look at the day, Bernice," he called. "Going to be a scorcher, let's lunch in the summerhouse."

Bernice was arranging pills and potions on the nightstand, Archie was far sicker than he made out and goodness knows what he had taken to give him today's boost of anxious energy. A clutch of magazines fell to the floor.

"It's going to rain later." She bent to retrieve the journals, spotting a pile of post under the bed.

"No way, not a cloud in the sky." Archie was struggling with the catch. Bernice went to help. They pushed it open together; despite his show of robustness, he had grown weak.

"Have you invited Eamon to lunch?" She avoided the glare that would no doubt follow the question.

"Have *you*?" Archie asked, sharply.

"I may've mentioned he should drop by. Things need sorting, you know that." She glanced towards the small mountain of unattended correspondence.

Archie sighed. "I want today to be a celebration, Eamon's such a killjoy."

"He's our solicitor, we need him here." Bernice was firm.

"Very well, as you wish." Archie waved her away. "But tell him it's just lunch, not a consultation, he needn't think he can send me a bill *and* eat my salmon."

Relieved, Bernice gave a small laugh. Archie, hopeless with money and generous to a fault, loved playing the curmudgeonly miser, fooling no one.

The taxi man asleep on a bench had a copy of the *Wexford People* over his face. A smart 4x4 stood at the rank. It was the only car there, the other passengers had been scooped away by the courtesy coach from The Harbour Spa Hotel, the new resort along the coast. The owner of the shiny vehicle was hoping to mop up any stragglers but seeing the coach full, resumed his nap.

"Taxi?" Fenella enquired of the supine figure stretched out in the sunshine. No response. "Taxi!"

A languid hand withdrew the newspaper and bright blue eyes crinkled at her.

"Ah, it's yourself is it?" Local dialect with a hint of somewhere else.

He swung his legs off the bench, rolled up chinos revealing tanned feet in deck shoes.

"I told him not to send a car." Fenella placed hands on hips but Mia noticed her eyes were sparkling too.

"You told him not to send me, you mean."

"No, but I heard you were back." She gave a smile, she was stunning when she smiled. "Where've you been thrown out of this time?"

The man just grinned.

"Don't tell me, this gorgeous creature … not Maeve?"

He was well-built, with a 'yachty' look about him; thick silver-fair hair curled at the collar of his polo shirt.

"Mia," she told him. Maeve had been ditched long ago.

"I'm Dominic Driscoll, an old friend of your mother's." He

twinkled his eyes at her.

"Old, without doubt," Fenella agreed. "Friend? Questionable. Now, can we get a move on please, I'm desperate to see Archie. How is he? Do you know?"

The man strolled to the car, zapped it and placed the bags inside.

"Not dead yet, anyway." He cast about. "Is this all there is?"

"Yes." Fenella climbed into the passenger seat.

"Ah, I get it. The truck with the ball gowns and state jewels is following behind." He opened the door for Mia. "She never did travel light," he stage whispered.

"We're not here to party," Fenella pulled the visor down against the sun. The vehicle swung out of the car park towards the crossroads, village to the right, coast road on the left.

"Straight there? Or can I buy you ladies a drink at the new resort first?"

"Is that the Harbour Spa Hotel?" Mia asked, remembering the card the shouty stress-head had given her mother.

"One and the same," Driscoll told her. "Very upmarket, not everyone's cup of tea, though. A lot complaining about the size of the development, impact on the coastline, marine life, all that kind of shite. Others saying, it's not 'real' Ireland. But sure, isn't it bringing in the tourists and jobs too? If they're coming to Ireland looking for *The Quiet Man*, they need to cop on, those days are long gone. Would you like to check it out?"

"Straight there, please, Driscoll, I've already said, we're not here to party." Fenella was snippy.

"Really? Anyone told Archie that?" he laughed, turning the wheel slowly towards the sea.

Ten minutes later they rounded a bend leading down to a large gateway flanked by crumbling stone pillars. Driscoll took the winding driveway carefully, avoiding clumps of weeds sprouting from potholes although the expansive lawns had been freshly mown, grass gleaming. Mia sat up, eager to catch a first glimpse of the house, basecamp for all her childhood holidays, lengthier stays too if Fenella was in a long run or filming somewhere exotic. It had been a while.

A glint of sunshine bounced off the summerhouse and as the car turned into the courtyard there it stood, the Fitzgerald country pile, Galty House, a glorious Georgian mansion, regal and resplendent on this perfect June day. The windows winked in welcome and as wheels crunched across the gravel, the huge hall door was flung wide and a lanky individual, clad in jeans and white shirt came charging down the steps, arms flailing wildly.

"Look, it's Archie!" Mia laughed.

"Good lord, so it is!" Fenella exclaimed, lifting her spectacles to check.

"Told you he wasn't dead yet," Driscoll confirmed, as Bernice appeared waving from the top of the steps. Fenella was out of the car before it stopped. The man and woman flew into each other's arms and clamped together began a little dance of delight. Mia was soon beside them and with Archie released, threw herself into his embrace. He felt wonderful, soft and sinewy. She stood back to look at him. Definitely thinner, freckles bright against his pale skin but it was all Archie, breathing and laughing, every inch of him alive.

"You old fraud." Fenella punched him in the chest. "I thought you were …"

"Dying?" Archie smirked, making the creases around his eyes deeper, cheekbones sharp.

"Dead," Driscoll told him, unloading the bags. "She thought you were dead."

"No, thank God, but if he doesn't stop chasing around he soon will be. Doesn't give his medication a chance." Bernice smiled, kissing Fenella on both cheeks.

Mia watched the women curiously, as close as sisters yet so very different. Bernice fair as Fenella was dark, with never a hair out of place, highly organised, pedantic. Fenella, on the other hand vague and dreamy, always changing her mind, unfathomable. Bernice pushed her sleek bob behind her ears, Mia watched the shrewd hazel eyes taking everything in.

"You must be jaded tired." Bernice took Fenella's arm, steering her towards the house. "And when is the last time you had a decent meal, young lady?" she said over her shoulder to Mia. Archie put his tongue out at Bernice's back. "I saw that!" she said, making Mia giggle.

"Am I invited for lunch?" Driscoll was hopeful.

"Have you *ever* been invited?" Archie pretended to look surprised.

"Nope."

"And don't we *always* give you lunch?" Archie rolled his eyes at Mia taking her by the hand. "Come with me, lovely girl, I've something really exciting to show you."

"Where are you going?" Fenella called from the steps. But Archie was running, towing Mia behind him.

"I'll bring the bags in, so," Driscoll said, as everyone disappeared.

Eamon Degan was worried. He put his 'out of office' message on, diverted the phone to his mobile and locked the door at the top of the stairs. He glanced at the lettering on the glass. Degan, Daly and Partners, Attorneys at La. The letter 'w' was long since rubbed away by an over-zealous cleaner trying to impress the charismatic Daly – now retired. Eamon knew he needed a new sign yet begrudged the cost of it, so few clients visited his tired little office these days, why bother? Yet it did bother him, bothered him every time he saw it and he saw several times a day. But Eamon was one to let things fester, always had been.

Checking his watch, he clattered downstairs and out into the brightness of a busy June day. It was the week before the bank holiday and the town was buzzing. Nothing brought the hordes to Rosshaven like a holiday weekend. Desperate to leave town as quickly as possible, he ran straight into Leela Brennan.

"Eamon, the very man." Leela lowered diamanté-framed shades. "Are you away to Galty?"

Eamon gave a grunt. "A lift, is it?"

Indicating the shopping bags, she bent to rub swollen ankles.

"Guests for lunch, I'm a bit behind schedule." She flashed what she hoped was a beguiling smile, the glare of her newly-whitened teeth nearly blinding him.

He shoved his briefcase under his arm as he helped load the shopping into the ancient Subaru, a temporary replacement for his beloved Mercedes. Things had been tight for some time, he was just waiting for a big deal to come in, then he would buy himself something decent, nothing flash, he had his reputation to consider. He sighed, the traffic was horrendous.

"Take the back road," Leela advised, checking her lipstick in the mirror. The way Eamon drove, the back road was by far the safer option. "This place is a total madhouse getting ready for the holiday." Leela had been Galty's housekeeper for as long as anyone could remember and considering she should have retired years ago, maintaining her job and her image at the same time was admirable.

"How did you know I was heading to Galty House?" Eamon asked, once they were on the road.

"I didn't want to say anything in town, you know how people

love a bit of gossip about 'The Seahorse Hotel'." Leela was referring to Galty's wartime codename, the name locals still used when discussing 'goings on' up at the big house. "But the Misses Flanagan are on their way and with Archie not in the best of health, I'm guessing the Fitzgeralds will need their attorney in attendance." Leela, perspicacious as ever, never missed a trick.

Eamon allowed himself a smile.

"That's very astute of you, Leela."

"Ah, I'm very acute, me Auntie Eileen always said that, avaricious too, she loved me, Auntie Eileen."

That word did not sit happily with Eamon. He crashed the gears.

"Vivacious, Leela, I think that's what she meant."

"That's what I said," Leela replied, pressing straying lashes to her eyelid as they bounced along the road.

Bernice was trying to prepare lunch – difficult without the ingredients – when Leela staggered in, Eamon bringing up the rear.

"At last!" She looked at the clock. "I did say lunch, Leela."

"Sorry Bernice, but with the traffic and the bus only running hourly because Jimmy Kenny is away on a stag … thought it best I came with Eamon but he was late."

Eamon plonked the bags on the kitchen table.

"Tut, tut, Eamon." A sultry voice drifted out.

He swung round. "Fenella Flanagan, look at you, gorgeous as ever, not remotely changed and it's been years."

"It has not, Eamon Degan, and stop trying to make me feel guilty for abandoning you to a life of debauched bachelorhood, pretending to be an overworked and underpaid lawyer of the parish."

"Ha!" Eamon laughed, embracing the world-famous actress warmly. "You have me rumbled, as always."

"Missed you," she whispered in his ear.

"And you." He kissed her on the nose. "And where's your beautiful daughter?"

"With Archie, of course, probably building a pirate ship in the boathouse, I'll go and drag them out in a minute." Fenella was at the fridge. "Who's locked the drink away?"

Bernice glanced at Leela. Archie had been ordered to cut down on alcohol but the bottles kept evaporating anyway.

"Replenishments are at hand." Eamon ferreted in the bags.

"Excellent. Are we outside?" Fenella asked.

"Of course." Bernice was taking trays out of the pantry. "The summerhouse, Archie always goes continental when the sun shines, you know that."

"Lovely." Fenella was straining to look out of the window, hoping Archie and Mia would soon return.

"You'll have to help me." Archie took the corner of the dust sheet in one hand, his excitement contagious. They were in the old boat house, Mia had helped push open the sliding door, wiping cobwebs from her hands as she stood breathing in the scent of heat and wood, fuel and fish. Closing her eyes she was sucked back in time, a curious little girl, let loose in Archie's adventure playground.

"Mia, a hand!"

She crossed to the large bulk hiding beneath a grubby canvas. It filled a vast area, as broad as it was long and so tall, it reached the roof.

"Ready?" Archie gave a grin as they hauled the tarpaulin up and away. "Ta dah!" He stood back, arms wide.

"Wow!" Mia touched the gleaming surface with her

fingertips. "It's a beauty, who owns it?"

"She's mine, ours, everyone's really. We've been too long without a boat and it's high time The Seahorse Hotel and its vagary of vagabonds had a seafaring vessel to make good our escape … should the need arise."

Mia walked around the boat. "Cool, what is she?"

"She's a motor sailor, I'm going to call her Banshee, after the mystical she-spirit that haunts these isles. She'll sail like a demon once the wind catches her and when it's calm we can anchor off the beach, swimming in the clear blue water to our hearts' content."

Mia gave him an indulgent smile; he seemed to have forgotten they were on the east coast of Ireland, the waters hereabouts rather cooler than the Caribbean. She watched him polish the bow-rail with his sleeve, Mia could not remember the last time she had been on board, wind whipping her hair, spray stinging her eyes, it was so long ago.

"You've not named her yet?" There was no lettering on the side.

"Not yet. She's a surprise. You're the first person I've introduced her to."

Mia folded her arms, smiling.

"So, Bernice doesn't know?"

Archie shook his head. "Not yet." He started to pull the cover back over the boat, she went to help; he did not look very strong at all.

"She'll go nuts." Bernice was always fretting about finance.

"Ah, she might indulge me, given the circumstances."

"She might. When will you tell everyone?"

"After lunch, wouldn't want anyone to suffer indigestion, now would I?" Archie clipped the cover neatly under the bow.

"How many for lunch? I saw a car arriving, Eamon?" Mia

said, subconsciously linking Eamon and indigestion.

"Bugger, I'd forgotten that crotchety old shite was coming. Bernice invited him, it'll be a touch of *The Last Supper* no doubt."

Mia widened her eyes. "Archie, please don't say things like that!"

"His not mine." Archie gave an impish grin. "I'll give him the sack, then the miserable fecker will have something to moan about." Satisfied Banshee was safely under wraps, he took Mia's arm.

"Now, not a word until I make my announcement."

"Of course," Mia laughed. Archie loved surprises. Surprises and secrets.

"And over lunch I want all the news, the sets you've been on, the bitchy *badinage*, who's sleeping with whom."

"No, Archie." Mia was stern. She had an unblemished reputation as one of the most trustworthy operators to ever wield a needle, she would never undermine that and certainly not for Archie's amusement – renowned as one of the biggest gossips in the business.

"Okay then, who are *you* sleeping with? Anyone I know?" he pressed.

"Stop it."

"There's someone in your life, I've guessed that much. You seem to have forgotten my legendary powers of deduction. For instance, there's a very odd looking lump of metal on your left hand, so you're probably secretly engaged to a cad and daren't tell your mother, especially as he doesn't have a pot to piss in."

"Archie!" Mia exclaimed, as the faded forget-me-not blue of the clapboard summerhouse came into view. She stopped and gave him a look. Archie had spies everywhere, always desperate to know who was plotting against him or worse threatening to entice Fenella away, well that's how it seemed.

"Spot on, aren't I?" And he laughed his craggy laugh, striding off towards the summerhouse. Mia followed frowning, the entire structure looked more unstable than ever, almost as if it were leaning towards the sea, longing to fall into the waves and float away, somehow teasingly playful and lethal at the same time – rather like Archie himself.

A LONG LUNCH

Typical of most meals taken *en masse* at Galty House, lunch was a far from sombre affair, despite Archie's prediction.

Driscoll and Eamon carried the picnic basket, followed by Fenella and Leela with trays. Bernice bore a large salmon on a platter, while Mia and Archie laid the table with the eclectic mix of Delft stored in the ancient sideboard, arranging a flagrant collection of glasses at each setting. Mia saw Bernice scan the tablecloth.

"Napkins!" she said, and went to the drawer where the antique linen was kept. As a child she used to help Bernice fold the mountain of fresh laundry which seemed to appear magically and without fail at Galty House, despite Leela's resistance to regular housework.

When Bernice was happy all was ready, Archie seated everyone in his usual haphazard fashion. Famous for often placing sworn enemies next to one another, Fenella complained Archie never thought anything through, while Mia suspected that was precisely what he did. Today Fenella sat to his left with Mia at his right and despite his best efforts, Eamon was placed at the far end of the table. In time-honoured fashion everyone helped themselves, passing dishes and while Archie made a great show of piling his plate, Mia noticed he ate hardly a bite.

The meal was delicious, a flavourful mix of luxurious and simple and Driscoll, assuming the role of wine waiter, seemed quite at home. Mia was intrigued, she was sure she had never met this man before – yet he was certainly one of the old guard, someone this tightknit inner circle knew well and accepted. And then, unbidden as usual, the same old question arose and she started to ponder, wondering if Driscoll was the shadowy secret they kept from her, the man who might be her real father.

Mia had been ten when she finally stopped asking but the question had never gone away. And though it seemed everyone else was happy to assume Archie was her father, she had never stopped wondering if the 'open secret' really was true. Yes, the clues all led back to the lovely man she had known all her life but sometimes in the middle of the night she would wake, convinced it was a myth and the reason Fenella had never told who her father was, was because in reality her mother did not know and if not Archie, then which of her mother's many admirers could it be?

She would try to guess his name, what he looked like and the hardest question of all, why he had left? Until longing for sleep she would push all thoughts away, desperate to quash the gnawing deep in her stomach, burrowing away like a worm ... a worm of doubt.

Lifting her knife, Mia caught her reflection in the blade and saw again that sad, anxious little girl who had never been told the truth ... and suddenly she was back, back to when she swore she would never, ever ask again.

Leela and Fenella were decorating the cake while Bernice took her to change. It was the first time she had ever invited anyone to the house and was bursting with excitement because two of the most popular girls in her class had agreed to come and share her birthday tea.

She remembered standing in front of the long looking glass, having opted for a violent pink froth of a dress, clashing dramatically with the wild red hair tied with ribbon. She pointed shiny toes and took a bow.

"What are you doing?" Bernice demanded.

"Thanking my audience," she beamed back.

"What for?"

"My ovation, I'm a great star," she told her.

Bernice drew her mouth into a thin line. Mia twirled and curtsied again.

"Stop it!" Bernice was sharp. *"Stop it now and come down."*

"One more encore." Mia blew kisses.

The woman grabbed her hand, pulling it from her mouth. *"Don't be silly, you could never be an actress!"*

"Why not?" Mia pouted.

"You'd always be compared to your mother, of course. She is a great star. We've enough with two in the same family, don't even think about it!"

"I want to be an actress!" Mia had wailed.

"But look at you!" Bernice dragged her in front of the mirror. *"Red hair, long nose, skinny legs. You'd be a laughing stock. You look nothing like her. A fate worse than death to be constantly compared with her. Sure you'd never be valued for yourself. Put it from your mind, I'm telling you for your own good."*

"But ..." Mia could feel her cheeks burning.

"Now listen to me." Bernice tried to speak kindly, crouching to look Mia in the eyes. *"Choose a sensible career, keep your expectations realistic. A good steady job and a nice reliable husband, you'll be lucky if you achieve that much."*

"But ..." Mia tried again.

"Don't delude yourself, child, heed my words, your heart will be broken, your hopes dashed."

Mia blinked at her reflection. It was true, she did not look at all like her mother, not one bit.

"Well, who do I look like?" she asked in a small voice, tears brimming, *"My father?"*

"You've asked that question often enough and what's the answer?"

"I'm not to ask. I'll be told when I'm bigger, old enough to understand." Mia repeated her mother's words precisely.

"Well, there's your answer." Bernice handed her a tissue. *"Now, go and splash water on your face. Your guests have arrived."* She pushed Mia towards the bathroom. *"And when you come down, be charming, totally charming."* Bernice's voice trailed after her.

Mia was ready for the consternation her outfit caused when she greeted her guests, deliberately late. She had ditched the party dress for her drab school uniform.

If she could not be a star, she would no longer dress as one. At the first opportunity, she would burn all her pretty clothes in the oil drum in the garden or give them away to the missions, even Sister Agnes would approve of that. She would show them, if they would not tell her who she looked like, she would not care what she looked like, so there!

"Wine, Maeve?" Driscoll asked, bringing her back to the present. She must have been staring at him for some time. Fenella was perfectly relaxed. No, Driscoll was not her father, she was sure of that.

"My name is Mia." She reminded him, curtly.

"What are you working on at the moment, Fenella?" Driscoll filled their glasses.

Fenella gave a small frown. "A dilemma, I want to chat it through with Archie." She turned navy blue eyes on her host. "I'm not sure what to do next."

"You always know precisely what to do, what nonsense!" Bernice chimed, sipping mineral water.

"You've a choice?" Archie was impressed, Fenella was still

much in demand.

"Not an easy one." Fenella played with her wine glass.

"Theatre or film?" Mia was interested.

"Neither, both television." Fenella sounded less than enthusiastic. "Haven't done any telly in an age."

"Go for the big bucks, Fenella. That's my advice," Eamon told her.

"Crass in the extreme," Archie whispered to Mia. "Most of his advice is."

"And?" Mia pressed; no one ever asked about her work. Well, Archie did, but he was only interested in gossip.

"One is a long running soap and I play an aging thespian looking for a rich husband." She glared around the table. "If anyone says 'typecasting' they're dead!"

Everyone laughed.

"In the other, a nun – imagine me and *my* attitude to religion, playing a nun? She decides life is passing her by and wants to have sex before it's too late."

They laughed even louder.

"A comedy?" Archie tried to straighten his face.

"A love story!" Fenella flicked him with her napkin.

"Do you know the director? Is there something that could sway you either way?" Archie was being unusually practical.

"That's the problem, they're all so young. I don't know anyone anymore," Fenella admitted.

"The male lead, would that help make up your mind?" Mia tried.

"They're asking James Quinn to be the nun's lover when he's finished your film, darling. But the actress in the soap falls for a much younger man, she deludes herself he loves her. Needless to say it ends badly. I've checked the list of executives but again, no one I really know." She gave Archie another frown. "I wish you'd come and be the nun's lover, I'd know what to do then."

"I'm sorry, dear heart, I'm really not up to it."

"Ravaging virgins or the part itself?" She slid him a look.

He gave a melancholy smile. "Neither, I'm afraid."

"He had to kick the habit!" Driscoll joked, lightening a sudden dip in the atmosphere.

Archie scowled. "Always stealing my lines!"

"The actress in the soap then?" Fenella asked.

"Regular money," Eamon interjected. "Make you a household name. Think of the revenue streams, advertising expensive face creams for mature women, for example."

"He has a point." Bernice sided with Eamon. "Who knows what's around the corner?"

They all knew what was around the corner, for Archie, anyway.

"I've always worked, I'm fine," Fenella replied, giving Bernice a pointed look.

Bernice shrugged. "So you have. There's many been in the business thirty years, yet barely worked for half of it."

Mia looked at one of her mother's closest friends. Bernice was very adept at making a compliment sound like a slight. She had a very low opinion of theatricals, despite being close to two of the most lauded thespians in the world. Mia considered acting, good acting, *extremely* gruelling and was grateful she had not followed Fenella into the limelight after all. She recalled the day she had made that decision distinctly. She and Archie had been sailing and returning to the summerhouse were thrilled to discover Fenella had arrived. Fenella however, was annoyed at being disturbed.

"Can't I get any peace?" She had said crankily, going back to her work. Mia was crestfallen, she had not seen her mother for months.

"Whatever you're doing, we'll help!" Archie was unfazed by her bad humour.

"Please don't," she grimaced. "I fear I may have to drop out, it's far too complicated and with so many brilliant actors involved I'm petrified I'll make a total balls of it."

"Even after all this time you're still petrified?" Mia had picked up the discarded script.

"Always. If I wasn't petrified I'd be terrified I wasn't." Fenella reopened her book.

"What do you mean?" Mia asked. They had had this conversation before, but she was pleased to have her mother's attention, however briefly.

Fenella put the book aside, she had been reading the novel the new movie was based on.

"Because I wouldn't be able to give my best," she explained.

"Does it always have to be your best?" Mia wondered, it was only acting after all.

"Of course, without question." Her mother was emphatic.

"Even something like a TV commercial?" Fenella did voiceovers, it paid well. "That must be very tiring."

"Exhausting." She closed her eyes to demonstrate the fact.

"Is that why actors rest so often?"

"Resting is a term used to describe an out of work actor, someone between roles," Archie explained helpfully.

"I can't ever remember you ever resting, Mother," Mia said.

"That's because I haven't been found out yet." Fenella tried to go back to her book.

"Oh, come on!" Decried Archie.

"It's true! I'm so petrified I learn all my lines and everyone else's and then try really hard to be the best I possibly can, you know I do, Archie, I'm renowned for it."

"But you're beautiful, surely that counts for something," Mia persisted.

"Worse if you're considered beautiful. They expect you to fail, want you to. So you have to try even harder. Totally exhausting." Fenella fell back into the chair to demonstrate her weariness.

"No wonder you're so often in bed," Mia replied, innocently.

"Sometimes that's for sex, darling." Archie laughed, being helpful again. "She has to try and fit that in as well." He ducked as Fenella threw the novel at him.

Mia blinked and the scene dissolved. She wondered fleetingly if Fenella might find a novel to throw at Bernice but Archie distracted everyone in the nick of time.

"Driscoll, grab some loungers, we'll head to the beach after lunch."

"I won't come," Bernice stood. "It's too hot today."

"Afraid you'll dry up even more," Fenella said, under her breath.

"You'd make a lovely nun," Bernice came back, giving Fenella an appraising glance. "Better than an actress in my opinion."

Mia saw Archie place his hand on her mother's wrist.

"You're probably right, Bernice." Fenella grinned openly at her old sparring partner. "Will I lift up the blinds, let in the sun? Any vampires lurking can leave now."

Archie coughed. This was Fenella's particularly cruel nickname for Bernice, implying that never having had a proper job she sucked him dry.

"Now, now precious one, no bad vibes, not today." Mia

heard Archie tell her mother. "Let's get some fresh air, it's rather stuffy in here." He shot Eamon a look. Eamon smiled back, Archie could be as rude as he liked; he was going nowhere.

It was indeed a glorious day; the tide was in and the sea, a barely rippling sheet of dark blue silk, stretched as far as the eye could see.

"Not too long, Archie," Bernice instructed, handing sundae dishes to Mia. "You don't want sunstroke on top of everything else."

He pulled a face at Fenella. She handed over her extravagant hat which Archie plonked on his head.

"Crisis averted." He gave his sister a gracious smile. Bernice held the scoop aloft.

"Only if you have a proper meeting with Eamon," she smiled back, eyes challenging. "Only then will the real crisis be averted."

"All in hand," Archie replied. "Mia, come and play in the sun, you're hardly ever here these days and I'm nearly dead."

"Archie!" Fenella exclaimed.

"Well, it's true and Bernice will let her do more housework than Leela if we're not careful."

"That wouldn't be hard," teased Fenella. Leela was taking her afternoon nap, one of the few habits she had never tried to give up.

Bernice took the dishes from Mia. "Go, Driscoll can bring the ice cream." Then, to Archie. "I never see her either, you know and I could easily die before you, you selfish old shite!"

Mia hesitated but Bernice was joking. Relieved she followed the others outside; relationships at Galty House could be volatile to say the least and Mia did not know the half of it.

SMOKE AND MIRRORS

Fenella and Archie were the first to return from the beach. Archie liked an early evening bath. It was an old habit, he learned his lines while soaking in the tub. She knew he was tired when she insisted on carrying her bag and he let her.

"Archie, I ..." She stopped.

"Please don't say you *need* to talk to me. I'm fed up with everyone needing to talk to me." He gave a weary smile.

"It's only ..."

"It's alright, honestly. You'll just have to trust me." He touched her cheek.

"I trust you, totally."

They had reached the landing as the phone rang. Fenella ran back down to the bureau that had nestled in the elegant curve of the staircase for as long as she could remember. Archie waited.

"It's Trixie, she says if you're not dead yet, remember you promised her the jewelled cigarette case?" Fenella held the receiver aloft so Trixie could hear.

Archie, together with the family portraits, peered down from the upper floor. Trixie had been friends with Fenella since the early days. He openly admitted he was jealous of their closeness, nearly having a fit when she moved into the actress's newly-refurbished London home.

Trixie had loathed Archie on sight, declaring he was a manipulative old queen who needed to come out of the closet and stop pretending Fenella was the unrequited love of his life. Thankfully, these days they maintained an amicable truce.

"Tell her to come whenever she likes, you've given me a new

lease of life, she can have anything she wants, always been my favourite."

"No, I have not." Trixie overheard him. "He's delirious on morphine, hated me for years."

"You've hated her for years." Fenella reminded Archie.

"Doesn't mean she's not a favourite though." He blew a kiss. "Now, I must take my bath." Archie strode briskly towards his room; he knew she was watching. The door closed heavily.

"He's gone," Fenella said into the phone.

"Gone?" Trixie gasped.

"To take a bath."

"Oh, for a minute I thought … anyway, old goat sounds perfectly alright to me. What do *you* think?"

"We're here for a reason, that's for sure. I thought it was to say goodbye but Archie's not quite ready to say goodbye yet by the looks of things."

"He always was an outrageous tease." Trixie had a smile in her voice. "Any hint on the Mia thing?"

"They had me worried, taking off to the boathouse when we arrived, then came back laughing, he hasn't told her anything he shouldn't have, not yet anyway."

"How can you stop him though?" Trixie was practical.

"Plead, beg, blackmail, I'll think of something." Fenella was not joking. "We've to meet in the library at seven, he wants to talk to all of us." She twisted the cord through her fingers.

"What about?"

"The future, I guess." She said it lightly, yet the words hung in the air.

Replacing the receiver Fenella noticed a silhouette flickering against the glass, the last of the sunset causing everything to shimmer. She ran to the door, swinging out in one movement. But the embodiment of the shadow had disappeared.

Running down the steps, she looked left and right. No one. She saw movement in the kitchen garden, a flash of yellow. As she sped towards it, her scarf came loose and pulling it free she lost an earring. Damn, she would have to go back, the earring was special. She was rattled, someone had been listening at the door, she was sure of it. Stopping to fix the scarf, she decided to look for her earring later and pushing on through the gate found Bernice stooped, yellow hat fastened tightly against the breeze.

"Beetroot," she said, holding out a clutch of bulbous vegetation. "Very good for blood pressure." She gave the actress a frown. "When did you take up running, Fenella? I'm full of admiration, fighting back the years the way you do, must be very draining."

Fenella tried to hide her breathlessness by turning to face the sea.

"Is … there … only … you here?" She dragged in air.

"No, you're here with me, aren't you?" Bernice lifted the brim of her hat to look intently at Fenella. "Has the sun got to you, again?" A euphemism she invoked whenever she suspected illegal substances had been imbibed.

"I thought someone was outside the hall door but they ran away."

"Did they ring the bell? Call out?" Bernice asked. Fenella could be fanciful at the best of times.

"No, I saw something, felt something … I'm not sure." She touched her ear, distracted. "Now I've lost an earring."

"Where?"

"Here, just now."

"Which earring?" Bernice asked, taking Fenella's chin in her hand.

"A gold one." Fenella touched the other earring mournfully.

"Do you mean the pair you keep here? The ones in the

mother of pearl jewellery box, you put them on when you come, yet leave them when you go. Why, I wonder?" Bernice was looking at her.

"They belong here, that's why." Fenella's eyes glittered.

"Surprised you haven't lost one before, you're so careless with everything." Bernice looked away, satisfied.

"Not these, I treasure these. Hope it's not a bad omen."

"What nonsense! Just time for a new pair, that's all." Bernice picked up the secateurs and started snipping at the mint, wild and unruly, taking over everything as usual.

"Fenella! Bernice!" A shout from the beach. The women looked at each other. Eamon was waving urgently. They ran towards him.

Mia was on the edge of a sun lounger at the bottom of the steps. Driscoll was crouched, wrapping a towel around her calf, the fabric dark with blood.

"What happened?" Bernice looked at the wound.

"Don't take the pressure off," Driscoll commanded. "A nasty gash, we've to stop the blood."

Fenella knelt beside Mia, white-faced beneath her shock of hair.

"What happened?" Fenella glared accusingly along the beach, where not half an hour since Mia had been strolling, waving back as they packed the day away. She had been gazing at the new development, the shiny marina filled with sparkling yachts, the elegant hotel on the cliff, wrapped in a terrace, its awning a billowing sail fluttering out to sea. She had never seen anything like it, certainly not in Ireland. Maybe the shouty stress-head had something about him after all.

"The ground seemed to fall away. I went down, panicked and something sharp cut my leg as I came up." She was wet up to her chest, her top sodden, splashed with sand.

"Your hands are freezing." Fenella rubbed her daughter's clenched fists. Mia started to shake.

"It's shock, back to the house, now!" Bernice ordered. "Eamon, help Driscoll carry her. Fenella keep the pressure on, I'll run ahead, ring the surgery."

"I don't think …" Mia tried to reassure everyone but no one was listening and besides she was just about to faint.

Strangely calm and nauseous at the same time, Mia tried to speak but her lips were numb and letting go she just drifted away in a swirl of grey cloud.

Fenella pulled a throw from a chair, eyes fixed on her child.

"What did she say?"

The doctor was replacing phials in his bag.

"It's the painkiller, she'll sleep awhile. Quite a scare, a lot of blood. I've given her tetanus and antibiotic just in case. Keep an eye on the wound, I'll take another look in a few days." He gave a reassuring smile. He had known the famous actress and her daughter for over thirty years.

Everyone loved Doctor Morrissey, trusted him implicitly. Besides he knew where all the skeletons were buried, Archie always quipped whenever the doctor was mentioned.

Once Mia was settled in the library, Bernice sent Eamon to see how Archie was faring.

"He won't let me in," Eamon announced, pushing the bell at the mantelpiece for more tea. He was wasting his time, Leela never responded to the bell. "The door's locked. Told me to go away. I reminded him we had unfinished business and he said to stick my unfinished business up my arse, preferably with the file still in my briefcase!"

"Head in the sand as usual," Bernice said wearily.

"And the business?" Fenella watched as Eamon leaned proprietorially against the fireplace.

"All of this!" he replied, encompassing the room. "We must make arrangements, sort out his affairs." He shook his head, hair springing from his scalp anxiously.

"You know Archie and paperwork." Bernice tucked the throw around Mia. "He hasn't made a will and won't tell us what he wants us to do. Wouldn't surprise me if we're to put him in a boat and set fire to the lot."

"A fitting end to the Viking he is." Driscoll had been flicking through Archie's sailing magazines.

"Wouldn't surprise me either." Eamon agreed, then looked sheepishly at Bernice.

"We need to know." She sounded desperate. "It's just that …" The door opened and Leela came in backwards carrying a tray freshly laden with tea and toast. "Dear Lord, Leela we're still stuffed, you've served everything in the kitchen," Bernice said, changing the subject.

"Ah sure, why not, with everyone here?" Leela replied.

Fenella stood.

"I'll go, he's probably just tired. It's been a long day and he's a sick man."

Bernice reached for her friend's hand.

"You do know how sick, don't you, Fenella? He wasn't being dramatic when he sent for you. It really *is* just a matter of time."

"Isn't that the case for all of us?" Fenella was brusque.

"Don't be in denial, please." Bernice looked into Fenella's eyes. "Don't, now."

"But … he looks so well, in such good form."

"He *is* one of the world's finest actors," Bernice reminded her. "And don't make a big deal of this either," she nodded at Mia buried under a throw. "He's so on edge these days, the slightest thing sets him off. He'd be mortified if he thought anything had happened to her here."

Fenella went to take the staircase at the far end of the library. The entrance had once been disguised as a bookcase but Mrs Fitzgerald had it removed, installing a plain oak door instead. It was strangely at odds with the rich mahogany shelves and leather tomes lining the walls.

"That's locked," Bernice looked up. "Haven't used it in years, dry rot or something."

"Of course," Fenella said. "I knew that. I'm all over the place today, must be the sun." She turned and walked the length of the room avoiding everyone's eyes.

Arriving at Archie's door, Fenella tapped. It was locked. She pushed the handle upwards with her hip. The manoeuvre, known only to the Fitzgeralds' inner circle, lifted the mechanism, releasing the lock. Putting her hand over her eyes, she stepped into the room. She could smell cigar smoke.

"For Christ's sake, woman, you've seen me naked before haven't you?" He was speaking from the ancient roll-top bath perched on a plinth before the window.

"Of course, but you're old and wrinkly now and I've just eaten," she told him, taking her fingers away, the frailty of his voice disturbing her.

"I could do with a hand." He lay half out of the water, translucent skin illuminated by the chandelier above the bath, the whole scene reflected eerily in the mirrored alcove. He had wedged himself between the tub and the wall. Grabbing a bathrobe, she ran to help.

"Should you be smoking these?" She took the cigar from his lips.

"Ran out of weed," he replied.

The bathwater, now cold, was a murky, brownish red.

Finding soap, she lathered his trapped shoulder and taking a towel threaded it behind his neck, holding each end separately.

"Now, when I count to three I want you to haul yourself up, I'll pull on the towel, okay?"

Fenella was praying this would work, his lips were purple.

"One, two, three ..."

His skin made a sucking sound and she gripped him as he fell forward, hugging him tightly. He had turned to stone. She rubbed his chest with the towel.

"How long have you been stuck here?"

"A good while, before that tosser of a solicitor came looking for me anyway."

"You were stuck and didn't ask Eamon to help you?"

"No way, that would have meant telling him how to open the door. That's a family secret."

"That's ridiculous, you've probably caught pneumonia. Anyway, Eamon *is* family."

"He thinks he is." Archie gave her one of his lizard looks.

"Now, a hot shower!" Fenella said, taking charge.

"Yes please, darling, that would be wonderful, one of the downsides of this bloody thing is incontinence." He gestured as the filthy water sluiced away.

Fiddling with the mixer tap, she wet her face in case of tears.

"I've played a nurse, don't forget, Sister Moriarty in *Angels of War*."

"Yes, you were an American, glad you didn't say 'no shit?' when I told you I was incontinent, I'd have wet myself laughing!"

Fenella smiled, Archie was warming up a bit.

Eamon was dozing as Bernice tidied away the remnants of tea, when the door swung back to reveal a perfectly groomed

Archie, resplendent in vintage smoking jacket and silk cravat. Fenella, on his arm, wore an embroidered tunic with matching bandana, a shimmer of crystals at her ears.

"I hope you haven't dressed for dinner," Bernice told the couple in the doorway. "Because there isn't any." There was a rattle and they parted, making way for Leela carrying the best glasses and a plastic bucket bearing a bottle of champagne.

Archie beamed as the housekeeper placed the bucket on the table. "Improvisation, the lifeblood of originality!" He scanned the room and seeing Mia motionless on the chaise, froze. "What's happened? Why was I not sent for?"

Her eyes opened. "I gashed my leg, that's all."

Archie looked at Fenella.

"Doctor Morrissey's been, dressed the wound, she'll be fine," she told him.

"Show me," he instructed. They drew back the throw, her leg swathed in a large dressing.

"How did it happen?"

"I was just paddling and seemed to fall, as if there was a hole in the sand."

"On our beach?" Archie frowned.

"Must have been a bit of rock or something," Driscoll offered, returning with a basket of peat.

Archie was momentarily distracted, Driscoll had been overtly helpful all day. "Does it hurt? Can you stand?"

"I'll be running tomorrow," Mia smiled into his worried face. "I won't let it spoil the fun."

"That's my girl! A drink, you must have a drink!"

"What're we celebrating?" Bernice asked, eyeing Leela hovering, hoping there would be a glass of champagne coming her way too.

"We've much to celebrate, have we not?" Archie opened the

bottle with a flourish, gesturing to Eamon to pour drinks while he took a glass to Mia.

"Just a sip," Fenella warned, pushing hair from Mia's face, blotchy with heat. "She's had strong painkillers."

"Champagne makes everything better," he told the patient.

"Archie, we're waiting!" Bernice was irked.

He waved a hand at her. She harrumphed, taking a glass from Eamon until her brother, satisfied Mia had enough champagne, took his place in front of the fireplace.

"Beloved family and friends." He was using his warm, speech-making voice. "A toast. The future."

They raised their glasses. Everyone except Bernice.

"I would really like to know what you mean by that," she said, quietly.

"I've no crystal ball, Bernice, no tarot telling me what's around the corner but here we are, all together and I think it's important to be optimistic, just because things change it doesn't mean they won't change for the better."

"At least tell me you've spoken to Eamon and made a will, tell me that much." Her eyes were pleading.

"No need to speak to Eamon." Archie took a cigar from his breast pocket. He sipped the wine. "Lovely vintage, don't you think?"

"But there is, Archie, a desperate need, you *have* to make a will!" Bernice urged.

"But I have, dearest sister."

"Have what?"

"Made a will."

"Eamon, is this true?" she asked their cousin.

Eamon put his glass down, flustered.

"Not with Eamon, I don't want Eamon to know what's in my will. Why would I? What's it to him?" Archie smiled, taking the sting out of his words.

"He's our solicitor." Bernice was beginning to despair.

"If I choose to tell anyone what's in my will that *will* be my decision. As it stands, until I've ditched this mortal coil, my will is my business. Now, close your mouth, Bernice, let's make plans for tomorrow and the unveiling of my supreme surprise."

With half his audience spellbound and the other half flummoxed, Archie lit his cigar and blowing smoke rings above his head, described the fabulous yacht he had recently acquired, inviting them all aboard for lunch the next day. A door slammed. He stopped mid-flow. Bernice had taken her leave.

"No matter. She'll know everything in the fullness of time," he said softly, pointing to his sister's abandoned glass. "Drink up, Eamon, waste not, want not. I'd hate you to say I never shared anything with you."

As the others chatted, making plans for tomorrow, their voices faded and Mia woozy again was dreaming of the beach, Galty's beautiful little bay, where she had learned to swim ...

... she was in the ocean now, the silky water caressed her and she was again a mermaid, twirling as the colours of the ocean floated past, stretching her arms, hair flowing, swishing her tail, wild and free. But the water grew cold and she started to shiver, in the distance she could see something dark, drawing her forwards. She felt her heart flutter and giving a huge flick of her tail started to swim away, away from the blackness as fast as she could. She knew she had to escape, because there, deep in the darkness, something evil lurked, something that ate mermaids for breakfast; particularly mermaids who had no protection, tasty little mermaids, whose fathers had abandoned them ... always a delicacy on the sea monster's menu.

"You're only a nightmare," she said into the darkness. "I've seen it all before." And though she was still half-asleep and longed to stretch the stiffness from her leg, she dare not move, not yet, not till it was light and there was undeniable proof that the sea monster really was just a figment of her imagination.

HER MAIDEN VOYAGE

Mia woke early; the wisp of nightmare evaporating as she opened her eyes, and although her leg throbbed, her head was clear. Throwing back the duvet – the same blue cotton scattered with buttercups that had draped her bed since her teenage – she pulled a sweater over her tee-shirt and hopped to the window. The sunlight was blinding, and shielding her eyes against the brightness, she pressed her forehead against the glass to absorb the warmth.

An early shower had left everything freshly washed; the yellow terrace, twisting path and lawns, shining all the way to golden sand and glittering sea. She pushed open the window, breathing deeply to drink in the air – calming, cleansing, cathartic.

The breeze pushed strands of hair about her face and taking it to twist into a knot, her fingers touched the metal braid on her left hand, the makeshift engagement ring … Rupert. She wrapped herself in an embrace, remembering gorgeous, outrageous, fabulous Rupert. How he had pursued and seduced her, peeling away her inhibitions and almost eating her alive. Just the memory made her shiver with pleasure, every inch kissed and caressed on that steamy September night. She recalled the scent of cypress, the smoothness of his skin, her fingers in his damp hair, his mouth at her breast as he murmured her name.

"Mia! Mia, are you up?" She jumped back, embarrassed. Archie was below in cut-off jeans and a Rolling Stones tee-shirt. "Fancy a walk on the beach?"

"My leg," she reminded him.

"A hop then? We'll go in, saltwater will do it good."

"That's how it happened!"

He gave her a grin. "Come on, let's plot an adventure like the old days, might discover a monster's lair."

She started laughing. He had always eased away the reticence, igniting her imagination with fascinations of mystery and intrigue.

"On my way," she told him.

By the time Mia hobbled through the kitchen, Archie was nowhere to be seen. Thoughtfully, a walking stick was propped against the back door but patience had never been one of Archie's virtues, he rarely waiting for anyone or anything. Mia recognised the stick, a family heirloom. It featured a fox head handle and bronze name plate above a slim length of golden wood. The elegant animal had amber eyes and the plate read 'Francis Fitzgerald', the rarely mentioned patriarch, now long gone.

Reaching the steps, she looked along the bright sand. Deserted. Archie would be in the boathouse, preparing for the great 'reveal' he had promised his guests the previous evening. Her leg ached, so taking Archie's advice she dragged herself to the water's edge and wriggling out of joggers, sat in the shallows, sending out sparkling ripples. The water was cold but it would help. Mia gritted her teeth and wiggling her toes, turned her gaze on the high, cloudless sky. Archie was right, the throbbing subsided.

Unwinding her hair, she let the sea lap lazily about her, as leaning back the coils of copper darkened, dipping in and out of the water. Turning on her side she looked across the barely quivering bay to Phoenix Island, a bumpy green mass, the mysterious hump-backed sea creature of her dreams, glowing like a dark emerald in the heat and finally relaxing she stretched out to let the ocean soothe her, the cry of the gulls swooping and swirling through her mind. At last all was calm.

"Is it a mermaid?" the little girl whispered.

"Never seen a mermaid round here before." A man's voice.

"No, but I'm sure they come here for holidays, Mama says all the best people do."

He laughed, deep in his chest. "Why don't you ask her?"

"I don't speak mermaid," she replied, cornflower blue eyes gazing at the figure, half in, half out of the sea, ropes of sodden hair splayed in the sand.

"She might speak English, they're very well educated, they travel a *lot.*"

Mia became aware of a presence at her shoulder.

"Excuse me," a young voice said. "Are you a mermaid?"

Mia dragged her brain out of cotton wool clouds and propped herself on an elbow. The little girl leaning towards her had such a look of innocent, hopefulness Mia really wished she could say yes. She lifted her good leg out of the water.

"Sorry, just an ordinary human." The little girl was about nine years old, golden hair tied up in a ponytail. She wore denim dungarees and sparkly sandals which she kept very deliberately out of the water. She looked familiar. "I'm Mia." She wiped her wet, sandy hand extending it to the little girl.

"I'm Pearl." The girl frowned, ignoring the hand offered. "You're definitely not a mermaid then?"

"Nope. No fishtail."

"Not always the case," said a soft brown voice.

Mia jumped. "Sorry?" Trying to stand, she forgot her injury and crumpled towards the ground. Two strong arms gripped her, gently standing her upright. She tried to take her own weight but her leg gave way and she fell against him, the warm skin through his shirt making her shiver.

"Sorry," she said again.

"Don't be." He gave a lazy smile.

Balancing on one leg, she took hold of her hair to wring out the water, trying to brush sand off her clothes at the same time. A wave washed over her feet.

"Look!" Pearl cried, pointing at the water. The walking stick with the fox head was being taken out to sea.

"I'll get it." He splashed into the waves.

Mia watched the man swim after the stick.

"Don't worry," Pearl called out. "He's a very good swimmer." In seconds the man held it aloft and, as if riding a wave, was back on the beach. Placing it across his arm, he presented it to Mia.

"Your walking cane, ma'am," he gave that smile again.

"Just borrowed. Bashed my leg, silly accident," she stammered, feeling foolish.

"Sorry to hear that." He turned the cane in his hand. "Lovely workmanship." He was looking directly at her. "We've met before, you're the girl on the train."

Pearl peered into her face. "Oh, yes the mad woman, the one who shouted at Ross in the bathroom."

Mia recognised the little girl now. But the man standing before her in a wet tee-shirt, damp shorts and a flop of dark wavy hair looked nothing like the fractious bundle she had encountered on the train.

"The *mad* woman?" Mia pulled on her sunglasses, avoiding his eyes.

"Yes, that's what Ross said, a mad woman was yelling at him in the bathroom on the train and I shouldn't have left my seat because I knew he'd be right back." Pearl gave the man a look. "Though some grownups say they'll be right back, then don't come back at all."

"Okay, Pearl, time to let the lady alone," he said.

"Thanks." Mia let the stick take the weight of her bad leg and started towards the boathouse. Archie would be wondering where she was.

"We're going that way too." Pearl skipped to catch up. "Going to see Archie."

"Do you mean Archie Fitzgerald?" Mia was surprised.

"I don't know his other name but we're going to see his new boat. I'm being the Queen." She pointed at her sparkly sandals. "I've to smash champagne over it."

"No crown?" Mia teased.

"It's in the bag." Pearl pointed at her backpack. "A tiara actually, I'm a bit young for a crown."

Mia hid a smile, the little girl was very serious. "Is your uncle royalty too?" She nodded at the man.

"No, he's just ordinary. I've ten."

"Ten what?"

"Uncles. Do you think that's enough?"

"Probably. Are they all like him?"

"He's one of the better ones," Pearl confirmed.

"I'm going to Archie's too," Mia told her. "He's *my* uncle in a way."

"He's one of *my* ten," Pearl said. "We're cousins then!"

Mia gave a quizzical look.

"Pearl likes to collect things, uncles, cousins, she's big into family." The man had overheard.

"Have you any brothers and sisters, Pearl?" Mia smiled.

"No," Pearl replied. "But I'm saving up for a sister."

Before Mia could comment, they were interrupted by a skinny man in a Rolling Stones tee-shirt.

"About bloody time. Where've you all been? I could have

launched an entire fleet by now." Archie waved them into the boathouse.

Pearl ran towards him, arms wide.

"Uncle Archie, this is Mia, are you her uncle too?"

He lifted her, spinning her round.

"Sort of, I've known her since she was even smaller than you."

"But I'm quite tall!" Pearl was indignant. The men shook hands heartily.

"So you've met Miss Flanagan here." Archie pulled Mia into the embrace.

"Not properly." The man extended his hand. "Ross, Ross Power, good to meet you."

"Mia," she said, not realising how cold her hand was until he touched it.

"Ross helped deliver Banshee, he's over from the States, running the family business."

Ross Power shrugged. "Just helping out really."

"The family business?" Mia asked.

"The new hotel, very upmarket, you know what these flashy Yanks are like." Archie was smiling warmly at the newcomers. Mia remembered, the man had given his business card to Fenella; she felt a twinge, shifted her weight.

"You must come visit," Ross Power said. "Be my pleasure to show you round."

Mia caught sight of herself bumpily reflected in the surface of the boat; straggly hair, sand-stained jogging bottoms. *Very upmarket*.

"Thanks, but I've to get back to work."

"Maybe next time." He gave her a sweeping look. "What do you do?"

"Mia's in the *business*, darling," Archie answered for her.

"An actor?" He sounded surprised.

"Just a dresser." Mia loathed being the focus of attention.

"No *just* about it! She's fabulous at her job, hides her light under a bushel. A costume designer's dream, makes everything look amazing and runs the show like clockwork." Archie was building her up, as was his way. She was about to protest when the large wooden doors slid back and Driscoll appeared, closely followed by Fenella and Bernice.

"Dear Lord, it's huge," Fenella exclaimed, looking at the vessel, half-hidden under the canvas.

"You said it was for pottering about the harbour?" Bernice was aghast. "You could live on this!"

"Not quite, sister dear," Archie replied. "But I'll never have another so, I thought I'd go for the best." He gave a sad look.

"Emotional blackmail," Bernice retorted. Her brother had always been a skilful manipulator. "Don't think I won't ask the price just because you're ill." She was teasing more than angry and tired of fighting.

"Shall we get her launched?" Archie's eyes danced with excitement. He started shouting instructions as they busied themselves, happy to play their part in this, the grand design of someone they all cared deeply about. They dragged off the canvas, fastening fenders and coiling sheets neatly on deck, lockers were searched for lifejackets and flares. Archie fired up the electrics, flicking switches as he listened to the hum of the engine. He called to Driscoll to check the propeller, declaring they were good to go.

Mia felt pretty helpless but pleased to be 'maid of honour' attending Pearl's regal role.

"If you'll fetch my tiara, I know where the champagne is," the little girl told her.

Satisfied all was ready, Archie instructed Fenella and Ross to open the doors as wide as possible. The young man gave Fenella a double take.

"Are you?" Ross remembered chatting to her on the train, totally unaware of who she was beyond a kind lady looking after his distraught niece.

"Am I who you think I am?" she fluttered.

"I keep forgetting who Archie is in real life. Are you his wife?" Ross opened the huge doors easily. The sunshine streamed in.

"The oldest friends," Fenella told him. "Family, really."

"I didn't recognise you on the train yet I've seen you in so many movies, I'm sorry."

"You were rather stressed." Fenella waved at the little girl with her daughter. "All's well that ends well, such a lovely child. The slightly bigger little girl is my daughter, Mia."

"We've met," Ross said.

"Before?" Fenella was hopeful, Mia was secretive about boyfriends.

"Just now on the beach. Pearl's convinced she's a mermaid." They stopped to watch Pearl brush sand from Mia's top, in an attempt to upgrade her to a passable lady-in-waiting.

"Are we nearly ready?" Archie appeared on deck and noticing Pearl's tiara, nipped below for his captain's hat. Pearl nodded approval. Mia saw them exchange a look. Archie smiled straight at her.

"Amazing, isn't she? Just like you at that age."

Mia relaxed into his smile; *do you grow out of being amazing?* She wondered.

"Chocks away!" Archie called as the boat started down the slipway. Pearl was counting, one, two, three, holding the bottle aloft. The boat glided towards them, sliding out of the shadows. It gleamed as the bow hit the sunshine.

"I name this boat Banshee, God bless her and all who sail in her," Pearl shouted in her biggest voice as she threw the bottle with as much force as she could muster.

"Thank you, ma'am," called Archie, saluting as they zipped down the ramp, faster and faster towards the water.

Pearl produced a hanky to wave after them. It made Mia laugh, she was such an old-fashioned little thing.

The boat slipped easily into the sea. Archie fired up the engine, it purred deliciously, lapping the water like milk as he powered away from the shore. Mia and Pearl scrambled down to the beach, stopping at the water's edge to watch.

"Is Archie coming back for you? I'm afraid I can't join you with this gammy leg," Mia said.

"No point coming back for me, I don't like boats."

A shout. Archie had swung Banshee round, bobbing happily off shore, everyone on deck, smiling in the sunshine, even Bernice.

"Are you coming aboard? There's a picnic and everything," he called. Mia felt a tug at her sleeve.

"I haven't told him," Pearl hissed.

Mia leaned on her stick, pointing at her leg.

"Bit sore, I'll have to head back," she shouted.

Archie frowned. Ross stood beside him.

"I'll stay with Mia, she's hurting," Pearl said.

"Wait!" Ross pulled off his top and dived into the sea, powering through the water, spray flashing. In minutes he was beside them, shaking himself. Mia looked away.

"Do you need a hand getting back? Your leg, must be painful …" Ross offered. Pearl had obviously decided she was going to make a friend of the mad woman.

"He could carry you, he's quite strong," Pearl piped up.

"Oh, no." Mia was mortified. "I'll …"

A bleep … another bleep. She reached inside a pocket for her phone. A text.

Call when you can. Sooner rather than later.

It was Lol. Mia scowled at the screen.

"Problem?" Ross asked.

"Work," she replied. "I have to go." She started limping back towards the house, leaning heavily on the stick as she went.

"See you real soon," Pearl called. Mia waved back and shuffled on. Pearl took Ross's hand. "Told you she's a mermaid," she nodded knowingly, watching Mia struggle through the sand. "Only just getting used to her legs."

TOTAL RECALL

"Where are you? It's been ages, what's going on?" Lol shouted down the phone.

"I can hear you. I'm not on Mars." Mia was sitting on the steps watching the waves grow restless.

"You could be, for all I know. When're you coming back, you're needed here!"

"Archie's ill, I'm needed here too." She had been away less than two days.

"He *is* an actor, you know. Could be milking it for all it's worth."

"Lol, please." Mia was in no mood for her colleague's petulance.

"Sorry Mia, but we're near to breaking point, loads of people are sick and everyone's arguing, accusing everyone else of holding things up, it's a total nightmare."

"You okay?"

"Yeah, I'm fine, I don't eat any of that catering crap." True, Lol mostly drank coffee and smoked. "It's probably Legionnaires."

"Serious then?" Mia grew concerned.

"Horrendous and as much as Archie needs you, we need you too. We'll never finish this flippin' thing without you."

Mia was torn; Archie was not quite at death's door; she could probably go back to work till the end of the week but her leg hurt more than she let on. She tried a different tack.

"You can cope, you're the best." Despite being some way down the pecking order, the costume department could make or break a schedule. The wrong earring on the wrong actress could mean reshooting an entire scene; if it involved a particular location or time of day the impact on budget, let alone the director's patience, could be devastating.

"We need you ... I need you. Archie's a pro, he'll understand." Lol almost pleaded.

Guilt rippled through her. "Okay, if Archie's happy for me to leave, I'll be on my way as soon as."

Mia heard Lol's exaggerated sigh of relief. It did not occur to either of them that Mia's return could be problematic. A national rail strike had been declared in time for the bank holiday and with all the taxi firms pushed to breaking point, the journey to a remote castle in the Wicklow Mountains might not be that easy.

Archie was in bed, propped on a mountain of pillows and snoring slightly. Mia reached out to touch the initials embroidered on the pocket of his pyjamas. She remembered working the twirl of letters in silk thread, a skill Bernice had taught her many years ago.

She looked about the room, somehow Archie managed to be old school and state-of-art at the same time. His computer stood on a eighteenth century desk, piles of books and an electronic tablet on the nightstand, the latest TV on the wall. Archie liked to keep up to speed with the world as much as he tried to shun it.

Eyeing the shape beneath the covers she frowned, he was wasting away. She made to leave, he looked so peaceful, the pain she had seen dug into his skin the previous evening, smoothed away.

"Must you go?" he murmured, taking her by surprise.

"It seems so," she told him. "Some sort of food poisoning has wiped out half the unit, they need me back on set."

He scowled. "But I need you *here*."

Mia pulled a face. Lying there he was thinner, translucent even, but Archie was as vibrant as ever, eyes sparkling with devilment, his raucous cackle spilling out at the merest joke. Until last night. Supper was a simple affair of soup and cheese in the kitchen but Archie had gone straight to bed, suddenly withdrawing to his room, the day at sea totally exhausting him.

"Does he need the doctor?" Mia had asked Bernice, as she bundled sheets into the washing machine.

"Not now." She slammed the door shut. "I've tried to explain to your mother, it *is* just a matter of time, despite the act, Archie won't be here for much longer."

Mia was shocked by the baldness of her words.

"I'm sorry but there it is. As much as I love the fact he is determined to enjoy every last drop of life he has left, I do despair at times." Bernice stared out of the window, biting back her frustration as the breeze whipped up, scudding clouds across a darkening sky.

Mia slipped her arm around the older woman. "It must be very hard." They were so close, the elegant sister and wayward brother; forever tussling and squabbling. Bernice always pleased to share their home, warmth, love – then anxious for them to leave, disgruntled others less deserving might receive the attention she craved.

Bernice stiffened. "How's your leg?"

"Loads better. The sea water helped. It was odd, as if the sand gave way. I've never known anything like that on our stretch of beach before."

"The coastline's always changing, tides, erosion."

"But it's safe here, that's why holidaymakers love it so much."

Bernice changed the subject. "Lay the table will you, Mia, there's a good girl."

Supper had been a subdued affair with Fenella excusing herself to spend the rest of the evening with Archie. Not unusual, they often took refuge in his room, watching movies, listening to music, immersing themselves in the sounds and pictures on which they had built their dreams; reminiscing a shared history.

"Make him tell you what he's up to," Bernice had insisted as Fenella left.

The actress raised perfect eyebrows.

"As if *I* could ever make Archie tell me anything," she said coolly, closing the door.

"More secrets and lies," Bernice had muttered, folding her napkin and pushing the soup away.

Upstairs they had lain side by side on Archie's huge French bed watching *Sophie's Choice*. Archie had been up for the Kevin Kline part or so he said, and therefore spent most of the movie criticising his rival's performance. It broke Fenella's heart every time she saw it, so having finished the wine she could feel her own bed calling.

"Shall I leave the door between us unlocked?" she asked, drowsily.

"Why not? I'm hardly going to pounce on you these days."

"I never locked it for that reason."

"No, you locked it so he wouldn't doubt you, I understand why."

"So you should, you had more or less told him we were lovers."

He paused the film.

"I'm sure we were, on more than one occasion."

"Nonsense, high jinks is all that was."

"Really," he gave her a soulful look. "Didn't feel like that to me."

"You've always been oversexed Archie, your auto-biography claims that in every chapter."

"Perhaps, but I admire your myth."

"Which myth?" she was becoming irritated now, she was tired.

"The Virgin Queen of the Screen … apparently you've never had sex with anyone before or since Mia's father."

"That's true!"

"Of course it is. Anyway why do you want the door left open, you're not still having those nightmares are you, after all these years?"

"No, no I have medication to help me sleep now, especially here. No, it's to keep an eye on you, my love. Why else?"

"Christ, I'm not that ill. And although I may have forgiven you for the dreadful names you called me last time we met, I still think Mia needs to know the truth."

Fenella sighed heavily.

"Why now? After all this time, it makes no sense."

"Because if she is to marry and have her own family she needs to know these things, it's disrespectful to keep them from her."

"What? And give her nightmares too?"

Archie shook his head. "Open your eyes, Fenella. Mia has always had the nightmares, she was in your womb when it happened. You can't believe she was immune, surely?"

The door from the landing opened slowly.

"Oh, there you are darling, what's wrong?" Fenella asked gently, Mia was standing tentatively in the doorway, just as she had as a little girl.

"Came to say goodnight." Mia crossed the room and kissed Archie. "Love you." And as she left. "Goodnight, mother, sleep well."

Fenella watched her go.

"Let sleeping dogs lie, Archie, don't be a selfish bastard there's a good boy, just because you want to die with a clear conscience. We're the ones who'll have to deal with the fallout when you've gone." Fenella also took her leave, closing the door between them. Archie listened for a moment, no lock turned.

It was still early but Mia was dressed and packed, standing in his room watching the rise and fall of his chest as dust mites flickered through the sunlit gap in the drapes. Archie's eyes were closed and here in the silence, she wondered how long she would have this precious, gorgeous man in her life and how, when he was gone, would she survive, pretending to carry on with a great, gaping hole in her heart.

He slid her a look. "We still haven't had a proper chat. I wanted us to go sailing, take a picnic like the old days." He took her hand, tapping the lump of metal on her finger. "And I want to hear all your plans, know you're going to be alright."

"Of course, I'll be alright." She tried a bright smile but her eyes were clouded.

"Tell me all about him then, I want to hear everything, make sure I approve."

But Archie knew all about Rupert Boniver, Archie knew most things about Mia. He had been keeping an eye on her ever since she left Ireland to attend college in London. Back then she was a young girl in the big city and Archie made it his business to know when she might need a little help. He wondered if his role as fairy-godfather could be required again soon. He lay back on the pillows, hands across his chest, as if awaiting a bedtime story.

Mia explained she had been contracted as wardrobe supervisor on the remake of *The Three Musketeers*. It was the most challenging job she had ever undertaken, not least because she was working with an inexperienced team who seemed determined to argue over every detail. There had been a freak heat wave, cast and crew were dropping like flies. It was all going horribly, irretrievably wrong when a handsome young actor, namely Rupert Boniver, came to her rescue, setting up a makeshift air conditioning system in the truck, having purloined some ancient refrigerators from the castle's kitchen.

"And thus beholden to the dear boy, you fell for him," Archie surmised. Being on location often kindled romantic alliances, most of which would not survive an hour once sets were dismantled and equipment packed away. "And?"

"We were friends first," Mia said, blushing at how brazen she had been, making sure Rupert knew she wanted to be seduced. Always professional, Mia could still be shocked by the antics of her co-workers but with Rupert she had thrown caution to the wind, flirting outrageously, teasing him at every opportunity, behaving totally out of character. For Rupert she had been wanton and wild, tempting him beyond reason until with her full permission he had completely and utterly devoured her, the most delicious deflowering she had ever experienced. She looked up, Archie was watching her.

"Back in London, the lease on his flat was up. I said he could stay until he found somewhere, it just went from there," she told him.

"How long have you been together?"

"Eight or nine months." She knew to the second. It was just after Fenella had told her about Archie's illness. He had been diagnosed with a rare form of cancer and although determined to fight tooth and nail, the prognosis was not good. Few with the illness lasted longer than twelve months. That was fourteen months ago, Archie was into extra time.

"Is it true love?" Archie asked. "Is he the one?"

"Yes."

"Does he feel the same?"

She nodded.

"You plan to marry?" Archie was using the patriarchal voice he saved for Victorian roles.

"One day. He's just starting out, needs the big break, you know how it is." She did not need to explain how difficult it was for actors to make a decent living, so many came into the business with stars in their eyes, only to leave broken and disillusioned after a few short years.

He patted her hand. "You light up when you talk about him, that's a good sign."

"Wait till you meet him, you'll love him, too."

"Once he makes you happy, my angel, I just want you to be happy. I can picture it now, a fairy-tale wedding to your prince and a wonderful, blissful marriage with hordes of babies, running barefoot on the beach."

"A fairy-tale wedding? I don't think so, not really me is it?"

Archie was prone to flights of fancy.

"Why not? It should be the one day you let rip, go for it, have all the glamour and romance you've ever wanted."

"But I don't want glamour and romance, never have," Mia insisted.

"Nonsense, of course you do, you used to love to dress up as a child, now you make others look fabulous instead. It's still the pursuit of gorgeous, fabulousness."

She gave him a crooked smile. He had hit a nerve.

"One day, just one day, with the spotlight on you. Everything wonderful and special, and all about you for a change. I do love a good wedding."

They giggled together. The door to the adjoining room opened and Fenella appeared. She had been straining her ears to catch what they were talking about and hearing them laugh, knew she had not been betrayed.

She and Archie had been inseparable ever since the Flanagans had moved to Galty House when they were both babies. Fenella's mother, a young widow had been struggling to make ends meet and when Mrs Fitzgerald heard about the woman's plight she sent for her, appointing her secretary to her husband and nanny to her infant son. It was not long before the Fitzgeralds had adopted the Flanagans and the Flanagans had fallen in love with the Fitzgeralds.

Galty House was the only home Fenella had ever known and she had been privileged to grow up in the midst of this delightfully disarming yet dysfunctional family, who loved every inch of her and made her believe, without a shadow of a doubt, she was born to be adored by the entire world. What could possibly go wrong?

"Why Archie, you old romantic." Fenella said, sweetly, the strains of a classic *Roxy Music* album drifting from her room. "Who's this you're talking about?"

Mia dug her fingernails into Archie's palm.

"Never you mind," he replied. "We're gossiping." Mia gave a relieved smile. She had not discussed her plans with anyone, least of all her mother.

"You were talking about marriage, Archie." Fenella was not put off. "Not regretting your relentless bachelorhood surely?"

"You know full well, you're the only woman for me and when you refused me, I just gave up all hope of ever being happy." He turned doleful eyes upon her.

"Outrageous claptrap," Fenella laughed. "No wonder poor Mia shows no sign of making me a grandmother. You've put her off marriage for life."

"I think we all have." Archie squeezed Mia's hand.

Fenella joined Archie on the bed.

"Did you sleep, darling?" she asked him, tightening the towel about her hair.

"I was awake all night, you never came back to check on me." He gave her an accusing look. "And now this one has been recalled."

Fenella pouted, pushing his hair from his brow.

"I do have to go," Mia was firm.

"It's a dreadful film," Archie complained. "But if you must, you must."

"She's a responsible girl, you know that." Fenella slapped his hand.

"Works too darn hard, always has." Archie pulled Mia closer.

"Her work is important. Don't be selfish," Fenella reprimanded, then frowned at her daughter. "Slight problem though, Mia ... transport."

"I only heard about the strike this morning," Mia said.

"You'll have to stay, so!" Archie was triumphant.

"I'll stay, my love," Fenella told him. "But Mia must go, for now."

This was looking more promising, Fenella thought. She wanted Archie to herself, she still needed to know what he wanted to say to Mia and if it was what she suspected, she had to prevent it; prevent it at all costs.

"Promise you'll come back once you've dealt with whatever crisis they have contrived to take you from me?" Archie's gaze searched Mia's face, she had a life elsewhere. "And if you must go, take the car, I insist."

Mia gave him a look. "You mean the Dame, you're actually lending me the Dame?"

He waved at the dressing table. "Keys are in the drawer, goes like a dream."

"Bloody liar." Fenella was incredulous. "You're taking your life in your hands going anywhere in that death trap."

"But, Archie, you love that car, you never let anyone borrow it." Mia was grinning.

"The sad fact is, my precious child, I'll never drive again. Take it, I want you to have it."

Despite her apprehension, Mia was excited. She adored the old car, it had featured solidly throughout her childhood, taking her to parties, dancing lessons, impromptu excursions into the mountains.

"Oh, Archie! Thank you, that's perfect." Then realising she had no idea how to drive it or even where she was going. "Does it have SatNav?"

Archie and Fenella were still laughing as she left.

SUFFERING SABOTAGE

Nervously easing the Daimler out of the garage, Mia drove in slow, jerky zigzags, anxious to avoid the huge potholes littering the drive. At the gateway, she lurched right towards Rosshaven and squirming as the gears squealed, finally let out her breath as the car began to warm up.

The sign to the Harbour Spa Hotel shimmered by the roadside as she drove and glancing through the impressive entrance, she caught sight of the new marina, palms swaying as shiny yachts bobbed on the water. It looked sophisticated, impressive – expensive.

Nearing the town she came upon a swishy new roundabout and slightly bemused, drove round it twice, barely recognising the place with its new shops and cafés; people milling about. She could hear music. She drove round again, it was Rosshaven alright. Maybe the fallout from the Harbour Spa Hotel was not so bad after all she considered, guiding the Daimler away from the coast and on towards the mountains.

Mia was red-eyed and weary by the time she arrived at Kilcohy Castle. Flashing her security pass at the gate she careered towards the costume truck, hardly noticing Courtney Wild desperately trying to flag her down. She screeched to a halt.

"Have you come into money?" He gave the car the once over.

"Belongs to a friend. You needed me back, food poisoning?"

"And the rest, this place is jinxed." He jumped in beside her. "Stuff's gone missing, props damaged, it's a right mess."

"Vandalism?" she asked.

"Seems like it, but targeted, like someone's making a point."

"Why? The project's hardly controversial." Parking next to the caravan, she switched off the engine.

"Dunno. Someone trying to spice things up? Give it more of a profile than it deserves?" Courtney looked even more stressed than usual. Mia punched him playfully in the chest.

"Hey, I'm here now, all will be well. Besides, you take things too seriously, Court. Always have." She changed the subject. "How's your beautiful baby girl?"

"Okay, I think. Rehearsals are going well but Shelley's so tired, she's usually asleep when I ring, so I try not to disturb her. I can't wait to get home and all this stuff just keeps holding things up." He gave her a grateful look. "Boy, am I glad to see you!"

Promising she would get things back on track Mia went to find Lol.

"What kept you?" Lol demanded, eyes bright with relief at the sight of her. "I'm guessing the old bugger is still going strong?"

"For now," Mia replied. Archie's penchant for drama off-stage was well known.

"Heard you were called to a meeting to see who's getting what and just for devilment he's made a will telling no one what's in it." Lol extracted herself from a rail of tailcoats. Mia was just about to ask how she knew, when spotting Mia's bandaged leg Lol shrieked.

"Fell down a hole on the beach, gashed it," Mia explained. "How do you know about the will?" Tittle-tattle travelled at the speed of light in this business.

"We'd fresh supplies delivered, driver came up from the harbour, said everyone's agog to know who's getting Galty

House, it's a stately home isn't it?" Despite her injury, Lol was thinking how well Mia looked; shining face brushed with freckles, turquoise eyes sparkling. "He knows the family lawyer, small world isn't it?"

"This is Ireland, it *is* a small world," Mia pointed out. "I hope they're in for a long wait, Archie's still running around, playing the squire, doing his 'country house by the sea' programme, you know the kind of thing, lunch in the summerhouse, tea in the library – he's even bought a new boat."

Lol chortled. "He's incorrigible, always has been." She lifted the kettle. "Tea?"

Mia gave their workspace a sweeping look; everything appeared orderly.

"Did you really need me back?" Mia started unloading the washing machine.

"Looks better than it is. It's been awful, first food poisoning – nearly everyone has had it – then this." She waved an arm encompassing the truck.

"What?" Mia was flummoxed.

"Sabotage, didn't want to go into details on the phone but someone's been interfering with the costumes."

"Interfering? In what way?"

"It's weird. We'd be shooting a scene and things would start to unravel, literally. Like all the buttons coming off a uniform or a gown splits apart, just like we're jinxed or the place is haunted."

"Nonsense," Mia laughed, but Lol was not joking. "You really think it's sabotage?"

"Has to be." Lol looked stricken, she took her work seriously, they both did. "We were shooting the ball, you know, the night before the wedding scene, the soldiers in uniform, full on, gowns, wigs, tiaras the lot when everyone and I mean everyone, from the leading man down to the dailies were squirming like crazy, no one in the entire cast could stand still."

"How come?" Mia had never heard anything like it.

"Itching powder. Old trick. Someone put itching powder in anything that would touch the skin. Cost a fortune to set that scene, lights, props, orchestra, everything. You know the script, it's pivotal to the whole movie."

Mia was picking through rails.

"Tried to salvage what I could but it's gone into the seams and with so much of it vintage, I can't just machine wash it." Lol was despairing.

"It *is* sabotage then?" Mia looked around gloomily. "And very expensive."

"And this gig was low budget to begin with, what do *you* think's gonna happen?" The kettle boiled.

"They'll never find the money to reshoot." Mia took the mug from Lol's slightly shaking hand. "We'll be out of work again."

"Short of sleeping on the truck, who could have stopped it? Especially if it's an inside job." Lol sighed.

"But we're the only ones with keys, aren't we ..?"

The door burst open. It was Courtney, looking worried and relieved at the same time.

"Everyone, sound stage two in ten." He made to dive back down the steps.

"Courtney!" Mia hobbled after him. "What's happening? It is over?"

"Just be there, Mia. I know you had to leave your post but it was a bad move. Your team fell apart, time to face the music, I'm afraid."

"Charming," Lol scoffed. "Trying to lay the blame at our door. Where was security, that's what I want to know?"

"Good point," Mia agreed, turning pale beneath her freckles.

She checked the door. "No sign of a break-in, unless they came in through the skylight." No response. Mia looked up, squinting at the ceiling. "Did they come through the skylight?"

"Er … I might have forgotten to lock up one evening." Lol muttered.

"What?" Mia was shocked. Lol was conscientious, she never forgot to lock up. "How could you? What was going on?" She looked directly at her colleague of more than ten years.

"Don't lay this one on me, you're the one who pissed off to a family reunion." Lol turned away.

"Lol, tell me the truth, now."

"What?"

"Were you … partying?"

"No, I wasn't 'partying' as you call it."

Mia gazed into her face. "Please don't say …"

Lol ferreted for sunglasses in her pocket. "We'd better go. Might not be as bad as we think."

Mia ran a hand over a rail checking her fingers for goodness knows what, what did itching powder even look like? Her leg ached and a band of tension was tightening over her eyes; despite Lol's uncharacteristic optimism, the situation was already far worse than she had imagined.

The entire crew – actors, technicians and every other movie trade – bustled into the large barn adjacent the castle. Mia cast about; many of the props; furniture, mirrors, chandeliers, were in crates by the door. It looked far from promising.

James, *sans* fangs and vampire cloak, nipped through the crowd to stand beside her.

"What about this then? You've only been gone five minutes …" He stopped. "And Fitz? What news of the old roué, is he really ill?"

"Very. In good spirits though. Asked after you particularly."

"Did he?" James was flattered. "He *must* be ill, we haven't spoken in years. Can't remember what we fell out about … probably your mother."

"Ancient history." Mia replied, she had more to concern her than their bygone grievances.

"Well, he scuppered my chances anyway, I recall that much." James was still miffed.

Michel de Banville, the director took centre stage. Renowned for his smooth, Gallic charm everyone could see he was struggling to maintain his cool in the light of recent events. He looked anxious, weary, he raised his hands.

"It is with a great sadness and 'eavy 'eart, I am today announcing the end of our project." Communal intake of breath. "I am sorry, but it is over."

Gasps. Mumbling.

"We have been the target of an unscrupulous prankster, who 'as determined to ruin the production. And now, we have run out of both time and money." He gave an expansive gesture of despair. "We will salvage what we can back in the studio but as of now, your services are being dispensed."

"What about our pay?" shouted the head electrician.

"'Eads of department will discuss the details, you will be paid and if we can secure any compensation, rest assured we will." The director gave a frowny smile, but anyone who had been in the industry for any length of time knew claims could wrangle on for years.

"If all department heads, could follow me," called Courtney, as De Banville made a hasty exit, his two assistants barely able to keep up.

Lol was on the steps of the truck, cigarette butts at her feet. "What's the story?"

Courtney had dropped Mia back in one of the estate's golf buggies. She limped towards her friend.

"Investigation," Mia said, dully.

"No way," Lol replied. "Insurance or police?"

"Both. We're not to touch anything."

"Too late," Lol told her. "We've fixed most of the damaged costumes already, the hired stock too. I've been through the inventory twice, we're more or less sorted."

Mia gave Lol a look. Cleaning, repairing and packing at the end of a shoot was proper procedure but all the dressers were involved. It was the wardrobe supervisor's responsibility to oversee things, Lol had overstepped the mark.

"I'm supposed to sign everything off, remember." Mia went into the truck, surprised at how empty it was, rails cleared, shelves tidied. Lol stood in the doorway.

"Thought we'd get on with it, we're ready to go home, no point hanging around."

"We'll have to give statements." Mia was uneasy.

"What'll you say? You weren't here. The quicker this is dealt with the better. Let's get done and gone." The base of Lol's throat glowed red.

"What aren't you telling me?" Mia was holding the clipboard with the inventory neatly ticked off. She waited.

"Look, I may have been duped, is all I'm saying." Lol was finding it hard to look her in the eye.

"In what way?" Mia glared back.

"It doesn't matter," Lol said.

"It obviously *does* matter and if you're involved we need to get our story straight, accidents happen, if that's what *did* happen?"

Lol sat down on a trunk.

"Alright, I got pissed. I went out for dinner with someone and before I knew it, I was drinking wine, dancing and one thing led to another and …"

Mia was stunned. She could not remember the last time Lol had gone out on a date but far more disturbing than that, Lol did not drink; could not drink. A recovering alcoholic, Lol had been dry for eight years. Mia knew this, because Mia had been there. They had been working on an epic historical drama, when Lol had fallen asleep in a drunken stupor with a cigarette in her hand. Mia arrived back in the nick of time and managed to douse the flames but valuable costumes had been damaged. It could have been worse, it could have been fatal.

It was a turning point; shocked by her actions, Lol made her mind up to take control and Mia had stood by her, helping her through her darkest moments, it had sealed their friendship.

"I guessed as much." Mia did not know what else to say, she was devastated. Lol's sharp little face had fallen in on itself. "And the man?"

Lol sighed. "Someone from years ago."

"One of the crew?" Mia was intrigued.

"No. He was long gone by the time I came round and when I got here the truck was unlocked, someone had taken the key and caused havoc."

"Your date?"

"Could have been. Or he distracted me and someone else seized the opportunity. I don't know, Mia, I was so blitzed I could hardly remember what day it was."

"Oh, Lol." Mia put her arms around her friend.

"I'm so sorry. I feel dreadful. I can't believe it of myself and worst of all I can't believe I let you down; us down." She looked at Mia, bitter tears spilling from her eyes.

"Hey, come on, we've been through worse," Mia said, pushing back a great despairing lump in her throat.

"Yeah, but if we tell the truth we've had it." Lol knew Mia was on the side of the angels, she always told the truth.

"Look, I need this job," Mia reminded her. "We both do. We can't have our reputation as the best goddamn dressers in the entire universe besmirched in any way. Someone wanted the movie stopped, not our problem. We'll tell whoever asks, the truck was vandalised. They broke in through the skylight and did their worst." She grabbed a pack of wet wipes and started cleaning the padlock and door handle. She wiped the key, passing it to Lol.

"Put your prints all over it, so there's only ours on everything," Mia instructed.

"But the skylight?" Lol was bemused.

Mia looked up. It was too high for them to reach. She raised her stick and bashed it against the frame. One of the panes of glass popped out. She pushed it to one side with the nose of the fox's head and dropped the latch.

"They broke in there, must have been wearing gloves and shoe covers, no prints anywhere."

"Genius!" Lol declared, beginning to look marginally less frazzled.

CASE CLOSED

Garda Regan was delighted; an investigation into a case of vandalism at Kilcohy Castle, that would certainly be a change from another afternoon filing at the station.

"Isn't that where they're making the movie?" he asked, reaching for his cap.

"It is." Sergeant O'Brien remained at his desk.

"Will we have to interview a few of them big name actors and the like? Or would the inspector have to do that, them being famous and all?"

"They're actors, ya eejit, when they appear in a film as the President or a member of the Royal Family, they're only acting. Hence the name, *actors*." The sergeant turned a page of the newspaper on the desk.

"I heard it's a horror film, we'll get to 'interview a vampire', so." Garda Regan rattled the keys to the patrol car, eager to be gone. He held the door ajar as the sergeant stood slowly, folded his newspaper and picked up his cap.

Outside in the yard the sun was blazing. "I hope they're up!" Joked the young guard, nodding skywards.

"Just get in and drive, will ye? The match is on, I was hoping for a quiet listen of it back at the station and now this, a crowd of luvvies wetting their knickers over a bit of an April Fool's joke in the dressing up box."

"But it's June, sergeant," Garda Regan pointed out.

"Did you never hear of a figure of speech?" The senior officer said irritated, he hated the heat.

"Of course I did, bet there's a few nice figures to look at

when we're up at the castle, too." Garda Regan had not had a girlfriend in a long time and there was little chance of one, the long hours and shifts he was expected to work in this so-called career.

The interviews were short. Mia and Lol as key-holders were questioned more fully but after examining the roof light, the police officers agreed this was how the vandals had entered and exited the scene of the crime.

"Easy enough to break in." The sergeant closed his notebook. "Have you no security on site?"

"Yes, twenty-four-seven," Mia replied. "There's a temporary perimeter fence all the way round, they're supposed to patrol that."

"Really?" The older officer gave his colleague a knowing look. He did not like security firms, shifty organisations populated by failed constabulary and 'lucky-not-to-be-inside' thugs. "Let's talk to them, Regan. If they were doing their job properly, these ladies would have been able to do theirs." He gave the ladies a denture-filled smile. "How's Archie, by the way?" The sergeant directed his question at Mia. "You're Fenella's daughter, aren't you? Just wondered how he's doing."

She was not surprised, the local constabulary would know all about the comings and goings at Galty House.

"He's bought a new boat," was all she could think to say.

"Good man," said the sergeant. "I'll warn the Coastguard, so."

"Are we free to go, officer?" Mia managed.

"Of course, just don't leave the country," he replied, then seeing their startled faces, "Only joking. You're fine, we've finished with you here." They tipped their caps and left.

"Blimey," Lol exclaimed. "Can't half tell you're from

theatrical aristocracy, they believed every word you said."

"Shush," Mia hissed. "Why wouldn't they? All perfectly plausible. Now, we just give the same statements to the insurance assessor and we're in the clear." Mia sounded a lot more confident than she felt but the encounter with the guards had gone well, it looked like she may have deflected the spotlight and saved the day.

The entire unit breathed a sigh of relief as the police drove away; the last few days had been a nightmare. Down to a man they just wanted to pack up and go home. Garda Regan was disappointed too, the whole scenario had been distinctly lacking in glamour, bright lights or indeed any action. He sighed heavily.

"What ails you?" Sergeant O'Brien sniped.

"I thought it would, you know, be more exciting."

"Exciting? I told you, it's only a bit of ole codology, makey-up stuff, it's only exciting when the backroom boys have weaved their magic, edited and polished. Then it hits the screen, that's the exciting bit."

"You seem to know a lot about it?"

"I've been around a long time, know lots of stuff about lots of things and that was an inside job if ever I saw one."

The young Garda nearly ran the car off the road.

"Steady," the sergeant warned, totally unfazed.

"How do you know?" Regan asked, when he found his voice.

"No one saw anything, all suddenly blinded by the bright lights. The security men had mixed their shifts up or been paid to disappear more like and the girls in the costume truck had the investigation all wrapped up before we even got there. Clever stuff. Nah, an inside job, someone wanted to cause trouble for some reason, so they did. Nobody's been murdered, no real damage, not even a proper crime really." He closed his eyes.

Garda Regan was going over the interviews in his mind. Sergeant O'Brien was right, no one knew anything, so how could he tell who was lying and who was telling truth? It was like he had a sixth sense, a proper copper. Sometimes he wondered if he would ever make a decent policeman, he had no idea it was an inside job.

"You never told me you knew Archie Fitzgerald and Fenella Flanagan, how come?" A hint of grudging admiration in the young man's tone.

"Ah, it was way before they were famous, I was a rookie on a job down at the harbour. A priest went missing. Senior fella, in charge of the seminary. Monsignor…Whelan that was it, Monsignor Sylvester Whelan. Another inside job if you ask me. Mind you, anything to do with that place on Phoenix Island has always been 'secret squirrel'." He tapped his nose. "You know what the clergy are like, worse than the mafia."

"That ole ruin of place? I've heard it's haunted. What happened the priest?"

"No one knows. Had a bad reputation though, right cruel bastard. They shut it down after that."

"I heard someone found a bomb, isn't that right?" There had always been myths and legends about Phoenix Island.

"God alone knows what you'd find over there."

"What did they have to do with it? Archie Fitz and the actress one?"

"They were just teenagers at the time, friends with one of the students, that's all. I was a young fella myself, only allowed help with the paperwork. But I do remember Fenella was a fabulous looking woman alright, made you hungry with lust just looking at her. Did me, anyway. Mind you, there were a few odd things happened around Rosshaven back then. Things before the priest went missing, unexplained things. But they're a tight crew that lot, if there was a conspiracy, which the inspector said there was, they conspired to keep it all secret, one way or another."

"I always thought it was just a sleepy little seaside town, nothing much happens there, surely?" said the young guard.

"Nothing much the likes of us would ever get to hear about anyway." Sergeant O'Brien laughed, pulling his cap over his eyes against the sun. "If it's excitement you're looking for, son, you're in the wrong business, that's for sure."

Lol was sorting through hire stock, special pieces to be returned intact. Luckily, the vintage collection had been safely locked away, awaiting the final scene, the breath-taking finale scheduled to take place in the ruined abbey. Sadly, with the project abandoned it had been scratched, the fabulous costumes destined never to be seen.

"Is that the last of it?" Mia asked.

"It is, except I've found something odd, just wanted to run it past you."

Mia limped to the rear of the truck, less cramped now with most of the garments labelled and bagged. She sat down wearily, pulling spectacles from her pocket.

"Look." Lol lifted a large box out of a packing case. Old yet immaculate. The cardboard was a pale turquoise edged in navy blue, with a flourish of gold lettering.

Mia read out loud. "Madame du Fouray, *Couturiere, robes de mariée et robes de bal*, Rue du Saint Martin, Paris."

She ran her fingers over the lettering, lifting the lid; tissue, as fresh as the day it had been folded, filled the box. Mia could see a piece of lace, creamy rich, the colour of buttermilk.

"Take a good look," Lol urged.

Mia patted the tissue back down.

"Shame to spoil it. Original?"

Lol had a particular flair with vintage pieces, her knowledge second to none.

"First World War, I'd say." She whipped the tissue away and taking folds of fabric lifted the gown from the box, stepping back so Mia could see the full effect.

It cascaded from Lol's fingers like a waterfall. Transparent, gossamer tulle, the palest hint of blush, draped behind a shimmering lace overlay. There was a scalloped hem just beneath the bust, another at the thigh, then below the knee, till it fell in soft folds to the floor. Each beautifully crafted curve sewn with pearls, crystals and tiny peach shells. Sheer sleeves featured a long cuff, decorated to match the scalloped edges of the gown. Satin covered buttons fastened the bodice at the back. It was exquisite.

In all her years in the business, Mia had never seen anything quite like it. She reached out to touch the dress, Lol swished it away. Holding it against her scrawny frame, turning and twirling, watching Mia smile as she danced, the elegant shimmering sheath contrasting with the billowing chiffon, visible only when the gown moved.

"Isn't it stunning?" Lol slowed to a stop.

Mia was suddenly sad. "What a pity we won't see it worn. Will they even film that scene now?"

"Who knows?" Lol shrugged. "But the real shame is, this has *never* been worn."

Mia lifted the gown, smoothing it with her palms. "You think the wedding was called off?"

"Judging by the date of the dress, worse than that."

"What could be worse?" Mia asked, running fingers over pearls and shells.

"My guess is the fiancé never came home from the war." Lol was serious. "Happened a lot."

Mia let the fabric fall.

"There's something else." Lol rummaged about and brought out an identical box. She lifted the turquoise lid with the same gold writing and there, amidst the delicate tissue lay another dress. Same size, same colour, same delicious design.

"They had a copy made?"

"I found this inside," Lol was holding up a delivery note; beautifully handwritten on headed paper, the same lettering as the box. She gave it to Mia, who started to read it in French. Lol poked her in the ribs.

"It says this is the fulfilment of an order placed by Madame Daphne Beaumont, on behalf of the Mademoiselles Lydia and Louisa Beaumont. Giving an address in Dublin, Lansdowne House, Ballsbridge." They stared at the note in silence.

"I don't get it," Mia said finally. "A woman orders identical dresses, for her daughters perhaps, but identical wedding dresses?"

"Maybe it was a double wedding. Looking at the gowns, the girls could have been twins, but neither of these dresses have been worn."

"You mean both fiancés died in the war?" Mia's eyes widened in horror.

"Highly likely and the poor Misses Beaumont lived out their lives waiting and hoping their beaux would return. I'd say a collector picked these up for a song."

Mia looked at Lol, her theory was perfectly plausible. She closed her eyes.

"That's too sad."

Lol folded the gowns away. "Bet I'm right, though."

Mia thought of Rupert, imagining herself in Lydia or

Louisa's shoes, waiting for him to come home, knowing they would be married as soon as he returned and then the gradual, cloying realisation, as the weeks, months, years went by, that he was not coming back. Suddenly she missed her gorgeous man very much indeed.

"Right," she said, tapping the clipboard to bring herself back. "Let's get this finished and go. I can't wait to get away now."

"Me too," Lol agreed, carefully storing one of the boxes with the other vintage originals. "But check that inventory for me, because something's not right."

Mia checked the list again. "Strange, only one of the wedding gowns is listed. It's not on another list, is it?"

Lol shook her head. "That's the only list, you know that."

"Think it's been missed off?"

"I think because it's the same thing twice, identical gown, packaging the lot, it's only been counted once. Just one wedding dress, right there." Lol pointed at the entry on the inventory.

"Most unusual," Mia said.

"It is unusual and there are two but we're only supposed to have one and that's why you ought to have the spare."

Mia was confused. "Spare what?"

Lol looked left and right. "Wedding dress, don't think anyone else is getting married around here."

"I couldn't do that, take something like that, I mean it must be worth a fortune. No way," Mia said.

"But no one knows it exists, one dress does, it's here on the list but the other, no one has any idea. Take it, give it a good home. A few minor alterations, it'll fit you perfectly. It's precisely what you would wear if you could afford it, so take it, you're meant to have it, *please* take it."

"But we'll have to report it, it must belong to someone."

"Yes, Lydia or Louisa but they couldn't wear it and you can.

It's far too beautiful to lie rotting in its box for another hundred years. I insist you take it." Lol thrust the box into Mia's hands.

"You can't insist, I'm senior to you." Mia had her there.

"Not where vintage originals are concerned. Check our contract, my department, you'll find. All repairs, renewals and disposals are at my discretion, and I 'discrete' you take it!" Lol was right. "You *are* still getting married to Prince Charming, aren't you?"

Mia laughed. "Don't call him that, he has to be charming, he's an actor."

Lol wanted to say she heard he was more than charming but decided against it. Besides, he was Mia's choice, *her* blushing bridegroom.

"It's beautiful but it wouldn't be right, it just isn't meant for me." Mia handed the box back to Lol. "Now, let's pack. I want to ring Rupert and tell him I'm coming home."

They locked the door together.

"You know what I could do with?" Lol said taking Mia's arm as they headed to the caravan. Mia stopped dead. "A nice cup of tea." And she laughed, tugging one of Mia's ever escaping ringlets, till she squealed.

The sun was setting over the mountains, the sky streaked silver as the amber glow dipped behind peaks to the west and evening deepened into night. Sitting on the steps of the ruined abbey, Mia took a moment to savour the stillness. She felt calm yet restless. The past few days had been a strain, everything weird, unreal, as if the axis of her life had slipped and she was very definitely off kilter. She rubbed her eyes … probably just tired.

Taking her phone from her pocket, she tried Rupert. They had not spoken for days and she was desperate to hear him. She wanted to go home now. She knew Archie was expecting her back, and she would go back but right now she needed Rupert, she longed to tell him she was on her way and would be in his arms in less than twenty-four hours.

The phone connected.

"Hello, hello." She was anxious.

"Mia, what gives?"

"Rupert, at last!" A breath.

"Has the old boy gone?" Rupert asked gravely.

"No, thank goodness but I'm back on set. We've been wrapped, I'm coming home."

"So soon? Isn't there an investigation or something?" Mia was not surprised Rupert was up to speed, even just a hint that a production was being pulled had everyone calling their agents, seeking a new start as soon as possible.

"We've done our bit, given statements. I just want to get back now. I miss you."

"Miss you too. I, however, have exciting news!"

"You do?" Mia did not need any more excitement.

"Yep, I've been called for a second audition for the soap opera gig."

"That's wonderful, when?"

"Tomorrow, Manchester. I'm heading up north in the morning."

"Oh." Mia pushed her disappointment away. "For how long?"

"As long as it takes." He was buoyant. Rupert had been looking for a decent TV role for ages. Deep down he was beginning to despair. To date his current job, a supporting role in a 'not quite the West End' musical, was the longest running gig he had ever had.

"Brilliant news, be sure to give it your best shot!" she told him, bracing up.

"Sure will. Look, why don't you stay in Ireland till the weekend, I should be back by then and we can spend some of that nice *quality time* together," he purred seductively, making her laugh.

Mia thought for a minute. A few sunny days in Rosshaven was infinitely more appealing than an early morning flight and Tube ride back to an empty flat.

"What's the weather doing?" she asked.

"Grey and hot at the same time, the city before a storm."

"That's decided then, see you at the weekend. But ring as soon as you're out of your audition. If you can't get me on the mobile, call the landline."

"Which landline?"

"Galty House, ask the butler to fetch me."

"Are you serious?" Rupert was impressed.

"Of course not but wait till you see it, you'll love it. Once we know your schedule maybe we can both come back for a few days? Archie will love you, I just know he will."

"Sorry, what was that?"

The signal was fading. Gone. No matter, Mia had a spring in her step.

The caravan was in darkness, Lol fast asleep. Mia did not fancy a long, winding drive through the night, nor would she leave without saying goodbye; who knew when she and Lol would work together again. Deciding to make an early start the following morning she crawled under the duvet, soon dreaming of Leela's full Irish breakfasts; local sausages, thick cut rashers, spicy white pudding with home grown tomatoes and eggs fresh from the hen house – her tummy rumbled – maybe that longing ache was just hunger after all?

THE KISS OF JUDAS

Not long after Mia had left Galty House the weather turned. Rosshaven Harbour had enjoyed unbroken sunshine for over a fortnight, but dawn's red sky warned of things to come and by breakfast dark purple clouds hung low out in the bay.

Fenella had spent the night nursing Archie. Unable to sleep, he had pleaded for more medication, more than Fenella dare administer, yet when she could no longer distract him she relented, topping up his morphine until he drifted off. Laying beside him, she remained awake, fearful. It was dawn when his eyelids flickered open. He gave her a weary smile.

"Not dead yet, darling." he said, through dry lips. She offered him water, he waved it away. "What time is it? I'm ravenous."

"You didn't eat yesterday," she reminded him. "What do you fancy? I'll make it, everyone else is asleep."

"*You* cook? That would surely finish me off!" He started to cough.

"Cheeky sod." She laughed, then seizing the opportunity. "I know you don't want to tell me, but why did you want to see Mia? What do you need to tell her?"

Archie struggled up, she placed a fresh pillow behind him.

"It's between Mia and myself. Besides, I've not discussed it with Bernice and I won't discuss it with you either, that would be unfair."

Fenella frowned, Archie's sense of fair play had increased a hundredfold since his diagnosis.

"Very well. Just assure me it's not something we have agreed *not* to tell her, ever."

Archie gave her one of his looks. "I might have guessed.

Haven't I promised I would never tell? Did we not stick pins in our veins till we bled, became blood brothers and sisters, making a pact on that very beach?" He pointed out of the window, then turned to her. "You do know your stupid secret has blighted that child all her life? And yours. You feel guilty that Mia not knowing the truth is holding her back, preventing her from making the ultimate commitment."

"Nonsense, we agreed never to tell. It was for the best."

"Then yes, but what about now?"

"All I know is if she wants a family, I want her to be married."

Archie sighed. "That's not a requirement these days."

"There would still be talk, like mother like daughter. I just couldn't bear her to go through what I went through."

There were tears in her eyes.

"That wouldn't happen, you're living in the past, besides it wasn't that bad." Archie took her hand.

"Wasn't that bad?" She stared at him in disbelief. "You've no idea. I was betrayed by those I consider my own family."

"Fenella, that never happened."

She was being dramatic, she did not know everything, he was sure of that.

"I asked Humphrey, when it was obvious I'd been abandoned, if he thought the letter was delivered. He didn't reply but I knew the answer by the look in his eyes."

"Not this again, please."

She let go of his hand. Silence. Then giving him a sideways glance, she gasped.

"*Humphrey,* of course, you *have* made a will, it's with Humphrey!" She jumped off the bed. Archie laughed, then coughed again. "And you better not have that stupid bitch Venetia Bailey singing at your funeral or I'll give you hell."

Fenella was wagging a finger at him.

Archie started to cry he was laughing so much. Fenella could certainly hold a grudge. Long ago he had been briefly engaged to the opera singer, when at the same time, Fenella announced she was marrying a sheik. They had all managed to escape, unscathed.

She poured water.

"I could murder some coffee."

He lied, the very thought made him nauseous but he wanted her to leave, he was in a mess. Fenella was part of his heart and soul, but there was only so much she needed to know, bear.

She pressed her mouth to his forehead.

"I won't be long." she whispered, tucking him beneath the eiderdown that had graced his bed since they were children.

As usual, being there had stirred her. She had been dreaming again, the same dream, watching it all over again, like a film that never quite reached the end. They were chasing along the landing, entwined as they tripped down the stairs, like butterflies dancing in a flutter of their own wings, until they fell through the door into a room full of people.

The Monsignor stood by the fireplace. Mrs Fitzgerald, the enigmatic mistress of the so-called Seahorse Hotel on the sofa with Bernice. Fenella's mother, Ursula, was serving tea. She held the cake slice aloft, unsure whether to hurl it at the couple who had just entered the room or plunge it deep into her own chest. Perhaps she would just die of shame right there and then; that would be by far the easiest, most convenient outcome.

The elegant man in black put his cup down and walked towards the stricken pair.

"Have you anything to say in your defence?"

His eyes were bright with emotion as the Monsignor

descended upon them. He found his voice. "If we've done anything wrong, I'm the one to blame. She's innocent."

The Monsignor raised an eyebrow. "We've been watching you both, she's far from innocent." His eyes lingered fleetingly on the girl's bare legs. "Go and get dressed, we'll deal with this back on the island."

"Deal with what?" She lifted her chin to challenge flinty eyes.

"This highly distasteful incident," the Monsignor replied, evenly.

"This incident, as you call it, is none of your damn business!" She swore to shock him, pompous prig.

"Now, now." Mrs Fitzgerald crossed the room. "Come, have some tea. You can tell me all about it in your own time."

"But it's not what you think ... it's not ..." she cried.

"Don't deny it," the young man said, softly. "Don't deny us."

Mrs Fitzgerald took her arm but she was holding his hand, holding on as tightly as she could, as if she knew, if she let go he would be gone forever.

"Get your things," the Monsignor told him. "We're leaving."

The young man released her, looking into her face, laughing eyes turned to stone.

"It'll be alright," he assured her.

"It will be far from alright," his superior said sharply. "Go, I can't bear to look at you a minute longer."

His touch scorched her shoulder as he left, she pressed the heat with her hand trying to hold it in. Mrs Fitzgerald led her to the couch.

The elegant priest started to pace, heels ricocheting off the polished floor. The young man reappeared at the library door. He was wearing the chambray shirt, open at the neck, her gift of love beads, turquoise and silver glowing on his tanned skin.

"I'll send my report," the Monsignor said.

"Your report?" Ursula asked, confused.

"I cannot emphasise enough how serious this is, Madam. This young man's life could be ruined. His vocation snatched away because of a moment's weakness. He may have committed a criminal offence for all we know."

"Ah, Sylvester," Mrs Fitzgerald protested. "They're young people in love, can't you see that?"

The man glared at his hostess. "His moral welfare is my responsibility. Would you took your duty of care as seriously!"

He strode into the hallway, pushing the young man ahead of him. Mrs Fitzgerald followed.

"Sylvester, you're being over-zealous. Playful fun is all it is." Mrs Fitzgerald kept her tone light. She wanted them to dine together, broker peace.

"This place doesn't change, Madam, I can see that much," he threw back.

"We have no reason to change." Mrs Fitzgerald folded her arms. "This has always been a safe house, you of all people should know that."

He had been captured during the war, The Seahorse Hotel providing sanctuary after his escape from a Nazi concentration camp.

A pillowcase stuffed with linen stood at the door, the Monsignor bent to pick it up.

"Leave that," Mrs Fitzgerald ordered.

"I beg your pardon?"

"Leave it." She pointed at the pillowcase. "Still have spies everywhere, I see." Somewhere a door closed. "You can't force him to become a priest if he doesn't want to."

"Temptation goes with the territory," the Monsignor smiled

grimly, looking directly at her. "He'll confess, ask for forgiveness."

"Beg, more like." She knew what she was talking about.

"Just doing my job." The Monsignor placed the black fedora firmly on his head and giving a brief bow, left.

That very day they had made their plan to escape. Under cover of darkness he would take a boat, send signal and she would know to steal out to the jetty and meet him. There was a safe bay close by, they would come onto the mainland there, head for the city and disappear.

Her face was pressed against the glass, watching them leave.

"Why the linen?" she whispered as the car swept away.

"Evidence, I suppose." Mrs Fitzgerald glanced sadly at the portraits looking down from the gallery.

Unseen hands had stripped her bed, she felt suddenly sick. The older woman locked the door and took her back to the library. She had started to weep, a stuttering sob, like hiccups. Her mother was lighting the fire; even in summer the house grew quickly cold come the evening.

"A holiday romance, hardly the end of the world." Mrs Fitzgerald told Ursula.

Fenella's insides had twisted into a ball. She would not give him up, they were in love, meant to be together; she would never, ever give him up. And then a tiny sliver of doubt. Unless he gave her up first, that was the only way she could accept it was over and then it would, without a shadow of a doubt, be the end of the world.

Passing the window on the landing Fenella shook her head, trying to shake away the ache in her heart as she forced herself not to look at the island. She kept it all here, the love, the joy, the anguish, this was where her past lived, separated from her present. She had never allowed it to seep into her real life but returning to Galty always had the same effect; longing to be here when she was away, yet always desperate to leave when she could bear the pain no more.

Leela found the actress in the kitchen staring out to sea. She failed to turn round even when the door closed and Leela's fluffy mules click-clacked across the floor.

"I've just checked, he's fast asleep," Leela said, quietly.

"A bad night," Fenella told her.

Leela looked away, steeling herself. Mrs Fitzgerald had left her in sole charge of the family; Archie, Bernice, Fenella and baby Mia. She had just slipped the maternal mantle over her shoulders. Mrs Fitzgerald had been like a mother to her, Leela would never let her down, dead or alive. She had to stay strong.

"Where's Bernice?" Fenella asked.

"Asleep too. You being here gives her a break, Archie's been play acting he's in fine fettle for years. Surely you guessed, seeing him over there in England?" Leela was making fresh coffee.

"I rarely see him," Fenella replied. "We might meet for a drink, have dinner, that's all."

"Does he never come to the Lodge? I believe you have a guest suite and all."

Fenella did not answer, Archie did not like Trixie and the Lodge was Trixie's home too. Besides, once Archie took against someone that was it, he could never be swayed, no matter how unfounded his misgivings.

"Some breakfast?" Fenella shook her head. Leela pitied her, she looked so small in the big bathrobe. "Will I do a reading for you? Always helps, takes your mind off things."

"Good idea," said Fenella, going to the drawer where Leela

kept the precious tarot cards hidden amongst her mystic accoutrements; the vagarious paraphernalia of the white witch.

"You haven't given a reading in a long time."

"Not publicly." Leela glanced at the door. "With Archie ill Bernice banned me. Said she didn't want any of that ole nonsense clouding the issue."

"She's changed her tune, always loved a reading, hoping for a tall, dark stranger to fall …" Fenella stopped, avoiding Leela's eyes, she handed over the cards, wrapping the bathrobe about her. "Cold in here."

Leela drew the curtains against the squall, indicating Fenella pull a chair alongside the range.

"I could do with a bit of guidance myself," she said, shuffling the cards. "There's a change coming, I can feel it."

"We know that," Fenella said.

"No, not Archie, bigger than that, way bigger than that."

Fenella felt her eyes burn. What could possibly be bigger than that, she wanted to ask. But she knew Leela too well. The passing from this life to another was as natural and as constant as the sun rising in the east and setting in the west to Leela's way of thinking. She always said those who live among us never leave us and requiring the physical presence of someone to believe they exist was naïve. Leela had always embraced other-worldliness, there was no such thing as supernatural; it was all natural, if you opened your mind to it.

Leela dealt until there were nine cards face down between them. Moving left to right, she turned the first card over.

"Remind me, which is this?" Fenella said.

Leela hushed her. "Wait until the hand is out. I need to see the complete picture."

Fenella sat back as Leela's fingers glided across the pack; gold and purple shapes and swirls. Turning them over she watched the jewel colours of the illustrations, faded now, corners worn, and was again the little girl in the library, entranced as Mrs Fitzgerald, diamonds flashing, tapped each card explaining every symbol and the impact it would have on the life of the person before her.

Mrs Fitzgerald loved the tarot. When war broke out, with everything uncertain, she became known for her readings, she had the gift. Her *soirées* grew in fame and popularity, especially during the dark days when the coastline was a very dangerous place.

The official Look-Out Posts were Ireland's first line of defence and the whole harbour breathed a sigh of relief when one was erected on Phoenix Island, manned by the newly-formed Coast Watching Service – ex-soldiers mainly, who had fought the bitter fight for Irish independence.

As hostilities deepened and fear of a German invasion increased, Galty was declared a 'safe house' and a young Irish officer, working under the Director of Military Intelligence, gave it a codename, The Seahorse Hotel. The pseudonym stuck and so did the legends that went with it. Mrs Fitzgerald had been proud to do her bit, providing sanctuary and succour for young men returning from the ravages of war.

Fenella adored Mrs Fitzgerald and tales of The Seahorse Hotel were her favourites. Sitting before the fire, she would regale them with wartime adventures. But the 'spy-priest' stories were the best. Some of the men went onto great things, others returned angry and broken, and a few never came back at all. But Galty House remained a safe haven, providing comfort for these clever, brave young men fighting for freedom all over again.

The storm railed outside as Fenella gazed at the cards spread before her. *He* had heard of The Seahorse Hotel, she recalled the conversation distinctly.

"You live at Galty House? Isn't that the Seahorse Hotel?" He had rowed over from the island, Archie and Humphrey helped pull the boat onto the beach.

The girls stopped reading to watch them. Archie bursting with energy, wild locks escaping from his coloured bandana; Humphrey big and broad, sporting the crew cut he favoured and the visitor, deep bronze skin, thick dark curls damp on his brow and his smile, sardonic, mocking.

"I've seen him on the island," Bernice whispered. "When I go to paint, he sits on the wall, reading." Bernice was the only female from the mainland allowed to go to the island, the Monsignor gave her special permission, saying her art must be encouraged, she was gifted after all.

"The Seahorse Hotel, haven't heard that in a long time," laughed Archie. "Don't tell me they still talk about the scandalous Mrs Fitzgerald and her safe house over on the island?"

"It's legendary. All sorts of things went on, apparently. Wexford's version of the Hellfire Club." He had an elegant voice, an English accent.

Bernice put her book away. "Do you need a hand?" She rose from her towel, going to help.

Fenella stayed where she was. She fluffed up her hair, biting her lips to colour them, then lay back, stretching her legs and placing sunglasses on her nose, hiding her face behind her novel. She was pleased she was reading 'Far From The Madding Crowd'. *If he was as educated as he sounded, he would know Thomas Hardy's classic, about a determinedly independent nineteenth century heiress. But cool as she wished to appear, she could feel her pulse starting to race; his voice had stirred her, it was most odd, no sound had ever made her feel like that.*

Leela clapped her hands, she was just about to speak when the door opened. Bernice appeared, in pink pyjamas.

"I've told you about that!" She pointed at the cards on the table.

"My fault," said Fenella defending the housekeeper. "Just trying to distract me." Leela kept her eyes fixed on the cards.

"What is it?" Fenella asked.

Bernice leaned in to look. "You may as well tell."

"You're at a crossroads." Leela pointed at the Hanged Man. "The road you decide to take will be life changing. There's turmoil, conflict in close relationships." She tapped the Ace of Cups. "I love this one, emotional happiness, home and family." She thought for a moment. The Seven of Swords. "Hmm, this fella, possibly betrayal, someone getting away with something."

"Anything say where my earring is? I can't find it anywhere." Losing the earring was driving Fenella mad, she even dreamt about it, the exact scenario over and over and when she woke she was trembling, desperate to find it … find *him*.

"I want you to have these." He handed her a small parcel. "They were my mother's." She opened the package and a pair of tiny gold hoops glinted in the sunshine. Her hands were trembling so much, she could not put them on.

"Here, let me." He stood close.

"Are they gold?"

"Think so, all I have anyway, all I have of her too." His breath tickled her throat.

She spun round to face him, lifting her hair so he could see.

"They never looked lovelier." He laughed. She took his face

in her hands.

"*I accept.*"

"*Accept what?*"

"*Your proposal. These are enough for me.*" *She touched her ears. He grinned, she had read his mind; he was going to propose that very afternoon. Wrapping her in his arms, he pressed his mouth against her lips.*

"*I love you, Fenella Flanagan, you are my heart and soul.*"

"*And you mine,*" *she said in a quiet voice, holding him as tightly as she could.*

The camera shutter closed. Bernice looked forward to developing that shot, she had people to show it to, her skill would be much admired.

"Fenella, have you gone deaf, I said you have any number of earrings." Bernice prodded her back to reality.

"They're special." Fenella looked away. Bernice would recall precisely how special they were.

Sensing a spat, Leela showed them the Three of Cups. "I wonder what this could mean, some sort of celebration, maybe and Judgement, here, this represents change, a transition, a calling to do something."

Fenella shuddered.

"Change doesn't have to be bad. There are changes for the better, happens all the time." Leela sounded more confident.

"That's true," Bernice agreed. She touched the Seven of Swords. "And I would rather know if someone was going to betray me, be prepared."

Leela looked up at her. "The way Judas betrayed Jesus, close as brothers they were, yet Jesus knew, knew that kiss would change everything forever."

The door opened. "What does a dying man have to do to get

a cup of coffee around here?" It was Archie. He spotted the cards. "Move over, haven't seen you with the cards in a long time, Leela. Not been banned in case they foretell something tragic?" He gave them all a grin. "Tell you what, let's have a champagne breakfast, it's filthy out there, scrambled eggs, tarot and champagne. That'll set us up." He sat down, rubbing his hands together.

"Why not?" Fenella said, going in search of champagne.

Sometime later Fenella found Bernice in her bedroom, an overnight bag on the bed.

"Was it something I said?" Fenella almost fell into the room, having imbibed the lion's share of the champagne.

"I need to go to Dublin the day after tomorrow, sort a few things out."

"I hope you're not annoyed with Leela." Bernice could be grumpy for days if the mood took her. "I wasn't in the best form, she was just trying to help."

"She told me you nursed Archie all night. Thanks for that, I slept for a change."

"You needed it." Fenella touched her shoulder. "You don't have to thank me, I love him too."

Bernice placed her hand over Fenella's. "We'll be much reduced when we lose him. Let's stay close, Fenella please."

"We will. I promise." She went to the mirror, fixing the sea green scarf tied around her head; it emphasised her eyes. She looked at Bernice through the glass, Bernice put her hand to her ear but it was too late, Fenella saw it glint.

"What's that?"

"What?"

"In your ear, something shiny? Take your hand away." Fenella ordered. "You found my earring and never told me!"

"I was just about to bring it to you."

"When did you find it?" Fenella glared at her.

"Only the other day."

"The other day?" Fenella cried, disbelieving. "I've been frantic. You know I have."

"Sorry I forgot." Bernice held it out to her. "I only tried it on." She turned away from the glaring eyes.

"You're pathetic, Bernice, after all this time, you'd still do anything to hurt me, anything. Even keeping an earring, just because he gave it to me. Christ, you're a sad, bad, old bitch." And although the words were harsh, her tone was despondent.

Bernice took a breath, letting the moment pass.

"You don't wear your hair down anymore. Why not? You've beautiful hair."

"It's very ageing," Fenella told her. "You've lovely hair too and Mia, we're very lucky."

"She's another one for always tying it up. Gorgeous, flowing locks, hidden away. Sometimes I think she doesn't want to be attractive."

"Maybe she doesn't." Fenella shrugged. "It's like a hangover from school, the way she wears her hair and dresses in tunics and trousers all the time and plain, always plain. Maybe she doesn't want to be noticed."

"She was mortified when she had to wear glasses, crying because it made her look different." Bernice recalled.

"Then she wouldn't take them off, hiding behind them, even when I paid a fortune for contact lenses. Hopeless." Fenella had prayed she and her only child would at least look alike, but they were so different; sometimes she looked at Mia and despaired, feeling only disappointment.

"It was how she was brought up." Bernice folded a cashmere cardigan into her bag. "Discipline and modesty, the school motto, remember."

Remember ... how could she ever forget? Fenella had rebelled against the nuns and their mottoes every step of the way. Watching Bernice frown as she packed, she remembered that frown and the lecture that went with it.

"Discipline, Fenella, someone has to instill discipline into the girl, she's at a dangerous age." Bernice had been painting in the summerhouse.

Sitting down on the bench, Fenella kicked off her shoes, admiring newly painted toenails.

"She's the most disciplined child I've ever met. Well mannered, tidy. Never swears or sulks, does her homework without being asked."

"And these are bad things?" Bernice was bemused.

"Where's her rebelliousness? I worry we're creating a monster, a replicant, you know, like in Blade Runner.*"*

"As usual, I haven't a clue what you're talking about. Maeve's fine. She is, despite everything, a lovely girl and that's because she knows how to behave."

"Despite what?" Fenella knew Bernice meant 'despite being illegitimate'.

"Her unconventional upbringing."

"Unconventional compared with what? The brainwashed robots sitting up in the Mary Magdalene?"

"Never did us any harm," Bernice told her.

"Are you mad? Look at us!" Fenella exclaimed.

"We're talking about Maeve. Let me keep her, Sister Agnes said she can stay for next term. You'll be on tour, one less thing for you to worry about," Bernice cajoled.

"But she's not a worry, that's the whole point!"

"Isn't that a blessing then?" Bernice was exasperated.

That very afternoon Mia had cycled into town, walked straight into the only beauty parlour in Rosshaven and had her waist-length hair cut to her ears. Her appearance at supper rendered the household speechless.

"I didn't know you were thinking of changing your image," Archie said gently, the first to find his voice.

"It wasn't up for discussion," Mia replied, unusually churlish.

"So it would seem." He continued slicing the ham.

"You could at least let me take you to a decent hairdresser, Maeve. I mean, a good haircut is so important." Fenella was near to tears eyeing the shapeless crop.

"Is it? Is it really important?" her daughter asked. "Half the world is starving, the other half dying of AIDS. No, you're probably right, Mother, a good haircut really is important."

"There's no need to be rude," she told the teenager, whose face was as red as what remained of her hair. "Who gave you permission to have your hair cut?"

"It's my hair."

"Fair point," said Archie, eyes dancing with merriment.

"What did you do with your hair?" Bernice demanded.

"Why, are you going to stick it back on?" the youngster snapped back.

"Maeve, that's enough," Fenella said. "I don't know what's got into you."

"If you must know, I sold it and gave the money to Oxfam."

"Very worthy." Archie announced.

"Archie!" Fenella exclaimed.

"And while I'm at it." The girl pushed her plate away. "My name is Mia, from this moment on I will no longer answer to Maeve, I've changed it."

"How?" Fenella squeaked.

"By Deed Poll," she replied. Not entirely true, she had acquired the official forms but could not affect the change without parental permission. And with that, the newly-named Mia, took the magazine she had been reading at the table – also not permitted – and swept out.

"I was never mad about Maeve as a name myself." Archie tried to smooth the frisson in the room. "I know she was named after that old doll you couldn't be parted from but ..."

"She wasn't named after my doll! Maeve is an ancient Irish name, the legendary warrior queen of Connaught. When I knew they wanted to take my child away I named her Maeve so someone, somewhere would know she was Irish. I gave my little princess, a name fit for a queen!" Fenella was furious.

Bernice sighed; she had lost her appetite.

"You don't think she heard us, do you?" Fenella reached for her wine.

"This afternoon?" Bernice said. "Maybe."

"You better keep her then," Fenella replied. "Looks like she could do with another term at Mary Magdalene."

"Poor thing," Archie said, lifting the teenager's plate to take it to wherever she was hiding.

SOMETHING BORROWED

Despite being up at dawn, Mia's plans to arrive at Galty House in time for breakfast were thwarted. Whispering farewell to Lol, she took her bags and the carrier stuffed with knits Leela insisted she take against the cold, and stole out of the caravan.

Throwing her luggage onto the back seat, she noticed someone sitting at the entrance to the yard. The figure waved as she turned on the headlights and putting the car into gear she crawled slowly towards the now redundant assistant director. Mia sighed; she could really do without a lengthy conversation about the failed project right now yet despite everything Courtney was a friend.

"Hey." He forced a smile. "Any chance of a lift to the airport? I've been kind of abandoned."

"How come?"

"The crew went into Wicklow last night, partying because we'd wrapped. I was trying to get in touch with Shelley, see if there's any money in our account. Anyway, they didn't come back, someone had a minibus going to Dublin, so they all went too." He gave a mournful look.

She indicated the passenger seat, he climbed in.

"I'm heading in the opposite direction, actually. Going back to Wexford till the weekend."

"Couldn't drop me at the station could you? Maybe lend me some money? If I miss my flight I've had it." He was giving her that look he could work so well.

"There's a train strike, no wonder the others grabbed a lift."

"Shit. I forgot. What am I going to do?" He was near to tears.

"Relax, I'll take you to the airport. Mind you, the road will be busy with the trains off, weather's bad too," she warned.

"Oh, the relief! What would I do without you?" He settled into his seat.

"You did very well without me, I seem to recall." She instantly regretted her words but it still rankled, he had never once mentioned marriage in all the time they had been together, yet the minute they parted he married someone else.

An uneasy silence descended as she eased the old Dame towards the motorway. The day was struggling to break free of the night, thunderous clouds clung to the mountains and the road was wet, rivulets of water spilling from the hillside. It was not going to be an easy ride.

Mia's mood darkened. The luggage on the back seat, combined with the twist of human angst beside her, deepened her irritation as they bumped along the route. She wished she had thrown the whole lot in the boot. However, if she had, she would have seen it contained an elegant turquoise box and a note scrawled with 'Something borrowed' in Lol's handwriting. But Mia just wanted to get to her destination as soon as possible, so put up with the annoying baggage all the way to the airport.

Leela must have heard the throaty thrum of the Daimler's six cylinder engine some way off because she was waving from the steps as Mia came along the drive.

"Why didn't you phone?" Leela asked, welcoming her with a California smile and yellow Marigold embrace.

"Didn't want to disturb anyone, it's late."

"Ah sure, you know this crowd. They're down in the summerhouse having coffee and liqueurs. What can I bring you?" Although Leela was allergic to housework, she could certainly cook.

"Not really hungry," Mia replied.

"Nonsense, I'll be down in a few minutes, go and see if you can keep the peace. Bernice's on a witch hunt about Archie's will, convinced Fenella knows all about it and as for Eamon, he's as crotchety as a toddler teething and I've no idea if that's because he knows what Archie's up to or he doesn't!"

Mia was weary, it had been a fractious few days. She had had to draw on a deep vein of inner strength to keep it all together, not daring to let Lol know how petrified she was during the police interview, terrified they would discover her entire story was a tissue of lies. Then adding to her anxiety, the mercy dash with Courtney, desperate to return to his wife and baby. She was at a low ebb. It would be better just to slope off and greet everyone afresh in the morning.

"Mia darling, is that you?" It was Archie, banished outside to smoke his cigar.

So be it, Mia thought, her spirits lifting a little. It was Archie she wanted to see after all, Archie she needed to spend precious time with. She followed the lanterns to the summerhouse, no more than an ancient clapboard shed with iron rails around the balcony, perched precariously overlooking the sea. Yet it had always been her very own fairy-tale castle.

"I spy a rat!" Archie called to his guests scattered about the room.

"Well, deal with it then!" Fenella shouted back; regulars at Galty House were not easily disturbed by rodents of any description.

"It's left a sinking ship," he laughed, throwing open his arms to Mia, returning his barb with a wonky smile.

"Darling, you must be exhausted." Fenella patted the sofa for Mia to join her. "You look totally drained."

"Is Leela fetching you something to eat?" Bernice asked.

On cue Leela appeared with food, enough to feed everyone all over again. Mia sat beside Fenella who arranged a throw around her, rubbing her shoulders gently while Bernice made drinks.

"Well, tell all," said Archie, striding through the door, having abandoned his cigar for port and gossip.

"Let the child have something first, Archie, she's white with tiredness." Bernice insisted, passing Mia a steaming mug.

"It was awful," Mia said, as they gathered to listen. "The worst experience of my career. Equipment stolen, the costume truck vandalised, clothes tampered with and, worst of all, itching powder. Someone had doused everything with itching powder, not one member of the cast could stand still for a minute."

"Oh dear." Archie rolled his eyes. "An old trick, haven't heard of anything like that in years."

"A prank, surely?" Fenella asked.

Bernice looked at Eamon, who had just knocked back his drink.

Mia's tummy rumbled, she had not had eaten properly since leaving Galty nearly forty-eight hours ago. She dived on Leela's mix of toasted cheese and ham.

"Definitely sabotage. Someone wanted the whole thing to dissolve in chaos and it did. No way could we carry on, ran out of time and money."

"Such a waste," Bernice sympathised.

"Hardly going to be a classic though, was it?" Fenella said, gently.

"That's not the point," Mia told her. "We worked really hard on that film, conditions weren't brilliant, the budget was tight but we gave it our best shot. We're a team, we wanted to see it through."

"I do understand, darling, we're nothing if not professional," Fenella said.

"Sounds like the sabotage was pretty professional too," Bernice interjected. "Could any of it have been accidental? Just one of those things?"

Mia's mouth was full.

"The food poisoning maybe," Archie filled in. "We've all suffered at the hands of mobile caterers. Even at five in the morning, pissed as a fart, I always demand to see a proper hygiene certificate."

Mia and Fenella exchanged a look.

Demanding to see paperwork was one of Archie's favourite pastimes. In reality he took scant notice of anything official. When he missed a premiere in New York because his passport was out of date, Bernice took responsibility for all documentation. Archie had no choice but to acquiesce – imagine if he had missed the Oscars?

"No, the stuff on the truck was calculated. They were thorough, knew what they were doing." Mia replied.

"What did the guards make of it?" Eamon lifted a slice of toast, checking the sandwich filling. "Anyone in the frame?"

"Whoever did it was long gone." Mia declined to mention Lol's lapse or the fact it was she had who had masterminded the cover-up. "I feel so guilty."

"Now, darling, that's enough," Fenella said.

"You weren't even there," Archie affirmed.

"I should have been, I'm in charge." She frowned into her mug.

"It's just a job," Eamon offered, licking his fingers. He had finished the last sandwich.

"It's my career!" Mia snapped. Archie knelt before her.

"It will all be alright, you'll still have a glorious career, you see if you don't." His eyes bored into hers. Mia softened; he spoke as if she were still a young girl. Mia had been in the business for years.

"Can I stay till the weekend, please? I don't think I'll be needed on set, anywhere, anytime soon." She gave him a limp smile.

"Of course, stay as long as you like, stay forever!"

"Just till the weekend will be lovely."

Archie pulled her to her feet.

"Very well, young lady, then I must order you to your bed, because if we are to have you, even just for a while, you must be nurtured and cherished so you leave with the happiest of memories, to return in all haste." Archie, who now looked totally jaded, led her to the door. It was a closing speech, he always gave one when he felt a particular scene should end.

Breakfast was cleared away by the time Mia surfaced. Leela was at the table with a huge slice of walnut cake and the tarot cards; she wiped her tears quickly as she put the cards away.

"Never known you sleep so late." She gave Mia her chair, the others piled with washing.

"Would you like a bacon sandwich? Salmon and scrambled eggs? Won't take me a minute," Leela said, selflessly abandoning the cake.

"Just toast, I can see you're busy," Mia replied, knowing Leela would be disappointed not to have an excuse to put the laundry off. "Where is everyone?" The place seemed deserted.

"Bernice and your mother have gone into Rosshaven, one of the new boutiques is giving a fashion show. Archie's in bed, wants to save himself for this evening."

"I'm surprised you're not at the fashion show," Mia

remarked. Leela loved a bit of style, even now she was wearing lacy tights under her pinafore.

"Wasn't invited," she said, without a hint of malice. "Too rich for my blood and to be honest, all that designer stuff is taupe and cream. I ask you? You need a hell of a spray tan to look anything other than half dead in taupe and cream." She took the cups to the Belfast sink.

"What's Archie saving himself for, another row with Eamon?"

"Ha, that would be easy enough. Eamon might be a lawyer, but he needs to give the interrogation a rest. If Archie's made his mind up about things, it's really nobody else's business."

Mia was surprised. Leela usually thought everything was everybody's business.

"What do you know about it?" She gave Leela an old-fashioned look.

"Nothing at all." Leela turned back to the sink. "I'm just the hired help, don't forget."

Mia smiled. "If no row with Eamon, what then?"

"A reception at the new hotel. They're opening the cocktail bar, live music, canapés, all that kind of nonsense." Leela had not been invited to this either. "It's all very salacious up there, I believe."

"I hope you mean salubrious, Leela," Mia said smiling. "Wonder who's going?" Mia was trying to plan her day. Supper in front of the TV after an afternoon on the beach would suit her perfectly.

"Well, you for one," Leela told her. "Archie wants you to escort him, said he'd ask you after breakfast but went straight back to bed."

Mia groaned as the bread popped out of the toaster.

"Do I have to go? Archie will keep us there till dawn."

"Ah, indulge him." Leela faced Mia, eyes pleading. Mia felt immediately guilty. It was Archie she wanted to spend time with and it was obvious, whatever time he had left, Archie wanted to spend it with her.

"Hey, a couple of hours on the beach will revive me, a bit of sea air and I'll be ready for anything," Mia confirmed, ramming a piece of toast in her mouth, as she stuffed her hair into a battered straw hat. Leela wiped her hands and leaving the dishes in the sink, went back to her cards. Mia stopped to look.

"Which is this one again?" She touched the Knight of Swords.

"One of my favourites, represents a young man, energetic, magnetic, a strong character." Leela tapped the card. "Might come across as a bit insensitive but he's forthright, refreshing. See, his horse is white, meaning his words are pure, certainly shakes things up, anyway."

Mia was fascinated, her fingers traced the dark knight, sword aloft, vaguely imagining him galloping along the beach, sweeping her up, crushing her in his arms, melting away all her worries.

"They say his influence is good when things need to change. Some think he's brusque but he wants people to see things as they really are. Yes, I like him a lot." Leela gave Mia a mysterious look. She turned the card over, hiding the knight. "You need a bit of sun, anyone would think you've been working down a coal mine, not up a mountain."

Closing the door, Mia took a large gulp of glorious fresh air and set off, striding through flower beds, air fragrant with scent. She strode past the fountain and stone Buddha, until she reached a cluster of palms each nodding gently in welcome.

Filled with childhood memories, Galty's garden was

eccentric. She remembered sailing boats on the pond, planting flowers and making gloopy soups from the vegetable patch. Although her stays were sporadic, Mia had lived here longer than anywhere else and soon, not today or tomorrow but soon, it could all be gone. No wonder Bernice was desperate to know what Archie had in mind.

Mia looked back at the house regally gracing the cliff, windows winking in the sunshine, shining ivy clutching the building in an embrace. Chimney pots were missing, the roof badly patched and the whole place rattled pitifully when a storm blew in off the sea, yet it was still the most beautiful house she had ever seen.

She closed her eyes and imagined it gone. Archie gone. All of it gone. And as she did a huge wave of sadness washed over her, chilling her very bones. Opening her eyes she stared at the house, willing it to remain, stand its ground and fight and as she did the icy dread began to trickle away, sliding down her body and into the ground at her feet. This was how she had been trained to deal with fear, loneliness and despair – one of Leela's many tricks – simply will the evil away. It always worked; that and treacle toffee, of course.

"Hey, you're back!" The voice made her jump. "Probably prime real estate once." Ross Power, the hotelier, was at the top of the steps.

Mia blinked.

"The house, prime real estate at one time, given the location and all."

"I think you'll find Galty House is one of the finest examples of the period in the area, probably the whole of Ireland." Mia used her haughtiest tone.

"*Was*," he replied. "People make that mistake. Think a period property's got to be valuable. But not maintained and upgraded, well, in most cases better to demolish and start again, site's probably worth a lot more."

Mia shuddered. Americans, always so bloody opinionated. The shouty stress-head had reverted to type.

"That's my home you're disparaging," she said pleasantly, given she felt like kicking him in the balls.

"Just my considered opinion, ma'am." He was cleaning his Aviator sunglasses on his tee-shirt. Mia looked at him; did he really think that patronising, false charm would wash?

"I too am opinionated," she told him. "I've an opinion on most things but try to consider, when in conversation, whether it's appropriate to air my opinion or not, in case it might offend."

"Sorry, didn't mean to offend you." He did not sound remotely sorry.

"You offended the house. I was merely defending a grand old lady." Again she kept her tone light. Ross, whatever his name was, was a neighbour after all, a newcomer and already a friend of the family. Mia had long since perfected the skill of being perfectly pleasant to people she found excruciatingly distasteful, one of the reasons she was so good at her job. She looked him up and down. "Looking for someone?" He was on private property after all.

"Archie. Invitation for tonight, said he'd like to bring someone along."

"He's resting at the moment, it's probably for me."

"You?"

Her grubby denim shorts and old sweatshirt would certainly not fit the Harbour Spa Hotel dress code.

"I'm escorting him." Again, her haughtiest intonation.

"Great, excellent." Ross tried to sound enthusiastic, but he was not looking forward to playing happy host at this evening's event. "There'll be dancing." He indicated her leg.

She pocketed the invitation.

"Time I shook the dust off my Irish dancing costume, anyway."

He looked uncomfortable. No homespun, skiddly-row at the Harbour Spa Hotel it would appear.

"Anything else?" Mia folded her arms.

"Your leg better?"

"Loads better, mystical healing power of the water." She nodded towards the sea, wanting him gone. "Where's Pearl?" she asked, hoping that would send him off to attend his niece.

"Summer school, she needs to keep up her studies."

"Local?" She started walking, he might take the hint and push off.

"The convent on the edge of town. Has a fine reputation, I believe."

"Must have changed then," she said, without thinking.

"You know it?" he was scowling again.

"Just voicing a considered opinion, you know, the way people do." She had steered him to the top of the steps. "See you." He stayed where he was. "Later? See you later?"

"Yes. Looking forward to it." He sounded unconvinced. Descending the steps he turned back. "*Is* it a good school?"

"One of the best," Mia assured him, not particularly convincingly either.

NOTHING TO WEAR

The wall curved, sweeping out towards the bay, its centrepiece a huge porthole window through which the entire harbour was visible. Sailing boats and fishing trawlers came in, liners and ferries pushed out, every minute the view changed, like watching a movie … a film of real life.

Yet more and more Ross Power seemed to see less of it. Glued to his computer screen, counting figures, checking statistics managing the daily grind of a multi-million-pound business from behind his glass-topped desk. If not tied to spreadsheets or back-to-back conference calls, he was trying to contact his sister, Tara. Sometimes an entire day could be lost, trying to find out it if she was surviving, alive even.

At first Pearl's anxiety had driven his quest but as time passed and Pearl's confidence grew, she hardly mentioned her mother. When Ross did manage to contact Tara, Pearl would dutifully mark the map tracing her mother's trip but that was all. Ross sometimes wondered if he should give up on Tara too, the way she seemed to have given up on them.

A discreet knock on the door.

"Mr Power, we're nearly ready, Miss Pearl's told everyone she's helping you host, is that okay?"

He dragged his eyes from the screen.

"Fine by me."

Caroline, Pearl's long-suffering English nanny sighed, it was a school night after all.

"And you, sir, will you be changing?"

Ross was still in the Levis and tee-shirt he had been wearing all day.

"Of course." He gave a smile. His whole face changed when he smiled, Caroline often thought, his smile rarer these days. Shutting off the computer he strode the length of the room. "Let's get 'all shimmied up' as Pearl says. Time to put our best foot forward." He guided her out, he had never felt less like hosting a party.

"What do you mean, I can't go like this?" Mia hid her smile, arranging Fenella's outfit on the bed.

"You just can't!" Fenella turned from her dressing table, Mia was still wearing the tatty shorts and top she had dragged on first thing.

"But I don't have anything for a party, let alone a smart one."

"We'll find something." They were the same size, although all similarity ended there. Fenella tied a scarf at her hair, curls wafting out from the exotic silk; the actress had impeccable taste, a master class in elegance.

Mia was dowdy by contrast but this had not always been the case. Young Maeve loved to dress up. Throughout childhood, the milky-skinned redhead cut a dash in her stylish outfits, choosing what to wear and when to wear it. If her cowboy hat was inappropriate or a tiara deemed outré, a steely wilfulness would surface behind the turquoise eyes and she would be left unchallenged. And besides everyone loved to indulge her, buying her clothes from faraway places, designer outfits way ahead of the latest trend. She really was a 'fashion plate' as the older ladies used to say.

Although still obsessed with fashion, teenage Mia appeared disinterested in her own appearance, tying her back her hair and wearing only plain, plain unadorned black. Instead, her interest took an academic turn, studying everything from the Tudors to *haute couture*. Fascinated by the myriad of techniques used to create, dye and decorate fabrics, she learned to make patterns, cut, sew, and embroider. Although she had decided not to follow fashion herself, she had fallen in love with the art of it and her passion engulfed her.

Graduating from the Courtauld Institute in London, it was no surprise when she announced she wanted go into show business but her decision to become a dresser was greeted with disappointment by the occupants of Galty House. Archie immediately offered to secure her an apprenticeship with a renowned costume designer but Mia refused point blank; this was her career, she was going to do it her way. So in fact, nothing had changed, the wilful five-year-old had just grown up.

Fenella was watching her in the mirror, so alike yet so different. Both determined and stubborn but Mia more sensible, less volatile than she. Mia rarely showed her feelings, slow to take people into her confidence and careful about relationships. Mia would choose to stay single rather than make a bad choice, Fenella admired that in her only child.

Finally happy with the outfit she had selected for her mother, Mia found Fenella riffling through a wardrobe. She withdrew a sheath of aquamarine silk, thigh length with a mandarin collar studded with opaque sequins, it looked like a jewel.

"This and capri pants?" She was trying to think of shoes; Mia would probably want to wear flip-flops.

"It's a bit bright," Mia said.

"It's a colour!" Fenella held it against her truculent child. "Gorgeous with your hair." She said, immediately sorry. Mia's copper mane was a moot point. "Lights your eyes." She tried.

"It's drinks in the local hotel, do I need my eyes 'lighting'?" She gave her mother a dark look. "I'll just change my top."

"But my outfit is gorgeous, we'll look out of sync!" Fenella exclaimed.

"We're not a matching set, we don't have to 'go together'." Mia was holding the tunic as Archie looked in.

He was wearing a midnight blue suit, white shirt. The sunshine had brought out his freckles, he looked boyish and suave at the same time.

"That'll suit you," he told Mia. "Get a move on though, we're guests of honour."

"What?" they exclaimed.

"I did tell you." He shook his head despairingly. "We're opening the new cocktail bar, Ross asked if we would, great publicity for the place, don't you think?"

"I just can't open a bar on a whim, it hasn't been booked, what will my agent say?" Fenella was waspish.

Archie shrugged. "Come on, Fen, it'll be fun. Besides, it's only neighbourly to support a new venture on our doorstep."

Mia frowned. "Opportunistic, considering the neighbours are international movie stars."

"Hurry up, now," Archie said, as he left.

Mia looked again at the garment on the hanger, deciding she had better make the effort. Nothing worse than the tabloids running a picture of Fenella and Archie looking fabulous with a monotone Mia in the background. She had made that mistake before, the columnists had had a field day.

The Daimler swung effortlessly into the gateway of the Harbour Spa Hotel. A domed portico graced the entrance, flanked either side by plinths bearing flame-filled bowls, the stone shimmered in the torchlight; solid, rich, expensive.

A red carpet across the gravel was cordoned off with thick rope swaying from gold struts. Guests streamed along the walkway as doormen, sleek in powder blue jackets, greeted the car. Archie, who had insisted on driving, was relieved to hand over the keys.

Bernice emerged first, elegant in bronze, a fitted cocktail dress and jacket, Mia followed wearing the aquamarine tunic with cream palazzo pants and unfamiliar heels. Fenella had twisted her daughter's copper mane into a twirling bun, finishing off the look with her own emerald earrings. Fenella, in turn, wore a slither of bitter chocolate, turquoise shoes and bandana, understated and opulent at the same time. The transformation was total, they each looked divine and all heads turned.

Archie stood back to admire the three women, looking forward to a night with his talented trio, they had not been out together in a long time, who knew when they would again. He hoped his medication would soon kick in, some alcohol might help, he had seen Mia watching him, sensing his pain.

"You came!" Pearl cried, leaping into Archie's arms. "I was worried. Ross said you had to rest in bed all day."

Archie kissed her, placing her on the ground. Pearl in a pink tutu, yellow wellingtons and sparkly tiara, danced a few steps and ran away.

"See," he said, eyes twinkling. "Just like you at that age." Mia looked at Pearl and smiled.

Had she ever been that self-assured?

Pearl ran up to a man and tugged his jacket. His face broke into a warm smile as he took her hand, striding through the crowd to greet them. Wild black hair smoothed back and dressed in a classically-cut dinner jacket with a perfect bow-tie, Ross Power cut a dash; a man in control. Strikingly handsome, the sun had darkened his skin making his smile bright white. Mia slipped into shadow.

"We're honoured to have you," he said in his soft American accent, giving Archie and Fenella a look of deference. "Your presence this evening will make it truly special."

Archie pumped his hand. "Delighted to lend our support, neighbour. Isn't that right, Fenella?"

"Totally," Fenella agreed. "This is all very impressive, a boost for the whole community and we're locals after all."

Ross was relieved. He had never seen Archie in professional mode and was unsure what to expect. Archie still had a 'wild man' reputation. When Archie asked if Fenella Flanagan could come along – meaning two famous movie stars in attendance – Ross could not believe his luck.

Within seconds the PR team had whisked them away and Mia could relax, she had never been fond of the limelight. An elegant young man was playing the piano, giving the whole scene a smooth, jazzy feel. With Bernice deep in conversation with Eamon, Mia took a glass of champagne and moved to the edge of the crowd. The artwork around the room had caught her eye, original pieces by a hand she had not seen before. She drifted over to a seascape, wild water, the spray so vivid she could almost taste salt, its vibrant primitive style enchanted her, just the sort of art she loved to get lost in …

"Hey, Mia, how's it going?" Driscoll looked surprised to see her. "What do you think to this place, amazing isn't it?" He had made a real effort, smart jacket, lots of aftershave. His eyes were on stalks, he had clearly been partying for some time.

"It is," Mia moved away, Driscoll was a nuisance, especially smashed.

"Thought you were called back to the job, Wicklow or somewhere, wasn't it?" he asked, loudly.

"Finished now." She looked for an escape.

"Heard there was a problem, you'd to go and sort out."

"It's wrapped, they'll do the edits in London." Driscoll used to be in the business, she would not discuss anything he could turn into tittle-tattle.

"I believe you had the police up there and everything," he continued. "Thought you'd be giving statements and stuff."

Nosy busy-body, Mia thought.

"Excuse me," she said. "Old friend … must say hello." And zigzagging through the crowd she slipped out onto a vast deck, framed by hundreds of fairy lights. Making for the farthest corner, she nestled into a chair to call Rupert. He picked up, she was thrilled to hear his voice.

"You on your way home yet?"

"Not yet. How did the audition go?" She so hoped he had positive news, Rupert was a good actor, he deserved a break.

"Still in Manchester, going out to dinner with the director, looks promising."

"You'll win them round, you see if you don't," she told him. Suddenly music piped through speakers on the deck.

"Where are you?" he asked.

"A do at a local hotel. Fenella and Archie are officiating, you know, 'Movie stars open cocktail bar', I'm in the backup team," she explained.

"Oh." Rupert sounded deflated. "I thought you were visiting someone who's terminally ill, not partying at flash hotels?"

"It's not how it sounds," Mia replied, then as if to belie her words, a huge fanfare blared out calling everyone to order, official proceedings were about to take place, glasses needed charging. "Rupert, I'll have to go."

"Yeah, go and enjoy yourself while I hold everything together back here. I mean it's not as if mingling with those guys could in anyway benefit my career, is it?" He was miffed.

"This wasn't planned. Anyway the one time you did meet my mother, it didn't go that well, I seem to remember." Mia wanted to bite her tongue, she had promised she would never mention that disastrous occasion again. "It's not like that anyway, I'll explain when I see you, just wanted to say good luck." He had already hung up.

Mia gave him the benefit of the doubt, he was obviously stressing about dinner and how much was riding on it; he needed the job. The music stopped, Mia downed her drink, Archie was about to make a speech, he loved making speeches.

Passing a porthole window, she spotted Ross Power and two other men. Ross checked his watch, folded something into a drawer and opened the door. Not wishing to be caught snooping, Mia sped away as fast as her heels would allow. One of the men saw her.

"Mia, this way." It was Eamon.

Mia turned back, feigning relief. "This place is vast, easy to get lost."

Ross did a double-take, the mad woman with the wild red hair certainly looked very different.

"Welcome to the Harbour Spa, do you know our esteemed mayor?" She felt a blush at her throat; *what was it about a man in a dinner jacket?*

"Of course we know each other," beamed the mayor. "Miss Flanagan went to the Mary Magdalene with my daughter."

Mia nodded at the mayor, while Ross, wearing a quizzical smile, guided them all out onto the deck.

The sky above the dark, shimmering sea was splashed with smears of tangerine; a light breeze trembled the lights, making them shiver in anticipation.

"Short and sweet," Fenella forewarned Archie.

"My Lord Mayor," Archie began, instantly promoting the small town official.

"Honoured guests, ladies and gentlemen, it's a great pleasure, along with my partner in crime, the beautiful Fenella Flanagan." Pause for applause. "To officially open this fabulous cocktail bar, here at the stunning Harbour Spa Hotel." He gave a megawatt smile. "My family, the Fitzgeralds, have been in this part of the world forever, it's our home, our family seat."

Bernice winced, Archie always built everything up.

"And no matter where we are in the world, this will *always* be home." More applause. "Now, before we release the Chinese lanterns into the sky, please raise your glasses and drink the health and good fortune of Ross and the Power family in its entirety, for their visionary investment in our sleepy, seaside town and giving us a fabulous five-star establishment to rival any in Europe, no, make that the world!" Archie lifted his glass.

"The Powers!"

Ross caught Mia's eye; he gave her an odd look, as if he not quite deserving of Archie's accolade but she was suddenly distracted.

"You came!" Pearl had thrown herself at her legs. "It is you, isn't it? You look so beautiful."

Mia unwrapped the little girl's embrace.

"Couldn't miss this. You look lovely, too."

Pearl took Mia's hand, pulling her to a table. "Everyone has a lantern with a number. We let them go and whoever owns the one landing farthest away, comes to stay at the hotel for free!"

Pearl's eyes were alight and although a PR stunt, Mia was not immune to the excitement as they stood side-by-side leaning out to sea, releasing their lanterns at the same time. Pearl squealed as the breeze carried them away.

"This kid bothering you, ma'am?" Ross stood behind them.

"Not at all but she's already beaten me." Mia pointed as her lantern floated gracefully towards the beach.

"It doesn't matter," Pearl announced. "Mermaids can stay

anytime they like, can't they Ross?" She flashed her eyes at her uncle. "It's in the Constitution."

"Mermaid or not," he turned to Mia, "you'd be very welcome, anytime."

"Probably a little out of my price bracket," Mia said.

Pearl took her hand again. "I'm sure we could accommodate you."

"There speaks a born hotelier, sorry but it's in the blood." Ross excused his niece. By now all the lanterns were afloat.

"Look, the sky's full of floating stars, millions of them, with angels steering them, I can see them, everywhere." Pearl gazed upwards.

"They're not stars, Pearl, and there aren't millions of them, you know that." Ross chided.

"There's a lot to be said for a vivid imagination, don't you think?" Mia defended Pearl.

"Reality's a good thing, too. Staying focused in the here and now, prevents disappointment, I often find." He raised his eyebrows at Pearl. "Now, I must go and mingle."

"Yes, go." Pearl waved him away. "I want Mia to turn her legs into a fishtail and she won't do that with you here."

So much for the reality check, Mia thought as she watched Ross disappear into the throng before joining the little girl in the wonky tiara to gaze at millions of stars with angels floating through the night sky.

MEMORY MAKING

Archie burst into Mia's room at an ungodly hour. Mia had been awake for some time. She was at the window, sunlight spilling in as a willow cast fluttering shadows on the yellow walls. Walls painted as a surprise the Easter she came to stay as a ten year old and left again at thirteen. The time Fenella had nearly married.

She was gazing across the ocean, a myriad of colours sparkling invitingly as she watched early risers hoist sails, chasing towards Phoenix Island then turning about in a flurry of creamy spray to swoop back to the harbour.

"Come on, let's go. It's perfect out there." He was wearing pink sailing trousers and a top with a hole in it. His deck shoes were ancient. Fenella bought them one Christmas, investing in the very best, knowing full well Archie would expect them to last forever. Mia looked at him, pale beneath his freckles. They had left early last night, Fenella said she had a headache but everyone knew it was Archie who needed to retire.

He spotted the phone in her lap. "Everything okay?"

She had tried to call Rupert, wanting to soothe troubled waters, assure him of her love and support. His audition was a big deal, he was bound to be tense.

"Just wanted to wish Rupert luck, big audition today."

"He'll knock 'em dead." He looked into her eyes. "If I can ever help?"

"Rupert wants to do things his way. He's really talented, you know."

Only a half-lie. Rupert regularly asked if Mia could inveigle the great Archie Fitzgerald to give him a leg up.

"I'm sure he is, my angel. I'm sure he's fabulous in every way, why else would you have fallen for him?"

Her frown faded.

"Now, let's make the best of our last day together. Leela's created an extravagant picnic and Pearl's on her way."

"Pearl?"

"Yep, just me and my two favourite girls. Let's go, surf's up!"

Mia grabbed a fleece, glancing briefly at the statue of the Virgin Mary in the alcove on the landing, she said a quick prayer that this would definitely *not* be their last day together.

Pearl looked very small, standing there in front of the large house, duffle bag in one hand, life jacket in the other. Leela rushed to greet her on hearing Driscoll's familiar honk of arrival, Mia hot on her heels. The little girl gave them a brave smile but her eyes looked larger than ever.

"You do know we're going sailing?" Mia reminded her. "I know you're not keen."

"I dislike it because I had a bad experience," Pearl said, cornflower-blue pools gazing at her. "Archie says I need a happy experience to balance the bad one, so I grow to like it."

"Okay." Mia guessed Pearl was repeating precisely what Archie had told her. "And how do you feel about that?"

Pearl thought for a moment. "It begins with A."

"Angry? No, anxious," Mia prompted. Pearl nodded.

"Archie says if at any time I want to come straight back, we can and when he said you were coming too, I knew I'd be fine." She gave Mia a smile. It was like a burst of sunshine.

"Really?" Mia was flattered.

"If anything bad happens you'll just call on the other mermaids and they'll take us to the secret Sea Palace until it's time to go home."

"Pearl, the thing is …" Mia started.

"So, you see," continued Pearl, picking up her bag. "I'm safe with you." And waving to Archie at the top of the steps, started running towards the house.

"You were frightened of the water, when you were a bit younger than her," Leela told her, tucking Pearl's brand new life jacket under her arm.

"I don't remember that, thought I always loved it."

They started back to the house together.

"Archie was determined you'd be a sailor and that's when we rediscovered the magic medicine I'd invented when he was little and determined to hate everything."

Mia laughed. "Now that I *do* remember. Jars of it, a different colour for every ailment."

Leela smiled, crimson lipstick dramatic in the morning sunshine. "That's right, blue for all water-related conditions." She was referring to her simple concoction, sugar transformed into exotic remedies with food colouring. The clever ploy worked for everything from sea sickness to fear of spiders.

With little formal education, Leela was professorial where common sense was concerned and not untalented when a small dose of witchcraft was required either. Appointed housekeeper, her only qualification being she had raised seven brothers and sisters single-handedly from the age of eleven, Leela was hard as nails and soft as putty. She ruled the kitchen with a rod of iron, with only one chink in her armour, Archie. The adored little boy, she had taken to her heart and who now totally owned her soul.

"Get out there and enjoy yourselves." Leela nodded towards the sea. "It's a fine boat, needs using."

"Rather extravagant though, don't you think? Archie buying

a brand new boat, just when …" Mia closed her mouth.

"When he's not going to be around to enjoy it? That's a very cheese-paring way of looking at things, Mia." Leela gave her a flinty look. "Did you never hear of a bucket list? Where would we be if those given the nod the Grim Reaper was waiting in the wings, didn't make the best of whatever time they had left?"

"I'm sorry. I just know Bernice was anti the boat, I wondered if it was because he's so ill, sailing might be too much for him?" They were in the kitchen now, Leela taking a mismatch of plates from the dresser, wrapping them in napkins before placing them in the picnic basket.

"Not at all." Leela was cross. "All Bernice wants him to do is sit quietly making lists of everything he owns, so as soon as he's gone she can sell the lot. She was mortified when he started spending like there was no tomorrow, sure, it cost thousands to get the old Dame back on the road, and I've no idea how much Banshee was, but she's worth every penny to see the smile on his face when he looks at her, and at you too, it has to be said."

Leela was yabbering away but Mia was not listening, the phrase, 'spending like no tomorrow' kept repeating in her mind. That's precisely what Archie was doing, he had no tomorrow; not even Leela had a magic medicine for what ailed him this time.

Pearl climbed onto the ancient carver. Leela produced, what she called 'emergency fruit cake' and was spreading thick yellow butter on a slice for the spindly little girl.

"This'll put a lining on your stomach. It's Padraig's favourite recipe." Leela said.

"Padrig?" Pearl mispronounced.

"Padraig the Pirate, fierce cake-eater, he is." Leela carried on with her work. Archie gave Pearl a knowing look, biting into cake. A gust of wind whipped through the open door, causing the brass chandelier above the table to creak as it moved. Pearl's eyes swivelled upwards, then silently she let her gaze absorb the room as she ate. Oil paintings of galleons on high seas adorned the walls; a collection of shark jaws rested on a shelf, a rusting anchor stood resolutely in an alcove.

"Is this house very old?" Pearl asked Leela, obviously the eldest in the room.

"Ancient," Leela confirmed. "Archie's great-great-grandfather built it."

"Probably need to add another couple of greats," Archie said. "But Leela's right, it's very old."

Pearl looked round again. "And do you *have* to live here?" She had a point, compared with the Harbour Spa Hotel, Galty House was positively decrepit.

"It's our home," Archie told her. "Old houses look like this, it's called character."

Pearl frowned. "Will you live in it until it falls down?"

"It's not going to fall down," Mia explained. "It's been here a long time, it'll be here a lot longer yet."

The little girl looked unconvinced. She pointed at a large metal sign above the range, it read *The Seahorse Hotel* in turquoise letters on a black background. It had been made by the local blacksmith, a gift to Mrs Fitzgerald from a grateful commanding officer at the end of the Second World War.

"Was this a hotel too?" Pearl's eyes widened.

"Sort of," Archie answered. "A story for another time."

"I still like it," Pearl announced, helping Mia carry the picnic. "It's a bit like *Hogwarts* by the sea."

"What is?"

Mia was distracted, Leela had supplied enough food to feed

an army.

"Galty." Pearl looked back at the house.

"I suppose it is," laughed Mia.

It certainly knew how to cast a spell, of that there was no doubt.

The Harbour Spa Hotel looked beautiful from out at sea, half submarine, half-Egyptian barge, porthole windows glimmered above the water, while awnings billowed gracefully in the breeze. Watched through half-closed eyes, it appeared to be moving, a glorious galleon, blazing in the sunshine, a shimmer in the moonlight. It was a lavish work of genius, no expense had been spared.

Ross Power's head was full to bursting, yet again he had worked through the night, examining spreadsheets and costings and something else, messages from staff about problems, equipment failure, maintenance issues; he was growing more and more anxious.

Pearl had slipped in earlier to say goodnight and despite her ever-growing repertoire of sophisticated airs and graces, in her pyjamas with her hair brushed out, she looked fragile, just how he remembered Tara at that age; charming and entertaining, wily and wilful, with the same vivid imagination that scared him.

Pearl had been at the window pointing out across the bay.

"That's where Uncle Archie's taking us, the island, the one that looks like a sea monster." She gave a sigh. "I hope I make it."

"Sure you want to try? You know I can't come tomorrow, I've an important meeting in Dublin," he explained again.

"Mia's coming, I'll be safe with her," she was going to expound her mermaid backup theory but changed her mind.

Ross seemed less appreciative of her storytelling these days; telling her she needed *true* stories, not make-believe; tales she could back up with hard facts. Pearl thought that was rich coming from him. Everyone said the hotel cost millions and the family, *her* family, owned it. But when she asked to see the money, imagining a treasure chest locked away in a cave, he had nothing to show her.

"How can I be a princess without any *actual* gold?" she had bleated, lower lip pushed out.

"You'll have to earn it and save it, like all the modern princesses do," Ross replied, ploughing through yet another file. Pearl gave a flick of her head.

"I'm nearly ten, I won't have time to save all the billions I need." He was not listening. "I'll just have to marry money the way Granny did."

Ross looked up. "Wherever did you hear such a thing?"

"Why, Granny of course." Pearl gave a little twirl and blew a kiss as she left.

Caroline had appeared at the door, wearing her 'time for bed' look. She had already been instructed to escort Pearl sailing on their neighbour's boat and was put out; she had been hoping for a day off.

"You guys have fun, you hear me?" Ross had called, slightly puzzled why Pearl thought the mad woman with the red hair could make everything okay but he chose not ask, he needed to focus, prepare for tomorrow. "And take real good care."

"We will," replied Pearl, but taking Caroline's hand, she knew the nanny would not be escorting her in the morning. Pearl had already paid Driscoll to take her directly to Galty House before Caroline even woke.

Now, with the sun high in the sky, Pearl, Archie and Mia were anchored off the far western point of Phoenix Island, devouring a scrumptious lunch of fresh crab salad with Leela's crunchy homemade coleslaw.

The three sat munching companionably on deck, the boat bobbing in a soft sea. Despite Pearl clinging to the bow rail and then to Mia, the little girl who hated water had been quiet and uncomplaining. Anchored off the small rocky bay, she seemed quite content, if a little subdued for the effervescent youngster Mia had grown fond of in so short a time.

"Are you here for the whole summer Pearl?" Mia asked.

"I think I live here now," Pearl replied, "I'm going to be a pupil at Mary Magdalene when vacation's over. I've to stay for my studies, Ross said."

"Quite right." Archie stretched out, dropping his battered panama over his eyes. "Education is very important, best stay as long as you can, make the most of it. The Good Sisters will give you a solid grounding, Mia went there too, got a first in her degree, though likes to keep that quiet."

Mia raised an eyebrow at him. Fenella's nomadic lifestyle meant her early education had been haphazard but it was true, she had spent the majority of her formal schooldays at the convent. It was most unlike Archie to deliver plaudits where education and in particular, a Catholic education was concerned. Always a firebrand revolutionary in the face of organised religion, Archie was a free thinking libertarian believing only in love and the arts. To his mind everything else was contrived and commercial, or so he had indoctrinated Mia from an early age.

"How do you know it never did me any harm?" Mia asked.

"You did better than I, imprisoned by the Christian Brothers up at The Holy Cross. Brother Aquinas beat everyone black and blue and Padre Thomas, delirious with sunstroke from the missions, wouldn't have known a syllabus if he ran into one.

Sure, he nearly fainted with shock when the school inspector demanded we sit the national exam papers. He considered such things beneath his boys." He gave a grim smile. "He was probably right."

"Surely things have moved on?" Mia teased, looking at Pearl who had edged a little closer to the side, a pool of aquamarine enticing her.

"I love the Good Sisters," Pearl said, not missing a thing. "When I tell Sister Agnes what Archie says about school, she says that was the Middle Ages and all the dragons have been slain, metro … metraphysically speaking."

"Metaphorically speaking," Archie corrected. "Do you know what that means?"

"It's a figure of speech, a descriptive example to explain something." Pearl replied.

Mia laughed. Pearl's education seemed more than adequate for one so young.

A boat buzzed by and Pearl jumped back, fearing she would be splashed. They watched it whiz towards the island, releasing its passengers into the water, who shrieked with delight. The swimmers, a group of tanned teenagers, were soon scrabbling up the cliffs, running excitedly across the grassy mound, shimmering in the sunshine. They were heading for what looked like a ruined fortress, a wide circular wall with turrets. The youngsters' voices faded as they disappeared.

"Where did they go?" Pearl pointed. "Is it a castle?"

"Been many things." Archie showed her how to focus the binoculars. "Has a very mysterious past." Archie was using his spooky, storytelling voice. "In olden days it was a meeting place for chieftains, ships were moored in the bay, ready to do battle with invaders on the high seas."

Pearl's eyes grew wider. "Was there a princess?" she asked,

enthralled.

"Ah, sure any amount," Archie countered, but he could not remember a legend featuring a royal female and pressing for names, Pearl was disappointed, the island losing its appeal.

"When did people last live there?"

"During the last war it was a seminary." Mia said. "A school for training priests."

"That was probably one of the island's most interesting periods," Archie declared, not wishing to lose his audience.

"Priests have to be trained? To do what?" Pearl asked.

Archie smiled, he was wooing her back.

"Well, apart from learning which vestments to wear on particular days, they're taught how to perform the Sacraments, let's see …" He tapped his chin. "Turning water into wine, for example."

Mia laughed. "Neat trick."

"Heal the sick, cleanse the souls of sinners." Archie continued.

Pearl raised her eyebrows.

"You know, people who've done bad things, their souls have black stains on them, priests help make them white again," Archie explained.

Pearl nodded. "Like the Laundromat."

"And the best of all is, they learn to exorcise demons." Archie confirmed. "Big job, someone's got to do it."

"No way!" Pearl *was* impressed. "Just like a school for wizards. They're taught magic and spells."

Mia coughed. "Archie might be exaggerating." Pearl's eyes were wide with wonderment. "Priests are taught to do good deeds and help others do the same. It's the same for imams, rabbis, preachers; they're priests too, trying to help people as best they can."

Pearl turned to Archie.

"So, why was the war the best bit?"

"Because during the war it was a very special kind of training camp. A secret one." Archie's 'man of mystery' voice came into play this time.

Mia's knew this tale, this was one of Sister Agnes's favourite stories.

"Training what?" asked Pearl.

"Spies!" Archie folded his arms, triumphantly.

"Wow, no way!" Pearl clapped her hands together. "Spells and spies? Can we go there, can we go there now?"

"You'll be disappointed," Mia warned. "It's not a theme park."

Pearl gave her a look. "I'm not a kid, Mia. It can be my summer project, I'll search for clues, take pictures, recordings, everything." She looked expectantly at Archie. He twinkled down at her. Mia was outnumbered.

"Your wish is my command, ma'am." Archie gave a salute. "Clear that picnic away, let's get shipshape, we're heading for the island."

"It's a bit late, maybe another time?" Mia suggested, but it was half-hearted; Pearl's excitement was contagious.

"No time like the present." Archie took the wheel. "Who knows when another opportunity will present itself, a perfect day for memory making."

Mia gave him a grin, it was one of their sayings. When she was little and needed cheering up, Archie would invent something, a treat, a trip, some kind of experience, calling it 'memory making'. Nothing else mattered while memories were being made, Archie always insisted.

Watching Pearl climb up beside him at the wheel, wind in her hair, beaming smile, Mia felt exactly as she had all those years ago; excited, uplifted and happy. It was such a wonderful feeling, a bit more memory making was definitely called for.

WELL, WELL, WELL

It was the second time Driscoll had been to Galty House that day and it was not yet noon. The call had come around ten o'clock, Fenella had to return to England, an urgent message from her agent, she needed to be at the studio as soon as possible.

The actress was showering when Bernice arrived with coffee. Checking her reflection in the mirror; smart linen trouser suit, tan brogues matching her silk scarf, a smear of colour on her lips, she looked well; she also looked worried.

Fenella padded through from the *en suite*. "Water's cold, never worked properly, bloody thing." She left footprints on the antique rug.

"Did you see Archie?" Bernice was stripping the bed.

"Came to kiss me goodbye before he left."

Bernice did not comment. Archie and Fenella had always been uncommonly close.

"Leave the bed," Fenella told her. "I'll be back once the schedules are sorted, no need to change it on my account." Bernice ignored her and continued; she decided when beds were changed.

"Do you mind if I come up to Dublin with you?" It was only then Fenella realised Bernice was dressed for town.

"I need to go straight to the airport."

"Drop me anywhere, I can pick up the DART."

The Fitzgeralds often used the commuter train that swept around the Dublin coast. Archie in particular loved to be recognised and would chat to fans while enjoying the journey, while Bernice preferred to remain buried in a book.

Fenella started throwing things in a bag – a bottle of Chanel, her jewel case.

"Have you a date?"

"Just some shopping, I've run out of ochre for a painting I'm working on and if Archie's to go into hospital, I can't let him take that old smoking jacket, whatever he thinks."

Fenella stopped what she was doing. "Surely he's had enough of hospital?"

Bernice shrugged. "I don't know Fenella, nobody does. I've discussed it with Doctor Morrissey – Archie won't let anyone near his consultant – and we just don't know how he'll be, what he'll need."

"He'll need to be here!" Fenella turned on her. "He'll need to be at home!"

"But what if we can't cope? I can't cope?" Bernice was standing at the end of the bed, Fenella's discarded shoes in her hands. Fenella was stunned. Bernice coped with everything, always, but there was mild panic behind her eyes.

"I'll help. We'll organise round the clock nursing, make sure everything's covered, there's Leela too," Fenella offered.

"I don't know if you've noticed but Leela's not in the best of health herself. She's crippled with arthritis these days and hopeless where Archie's concerned. Gives into him all the time, never backs me up." Bernice's voice caught in her throat.

"Ah, Bernice, give her a break, he's her baby, always has been." Fenella was applying moisturiser.

"He's a middle-aged man with responsibilities, it's high time he and indeed everyone else around here realised that!" She let the shoes clatter to the floor.

Leela was polishing the Daimler when Driscoll arrived. He swung the taxi in beside the old girl, her rich ruby body and shiny chrome gleaming in the sun.

"You're to take this," Leela said, not a bit happy. Driscoll had always been too borderline bad in her opinion. "Archie said she could do with a run and if you're taking the girls, you're to do it in style."

"The girls?"

"Miss Bernice needs to go to town and Miss Fenella the airport, they'll be company for each other." Driscoll rolled his eyes. The batty old housekeeper always referred to the women as Miss, as if they were the young daughters of somebody grand.

Driscoll was delighted he could take the Daimler but disappointed he would not have Fenella to himself. Having worked together back in the day, she might know of something going, just a small part would do; he would not broach the subject in front of Bernice. Things were not working out, he had been wooing Bernice ever since his return and was getting nowhere. Eamon intimated she was going to inherit everything but he was not so sure, wondering should he hang around or move on, again.

"Keys are in it," Leela told him, and taking a large box from the trunk, waddled off in the direction of the house.

"Any coffee going?" Driscoll called.

Leela did not reply, the box had her intrigued. Was it a costume, some fabric, an *objet d'art*? Mia was a collector, Leela knew her little flat was a palace, a treasure trove filled with exotic pieces from everywhere she had ever been. She could not wait to see what was in the box, what little piece of paradise Mia had secreted away.

Checking the coast was clear, Leela placed the box on the kitchen table. It was old, she could tell by style of the script scrolled across the turquoise surface. She ran her fingers over the lettering, noticing the note.

"Something borrowed," she read aloud.

Removing the lid she gazed down at a swirl of tissue. As deftly as her twisted fingers would allow, she drew the wrapping back to reveal a glorious creamy froth of fabric and taking it out, held it up. The gown fell away in a whisper of gossamer, the faintest tinkle as embroidered pearls and shells swung free. A piece of paper fluttered to the floor, the delivery note. Lol had left the vital clue to gown's provenance intact. Reading it Leela gasped. The door opened. Spinning round, she whipped the gown away and scurried into the back kitchen.

"Be right with you," she called, shoving the box into the cupboard along with tennis shoes and abandoned riding boots. Driscoll was at the sink, washing his hands.

"What was that?" he asked.

"What?"

"Whatever you were stuffing away in the cupboard?"

Leela rubbed her hands on her apron. "Just some old clothes." Not a lie, the dress was obviously an original, it had a look of the nineteen twenties about it, like something from an old film.

"Valuable?" Driscoll queried. Leela stood in front of the cupboard door.

"What's it to you?" She was mightily fed up with people asking her how much this or that was worth. There had always been speculation on how wealthy the Fitzgeralds were. Was there money stuffed under every mattress? Were the paintings and antiques really worth more than anything on display in the national museum? To some extent she had perpetrated the myth; wanting the family and especially her beloved Archie, to appear a cut above. But since Archie's diagnosis the speculation was rampant and the questions downright rude.

"I'll get you some coffee." She pushed a towel at him.

"Any emergency fruitcake going begging?" he asked.

Leela tutted, he could have the stale stuff she was saving for the birds, she would not butter it either, always after something, that fella.

Bernice was at the coffee pot, freshening the brew.

"I'll stay over, up above," she announced as Leela and Driscoll appeared. "There's a play on at the Gaiety, I'd like to see, Archie's friend, Gordon O'Toole is in it."

Leela sliced a piece of elderly cake for Driscoll but Bernice was eating it before she could stop her.

"Good enough," Leela replied.

Bernice pulled a face at the cake. "I'll be back for supper tomorrow."

"Good enough," Leela repeated, giving Driscoll the last of the cake on a plate. The door opened, it was Fenella, dressed head to toe in cream, a tangerine scarf around her hair, amber drops in her ears.

"Breakfast?" Leela asked.

"No time." Fenella swooped on Driscoll's plate, swiping the stale cake. "Could you put a drop of hot chocolate in a flask?"

"The coffee's fresh," Bernice told her.

"Of course, won't take a minute," Leela said.

Bernice sighed. "I'll be in the car."

"Is she staying over?" Fenella asked, biting into and then abandoning the cake.

"There's a play," Leela said.

"Don't tell me, Gordon O'Toole's in it?" Fenella gave an old-fashioned look.

Leela changed the subject.

"Any idea how long Mia will be staying? Anyone to get back to?" She could not get the dress out of her mind. It looked like a wedding dress to her way of thinking.

"How would I know? She plays things very close to her chest. Especially after Courtney, he hurt her more than she let on."

"Ah, that was a long time ago." Leela looked wistful. "Lovely boy, very exotic. She gave him up though, then he turned round and got married just like that." She snapped her fingers. Leela has seen it in the cards, Courtney was not 'the one'.

"Introduced me to a guy at a party a while ago, very good-looking. Flirted with me like mad, most inappropriate." Leela was not surprised, men of all ages pursued Fenella. "An actor, what can I say?" Fenella gestured despair. "Don't think I'm going to be a granny anytime soon."

"Well, that would hardly suit your image, now would it?" Driscoll piped up. They had forgotten he was there.

Leela gave Fenella a flask with a wink indicating there was a good slug of whiskey in it. Her eyes were misting over, she hated them, any of them, leaving.

"You'd better go." She looked up at the school-house clock over the range. Fenella hugged her.

"I'll be back soon."

"Make sure of it." Leela turned away, rubbing at her eyes.

The intrepid trio had made great progress over on Phoenix Island. Banshee was moored at the end of the old jetty and once Archie was happy she was secure, they took the cliff path up to the brow of the hill with the ruins on the far side. Passing the teenagers heading back, one of them recognised Archie and stopped.

"Hello, sir, heard you lived around here. I'm a great admirer of your work," the young man said, politely.

"Dear boy!" Archie shook his hand, glad to take a breather. "How very kind. Are you in the business of theatrics?"

"I'm a student, sir, final year at the Gaiety School of Drama."

Archie studied him. Handsome, fine nose, clear eyes. He would do well.

"Are these all drama students too?" He waved at the gaggle of youngsters who had gathered round.

"A couple, the rest are doing creative writing, and Joe over there, he's English Literature at Trinity." The others jeered Joe, pushing him playfully.

"Ah, mock not the pen pushers," Archie warned. "For they write the words we speak, life would be a lot less without them. Someone had to scribe, 'all the world's a stage'." He turned to walk on.

"I hope you get better, sir," the young man said.

"I'll keep trying, promise me you'll do the same."

The student laughed and ran after his friends.

"I think he meant your health," Mia said.

"I hoped he meant my art." Archie gave her a broad grin.

Arriving at the entrance of what had been the monastery, they were disappointed to find a metal fence barring the way. There were signs declaring the building unsafe, the land private property and trespassers would be 'Persecuted' – some wag had messed with the sign.

"It'll be health and safety. Everyone's so scared of being sued, wiser just to ban everything," Mia said. Pearl was poking around the entrance, pushing at the gate hopefully. Her shoulders drooped in disappointment and then something caught her eye, she ran off, disappearing round the building.

"Look, I'm in." Pearl was jumping up and down behind the gate.

"How?" Mia was bemused.

"Go round, the wall has a hole in it," she hissed through a crack.

"Where?" Mia could not see an opening anywhere.

"Behind the hedge."

Archie was already there.

"Come on," he called. "Breathe in." He grabbed Mia's hand and they slipped through the crumbling stone. Pearl ran towards them.

"It's not half as ruined once you're inside the wall," she exclaimed. "Look at all this!"

They were in a flagstone courtyard; a corridor of beautifully carved eaves ran along one side leading to what looked like a school room and on the other a church. Although windows were broken and the roof had collapsed, the crumbling eaves gave the place a gothic grandeur.

"It's lovely," Mia said, struggling to remember what it had looked like on her one and only visit many years ago.

"And there's the well," Archie announced, striding off to a circle of bronze stone in the centre of the courtyard. He took a pebble dropping it into the darkness, turning his head to listen. A splash.

"Aha, still water in there!"

"I'm thirsty," said Pearl. They had left everything on the boat. Leaning in Mia could just make out rough steps circling downwards, disappearing into the gloom.

"I remember!" Archie yelled. "Count thirteen stones round from this one and then thirteen down."

"Really?" Mia thought this was one of Archie's fairy stories.

Pearl was there in a flash.

"I can only reach down eight." She was on tip toes.

Mia grabbed her by the waist, making her squeal. "I'll do it."

She leaned in and counted. "I've found something."

"Good, pull it out," Archie said. Sure enough, Mia grappled with the object and pulled out a small bucket attached to the wall of the well by a chain.

Archie went to help. "Keep hold of the chain, let the bucket drop." Mia did as she was told. They heard a clunk and a splash. "Now, pull it up." They drew the bucket up together. It was full of water.

"Looks clear enough," he said, lifting to taste it.

"Archie," Mia went to protest.

"Delicious," he exclaimed. "Fresh as can be. I thought it might be sea water after all this time but no, here." Mia took a tentative sip. "You've lost your sense of adventure, young lady."

"I've never had water straight from a well, especially not a holy well." Pearl took the bucket and drank.

"Not too much now," Mia warned. "It might not be that clean, don't want you going back with an upset stomach."

"It can't harm me if it's holy water, now can it?" Pearl reasoned, drinking heartily.

"Who said it was a holy well?" Mia asked.

Pearl gestured their surroundings. "Go figure," she said and they laughed.

Mia checked her watch, the sun was high.

"Better head back, you told Ross a couple of hours if Pearl was okay on the water. We left ages ago."

Taking the bucket, Archie placed it back on the ledge where Mia had found it. Pearl took his hand as they slid out from behind the bush and onto the track.

"We can come back can't we, Uncle Archie?" Pearl asked, as they walked towards the sea. "I've loads of ideas for my project."

"Of course. Now we know how to get in, I'll remember lots of things to show you, we'll find artefacts and relics all over the place."

"Did we go there much when I was a kid?" Mia asked, running to catch up. She could only remember Sister Agnes's history class and the row when Fenella discovered she had been to the island, demanding all future trips were cleared beforehand.

They were in the kitchen, Mia was under the table, playing with the tarot cards. Leela had stood her ground, saying the trips were part of her education.

"I need to know what those nuns are teaching my child, anything off curricular needs my specific permission from now on." Fenella had insisted.

"Sometimes it's hard to know where you are." Leela was snippy.

"You could find me if you wanted to."

"So you can stop her doing things and make her stand out even more than she already does," Leela had snapped back.

Mia cringed at the memory. Fenella and Leela rarely argued but when they did it was only ever about her and usually involved her mother trying to influence her life, without really being there at all.

"Not when you were little," Archie replied, linking Mia's arm. "But yes, at one time we came here a lot."

"Were you nearly ten like me?" Pearl queried, hoping she had discovered the island at the same time as her newly adopted uncle.

"About the same age as the students we met earlier."

"Bonfires and midnight barbecues, I know what must have

gone on." Mia joked.

"Not at all." Archie pretended to be serious. "We came to recitals. The students' Gregorian chant was sublime, never heard a choir like it. Depending on the wind, it would drift across the bay, you could hear it in Galty, like a mystical heavenly host." Archie had either had too much sun or not enough medication.

Mia watched Pearl taking in every word, Archie was fascinating company, especially if you were young and impressionable with an overactive imagination … she should know.

THE PIRATE

Archie was trying to fight the deep, dark depression that had been seeping into his psyche ever since they left the island. Not only did he have to face the frenzied anguish of Pearl's furious nanny, storming along the shore as they arrived but he was crestfallen Bernice and Fenella had left. He felt abandoned.

The ritual of his bath had not soothed him, so instead of seeking company he buried himself in the library. Looking at the awards adorning the walls, the poster of the film he had starred in to spectacularly win the Oscar, he was overcome with remorse.

"Good-looking bastard, you were," he told his image. Then gazing into his brandy balloon, "Lonely old bastard, now."

Mia had slipped into the room. She stood watching him, head bent, the evening sun lighting the mix of copper and silver in his hair, his usually smiling mouth turned down.

"Who're you talking to?" she asked.

"That sad eejit." He nodded at his portrait. The picture looked far from sad.

It was fusty in the library. Mia opened the French windows onto the terrace, a light breeze drifted in, fragrant with roses and the scent of the sea. There was nowhere as lovely as Galty with the weather as perfect as this.

She poured drinks, passing Archie his glass; he looked drawn beneath his tan. "We'd a great day."

"Isn't she lovely?" Mia was unsure whether he meant Pearl or the boat. "Now," Archie pulled himself upright, "Before we're called into dinner, some business."

His voice was weak. Mia leaned in to listen. Archie's

'business' was usually a series of lectures telling her to misbehave, go a bit wild and even, if only now and then, throw caution to the wind. Considering his limited time frame, she expected the works.

"This young man you want to marry, what's the holdup? Is he already married?" Archie took a sip of his drink.

Mia shook her head, recalling she had not even checked whether Rupert had a partner when they were first introduced. Her love life had been non-existent for so long and he so totally charming, that from the very moment they had kissed, they had tried to devour every inch of each other at every opportunity. She blushed.

Archie gave a cough, pulling Mia back out of Rupert's arms.

"Finance then? You don't have enough money?"

"Hmm," Mia replied. "Although, I don't want anything grand or over the top."

"Why don't you want anything grand? A wedding should be grand, special, mean everything to you, to you both."

Mia smiled; if she were honest, she would like something special, something that set the day apart, made it about what she wanted for a change.

"Then we will not let a small and rather vulgar detail like finance prevent you from having the wedding of your dreams."

"But I ..." Mia tried to protest.

Archie raised his hand. "Nonsense, every girl dreams of a fairy-tale wedding in a castle, to a handsome, shining knight. I shall be your fairy godfather, wave a magic wand and all you've ever wished for will be yours. The wedding, the castle, the prince."

"But, Archie ..."

"No buts. How old are you now? Time you had someone special in your life, made plans, had your own family. You've been hanging around with this crowd of decrepit old yokes for far too long. It shall be done."

He closed his eyes.

"I was wondering," he murmured. "Would you ever come home?" He turned to look at her, sharp eyes drilling into her for an honest answer.

She looked away, across the lawn to the sea. "I've always said no, but now, I'm not so sure." Her gaze followed two gulls swirling in the smooth, blue sky. "London feels like home too, so many of the theatres are where I grew up."

In the early days Fenella had taken her daughter everywhere, no nanny or *au pair* for little Maeve. Fenella had battled to keep her child. Back then, even in England, a single mother was frowned upon. In rural Ireland far worse – a scandal – the girl had committed a mortal sin, disgracing the whole family and if Fenella had ever named her child's father, the shame and derision would have been unbearable and they all would have been ostracised, forever.

Archie remembered those bad old days only too well. Thank goodness London's thespian community was more accepting of the beautiful actress and her fatherless child. Fenella and her baby had stayed away from Rosshaven Harbour for a long time and with good reason.

"And now?" Archie pressed, Mia had still not told him what he wanted to hear.

"If I were married and well, you know …" She did not want to put her dreams into words … not yet.

"Be a great place to bring up a family." Archie placed his hands in his lap. "Which is why I'm leaving you the house." He leaned forward making sure she heard him, understood his words.

"What?!" Mia was flummoxed. "What about Bernice? Leela?

Fenella?"

"They're all catered for one way or another. But the house needs you – young blood, vigour, enthusiasm – the next generation." He gave a smile but his eyes were serious. "This is confidential, just between you and me, until well, the inevitable …"

"But …" Mia felt sick.

Archie clapped his hands together. "No buts." He could see she was shocked. "I know it's the right thing to do, my angel, the right thing for you and the house."

Mia was just about to tell Archie she was very grateful for the offer of help with the wedding but leaving her Galty House was too much, too much to take in and far too much responsibility, when Leela poked her head in; Ross Power was waiting in the hall.

"Show him in," insisted Archie, indicating that Mia fix more drinks. "There's enough supper, isn't there?"

"Of course," Leela replied, affronted. Archie was hardly eating anything these days, anyway.

Mia hoped the visitor would not stay; she was pleased to have Archie to herself at last and needed to speak to him properly, insist he did *not* leave her Galty, she did not want it, could not cope with it, but Ross Power seemed oblivious he might be intruding.

"Sorry it's late, I'm just back from Dublin but Pearl stayed up to tell me she'll never be afraid of the water again and I just had to thank you, it means a lot."

Archie rallied. "Not at all, dear boy. Now, supper's ready will you join us?"

"If that's okay with you?" The visitor turned to Mia. "I'm guessing you two don't get to see each other much, if I'm intruding just say the word, I can come and bother this guy any old time."

"Fine by me," she shrugged, avoiding the American's eyes. She would never make anyone feel unwelcome at Galty House.

Ross had a hearty appetite, which pleased Leela greatly, and his conversation was far more entertaining than Mia had expected. He was making Archie laugh about some of the antics up at the hotel, explaining his policy of recruiting local people to work in the five-star establishment was not without its challenges.

"When I asked for the *à la carte* menu to be in both languages, I expected English and French," Ross explained.

"What did you get?" asked Archie.

"Why English and Gaelic, of course!" He laughed, using soda bread to mop up Leela's delicious onion sauce. Mia found herself watching him, he reminded of her someone.

"How did you resolve that?" Archie imagined a serious run-in with the local branch of *An Cumann Gaelach* if he had dispensed with the Irish translation.

"Just made the menus bigger and included all three!" Ross replied, laughing again.

A pirate, Mia thought, as mirth caused dark hair to fall across his eyes. *Just needs an earring.* It was a trick she used, choosing a character and imagining them in full costume. She could deal with all sorts of personalities that way, it put them in their place, gave her more confidence. Yes, making him a pirate suited, for now.

Leela was serving coffee when Mia decided to take her leave. Archie had drifted off again and their guest had refused a nightcap, time to go. Mia leaned over and kissed Archie. He opened his eyes.

"I'm taking the first train tomorrow, you stay in bed," she instructed.

"Have you business in Dublin too?" Ross asked.

"Plane to catch, time to return to reality." She stood. He stood too. He towered over her. She made him a pirate again.

"Pearl will be disappointed, worse she'll be devastated you've gone."

"Tell her I'll come back, when I can."

Ross put a finger to his lips, Archie had closed his eyes again.

Leela was at the door. "I'll get him to bed once I've cleared away. Off you go now." She shooed them away, leaving them in the half-dark of the hall.

"I meant what I said. Pearl's been through a tough time, you and Archie have helped her turn a corner."

"She's a great kid."

"Big responsibility. Then there's the hotel and everything." He stared into the darkness.

Mia opened the door, a gust of wind burst in whipping up her hair, slashing strands across her face. He caught the curls in his fingers, smoothing the tendrils back. She froze. Did she imagine it or did he cup her chin lightly, lifting her face towards his. She drew in a breath, catching the scent of him, sea, salt, heat, wine. She swallowed.

The porch light made his black eyes glint, he was standing very close, blocking the wind.

"Promise you'll stay in touch," he whispered. "It would mean a lot."

"I will." She felt a chill at the base of her spine. He looked straight into her eyes, questioning yet confident, his musky scent tingling her nostrils; she stopped breathing. She tried to drag her gaze away, find her voice, the right words. "I'm engaged, you know."

"Congratulations," he said softly, his lips so close to her

mouth, she knew if he just drew her to him, she would let him kiss her, hard. A pirate's kiss. She closed her eyes, anticipating … Ross had turned on his heel to stride off into the dark.

Mia closed the door quickly, despite the coolness of the night, she felt hot. What was she even thinking? She was missing Rupert, of course, her hormones were all over the place. She glanced up at the portraits, the entire gallery gave her a knowing look.

Mia did not sleep well, her usual mermaid nightmares twisted into dreams of black-eyed pirates and when she woke it took a while to drag herself out of bed, even though she had a plane to catch. Stumbling drowsily into the kitchen, she noticed Leela had left everything as it was, the only difference being there was a large, turquoise box at the far end of the table. She jolted at the sight of it. Giving it a shake, she listened for the tell-tale rustle inside, then spotting the note, 'Something borrowed.'

It was the dress. Lol must have sneaked it into the car. She lifted the lid and spying a fragment of fabric knew it was there; unworn, pristine, perfect.

There was an envelope on top of the tissue, she opened it, a print out of two airline tickets were folded inside. First class, no restrictions, London to Florence. She could feel her heart beating hard as she read.

'Here's to your fairy-tale wedding, my angel. I believe you have your gown! Be happy, forever.'

It was signed with a flamboyant *A* followed by a huge *X*.

She started to laugh.

A car horn sounded. Taking the box, Mia picked up her bag and trotted down the steps, relieved the driver was unknown to her, no conversation required.

"The station please." She carefully placed the box beside her.

"Want a pick up?" the driver asked.

"Sorry?"

"Coming back, want to be picked up?"

"No thanks."

Maybe Archie was right, maybe it was time to do her own thing, start a new life; for better or worse. And Rupert was 'the one' she was sure of it.

She stared ahead as they drove away, a habit developed over the years, never looking back, never saying goodbye. Leaving was no big deal, she would be back any time. But deep down something always nagged.

Who knew when she would be back, ever be back; this happened every time she left Galty House too.

CALLED TO THE BAR

"Would you send in Miss Fitzgerald, please?" The cultured Dublin accent came over the intercom.

Bernice followed the receptionist through the mahogany door into his office. He came out from behind the elegant desk which had sat before the window overlooking St Stephen's Green for over a century. The door closed with a satisfying clunk and she flew into his arms, as fragile as a bird in his embrace.

He pressed her hair with a kiss as she clung to him. She was trying not to cry, but the tears came anyway. Reaching into his pocket, he withdrew a spotless handkerchief and dabbed her face.

"Come and sit," the gentle voice again. "There's fresh tea, scones from Bewley's, I sent out for them specially." Bernice wanted to weep again, his little kindnesses always touched her, whenever she was with him she felt the cold slab of contrast between her life now and what could have been.

She dried her eyes, looking out across the busy road to the park, trees bright in the sunshine, the monolithic sculpture of the Irish patriot Wolf Tone at the entrance, shining and solid. How she loved Dublin, a fascinating contrast, sometimes slightly pompous, set in its ways yet always vibrant, fresh and surprising. Like him. She sat, the couch angled to look out of the window and back into the room easily.

He poured tea, the china dwarfed in his tanned countryman hands; his sparkling white shirt, gold cufflinks. She looked around the office, framed certificates on walls, the painting of his grandfather over the fireplace, his father's portrait near the door. Everything oozed solid, traditional, reliability and indeed, he was totally, utterly trustworthy. Except for one tiny, hardly noticeable flaw, this was completely the case.

"Now, tell me all." Humphrey Beaumont, barrister-at-law sat back, a slight crease to his brow though his eyes glittered, alight at the pleasure of seeing her, Miss Bernice Fitzgerald, the love of his life.

The Beaumonts and the Fitzgeralds went way back, each generation harbouring at least one tale of unrequited love between the two families, Humphrey however, was not quite ready to give up hope yet.

Relieved beyond measure Bernice told him everything, the sudden deterioration of Archie's health, Fenella's visit, Mia's coming and going, Archie's new and ridiculously expensive boat and then, the earth-shattering revelation that he had already made a will, signed, sealed, done.

"And is it not to your liking?" Humphrey asked. She had not touched her tea.

"How would I know?" she declared. "He's told *me* none of it! He didn't even go to Eamon."

"Eamon?"

"Eamon Degan, our cousin, you know the solicitor."

"Perhaps Archie felt his affairs were more complex, beyond Eamon's experience?" He was cajoling.

"Not at all." Bernice was angry. "He just doesn't want us to know what he's up to."

"Well, it *is* his prerogative."

"What is?" she asked, crossly.

"To engage the services of a solicitor he trusts to keep his confidence. I don't need to remind you the property *is* his. Your mother, considering he would fail as an actor and end up homeless, rightly or wrongly left Galty House to him." Humphrey spoke slowly, they had had this conversation many times.

Escaping his words, Bernice abandoned her tea and stood at the window.

"But what about me? Am I to be left homeless?"

Humphrey joined her. "You were engaged at the time, I'm sure your mother thought you would be married and settled in your own home."

He took her hand in his.

She looked away. "Don't bring all that up again, please."

He gave a melancholy smile. "Come, it's a lovely day, let's walk through the Green, I'll stand you lunch. You haven't touched the delicious scones I sent out for, maybe a glass of champagne in the Shelbourne will perk you up?"

She squeezed his hand, the one with the wedding ring, his only flaw.

"Very well, and over lunch you can tell me how I can find out what's in my brother's will."

"I don't think I can do that." He gave a soft laugh and picking up her bag, opened the door.

"Or help me find out who his solicitor is, I could try and get to it that way."

He held her arm as they descended the stair, so he could drink in the scent of her.

"Not a chance," he said, taking her hand lest he lose her in the buzzy, city sunshine.

After dropping Bernice off at Dalkey station, Fenella settled back into the comfort of the old car. Bernice had tried, unsuccessfully, to find out what Fenella knew about Archie's will. Unsuccessfully because Fenella genuinely knew nothing and despite Bernice's obsession with the subject, was only mildly interested.

"Whatever happens, happens. You'll be fine, Archie will look after you, you know that."

"How come you're so sure? What's he told you?"

"Nothing." She flashed a look at the back of Driscoll's head, he was taking in every word.

"Oh, *please*." Bernice turned away.

"You'll be fine," Fenella told her quietly. "Archie loves you."

"He loves you more."

Fenella sighed. "It's not a competition, you're getting yourself into a state. Come on now, let's not part on bad terms, we've enough to contend with, our lovely fella so ill and all."

Bernice shrank in her seat, as if all the air had been let out of her.

"You're right." She looked down at her hands clamped together in her lap. Tense, angry hands. "Oh, Fenella."

The actress folded her in an embrace. Bernice hugged her back and they stayed locked together for a long moment, united in their pain.

With Bernice despatched, Driscoll seized his chance.

"Afraid he's left everything to you isn't she? Or Mia? Probably thinks his Last Will and Testament will finally prove Mia is his daughter. Mind you a lot of people think that."

"What the *hell* do you know about it?" Fenella was ready for a row, she had been biting back a lot of anger for a very long time. "And how is it any of your business anyway?" She slammed the glass partition closed. Then noticing the chauffeur's hat on the parcel shelf, flung the glass open and rammed it on his head. "Now shut up and drive, if I miss my plane you don't get paid!"

She tried to calm herself but she could not stop thinking

about Archie and Bernice and their interminable love-hate relationship. The way Bernice vied for his attention, challenging him to demonstrate who he loved more, his sister or his best friend; because they were best friends, always had been. And now Driscoll, making inane comments. She knew he was only voicing what people thought, the tittle-tattle still repeated after all these years. It was raining again, another bloody reason why she hated the place.

Closing her eyes she was back at Galty House barely eighteen, at her dressing table, taking out the heated rollers Archie had bought her for Christmas. He liked her to look her best, as near to one of Pan's People as she could, she could never remember which one.

"There is a difference between vanity and taking pride in one's appearance," she told Bernice, glaring at the intruder.

"Really?" Bernice had replied. "That would be hard to measure where you're concerned. Vanity is one of the seven deadly sins."

"Ah, fuck off with your sins," Fenella threw back. "I don't know why you don't take yourself up to the convent and stay there, you're so bloody pious all the time."

"Lock myself away in the Mary Magdalene? That would suit you right down to the ground. Then you'd have everything, the house, the land, Archie."

Fenella turned to look Bernice in the eye. "I don't want Archie!"

"No, but he wants you, it's pathetic to watch, fawning all over you like a puppy."

"Stop it, you bad-minded bitch. And I don't want the house either, it's your home, yours and Archie's. Besides, I'm going to be a great actress and will, no doubt, have a number of beautiful homes scattered about the globe. So you can stick this shambling, old wreck up your ..."

"Trilogy!" Archie slammed the dictionary shut. "That's the word I was looking for, 'a set of three related artistic works'." He stuck his head through the doorway. "Rather like us."

As ever, Archie was oblivious to the atmosphere in the room and had not heard a word of their bickering. He threw himself on the bed.

"Bernice, put something on by that Marc Bolan fella Fen likes so much, she might dance for me." He licked his lips, attempting to appear louche.

"She's going to be a great actress. You'll get no more free shows around here," his sister told him.

"That's interesting." Archie sat up. "I've decided to become an actor too. I'm made for it, wouldn't even have to try very hard. This playwriting is really draining, I don't know how father made a living at it."

"He didn't," Bernice confirmed, sweeping out of the room.

Fenella returned to her toilette. "I'll be far more famous than you."

"You already are, darling." Archie replied, eyeing her neat curves and wondering if he would be able to tell when she were no longer a virgin.

"Now she's gone, you can kiss me if you wish." Archie watched her in the mirror. She saw the glint, the lust he was trying to douse whenever they were alone these days. "I do have the most fabulous cheekbones, don't I?" He turned his head sideways so she could admire them more fully.

"I don't know what's got into you lately, Archie Fitzgerald, but as far as I'm concerned you can stick your fecking cheekbones up your arse."

He lifted an eyebrow. 'Even I, lithe as I am, darling girl,

would find that a contortion too far." And kissing her anyway, exited stage right just before a snakeskin shoe hit the door frame.

She felt the car swing left, they were at the airport; she would be through security and home very soon. She was ready to go, as much as she loved being back, if she stayed too long she began to despair, finding herself late at night, staring across to Phoenix Island and wondering, always wondering, what became of him, the dark, clever, handsome one, the one who had taken her love and thrown it back in her face.

FOOD FOR THOUGHT

Standing in the VIP car park, shades on, arms folded across his pale green thousand dollar suit, Ross Power imagined himself a tourist. He watched a man about his age in a rugby shirt, pulling a trolley piled high with luggage and children; broad grins, excited faces. A woman in cropped jeans and bangles caught up with him. He slipped an arm around her, she pushed hair from his eyes; his mouth brushed her forehead. Ross was suddenly saddened. In that moment he caught a glimpse of something he felt sure he would never have.

A vintage Daimler purred by and recognising it immediately, he waved the driver down. The movie star sitting in the back gathered her things.

"I could have given you a ride," he said, as the actress emerged.

"I came up with Bernice, a mass exodus with you here too." Fenella Flanagan scanned the crowds clamouring for buses, queuing for taxis. "Still, with this lot descending for the holidays the hotel should be good and busy." Fenella had always made her own way in the world, working hard as a single parent, running the 'family' business as she mockingly called her career.

"The more the merrier." Ross took her bag. "We haven't had a complete season yet, it's taking us a while to get going."

Fenella gave him an admiring glance; he had dismissed Driscoll, effortlessly taking charge, guiding her towards departures. "Who are you meeting? Some well-heeled guests, I hope?"

"Chairman of the board, he's bringing over an architect from the States." Ross strode on, she trotted to catch up.

"An architect? Planning more development at the Harbour Spa? I imagine it's been a massive investment so far, apart from the building itself, the infrastructure for that stretch of coast must have been a phenomenal project," Fenella said.

Ross was surprised, the actress sounded very knowledgeable.

"I nearly married a developer once, lovely man, very talented," she explained.

"Really? What did he build?"

"Most of Dubai, I think."

Fenella declined the VIP lounge, choosing to stand in line to check her bags.

"I don't bother with all that, I've been travelling backwards and forwards for over forty years. I'm not paying for status as well as my ticket, money's too hard earned." Nevertheless, a man in airline uniform arrived to escort her through security. Fenella warranted superstar treatment, whether she wanted it or not.

"I'll say goodbye, ma'am." Ross offered his hand.

"Things will work out, Ross, you seem a pretty determined young man to me, just give it time."

She leaned in to be kissed; he caught an aroma of lilies and cocoa and instantly the enigmatic redhead Pearl was convinced was a mermaid came to mind, though Mia and her mother could not be more different.

Ross went to greet the airplane he was dreading, his mind a swirl of unanswered questions; he was tired, was all. Besides, they were in too deep to pull the plug now. The Harbour Spa Hotel had cost millions, if they were to sell they would lose a fortune but if they could not keep to the repayment schedule investors would walk away and they would be left with less than nothing. Everything would have to be sold. The Harbour Spa was already draining money from the corporation's existing businesses just to stay afloat, no wonder the gnawing anxiety in the pit of his stomach never left him.

Fenella was right, it had everything going for it and it was just a matter of time but as usual time was the one thing Ross Power did not have and pretty soon he would need a miracle to save him and miracles were hard to come by, nearly as rare as mermaids.

Scanning the screen, the plane had landed; he smoothed his hair, straightened his tie; time to face the music.

Driscoll was dawdling along the motorway towards the city. He kept the great Dame in the slow lane, pootling gently southwards. She was a pleasure to drive, a soothing sort and he needed soothing, so far very little in his life was going according to plan.

Dominic Driscoll had always played it fast and loose, a gambler just like his father, a risk taker with an eye on the main chance; the sort of guy who made the best of every opportunity. After a brief career in a show band, Driscoll left Ireland to join the cruise ships, sailing the seven seas entertaining wealthy passengers who visited exotic places without the requirement to leave their five-star, air-conditioned cabins.

A native of Rosshaven, his father was a fisherman lost at sea during the terrible storm that had taken Fenella's father, Captain Seamus Flanagan; the man who had stolen the Driscoll family boat and who was no doubt drunk at the helm that fateful day. He tried not to think about it, but the past always seem to creep up on him and in no time at all he was fuming, livid with anger at his loss, his pain as raw as the day it had happened.

By now he was way over the speed limit. Coming to a sharp bend he slowed the car abruptly, a horn blasted behind him. He gave the driver the finger in the rear-view mirror.

What was it about Fenella Flanagan that always wound him up? She had been silent all the way to the airport, doing that high and mighty act she was so good at. He only wanted a couple of contacts to get him back on track. It was the least she could do. The Flanagans owed him, he could have been Archie Fitzgerald up in the big house if it had not been for them … all of them.

He passed the sign for Glen o' the Downs; he could stop, give his old flame a call, she might enjoy a ride to the coast, they could have lunch, a romantic interlude on the beach, just for old time's sake. She may have some news, a juicy titbit about Fenella's daughter, the unassuming redhead who spent most of her time with Archie. Maybe she knew something he could use to exert a little pressure. It was the least she could do. They *all* owed him anyway.

He swung the car off the road before he missed the turning, the driver behind him honked again. *Arsehole.*

Humphrey had ordered, choosing something she insisted she would not like and promptly loved, and he always made her laugh, flirting decorously, eating her with his warm brown eyes, touching her fingers at every opportunity; dear Humphrey.

"So, what's the worse-case scenario?" he asked. She had sipped two glasses of champagne and had become quite skittish. "What're your plans, if as you fear, Archie has left everything to someone else?"

"I'll contest the will of course, say he wasn't in his right mind, he'd never leave his only living relative homeless."

Humphrey gave her one of his legal eagle looks.

"You have evidence?" the barrister persisted.

"His medication, Doctor Morrisey will verify he hadn't taken it, or taken too much, he'd do that for me."

"Would he?" Humphrey stirred his coffee. "You might be scuppered if it was the good doctor who'd witnessed the will."

"Oh, I hadn't thought of that. Do you *know* he's witnessed it?"

Humphrey sipped his espresso.

"Just playing Devil's advocate, to see if you've really thought this through."

She looked away.

"Now, worse-case scenario? Answer please," he prompted.

"I'm left homeless and I've to pack up and move out."

"And if you were left with that choice, that freedom, where would you chose to go? No ties, no demands. Where?" He watched her intently.

She thought for a moment.

"Well, Tuscany first of course, a month there at least and then Dublin, that would be my choice. Why would I stay in Rosshaven, what would be there for me?"

"Precisely!" He slapped his napkin on the table. "The worse-case scenario is actually a lovely alternative to rattling around a falling down mausoleum, struggling to keep warm and pay the bills. Perhaps if this worse-case scenario comes to pass, you'll stop cursing your brother and thank him for setting you free."

"But …" Bernice was bemused.

"Think about it," he said. "Might be the best thing that ever happened to you." He took her hand. "Us."

She kept her eyes fixed on the tablecloth.

"I've a meeting," he told her. "I'll see you at the theatre later?"

She nodded, avoiding his gaze.

"Good, I'll ring Gordon, tell him we're coming. I'll book a

table so we can all have supper together."

Sometimes it was such a relief leaving everything to him. Since her mother died she ran the house, paid the bills, kept up appearances. What was wrong with the worse-case scenario, she began to wonder?

Yet there was always that barbed wire in her heart where Fenella was concerned. She had taken everything from her once before, all she had ever loved or wanted, she was damned if she was going to let her do it again.

Bernice waited for Humphrey to leave, then took out her phone and dialled.

"We've a serious problem." She pressed the phone to her ear. "We need proof Archie's been coerced into signing this will, watertight evidence and quickly, very quickly." She waited.

"Okay. Ring the other fellow and organise a meeting, there's no time to lose." She waited again.

"Tell him we'll pay the going rate and not a penny more. I'm not sure if we can trust him but I agree we've no choice." She shut the phone off.

It was a short walk to the small hotel she favoured in Harcourt Street. She needed a lie down, her head was thumping and her lunch was not agreeing with her one bit.

UNDRESSED REHEARSAL

Mia leapt from the taxi as deftly as she could, considering the precious cargo she was carrying. She rammed the box between her legs while she paid. She could not believe how expensive the cab fare was, she was left with the grand total of fifty-two pence and four euro in her purse. But she could not risk the Tube, she needed to get herself and the dress home as quickly as possible, cost did not matter, she and the package were safe. She was just bursting to see Rupert and tell him all her wonderful news. This was going to change everything, forever.

Mia fumbled for her keys. She very nearly pressed the buzzer to announce her arrival, but stopped herself. That would spoil the surprise and although she could not show Rupert the contents of the box – that would never do – she could tell him all about it. And then the best bit – revealed after a frenzy of passionate love-making – her promised inheritance. How dearest Archie had made sure she, and therefore her gorgeous husband-to-be, would have nothing to worry about.

Rupert would be free to pursue a glittering career, while she kept house, cooked delicious meals, walked the puppy, took care of … she cut her reverie short, not wishing to tempt fate.

Mia and her precious 'something borrowed' clambered into the lift. Arriving at her floor, she was relieved to find the door to the apartment slightly ajar. Arms full, reversing into the hallway, she caught sight of herself in the Venetian mirror; eyes shining, cheeks pink with excitement.

Rupert's denim jacket was on the chair. He was back. Returned from Manchester. Excellent. She was just about to tiptoe through the flat to find him when she heard a noise, a kind of mew, coming from the sitting room. Gently opening the door, she scanned the room for an escaped moggy. She followed the noise. A Moses basket stood by the window and there lay a beautiful, gurgling baby, kicking its feet and squeaking at the mobile above its head.

Mia smiled at the child and looked round the room; chandelier, velvet winged chair. It was definitely her apartment.

"What're you doing here?" she asked, it was then she heard voices, muffled laughter. She followed the sound. Her foot caught on something, she shook it free. Discarded clothing plotted the route to the bedroom. Silently she half-opened the door; the room was dark, candles glowed, throwing shadows. She could just make out the bed, full of people.

Mortified, she jumped back onto the landing, desperately trying to recall if they had invited people to stay. Brain whirring, she peered back into the room. A naked woman climbed out of bed, and wriggling her behind sashayed into the bathroom.

Mia could feel her heart push up to her throat. She adjusted her viewpoint, there was only one other person in the bed, with arms and legs everywhere, she had been convinced there were more. A hand threw back the duvet, a toned, tanned chest exposed. Mia dragged her gaze up to his throat, his jaw, his sweetly smiling mouth.

The floor, the building, the whole world seemed to tilt. She placed her palms flat against the wall, scared she would slip away, fall into oblivion. Gone.

"Hey, Mama, this baby could do with some more of what you got!" he called in the rich accent of America's Deep South.

"Wait a minute, honey. I'm just getting all hot and silky for you!" came the voice from the bathroom.

Mia recognised the lines. It was from the musical, the one set in New Orleans and despite the accent she recognised his voice, the delicious, distinguished unmistakable timbre of her very own, beloved fiancé. The woman reappeared. Sheeny coffee-coloured skin, glossy hair, shoulders thrown back to display perfect breasts to their greatest effect. Mia felt the floor move again. Her throat had closed up and her head was throbbing, but she could not drag herself away.

In her mind's eye the door flew open.

"I didn't know we had guests."

Mia imagined the woman fleeing back into the bathroom. Rupert wrapping the sheet around himself.

"Mia, you're back. Brilliant. Why didn't you call?"

"You bastard!"

"Rehearsing, that's all. The production, we're in it together."

"I can see that."

"Now, come on." He opened his arms.

Mia hauled herself back into the real world. Rupert had his arms open alright, welcoming the other woman. She looked at his outstretched fingers. The ring was gone. The rings he had made. They were going to wear them until they could afford wedding bands.

"Guessing this is your girlfriend's?"

The woman was oiling her skin with Mia's body lotion.

"How's it going with the actress's daughter anyway? Heard you guys were engaged or something?"

"Just roommates really."

He lay back, hands behind his head. "Mia's great, but not such a fast-track to fame as I'd hoped. Might have to work my devastating charisma on her mother, women find me irresistible as well you know, and a lady of a certain age is bound to fall for my natural charms." He slid from the bed, standing to attention so she could see his 'natural charm' in all its glory. Mia tried to look away.

A loud squall erupted. The woman disappeared, reappearing in Mia's robe.

"Can I borrow this, I need to feed her?" Cultured RADA voice now, all trace of New Orleans disappeared.

In her head, Mia heard herself say, *"Take it, take him, keep the lot, I'm done." She saw herself push her left hand in front of his face and tearing the band from her finger, threw it at him with as much force as she could muster.*

But in reality she did not make a sound.

The child was screaming by the time Mia dragged herself and her luggage out of the building. She was racking her brain, where to go? She had lived in London for years but when the chips were down, only Lol and her mother came to mind and Lol was in Ireland. Besides, she was broke, she had no choice but to hail a cab to the one place where someone could pay for it and where, once the taxi has been paid, she could stay free of charge.

The cabbie asked her twice for the address, her mouth was so dry she could hardly speak.

"Morleigh Lodge, Montague Street, Islington." Her eyes were dry too. *Good,* she thought. *Keep it that way. Only dry eyes in this house,* she misquoted, clutching the box to her chest as the cab pulled into the traffic.

Rupert had given up on the idea of another session of lovemaking, the wails of the child dissipating all desire. He dressed, deciding once Shelley had finished feeding the baby, he would take her out for supper; they were buddies after all and besides, Shelley's star was in the ascendant, her husband was a director, she would be useful.

In search of socks, Rupert trod on something hard and sharp outside the bedroom door. He grimaced, bending to retrieve a circle of twisted metal. It looked vaguely familiar, but he had no idea where he had seen it before. Bloody hurt, though.

Trixie ran out to greet her. At first she thought Archie was dead, as the young woman before her looked so devastated; something truly dreadful had happened.

"Meter's running, love," called the cab driver. "She didn't know if anyone was in."

"Alright, keep your hair on," Trixie barked. She took Mia's bag, trying to help with the large box but Mia would not release it. Guiding her along the path, Trixie pushed her through the door and went to fetch her purse.

"Where did you pick her up?" she asked the cabbie.

"Clapham, just off the High Street."

"Anyone with her?"

"No, looked pale, mind, like she'd had a bit of a scare."

Trixie waited for her change, he wasn't getting a tip.

"Did she say anything?"

"Nah, could barely give me the address. Wouldn't let go of that box though, hung onto it all the way here." He pulled away before the lights changed.

Mia had not moved from where Trixie had left her, rooted to the bright Afghan rug in the hall. Trixie closed the door softly, afraid any sudden movement might send the stricken girl scurrying away like a frightened animal.

"Let's get you a drink."

Mia followed wordlessly.

Seated at the kitchen table, she ignored the glass of wine Trixie put before her.

"Is it Archie?" Trixie finally asked. "Has he died, sweetheart?" Mia shook her head, and despite her long-running feud with the actor, Trixie was relieved.

"Is my mother here?" Mia found her voice.

"No, came back from Ireland and went straight up north, had a meeting about a soap, didn't she mention it?"

Mia vaguely remembered her mother was between jobs.

"Can I stay?"

"Of course. Why? Lost your key? Been evicted?" Trixie tried to make a joke but Mia was close to tears.

"Did you ever catch someone in bed with someone else?" Her voice was quite controlled.

"You mean someone you thought you were having a relationship with?"

Mia nodded.

"Ah." Trixie drew up her chair. "Once, no, twice now I think of it."

"What did you do?" Mia was looking at her intently.

"Let me see." Trixie picked up her wine. "First time I forgave him, believed his bullshit and took him back. The second time, I wanted to kill him, I really wanted the bastard dead."

"What happened?"

"Your mother hid the gun," Trixie said glumly.

Mia was not remotely surprised she had a gun, Trixie was very self-sufficient. "So, we burned his clothes instead. He never came back anyway." Mia looked up at Trixie, shock draining away as anger started to seep up from her chest.

"Do you still have the gun?" she asked.

SENDING THE GIRLS IN

Opening her eyes in the cool, blonde room, Mia was amazed to find it was nearly ten o'clock. Refusing everything except tea, she had soaked in Fenella's deep, claw-footed bath and pulling on a silk nightdress Trixie had found, crawled gratefully beneath the duvet sliding into a soft, warm tunnel of sleep.

She checked her phone. No missed calls. No text messages. No emails. Good.

Let the world leave her alone. The whole fucking world.

The door opened. Trixie had been waiting for signs of life to come and tell Mia what had transpired while she slept, she thought it best not to mention the sleeping pill she had dissolved in last night's tea.

The scrambled eggs and freshly buttered toast made Mia's mouth water, she could not remember the last time she had eaten.

Trixie passed her a glass. Mia protested. Trixie was firm.

"Buck's Fizz – at times like these a girl needs three things, champagne, vitamin C and good mates." Mia nearly smiled. "See, it's working already." Trixie pulled a notepad out of her chef's apron.

"Have you a plan?" Trixie's sharp eyes searched Mia's face.
"Apart from the gun?"
"Not worth doing time for."
"So?" Mia ventured. She knew Trixie was on the case.
"I've spoken to Fenella, she's on her way."
Mia groaned.

"She's fine, glad you came to us. A little surprised though, she didn't know you were seeing someone. Now," she picked up her pen. "Where does he live?"

Mia felt her tummy flip.

"That's part of the problem."

Trixie raised an eyebrow.

"He lives with me."

"What? You found him in bed with someone else in your own apartment? The absolute bastard. How long has he been living with you?"

"A few months." Mia was feeling nauseous.

"How long have you known the little shit?" Trixie was angry.

"A few months."

Trixie tutted. This was not like Mia, she took things slowly where relationships were concerned.

"What does he do?" Trixie was suspicious now.

"Oh, God." Mia put her hands to her face.

"He's a frigging actor isn't he?"

Mia nodded.

"Bloody hell, Mia! Have we taught you nothing? Have you never listened to one single sodding piece of advice we've ever given you?" She threw the notepad on the bed. "Useless wastrels the whole bloody lot of them."

A door slammed, a cab pulled away. Trixie was at the window.

"Don't tell her, Trix, please. I feel bad enough as it is," Mia said.

Footsteps thundered upstairs. Fenella flew through the door, running to her daughter propped up in bed.

"I know all about it, everything. And don't you worry, my darling, he'll be so, so sorry he's done this to you. Who does he think he is? Where does he live? I'm going to pay him a visit, give him a piece of my mind!"

Mia slid out of bed and went into the bathroom. They could hear vomiting.

Fenella put her hand to her mouth. "This is worse than I imagined."

"It's probably quite a bit worse," Trixie said in a whisper. "I think there's a lot she didn't want us to know."

"If she's come to us for help, we'll have to know. She's my daughter, I *need* to know."

Ghostlike, Mia came back into the room.

"Trixie, would you mind? I'd like to talk to my mother."

Stationed outside the door, Trixie heard every word.

"Why haven't I met this man you're living with?" Fenella kept her voice level.

"You have, you didn't like him." Mia was equally controlled.

"An actor? At the start of his career no doubt."

Mia nodded.

"Where did you meet?"

"Tuscany, *The Three Musketeers*."

"Not known him long then, wasn't it only a few months ago you were filming that?"

"Not long."

"Moved in pretty quickly, didn't he?" Fenella was trying not to sound shocked, this was so unlike her daughter.

"His lease had run out."

"Classic. Just been kicked off someone else's couch by the sound of things."

Mia sighed.

"Trixie seems to think it was serious?"

"I thought we were engaged," Mia said it quickly to lessen the impact.

"Engaged? Oh, my God, you're not ..?" Fenella had just heard her daughter being sick.

"No, Mother I'm not pregnant."

"Oh,"

Fenella was unsure whether she was relieved or disappointed.

"Did you know about the affair?" She tried a dispassionate tone, hoping to make things sound less seedy.

"The affair?"

"The other woman. Who is she?"

Mia had been giving this some thought. She was convinced the stunning woman with the beautiful child was familiar.

"Trixie said you caught them at it, you surprised them when you came home."

This was the bit Mia had been dreading.

"Not exactly. They surprised me. I could see what was going on through the bedroom door."

"And?" Fenella was impatient for facts, the sordid details, so they could throw them back in Mia's so-called fiancé's face.

"I just left."

"Left what? A dagger in his chest? Poison in his glass? A bomb under the bed?" Fenella was warming to the scene.

"No, I just went back downstairs and left." Mia felt her shoulders sag, she was embarrassed, she had let the Flanagans down; a proud Irish clan, they would never be dishonoured in such a way. She felt sure she saw her mother shudder at such a shameful revelation.

"Obviously it's over. He needs to leave and you need your home and your life back." She looked at her daughter. "No tears now, there's a good girl." She patted her hand. Mia remained rigid, holding every emotion in check, the way she had always done, been trained to.

Fenella called Trixie, who made no show of the fact she had

been listening outside the whole time.

"What's the plan?" Trixie spoke first.

"I was hoping you might have one?" Fenella replied.

"Wine, let's start with wine and take it from there. And don't look at your watch." It was ten thirty. "This is a crisis, we need planning fuel – a nice Sauvignon Blanc and chocolate, definitely chocolate. Get dressed Mia we'll sort the bastard out, you see if we don't."

"What are you going to do, send the boys round?" Mia asked, lamely.

"No need, we're well up to the job. Now get a move on, we don't want the little shit escaping before we've torn him limb from limb." Trixie disappeared.

Mia dressed as quickly as she could; who knew what those two would come up with if she were not there to stem the flow of their combined venom? Poor Rupert would become every man who had ever wronged them. She checked her reflection in the mirror.

Stop that, stop being so fucking nice. Poor you! The bastard betrayed you, took you for a complete fool ... he deserves to die.

HONESTY IS THE BEST POLICY

A few hundred miles west across the Irish sea, Ross Power was enduring an awkward dinner with his uncle Christie and Daniel Keeley, the renowned New York architect. Seated in the VIP area of the hotel's acclaimed restaurant, he had little appetite.

"So far Daniel's mightily impressed, reckons we stand a good chance when the award is judged." His uncle smiled broadly. "Told him I expect first prize, we all do, wouldn't you agree, Ross?"

Christie gave the impression he was quite relaxed about the hotel's shortlisting for one of tourism's most prestigious awards but Ross knew this was far from the case, he was determined the Harbour Spa Hotel would win the coveted title, a huge prize that would bring global publicity, a high profile and guaranteed investment for the group.

"Stands as good a chance as any," Daniel said. "I'm looking forward to my tour tomorrow, when Ross can talk me through the finer points. I want to be sure all the boxes are ticked, this must have been a particularly challenging project, given the hotel's proximity to the ocean. I'm guessing the infrastructure combined with the work carried out to preserve marine life will make fascinating reading."

"All in Ross's report." Christie did not skip a beat. "And we score over and above, I think you'll find. Ross and the rest of the family want this to be our flagship, our way of giving something lasting to our homeland. We're back to make a difference, a positive contribution to the livelihoods of local people and the economy as a whole. That's far more important than ticking a few boxes, surely?"

Ross had heard this speech many times and while the principles were sound enough, the reality was not quite as it seemed.

"I'm sure Mr Keeley appreciates what we're trying to achieve here," Ross interjected. "But he has his job to do, right?"

"Indeed." Daniel Keely stood. "And if it's okay with you, gentlemen, I'll turn in."

Christie protested, keen for their guest to enjoy more hospitality but thanking them for a first class meal, the award judge took his leave. Ross wanted to call it a day too; his performance tomorrow was crucial, the presentation all planned, another run through after a good night's sleep and he would be primed to give it his best shot.

Ross looked across at his father's younger brother. Christie was a good man, who had worked hard to ensure the family business provided a livelihood for them all. It had been his life's work and this, the Harbour Spa Hotel in Rosshaven – the long-ago home of the Powers – a dream he had shared with his brother. Now it looked like the pursuit of that dream could bring the whole corporation crashing down around their ears. Ross could see worry etched on the broad handsome face, eyes clouding with concern whenever he thought he was under the radar. Ross recognised the signs, he knew them all too well, saw them every time he looked in a mirror.

Christie had been watching Ross, so like his father before him; the worrier, planner, perfectionist. But life could not be planned or perfect. Christie still felt the pain of losing his only brother way too young and he knew Ross felt it too. Sometimes he feared he had placed too much on his nephew's shoulders, but Ross had been hungry to fill his father's shoes. Now with

Pearl under his wing, maybe Ross had taken on too much, there was more to life than business and responsibility. And as for family, the Powers were obsessed with protecting their own.

"How's Pearl doing? I'm longing to see her," Christie said, hoping his vivacious great-niece had settled and that distancing her from her mother was having the desired effect. Following her father's death, Tara had taken up with a weird cult, traipsing the globe, hoping it would assuage the grief of losing the only man she truly loved.

Then there was Imelda, the girl they hoped Ross would marry only to change her mind at the last minute and vanish out of his life completely – no goodbye, no explanation – or not one Ross had shared with anyone anyway.

It had been a trying couple of years.

"Pearl's doing really well," Ross told him, hoping it would give Christie one less thing to worry about.

"And how're you getting on with the neighbours?" the older man smiled at him. "You did a good job getting those movie stars to open the bar, great PR, making people think they'd be rubbing shoulders with the rich and famous as a matter of course. I believe there's a young niece staying there at the moment." Nothing much passed Christie. "Might be just your type? Worth cultivating anyway, just being neighbourly, you might say."

Ross flashed him a look. "You know I never mix business with pleasure, besides she is *so* not my type."

Christie raised his hands in surrender. "Okay, I get it." He stood. "You all set for tomorrow? Big deal, you know."

"I think I know that, sir," Ross replied coolly. He had thought of nothing else for weeks.

"You sleep well now, like I said big day coming up." He gave Ross a casual salute as the headwaiter guided him to the elevator.

Ross threw his napkin down, and shrugging out of his jacket walked onto the deck to take some air. It was a beautiful evening, moonlight on the water, the soft shush of waves landing on the shore. Placing his hands on the rail, he took a deep breath and throwing back his head let out a long, piercing howl … the cry of a lone wolf.

"Is this a dagger which I see before me?"

The unmistakable enunciation of the world-famous actor, Archie Fitzgerald, drifted towards him and emerging from the shadows, Ross watched as he took another long pull on his cigarette.

"Gauloises, dear boy, hard to find these days, I rather greedily smoke them alone, another of my guilty pleasures." He looked at the younger man intently.

"I wonder about yours?"

Ross pulled a face. "Don't flirt with me, Archie, it freaks me out."

Archie laughed. "Sorry, dear chap, but you are so devilishly handsome." He waggled his eyebrows.

"Stop it!" Ross laughed with him. "Damn actors, never know when you're for real."

"Fair enough," Archie resumed his everyday voice. "But I'm sure it's a skill you've called upon on more than one occasion. A tense boardroom take over or the seduction of a fair maid, perhaps?"

"Guess so," Ross conceded. "Pity we couldn't all be a bit more honest though and ditch all the bullshit."

Archie gave an exaggerated shudder.

"'A little sincerity is a dangerous thing, and a great deal of it is absolutely fatal.' Oscar Wilde," he said. "And I agree, one's life could be threatened, going around telling the truth. No, let's keep the pretence, the dark secrets." Archie flicked his cigarette into the sea, coughing with the effort. Ross waited for the hacking to subside. "Please don't ask about my health, bores me witless, people have been talking about nothing else for months. I'm starting a campaign, if you know someone who's dying, stop the fuck asking them how they are. They're dying, talk about something else, something interesting, for the love of God!"

Ross watched Archie leaning on the rail, wheezing after his outburst.

"Something pissing you off, Archie?"

"What makes you say that?" Archie was snippy.

"You're here again, second time today, this time alone."

They started back towards the bar. Ross was tired, ready to go to bed but he was fond of Archie and found him fascinating, he would rather spend some time with him if he could.

"Just needed some thinking time. Nice place you have here."

"Cognac, Mr Fitzgerald?" Ross guided the older man to a stool.

"A beer if that's okay, Ross. A few beers would do us both good."

Considering what Ross had to face tomorrow a few beers was a very bad idea, there again considering what he had to face tomorrow, a few beers was probably the best idea in the universe.

They were sitting companionably on the terrace, Ross laughing at one of Archie's many anecdotes when two girls in gowns designed to show off their shapeliness gave them a lingering look.

"Bet you have to put up with a lot of that." Ross raised an eyebrow at his guest.

Archie frowned. "Lovely young things like that are way out of my league these days. You're in denial, young man if you don't think they were looking at you."

Ross shrugged.

"You don't have an eye for the ladies? Didn't think you were gay, am I wrong?" Archie had lots of gay friends, men and women but Ross was an enigma, hard to define, not a pack animal at all.

"I'm 'resting'." He was smiling but a sadness had seeped in.

"Bad experience?"

"You could say that."

"Divorced?" Archie kept his voice to a whisper.

"Worse."

"Jilted?"

Archie knew he was onto something.

"I wanted out. So for her sake I let everyone think she jilted me."

"Gallant." Archie approved. "Had a similar experience myself. Beautiful girl, opera singer, everything booked, cathedral, honeymoon, the lot. Guess what? She wanted to stay in Florence, when it came to it, wouldn't hear of living at Galty House."

"Shocking," Ross mocked. "What's not to like?" Galty House was more like a gothic film set than a family home.

"Married a Duke in the end. It wouldn't have worked, she didn't like Bernice and *hated* Fenella. One shouldn't marry a person who hates one's best friend," Archie stated, remembering the rows about 'that other woman in his life'.

"Or marry a person who likes one's best friend too much," Ross replied, mimicking Archie perfectly.

"Hmmm, I see. Such deep cynicism for one so young." Archie considered. "Women eh? Can't live with 'em ..."

"Can't live without 'em!" Ross finished the cliché.

"Would you try again?"

"Dunno. Right girl, right time, right place," Ross looked away.

Archie raised his glass. "Here's to swimmin' with bow-legged women." He quoted Robert Shaw's character in *Jaws*.

Ross threw his head back and laughed. "I love that movie, no sharks around here, I hope."

"I wouldn't be too sure about that!" Archie growled, knocking his beer back.

Ross's initial appraisal was correct, something and indeed somebody was seriously pissing Archie off … and it was something to do with Bernice. Despite their earlier friendliness, Ross was sure there had been a disagreement at lunch. It was a warm summer's day but the atmosphere between brother and sister was positively icy. Mulling things over while Ross fetched more beers, Archie was still annoyed by the way events had panned out.

He had been in his robe when Bernice had telephoned to say she would be arriving at noon from Dublin and needed to discuss an urgent matter in private. Archie was to collect her from the station and take her to lunch.

"Of course," Archie told her, trying to calculate the drive, even the shortest journey exhausted him these days. "But who's at home to overhear us?" Wednesday was Leela's day off.

"That house has ears," was all she said, ending the call.

He replaced the handset gently, yet the click reverberated around the hall. He looked up at the portraits; eyes and ears everywhere, the house knew everybody's secrets. He had guessed what she wanted to talk about, the only item on the agenda lately. He dialled the offices of Beaumont & Co.

"Goodness me, you're like buses, don't see a Fitzgerald for ages and then you all turn up at once." Humphrey Beaumont's velvet voice warmed his heart, there was something uncommonly reassuring about his childhood friend.

"You've seen Bernice then?" Archie was hoping Humphrey could talk, he was a busy man.

"We had lunch. Went to see Gordon act his heart out in that awful shite he's in at the Gaiety. Had supper together, one of these buzzy Italian places on Chatham Street. Gordon had a pizza, I ask you? He's lost the run of himself altogether."

Archie laughed – Humphrey could be such a snob – he started to cough.

"I hope you've stopped smoking," Humphrey remarked, once Archie could breathe again. "You're not going to ask me if I told her anything, are you? You know me better than that."

"Of course not. One thing though and I need to be absolutely and unutterably clear on this, you still feel the same, don't you? She is and always will be the love of your life?"

"I'd be lying if I said Isabella and I weren't happy for a while. But she grew to hate living here, me working all the time, no family close by. Spending more and more time in Italy, she was bound to meet someone sooner or later and Giovanni's a nice guy."

"And Bernice?" Archie had always wanted his dear friend and sister to be together, but affairs of the heart never did run smoothly for the Fitzgeralds.

"I've always felt things were unfinished where Bernice and I were concerned. We parted badly, she blew everything out of proportion."

"She hasn't changed in that respect," Archie warned.

"She hasn't changed in lots of other ways too. So yes,

Archie, I still feel the same."

"I have your word?"

"My bond," Humphrey confirmed. "Sorry, due in court."

"Before you go, what you said about all the Fitzgeralds turning up, have you seen Eamon too?"

"Got it in one. Bernice and I met for breakfast in Bewley's and that bad penny showed up. He was giving her a lift home."

"Interesting, she told me to pick her up at the station, but now I come to think of it, she didn't say she was taking the train."

"Aha, a criminal mastermind at work," Humphrey said.

"Me or Bernice?"

"Two peas from the same pod," Humphrey laughed.

"Humphrey, one last thing."

"Who are you now, Columbo?"

"About the letter. Fenella, she doesn't know does she?"

"Not from me. She did ask though, whether I thought he ever got it. She wondered if it had been delivered at all. I told her I couldn't say and that was the truth, I couldn't say. Bernice would have killed me. She broke down, I was comforting her when Bernice came in put and two and two together coming up with a hundred and ten! Why? You know all this, Archie."

"Just want to be sure, get my facts absolutely straight."

"You're not writing us all into one of your fecking plays, are you? I'll have to see my lawyer about that one." Humphrey gave a loud guffaw. The line went dead.

Archie looked at the phone; the conversation had made him melancholy. He would probably never see his long-time friend again, not in this life anyway.

What Archie did not know was, that by the time he saw his sister that day, she too had been frazzled from spending too much time in Eamon's company. Eamon was a hopeless driver, the luxurious appointment of his old Mercedes had compensated a little but this elderly Subaru was totally unforgiving, Bernice thought she would be physically sick as he tried to navigate from the city centre towards Dun Laoghaire.

She did not want to engage him in conversation while he drove but she had no choice, time was running out. She knew Humphrey Beaumont well enough to know he had not been telling the truth, although he had not been telling untruths either. Humphrey had told her precisely nothing, other than confirming Archie had made a will, and she was not entitled to see what was in it. Damn him.

"Any news?" she asked.

"About what?" Eamon squinted at her.

"The property. Did you have it valued?"

"I did indeed. That was a masterstroke getting rid of Mia so she wouldn't suspect anything. Imagine a couple of auctioneers turning up, measuring, tapping walls et cetera and her asking Archie what was going on."

"For God's sake Eamon, watch the road," Bernice snapped. "Well?"

"It's a big estate. I'd to make sure the coast was clear." Eamon grew irritated, it was always questions with Bernice, drove him mad.

"And where was Archie, while people were tapping on walls et cetera?"

"With his consultant," Eamon replied, it had worked out well.

"Leela?"

"She drove Archie, those needles and tests tire him out. Bound to, I suppose." He slammed the brakes on.

"Good God, Eamon, it's amber!" Bernice was flustered. They jerked forward as the lights changed. "And?"

"And what?"

"What did the auctioneer say?"

"Not had the report yet. But worth a good bit alright." Eamon found the right gear at last, he shot her a look; he had his own reasons for appointing an auctioneer who was notoriously slow.

"Very helpful." Bernice glared out of the window. "I could do with a bit more detail than 'a good bit, alright,' if I'm to have ammunition for a counter-claim."

"Counter claim? Sounds expensive," Eamon mused.

"It would all be in the bag if Archie had instructed you. But as usual you let me down," Bernice huffed.

"I got Mia out of the way, didn't I?"

"She's very committed to her work, brave of her to go back with that bad wound in her leg." Bernice softened. "That was strange, never had any kind of accident like that before." Not entirely true, Bernice recalled, but the near disaster she had in mind had not been accidental, there were a number of people to blame for what happened that terrible night.

Eamon swerved round a bend, Bernice held onto the dashboard. "That was just a fluke. Good job she was well enough to go back to work though, we didn't want her hopping around telling the auctioneer the beach was unsafe either. That stretch of coast adds quite a bit to the property." He was driving too fast now.

"So he has given you a price?" Bernice was sharp.

"No, no, just said that in passing." Eamon kept his eyes on the road, he could taste perspiration on his upper lip but he dare not take his hand off the wheel to wipe it away.

"I'm going to ask Archie point blank what's in the will and if he won't tell me, I'll make sure he knows I'll contest it if it's not to my liking." Bernice had checked on what grounds a will could be contested. "We need to see a copy of the actual paperwork to find out who witnessed it, see if we can get them to testify to coercion, say Archie was not of sound mind when he signed it."

"Tricky." Eamon swallowed. "You do appreciate if someone is a beneficiary they cannot witness a will, might not be anyone we know."

"I know that," she snapped, this was difficult enough; she was talking about something that was going to happen after her brother's death. "That's why we need Driscoll, we want the signatories' names so he can track them down, you've said he can be very good at exerting a little pressure if required. They'd be well rewarded for their statements."

Eamon sighed heavily. If what he had been up to regarding the Fitzgerald estate came to light he would be in enough trouble, he could barely contemplate the outcome if they had to contest the will on top of everything else. Was that a red light he had just gone through? Bernice was screaming, probably was, so.

Bernice had Eamon drop her at the station, the less Archie knew about their liaison the better. She was surprised to see Galty's battered 'run-around' swing into the station car park with Archie at the wheel. Bernice did not want a row, they had so little time left, but she would not be side-lined into allowing him to control what remained of her life. It made her boil with rage the more she thought about it.

Archie looked as if he had slept in his clothes, they were hanging off him he had grown so thin. He wheezed as he opened the door, hoping she was not planning anything more adventurous than a sandwich in Rosshaven, what with the heat and everything else, he was totally wiped out.

She had timed her arrival to coincide with the Dublin train, just like Bernice to be thorough, he thought. She was immaculate too, navy linen trouser suit, pearls, low-heeled courts. Archie and Fenella used to tease her, asking her how someone so artistic could be so conservative at the same time. Pushed too far, she would rail at them.

"I don't have to paint my face and put on a flouncy top to be creative, I'm not play-acting at it, I'm creative where it counts, in my soul!"

Fenella would give a dreamy smile. Artistic or not, Fenella was sure if she could afford the same level of instruction in speech and drama as Bernice undertook in art, she would be the greatest thespian the world had ever seen. Archie assured her the money would be wasted, Fenella was a natural. Not true, Archie was the natural, they all knew that, Fenella worked very hard at her art, hoping she was making the whole thing look completely natural too.

Bernice wanted lunch at the Harbour Spa Hotel, saying they ought to support their neighbour. Archie was relieved, the hotel was on the way home.

"You're going a bit wild with yourself, aren't you?" he had remarked. Bernice watched her weight like a hawk, unlike Fenella who ate like a horse yet remained slim. "Dinner in a fancy restaurant last night, breakfast in Bewley's and now lunch in a five-star hotel."

"How do you know all that?"

Archie smiled. "Just a guess, sis. You're a creature of habit, after all."

After lunch, they settled in a corner of the deck café, gazing out to sea through a soft haze of heat. Archie rolled up his sleeves, Bernice took off her jacket. She had not touched her wine.

"Archie, the will," she said firmly. "I've taken legal advice and I'm entitled to know what's in it." She kept her eyes fixed on the ocean.

"I hope you didn't pay for that legal advice because it's inaccurate," he told her, matter-of-factly. "It's not *the* will, it's *my* will and what's in it, indeed what's in anybody's will, is entirely their business. The only thing anyone can hope for, following the demise of a loved one, is that they will be taken care of. So rest assured, dear sister, you will be taken care of."

"But what kind of 'taken care', my kind or your kind? Will whatever arrangements you have made, suit me?"

He reached out and touched her hand.

"Of course they will. I only ever have your best interests at heart, you know that."

"That's what worries me. How can someone who doesn't even know what I want for Christmas, know what I want for the rest of my life?"

He laughed but she was serious.

"Just tell me you haven't left Galty House, *our* family home to Fenella. Please assure me of that."

Archie was ready for this. He took a deep breath. Thank goodness they were outside, the fresh air clearing his head, the sound of the waves soothing him.

"Fenella *is* family as far as I'm concerned." He raised a hand to deflect any response. "And so is Mia. She's our little girl, representing the next generation for all of us. Galty House belongs to Mia, that's my decision, it will be hers."

Bernice clenched her hands in her lap, a seesaw of emotion making her head spin. Not Fenella. She released her grip. Not herself, but not Fenella either. She was furious and relieved at the same time. Fenella would have been a whole other issue. She would have had no choice but to contest it, take it to the highest court in the land. But Mia would be easier, more malleable; even so, she could not let Archie off the hook.

"But she's not really a Fitzgerald, there's no blood there. I know you've always intimated ... for the sake of the child ... because of what happened ... but surely you're not going to tell me after all this time you really are her father, that would be too outrageous for words."

"Bernice, sometimes you try my patience, you really do!" Archie folded his arms across his chest to hold his anger in check. "Anyway, it's not up for discussion, I'm not leaving you homeless, the house in London will be yours, sell it, buy a place in Dublin, you've always wanted to live there."

"But Galty is my home."

"You hate the place. If you stay you'll just grow old and decrepit with it. I'm doing you a favour, go away and live a little," he said, encouragingly.

"I have a life, it's here!"

Archie shrugged. "Galty needs a new mistress, someone with energy and vision."

"Is this what Mia wants? Have you discussed it with her? You could be making a big mistake." Bernice was glaring at him.

"Of course I have, the decision whether to make Galty House her home is hers, but I have told her she *is* the next generation and the only one who really loves the place deep down."

"Ach, you're only trying to make up for the past, you still blame yourself for what happened. But believe me, leaving Galty House to Mia is the worst thing you could do. Because if she does make it her home, the truth will come out and then where will we be? You'll be long gone but the rest of us ... Mia would never forgive us, it would open old wounds, there'd be an investigation, the police involved, we could all be ruined."

Her anger had turned to fear, her eyes glazed with mounting panic and looking straight at her, he knew she was remembering that same dark, stormy night as vividly as if it were yesterday.

Archie had walked up from the beach. Humphrey was mooring the boat, their trip to the island had been unsuccessful. Postulant Gregory was on retreat. He could not be reached, never mind disturbed. Of course they could leave a message, but what business a couple of young bouzies could possibly have with the soon to be fully ordained priest, Brother Aquinas could not imagine. Waving them off, he drew the gate across the entrance and locked it noisily.

"Go in peace, now boys." The man gave them a sneery smile, showing broken yellow teeth.

"That place gives me the creeps," Humphrey said as they scrambled down the hillside.

"It's supposed to," Archie replied, pulling on his jacket. The sea was a grey swirl about the boat, the mist building.

"There's no way I'm giving this letter to anyone but Gregory."

"What does it say, anyway?"

"It's from Fenella, I guess it's telling him about the baby."

"Best he doesn't get it then."

"Why do you say that?" Archie did not understand Humphrey sometimes, he could be very hard hearted.

"How will knowing make anything any better? Probably just make things a whole lot worse."

"You always were a real romantic, Humphrey."

"There's enough of you poncey poets around, sometimes you just have to be practical for everyone's sake. The happy couple sailing off into the sunset is a load of old bull. No money, no job, no future. A disaster waiting to happen."

Desperate to get back and find out what was going on, Archie left Humphrey at the boat and was just about to run up the steps when he heard voices. There were sheets on the line, he could make out two pairs of legs, one in riding boots, the other stockinged, in stout brown shoes.

"But what about hell and damnation? Mortal sin?"

"What are you talking about? Nobody believes all that stuff anymore. That was made up to keep the medieval masses guilt-ridden and in emotional chains, where have you been Ursula, have you never read a book?"

"Of course I've read a book."

"That wasn't the life of a saint?"

"Please, don't mock my faith, Noleen."

"I'm not mocking your faith, I'm questioning your sanity!"

"I think we should send her away. You've a sister in Galway."

"Don't be ridiculous, what do you want my sister to do, keep her in the barn until she has the baby then sell it on the black market?"

"I don't know ... I ..."

"Anyway, she's staying here where she's safe. I've just had Monsignor Whelan on the phone. I don't know how he found out but he knows and he's talking like a madman, I dread to think what's going through his mind."

"Oh God! How did he find out?"

"Does Gregory know? Has anyone got to him yet?"

"I saw the boys go off in the boat."

"To the island?"

"I don't know. I went into town."

"I told you to stay with Fenella. I'm worried about her, she could do something irrational."

"Bernice was here. I ... I had to go and talk to someone. I

saw Sister Agnes."

"Sister Agnes? What about?"

"To see if she could help – she's a nun after all."

"For God's sake, she's a brainwashed young woman in a long black frock, how can she help?"

"Then I went to Confession."

"It gets worse. What on earth have you to confess?" It went quiet. Archie strained his ears. Then a shout. "You idiot! That's how the Monsignor knows, you told the bloody priest!"

"Ah no, the sanctity of the confessional ... it's sacred."

"Sacred my arse." Mrs Fitzgerald started dragging sheets off the line. "Get this washing in, I'm going to make sure every door in this house locks and I want all the keys. Bernice! Bernice!" She was striding off towards the kitchen.

Humphrey had joined Archie behind the wall.

"Sounds bad," he whispered. Archie put a finger to his lips. He hotched up to look over the wall. There was a pile of linen crumpled on the ground, Ursula was kneeling in the middle of it, crying. She was tearing the sheets into tiny shreds as she sobbed. Archie stared at her hands, her fingers were leaving bright red stains on the linen as she ripped. He moved closer, it looked as if her nails had been chewed till they bled.

Blinking the memory away, Archie leaned across the table.

"Quite right, darling sister. That child was denied her father and that father his child because of you, because of what *you* did."

Bernice leaned in to him, their noses almost touching.

"No, Archie, because of what *we* did, that's the truth of it, that's what's tearing you up inside, always has and always will!"

And because the memory had touched her too, she reached

into her bag and pulling out her keys threw them at him. He ducked as they landed with a crash on the floor.

"Keep it, keep the lot, you miserable bastard, and may you rot in hell!"

Archie's mouth twisted; sometimes he wondered if Bernice should have been the actor. She was just about to storm off when Ross Power strode over to them.

"Hey you guys, how was lunch?"

Bernice quickly rearranged her face into a welcoming smile. Ross was very easy on the eye.

"Delicious, we're just having a drink. Join us why don't you?" Archie charmed. "Not many dining today?"

Ross shrugged. "Everyone's on the beach, we'll be busier later."

"Perhaps just as well," Bernice said, sipping her wine now Ross had joined them. "Not sure how many people this could take." She pointed at the rails fixed around the decking. Ross's gaze followed her finger. There was a large crack to one side of a concrete strut, the metal had worked loose. He stood up slowly.

"Let's take that drink inside, sun's pretty fierce out here." He turned to Bernice, "I'll get maintenance on it straight away, ma'am."

"Ah, sure we have cracks and splits all over Galty House," Archie told him. "As soon as one gets filled in a new one appears."

Bernice laughed despite their quarrel.

"Filled in? That's news to me. Galty House has been falling down since it was built."

"Still worth a fortune though," Archie said good-naturedly. "Just like the Harbour Spa Hotel, a quality building will always stand the test of time. Isn't that right, Ross?"

But Ross Power was already on his phone.

Back in the now, Archie watched Ross stride across the decking, a tray laden with beer and sandwiches in his hands.

"Did you manage to sort out that little problem we noticed earlier?" he asked.

Ross glanced at an area of terrace, cordoned off for repair.

"Maintenance will be on it first thing. Be sorted in no time."

"Excellent," Archie said, taking a beer and ignoring the food. "I'm very impressed with how you operate Ross. Calm, efficient, professional. You're certainly making your mark on Rosshaven, of that there's no doubt."

Ross felt the bite of sandwich he had just taken stick in his throat.

TRIXIE'S PLAN

The discussion about Rupert and their relationship was one of the most difficult Mia had ever had. She was grateful for Trixie's intervention as Fenella grew more and more fractious, pacing the floor, twisting and untwisting the long strand of pearls she wore over her flowing jumpsuit.

"You planned to marry? I had no idea."

Trixie went to the fridge, took out another bottle of wine and poured them each a glass.

"It's so unlike you," Fenella declared. "Why the big secret, why keep this from me?"

Mia's eyes widened. Despite living in the same city and working in the same industry as her mother, they were not close. Things were easier now Trixie was in residence, Mia could at least communicate, ask where Fenella might be spending her birthday or Christmas, but her mother never phoned just to see how she was, never asked what she was working on, were things okay in her life? And she could never remember Fenella ever arranging a trip, a jaunt, even just a meal together to celebrate her own birthday. She knew Fenella loved her, of that there was no doubt, but sometimes she wondered if her mother *liked* her, and if just the sight of her reminded her of something, someone she longed to forget.

"Maybe she just wanted something for her and Rupert. No big deal," Trixie offered. "Is the right, Mia?"

Mia took a deep breath.

"Not entirely. I did want something just for me and Rupert *but* I did want it to be a big deal. I wanted a beautiful dress, a fabulous venue and a glorious marriage. I wanted all of that. Not to impress anyone else, not to make anyone else happy, I just wanted it for me. Something to treasure and remember for the rest of my life." Her mouth turned down at the sides as she finished her speech. Trixie patted her hand.

"Oh." Fenella looked sheepish. "Well, that *is* surprising." She sat down again, staring blankly out of the window.

"Have you heard from him yet?" Trixie asked.

"Phone's flat." Mia gave Trixie a look. She did not want speak to Rupert ever again.

"Have you anything else on the agenda? I heard they wrapped your movie early." Trixie was trying to find something practical to focus on. "Found anything yet?"

Mia shook her head. Bills would be mounting up, she needed a job sooner rather than later.

"Why don't you take the rest of the summer off, darling? You're always working and with so much going on, Archie and now this, you've a lot on your plate." Fenella advised. "I've agreed to take the soap, perhaps I can find you something there? They're a good production company, nice crowd ..."

Mia did not answer; she had never used her mother's connections for business. She had built her own reputation but could not even think about work at the moment, right now all she could think about was how shell-shocked she felt ... shell-shocked and foolish. Maybe a job on a long-running soap might be a good idea, perhaps it was time for a change. But Mia just felt leaden, hardly able to muster the energy to change a light bulb, let alone her life.

Trixie took the glasses away. "Fetch your phone, Mia, I've a charger in the office, we need to know where Rupert is."

Fenella looked up. Trixie had a plan.

"He had an audition, Manchester I think, out of town anyway." Mia could barely remember the last conversation she had with Rupert everything in her head was such a jumble.

"Good we need to go to the apartment, collect all his stuff and take it straight to the tip." Trixie was already on her way to the office.

Fenella was thinking; she turned to Mia.

"What was his surname again? Did you say Boniver … Rupert Boniver?" The actress did not wait for an answer, she was on her way to the office too, an email needed to be sent, urgently.

Four hours later all the locks had been changed and Rupert's meagre belongings were in two bin bags in the back of Trixie's Golf on the way to the municipal tip.

Mia dreaded getting in touch with him. His picture appeared when she dialled his number; she could not bear to see his handsome, smiley, two-timing-bastard face. Mia dictated, Trixie texted. He came straight back, oblivious he had not heard from her in days, saying he had been recalled to Manchester, another run-through, he was pretty sure he had the part.

The flat was spotless when they arrived. Classic behaviour, according to Trixie. Rupert *had* to change the sheets, which would have looked suspicious if he had *not* cleaned the whole apartment. She did not read Mia the message that pinged back.

Hope you're pleased when you get home, I've been a REALLY good boy.

But Mia saw it. Handing the phone back to Trixie, she went to fetch the spare duvet for the sofa; she would never sleep in her beautiful brass bed again.

Archie was in the library when Leela announced Trixie was on hold.

"Sounds a bit anxious," Leela told him. Trixie was not easily fazed, there was something wrong. Archie went to the hall, the only extension was in his bedroom. Bernice's theory was Archie liked to keep tabs on everybody, the hall phone meant conversations were never private but these days even Leela had a mobile. Archie, however, despite his penchant for gizmos still eschewed the cell-phone, 'for emergencies only' he stubbornly insisted.

"What gives Trix?" He and Trixie kept a wary alliance for Fenella's sake.

Trixie explained the situation regarding Mia and her so-called fiancé in her usual uncompromising fashion. Archie listened. Trixie was concerned about practical details; did they have a joint bank account, did Rupert owe Mia money, had any deposits been paid for the secret wedding?

"Not entirely secret," Archie said. "I knew. But Mia insisted I said nothing. This *is* bad news, he hasn't changed then, the despicable bastard."

"You know him?" Trixie asked.

"I've come across him before, he was sacked from a job I was on a couple of years ago, lazy, belligerent, caused mayhem sleeping with two sisters playing twins, the director tried to throttle him."

"You told Mia all this?"

"Of course not!" Archie was aghast. "She was obviously besotted, totally caught up in the whole idea. My plan was to support her as best I could and hope against hope he had either changed, or she would see him for what he is *before* the big day. The worst thing anyone can do when someone is infatuated is decry the match, sends them rushing straight into the undesirable's arms, surely you know that?

Trixie knew that only too well.

"You're right," she agreed. "But she's devastated, Archie. It's terrible to see her like this, all the wind knocked out of her. She can't even bear to stay in her own flat, he's spoiled her special place, her sanctuary. If I ever meet him, I'll kill him."

"Get in the queue," Archie told her, wondering now if he should have come clean about Rupert Boniver's reputation in the first place.

The news that Mia's dream lay in tatters saddened him, he so wanted his backstage girl to have her moment in the spotlight. The wedding would have set Mia on a different path, a new future, because as independent as she tried to be Archie felt she was at a stage in her life when she needed a partner. The Galty House clan had always had each other, whenever any of them seemed about to break free, something prevented it. Now the pattern was repeating itself, although slightly differently. Mia's relationship was being thwarted by outside influences, whereas Archie, Bernice and Fenella had always scuppered one another's plans – unwittingly of course.

"Are you still there?" Trixie barked.

Archie did not like his thought process being interrupted.

"I'm trying to work out how can we help? Surely, she needs time to lick her wounds, heal her broken heart."

"I agree," Trixie said. "But the wedding plans were well underway. Mia arrived with a dress box, after she left I found it abandoned under the bed. I opened it of course, there's a beautiful gown inside and a note from you."

"Ah."

As usual Trixie knew more than she let on. "Well?"

"She had taken me into her confidence, they were broke. I couldn't not help, could I?"

"I suppose." Trixie went quiet. She probably would have

done the same, she loved Mia too.

"Well, with all that's happened, I think you're the best person for her to spend time with right now. I found Fenella crying in the garden, she's hopeless when anyone is having an emotional crisis."

"Unless it's her own," Archie replied, tartly. Trixie laughed. They did all try to keep Fenella on an even keel; having suffered from depression in the past she could be unpredictable, especially without her medication.

"Okay, I'll ring Mia, tell her to come home. We'll keep the tickets for Tuscany, we'll all be ready for a nice holiday by September." Archie was trying to be upbeat. "Could be the perfect ending, closing the chapter where it began, what do you think?"

"First things first, let's get her back to Ireland and see where we go from there, anything could happen between now and then." She ended the call. Archie was being very optimistic, it was June, who knew if he would be able to travel by the time September came. Who knew if he would still be here, who knew if any of them would? Trixie was a realist if nothing else.

Archie chose not to disclose the conversation with Trixie in front of Bernice, who was poking about in the butler's pantry when he went to ask if Mia's room could be made ready for her return.

His sister followed him into the kitchen, the aroma of Leela's freshly-made ham and pea soup making him nauseous.

"Find what you're looking for?" Leela asked. Bernice was empty-handed.

"Who was on the phone?" Bernice ignored her.

"Trixie, she thinks we ought to have Mia over, she's between jobs, needs a break and London's as hot as hell." Archie buttered some bread, he needed something in his stomach.

"You and Trixie are very cosy all of a sudden." Bernice was at the mirror, fixing on a large hat. The sun was intermittent, but Bernice did not take chances.

"Not at all," Archie replied. "We both love the child and love is very unifying, don't you think?"

She raised an eyebrow at him through the glass.

"I'm not in for lunch," Bernice told Leela. "I've a meeting in town."

Leela continued to stir the soup.

"Hope you find what you're looking for there," she murmured.

"What?" Bernice was impatient to be gone. Things had moved on. She wanted to see Eamon, tell him Archie was leaving Galty House to Mia. The will would *have* to be challenged.

Eamon should have found Driscoll by now and as much as it was distasteful they needed him, because whatever they had to do next, was going to be rather more dangerous than sprinkling a box of itching powder into a few costumes on a movie set, of that there was no doubt.

Archie spent the rest of the day deep in thought. He had taken a long walk on the beach and as evening fell found himself on the steps of the summerhouse, the sun dipping over the horizon as night's velvet promise smeared the purple sky. He was weary now. He sat, gazing out at a calm sea, the bay shimmering before him as a lone gull swirled elegantly through the dusk before taking a deep swoop to disappear into the dark. A final bow.

Today had felt closer to the end than ever before; he had been going through his checklist, relieved he had managed to tell Mia his plans face-to-face, the rest she would have to discover for herself.

He looked across the water, out to the island and imagined he heard again the glorious choir, the young priests practicing Gregorian chant. He recalled the summer they had all fallen in love and the shock and fear, followed by the joy of the gift of Mia, their little girl. He could hear his mother, laughing as they built castles in the sand, singing soft lullabies to the baby they adored.

He remembered too how brave his mother was, a woman ahead of her time, a real warrior in her own way; she would not be cowed down. He recalled the conversation the night he realised she was going to stand by Fenella and the baby whatever the world wanted to throw at them.

"I won't go, why should I? I've done nothing to be ashamed of. You're the ones not allowing us to be together, you're the ones in the wrong!" Fenella was shouting at her mother. Mrs Fitzgerald had just walked into the room.

"You don't have to go anywhere, love. This is your home. The best place for you and the baby. We'll sort it out and if you're to be together, you and the baby's father, then that's okay too. Your mother's just in shock, that's it isn't it Ursula?"

"In shock? In shock is it?" Ursula flared back. "I will not live with the shame and disgrace she has brought on us, brought to you and this house. You gave us a home when we had none, you've cared for us all these years and this is how she repays you ... us! She'll have to go, she's my responsibility and if you won't help me, I'll make my own arrangements."

"But ..." Fenella was used to having her own way.

"Enough!" Ursula snapped at her. "You're a traitor and a liar! Get out so I don't have to look at you a moment longer."

Archie listening at the door disappeared into the kitchen as Fenella ran upstairs crying, his mother followed. A few minutes later he heard someone on the phone.

"The best thing for her and the baby is to go away, far away. But she's very stubborn." It was Ursula, she was listening to the response. *"What kind of scare? ... Oh, I see a little fright so she comes to the conclusion herself. Well, that might be the best idea. How will we do that?"*

She listened again.

"I'm to leave it with you. Alright. Sooner rather than later, oh I agree with you, that'll be for the best. What about him? Has he confessed yet? Did he ... you know ... take her without her consent?" She listened again. *"I see, of course, it's a terrible mess, I hope we don't have to involve the police. I'd die of shame, I'm dying inside already."*

Sitting on the step Archie lit another cigarette. He was cold now and zipping his jacket up to his chin wondered if there was any whiskey in the summerhouse. At the same time his handsome, feckless father came to mind, it was here he had poured him his first real drink and they had sat, father and son, watching the sunset as they drank.

He was remembering the stories he had struggled to understand. Rumours of a lover in Dublin, a young man his father would not give up and he recalled Leela's eyes, hard as stone on the rare occasions his father appeared, until he stopped coming home altogether.

He needed a drink now. Relieved to find the door unlocked he slipped into the summerhouse, flicking on a lamp. He found a half bottle of whiskey nestling behind a selection of elderly liqueurs and tipping the contents into a tumbler took a gulp. The lone lamp doused the room in a soft pool of light, illuminating a haphazard gallery of posters on the wall above the old-fashioned cocktail cabinet. He gazed at them smiling, the whiskey warming his chest, some huge hits, some massive flops, one crazy career; the films, the fights, the fun. A great life.

He had played so many parts but if asked which had been his favourite role, his most accomplished, he would have to say, in all honesty – father to Mia. Making up for the father she had been denied? Perhaps. But more likely seizing the opportunity presented, embracing the gift he might never have had. His beautiful, gorgeous girl, her happy childhood, her loveliness as a grown woman his greatest achievement, his finest hour.

Taking his drink, he stood at the door facing the sea. He looked round taking in the beach, the garden, the house, lights glinting here and there as the night set in; this would, *should*, all be hers. His legacy to his precious darling girl.

"Archie, Archie are you there?" Leela called through the dark. "Your medication, time to come in now."

Archie took another pull on his cigarette and closing his eyes stayed precisely where he was.

NEEDS MUST

Twisted like a corkscrew in the duvet on the sofa Mia could not sleep. She was too angry. She had been so naïve. She kept reliving how Rupert had targeted his prey and she had played right into his hands. Reeling from a broken relationship and the recent news of Archie's illness, she was so fragile, so vulnerable, how could she not fall for the dashing young actor, who had pursued her so relentlessly?

She remembered vividly the intimate dinner, the bottle of Chianti encased in mesh and Rupert looking deep into her eyes, before taking pieces of the gold wire to turn into make-shift rings to propose to her so irresistibly.

"As soon as I saw you, I knew you were the one." He placed the rings in the palm of his hand. "Here, take one," he said, looking at her intently. "A symbol of my love. Wear it, show the world you're mine and I'm yours."

She heard herself say "Rupert, this is mad! We hardly know each other."

"I've never been saner. Don't you believe in love at first sight?" He gave her that smile again. "I'm serious Mia, I'm crazy about you. Wear my ring – until I can afford to buy you a proper one – and we'll get married and be together forever. Say yes, all you have to do is say yes."

And so she did. The wine, the moonlight, the ring and his kisses all merged into the most delicious feeling of perfect romance. And she woke the next morning, in his room, in his arms and in love. *The absolute and utter bastard.*

The trill of the landline woke her. She staggered to the sideboard, the phone nestling beside her precious Clarice Cliff vase.

"It's Leela!"

The caller shouted, surmising the distance between Wexford and London warranted full volume. Mia's heart lurched.

"Now, Archie's after telling me what's gone on and you're to come home at once." *Relief, Archie was not dead.*

On hearing that Mia had been betrayed Leela had been unable to rest, a vision of that beautiful dress kept flashing before her eyes. She had scanned the cards for answers.

When the dress arrived, she had recognised the name on the delivery note, the Beaumonts of Ballsbridge; Humphrey's family. It was an agonising story, the sisters, Lydia and Louisa had been engaged to Mrs Fitzgerald's brothers. Two handsome boys, their picture in the library, taken the very day they had left for war, never to return.

But the dress had somehow found its way back and Leela was convinced it had been sent to fulfil its original purpose, to play a vital role in a wedding, a wedding at Galty House, she was sure of it.

Mia was quiet.

"Did you hear me, love?"

"Leela, I need to be looking for a job."

"You need to be looking after yourself." Leela replied.

"It's not a good time," Mia protested.

"No, it's not. Your boyfriend is a cheating bastard but at least you found out before you married the little shite. Now, the sun's shining." Silence. "The boat's ready to sail." Still silence. "I've no one here but a sick, grumpy old man to mind, so if I'm allowed to be just a little bit selfish, Mia, you're badly needed and I'm praying to Our Lady and all the saints you'll come. So please say you're on your way and make one tired old woman very happy."

Mia looked around the room that used to fill her with such pride, now it just felt sullied, sullied and sad.

"Okay, tired old lady, tell the grumpy old man I'm on my way."

Leela let out a yelp. "Praise be, I knew that novena would work." And promising to arrive at Rosshaven later that day, Mia said goodbye.

Crossing her fingers the credit card would work, she booked the next flight to Dublin and without even stopping to pack, gave the apartment one last look before slamming the door with the new lock shut. Mia Flanagan was needed elsewhere; thanks to Leela Brennan and all her saints.

By the time Mia was on the train pulling out of Connolly Station with a cup of coffee and a bacon sandwich, Rupert had phoned six times. Not a word for days and then six calls in less than six minutes. When she failed to pick up, he started texting; complaining he had gone to Manchester to discover the producer had been called away and then, the final straw, on his way back to London – it really was the most horrendous journey – his agent rang to say the part had gone to someone else.

She read the message again, no enquiry of how things were in her world, no hint that while she was away supporting Archie through his last days, he was shagging someone else senseless in her very bed. She trashed the message, was just about to block his number when the phone went to voicemail.

"I can't get into the flat. Why won't my keys work?"

His beautiful voice shouted at her. Mia gazed out as the train trundled through Dublin, graceful buildings, broad streets, green parks resplendent in the sunshine. She looked back at the phone, hit delete and closed her eyes. She was tired, she had been tired for a long time, a nice quiet holiday and a rest would do her the world of good.

Mia was jolted awake just before they pulled into Rosshaven. The train manager, concerned the winding journey in hot carriages would leave half his passengers in the land of nod, called out the stop repeatedly. She could not believe she had slept, missing all the landmarks she loved.

Grabbing a carrier of hastily purchased essentials – Archie's favourite whiskey, Leela's luxury chocolates and a toothbrush – she leapt from the carriage onto the sandy platform.

Dusk was falling, the sky streaked with echoes of the setting sun, the air warm; a delicious aroma made her mouth water. Fish and chips, perfect, a tempting treat for Archie and nice surprise for Leela. She looked round the deserted car park, taxi rank empty. A liveried minibus was reversing out, she would have to walk into town.

"Need a ride?"

A now familiar accent drifted towards her. Mia looked up. Ross Power was leaning out of the window.

"Sorry?"

"Hop in, no cabs in sight and if you're heading to Galty House, it's on my way."

He opened the door. She did not move.

"Other plans?" he asked. She looked drawn, pale beneath her freckles.

"I was going to the chip shop. Thought I'd take supper with me."

He sniffed the air. "Smells good. Okay, let's go there first, then I'll take you home."

She felt awkward, he was always so busy, no time for anything but the hotel ... and maybe Pearl.

"Come on, it's making me hungry too." He gave her a bright smile. She nearly fell up the step.

"You driving?" This seemed a very menial role for such a high-powered businessman.

"Yep, that guy Driscoll has gone AWOL so I'm ferrying guests. Enjoying it, if I'm honest. Might be better to stick at this." He gave a wry smile as he turned towards town. Mia leaned across, instinctively pushing the wheel away.

"Only if you remember we drive on the left," she told him and he started to laugh, making her laugh too. The sound surprised her; she had not heard herself laugh in a long time.

Leela must have been on tenterhooks, because she came flying out as fast as her swollen ankles would allow, pointing at the bundle Ross held in his arms.

"Knew you'd stop off at the chipper, I said as much to Archie. She'll stop at the chipper the way she used to, I told him. 'I hope she remembers a pickled onion with my ray', he said. I bet you did, didn't you?"

Mia threw her arms around her.

"You're such an old witch!"

"I'm sorry?" Ross thought he misheard.

"Term of endearment in these parts." Mia followed Leela into the house.

"You'll stay and share the fish supper with us?" Leela called back at Ross and then whispered conspiratorially to Mia. "You'd wear your eyes out looking at that fella, he's only gorgeous isn't he?"

"Can't say I've noticed," Mia hissed back. "Does a lot of

scowling though ... a right stress-head if you ask me."

"Many thanks, ma'am but I've to be back at the hotel." Ross still had the food in his arms.

"Not at all, even the Rockefellers had to eat," Leela said, and the hotelier had no choice but traipse through to the 'engine-room' as Galty House residents called the kitchen.

Archie was in a rocking chair smoking a French cigarette. Smoking was banned but Leela rarely upheld any of Bernice's rules and regulations, especially where Archie was concerned. He jumped up to greet them.

"I see Bernice is away," Mia smiled as Archie tried to kiss her with the cigarette still in his mouth.

"In Dublin. She had a meeting in Rosshaven earlier and then off to a black-tie dinner in the Westbury. Left with a cocktail gown on a hanger!" Humphrey was wooing her back, Archie was pleased to note. "Turning into quite the jet-setter, rarely here these days."

"Does her good to get away and you having visitors gives her a break," Leela reminded him. Much as she loved Bernice, having Archie to herself was by far her favourite arrangement. Just Archie and Mia, suited her perfectly.

Archie took Mia to one side, looking into her face.

"Tough time, darling one, most unpleasant state of affairs. How're you bearing up?"

"I'm fine." She gave him a small smile. "We took his clothes to the tip and changed all the locks."

"Had to be done and ..?" he whispered.

"He didn't get the part he went after. Fenella's influence, I imagine."

"Gook work," Archie agreed. "And ..?"

"I slept the whole way on the train and am about to eat the best fish and chips in the world!"

"That's my girl!" Archie kissed her forehead. "Rosshaven fish and chips, the perfect remedy for a broken heart. Now, drinks."

"Shall I fetch plates?" Ross put the food on the table.

"Not at all," said Leela. "Sure, that spoils the taste. We eat them out of the paper. Who wants bread and butter?"

Ross's eyes widened.

"To make chip sandwiches," Mia enlightened him.

"Of course," Ross replied and laughed again, land of his forefathers it maybe but sometimes this really did feel like a foreign country.

Archie hardly ate a thing, though he was certainly enjoying the impromptu supper party, eyes twinkling as he explained to Ross that *ray* was not 'stingray' as the American had assumed but skate wing, a delicious meaty white fish. Mia knew what was coming next, Archie's anguished bemoaning of the failing fishing industry, devastated by European Union rules and regulations.

"Was your father a seafaring man?" Ross asked, assuming the grandeur of Galty House had been the result of a thriving fishing enterprise.

"No, my father was a playwright, my grandfather was a shipbuilder though, that was the family business," Archie said.

Ross looked at Mia.

 "And your family business?"

"Show business," she replied; her stock answer.

"Even the men?" Ross was interested.

"Mia's grandfather was a fishing captain, lost at sea long before she was born," Leela cut in. Mia had already left the table, taking the wrappings out to the bin. Leela busied herself pouring cups of strong tea but Ross requested milk, he had never taken to the blackish brew the Irish seemed to drink by the gallon.

"Mia likes milk too." Leela handed him a glass. He had good hands, she noticed, long fingers. She liked hands, indulging in a weekly manicure herself, although Bernice baulked at the electric blue varnish she favoured, saying she could not eat a thing served with such garish talons. Archie advised Leela leave the varnish on, his sister needed to lose a bit of weight anyway.

"I only like the full fat version, none of that skimmed rubbish for me," Mia confirmed, pouring herself a glass. "It's a wonder I'm not the size of a house."

Difficult to know what size Mia was beneath her layers, Leela considered, watching their guest give her an appreciative glance. Ross was remembering the night at the hotel, when Pearl had been transfixed by her beautiful mermaid friend and despite all the angst in his life – head crammed with finance, worries about Tara – this was not the first time the image of Mia that night crept into his mind, momentarily transfixing him too.

"You can't fatten a thoroughbred, as they say," Leela laughed and Archie agreed, he had also noticed Ross looking at the mermaid.

The attention was making Mia uncomfortable, she had been thinking about the meeting on the train, when she had given everyone the impression Ross was a pervert; she still blenched at the memory.

"How's Pearl?" she asked.

"Having the best time." He gave that rare smile again. "Irish dancing classes, barbecues on the beach and her school project, she's obsessed with anything to do with the island. It's great to see her so engaged."

"The island?" Leela asked.

"Yeah, the one out past the harbour, Phoenix Island, isn't that what it's called?"

Mia laughed. "Archie's fault. We went exploring the day we were out in the boat, Archie's history lesson sounded like a cross between Harry Potter and James Bond."

Leela shot Archie a look.

"Just entertaining my guests," he explained. "Everyone loves a legend."

"Well, Pearl says it's more than a legend. She's keen to get back there, carry out field research, as she calls it, very determined once she gets an idea in her head."

"Must be a family trait." Archie lit another illicit cigarette. "Shame I can't take her, but I'm out of action for a while, medics running tests, confined to base I'm afraid."

"I'll take her," Mia cut in. "Not in Banshee though, too much for me but I can take the tender, can't I?"

"Of course, she's old but sturdy," Archie replied.

Leela flicked him with a tea towel. "Don't be cheeky, a bit of respect for the elderly ladies around here if you don't mind."

The clock struck.

"I've outstayed my welcome as usual." Ross shook hands with his host, looking hopefully at Mia. "Pearl would love you to take her, you're a mermaid in disguise, don't forget, she feels safe with you."

Mia felt herself blush. "I'll call her."

"You guys stay put, I'll see myself out." He looked back at Mia. "Maybe I could come along?"

"Sure, why not?"

But she was not sure, not sure at all, there was something disturbing about Ross Power, if she was in his presence for too long her nerves seemed to jangle. Her own fault, she forgot to make him a pirate, she needed to remember to do that the next time.

Cruising along the coast road heading south, Mia's erstwhile colleague Lol Battersby was having a lovely time. Convinced the night of passion with her old flame had been no more than drinks and a tumble in the hay for old times' sake, she was more than surprised when Dominic Driscoll called.

"Funnily enough, I was planning to stay for a few days. Take in some sea air before I drag my sorry arse back to the smoke looking for another job to drive me crazy."

Driscoll stifled a sigh, Lol could be a right whinge once she started. He had picked her up at Brittas Bay; she looked like an elderly student, backpack, baseball cap, skinny jeans.

"Bloody hell," she cried when the beautiful car drew up beside her. "Did you win the lottery or is it stolen?"

Driscoll gave her a slimy smile. "Neither, someone with more money than sense lent it to me. To be honest he won't need it for much longer."

"Why, been nicked for drunk driving?" she asked, climbing in.

"No, he's terminally ill." Driscoll pulled away. The penny dropped.

"It's Archie Fitzgerald's, isn't it? Poor old bugger. Mia was driving this, last time I saw it."

Driscoll did not reply. Lol slid him a look.

"Does he know you have it?"

"Of course, I gave Fenella Flanagan a lift to the airport, so I thought I'd look up an old friend." He squeezed her knee.

Lol was not falling for it. All a bit too close to home.

"So, what's the story?"

"No story." Driscoll kept his eyes on the road. "You've been working with her daughter Mia, haven't you? Nice kid ... is she seeing anyone do you know?"

Lol bit her lip. Mia's engagement was hush, hush.

"Why do you ask?"

He thought for a minute.

"There's a chance she may be in for a very large inheritance and I was just wondering if this inheritance came to pass, would she take it up or carry on her life elsewhere, you know, take the money and run?"

Lol twigged that Driscoll was talking about what Archie might leave Mia.

"I think you might be a bit old for her," she told him.

"Ha, I'm not interested in her, lovely girl though she is." Driscoll forced jollity. "It's just that I've friends who'd be interested to know what she'd do with the property, *if* she inherited it, that is." Eamon had been most insistent Driscoll find out if Mia would stay; they stood a far better chance if the property was uninhabited, Bernice could gain squatters rights while they fought the case, although Eamon would never dare suggest that in front of Bernice.

"You mean, someone wants to try and do Mia out of her inheritance?" Lol's brain flicked into overdrive. That's why Driscoll had reappeared. The reason he had sabotaged the set. Someone wanted Mia out of the way and Driscoll was being paid to make it happen, he had always been trouble. "I'm sure whoever is bequeathing such an inheritance would have enough about them to take proper legal advice, your friend could be on a hiding to nothing."

Driscoll was quiet for a while.

"That's as maybe, but if she does end up with the property, my question is, would she sell it? Are the ties over in England enough to keep her there? You know the job, a fella if she has one?"

Lol sat back, watching the beautiful landscape fall away from the road as they motored on; rolling hills; fields of every shade of green bordered with soft grey stone; the hand-built walls a signature sealing its heritage. She hoped if Mia did inherit a house there would be room for her, nothing grand, just somewhere to live out her retirement in peace on this beautiful island, she felt ready for it now.

"Don't know, none of my business." She was not happy with this line of questioning.

"Come on, Lol, spill. Wouldn't want me to start any rumours now would you? About how you might have got pissed and forgotten to lock the truck. People might think it was your fault the shoot was wrapped, why they all lost their jobs."

Lol bridled. She remembered now why she had finished with him. He was a shit, a snidey, blackmailing, dirty low-down piece of shit.

"If it's anything to you, Mia loves her job and she's bloody good at it. Directors breathe a sigh of relief if she's in charge of wardrobe. Not sure how much work she'd get based here but with an inheritance she might not need to work."

"And with a man in the picture?" Driscoll pushed.

"Might make a difference." Lol was thinking about Rupert. She had only met him a couple of times but was unimpressed. He had dismissed her as soon as Mia introduced them, looking over her shoulder, seeking out someone far more important to talk to. She had heard rumours too, one of the reasons Courtney looked so stressed was because his wife was having an affair with another actor, some guy called Russell or Rupert. But the business was so riddled with gossip who knew if it was Mia's Rupert, or even true.

"Depending on the guy, of course. Someone ambitious,

building a career, would definitely have to be based in London," she said.

"And she'd stay with him? Does she want kids, family all that stuff?" Driscoll felt sure Lol knew the score.

"As I said, depends on the guy. If she inherits loads maybe he won't need a career and she can keep the both of them." Lol could just imagine Rupert, the little prick, poncing about some country estate. But he would soon be off, stuffing a load of Mia's money in his back pocket and disappearing to New York or Los Angeles, she knew the type, knew the type only too well. She looked at Driscoll.

"Where are we going?"

"I thought we'd head to Kinsale, some fabulous gourmet restaurants there, nice hotels."

"Bit beyond my budget I'm afraid."

"You short of funds then?"

"Flat broke," Lol told him. "I'm backpacking, nothing fancy, just a couple of days taking in the scenery, you know the stuff that's free." *He wants me to pay as usual,* she thought.

Driscoll squirmed in the leather seat; he always borrowed off his girlfriends, it sounded like Lol had closed his account.

By the time they stopped at The Bridge Inn in Arklow their initial banter had become strained. He was put out when Lol refused a beer. She was back on the wagon and despite enjoying what she could remember of their intimacy, she was not prepared to let it happen again. No way.

They were finishing lunch when it started to rain. Driscoll's plan of fun in the sun was beginning to dissolve. Relief, he had a voicemail from Eamon, requesting a meeting; they had important business to discuss.

"Sorry, sweet thing, I'll have to drop you at the nearest

station." He gave a sad smile. "Just had a call. I've to get back."

Lol was nonplussed. "Didn't think you'd be allowed to keep that car for long."

TREASURE ISLAND

Mia had her head in the cupboard under the stairs, seeking out lifejackets and the spare can of fuel when she heard wheels screech on the gravel and the whole house rattle with the loud banging of someone at the door. The letterbox lifted.

"Quick let me in!"

Pearl threw her arms around her, clinging like a limpet.

"You never said goodbye, didn't think I'd ever see you again." The huge cornflower blue eyes stared up at her. Mia returned the hug.

"Silly thing." She smiled. "House rule, no one here ever says goodbye, because we never leave, not for good anyway."

Ross Power appeared in the doorway.

"You trying to give me the slip?" he scowled at his niece.

"Yep." Pearl was defiant.

"Because of Caroline?"

"Yep," she said again.

"What have I told you about eavesdropping? I was only saying things might change, you have to give people notice if their services are no longer required." Ross was serious.

"But if Caroline's no longer required it only means one thing." Pearl was glaring at him. "You're sending me away."

Mia gestured for Ross to come in. Pearl edged back, gripping Mia tightly.

"The family think it might be good if you went home, just for term time, you can come back on vacation."

"There *is* no home," she said, baldly.

Ross dropped to his knees. "Come on now, that's not true …"

Mia watched as he knelt there, worry etched across his face.

He felt her gaze.

"Pearl, can we discuss this later?"

"I won't change my mind. There isn't anyone back home, you're here." A large tear rolled down her cheek. Ross looked desperate. Mia felt a stab of pity, concern for the scared little girl and the worried man, their hearts breaking right there in the hallway of the big house.

"That's enough." She took the child by the hand. "Let's fetch our picnic. It's high summer, far too soon to be talking about school or anyone going anywhere. Now, field research, that's the only thing on the agenda today, okay?" She guided Pearl towards the kitchen, Ross was leaning heavily against the grandfather clock.

"Don't just stand there, get in here and help. All hands on deck if you want to be part of this crew." She threw a lifejacket at him.

"I'm not sure … I have a meeting …"

"Make a call. Cancel. You're needed elsewhere today," Mia told him.

Pearl was in the bow, Mia at the tiller as Ross pushed them off the beach. The water was streaked with mist, a hazy sun shimmering in the distance, another fine day. Pearl seemed totally unfazed as she sat boldly upfront in her life vest, bag slung over her shoulder, pointing straight at the island in case Mia might miss it.

Mia was just about to tell Ross they were afloat when he disappeared. She killed the engine. He bobbed up, spluttering as he wiped his eyes, then hauling himself over the side, landed full length in the boat like a huge, wet fish. He sat up, coughing. Pearl started to giggle.

"What's so funny?" He smirked, pulling his sweatshirt over his head. He threw it at Pearl. She was laughing now, the sound was infectious. He tugged off his tee-shirt, Mia looked away.

"What happened?" She busied herself at the tiller.

"Lost my footing." He moved up beside her. "Here, let me do that, I'm fine, no need to go back."

"You're wet through." Water ran from his shorts down his long, tanned legs. He pushed dripping hair out of his eyes.

"I'll dry by the time we get to the island, sun's coming out." He smiled. Mia pulled the zip of her sailing jacket down a little, the temperature was rising, alright.

"See what I've brought for the project," Pearl called. "We can make a map and everything."

Mia let Ross take the helm.

"Be careful, hidden rocks, stay in the channel," she warned.

"I will."

He stretched out as he guided the tender skilfully through the water. Mia kept her gaze fixed over the side, straying from the channel could be dangerous.

Pearl held the paper as Mia drew the shape of the island. They had spread the rug in the courtyard near the well. Ross was busy unwrapping food; homemade scotch eggs, baked ham and tomato in soda bread with chunks of syrupy apple cake for dessert, a flask of Leela's bitter-sweet lemonade to drink. The sea air made him ravenous, having been holed up in his office for days; preparing reports, attending meetings and now this latest scenario, the debate over Pearl's education.

"Save some for us!" Pearl reached to pluck a scotch egg. "I've never had these before." She nibbled at the spicy sausage meat.

"This place is amazing." Ross took a swig of lemonade. They had already trudged the path circling the island. "I'm guessing you know every inch of it, coming here as a kid?" he said to Mia.

"It was off limits. Only came once, history field trip with Sister Agnes. The seminary's been derelict for years, someone found an unexploded bomb, whole place was fenced off."

Ross pushed his shades up. "A bomb?"

"See that?" Mia pointed at a disused shed. "It's a Look-Out post. They're dotted all around the coast. Ireland was neutral during the war, not surprising given our proximity to the UK, these were manned by a special army division, guarding against invasion."

Ross nodded. "Makes sense."

"Phoenix Island was more than just a Look-Out post though, it had the seminary too. Sister Agnes said during the war the clergy could move quite freely throughout Europe, so the Irish Army worked with British Intelligence to train priests."

"To do what?"

"Spy, of course. The art of espionage."

"Interesting, a bit like the Knights Templar," Ross said. "Christian soldiers with a special agenda."

Mia was impressed, for her history and art were inextricably linked, feeding her passion, Ross Power seemed to have an appreciation of this fascinating connection too.

"The bomb was left over from the spy school, they were probably being taught how to disarm it."

"Or make one." Ross was intrigued.

"Told you." Pearl tapped the chart with her magic marker. "A school for spies and wizards."

"Wizards?" Ross was bemused.

"Priests have to learn how to do miracles, you know water

into wine, that kind of thing." Pearl explained. "The bomb was probably a turtle." Pearl was off on one of her flights of fancy.

"We don't have turtles, Pearl," Mia told her. "Sea's too cold."

Pearl shrugged. "Get real Mia, anyone who can change water into wine could easily heat it up a bit." She went back to drawing the map. Mia gave Ross a look. He was trying hard not to laugh out loud.

Pearl had disappeared to take rubbings while Mia and Ross took shelter in the shade of the ruined church.

"Does she have to go back?" Mia rested against the cool wall.

"They've chosen a very good school," he said.

"They?"

"The family trust."

"Is her mother not coming back?" Mia was surprised.

"On her way to Australia."

"Her father?" Ross shrugged.

"Tara's never spoken about him. She was something of a wild child around the time she got pregnant, wonder if she even knows who he is." He looked out to sea.

Poor Pearl. Mia knew what that felt like, trying to plaster over a huge fatherless hole in your heart. "Can't you keep her here?"

"Not sure if I'm staying," he said.

Mia could see he was tired, nearly beaten. "Archie told me the hotel was your father's dream. He died before he saw it finished, I'm sorry."

"Who's to say it's not my dream too?"

"Oh, I didn't realise."

Ross gave her a look, she could have a point. He plucked idly at the grass between them.

"What about your father?" he asked, eventually.

"What about him?" She was practiced at changing the subject when asked a direct question about her parentage but she had nowhere to hide with Ross.

"Did he follow his dreams?" Ross might have been talking about Archie, the general consensus presumed he was Mia's father but dig a bit deeper and older folk might cast a different light and besides, locals shut up like a clam when asked about the Fitzgeralds. They were like royalty. Fascinating, mysterious; revered and despised in equal measure.

"We don't talk about my father." Her voice was dull. "My mother … gets upset." She looked away, blinking at the sun with watery eyes.

"That must be hard."

"Only if I think about it." She was already shutting down the compartment in her brain where the questions lay buried beneath legends and fairy tales.

"Still, you only had your own dreams to follow." He was looking at her.

Mia tried not to dream. Dreams while she slept turned into nightmares, daydreams a waste of time. Until Rupert that is, something about him had made her dream; a fairy-tale wedding, marriage, family, a bustling busy home. See how that had ended, her confidence rocked, pride smashed, dreams shattered.

She looked down; Ross's fingers were a hair's breadth from hers.

"You have to be brave to dare to dream," he said.

"That sounds like something Archie might say." She took her hand away, brushing crumbs from her top, watching him under her eyelashes, wondering if Ross had also dared to dream and now had no idea where the future lay. "Best stick to reality, less chance of getting hurt that way."

"You okay now, with everything?" Ross recalled Archie declaring fish and chips healed broken hearts.

"Why do you ask?" Mia was defensive.

"When I picked you up the other day … you seemed …"

She must have looked in a bad way. She guessed what he was thinking.

"I left London in a hurry, Leela needed me." She shielded her eyes, the sea a soothing stretch of dark velvet, sails shining like pearls; a smooth, deep space between her and that bastard who broke her heart. She stood up to shake the rug and the bitterness away.

"What will you do, you know, after Archie ..?" He had no idea how tough this was for her to hear.

She could not talk about it, think about it even. The more time passed, the more she could feel a future without Archie pressing down upon her and all she wanted to do was push what was coming further away. But Ross was anxious to know what would happen to Galty House, the fate of the Fitzgerald estate would impact on the future of the hotel, the whole area come to that.

A yelp.

"Look! Look what I've found." Pearl ran towards them, holding what looked like a coloured worm in her hand, turquoise beads interspersed with rings of silver. "Is it treasure?"

"Could be a necklace." Ross examined it.

"Is it antique?" Pearl asked excitedly, pointing at the well. "I was taking a rubbing of the date stone when I saw it glinting, behind the bucket on the ledge."

"Maybe someone leaning in to get a drink lost it, see, the clasp is broken." Mia showed her.

Pearl produced a small plastic bag.

"I can put a card in the post office, lost and found." Pearl had recently discovered this 'old school' service and visited the post office regularly, fascinated by the weird and wonderful items people advertised.

"Won't be worth much," Ross told her.

"There's more to life than money, so you always say," Pearl reminded him.

"Very true," Mia agreed, as Pearl put the trinket safely in the bag.

Ross had been trying to focus on that premise for some time now. Struggling with the desire to cut and run, escape the pressure; or stay and fight his corner, make the dream work, whatever the cost, for all their sakes. Growing anxious, he checked his watch, they had been gone for some time.

"Time to head back."

Mia was ready to leave too, their conversation had made her uncomfortable. She zipped her jacket, the wind was getting up.

"Can't we stay? The island would be wonderfully spooky in a storm," Pearl pleaded. But the grownups had already disappeared out through the wall, the squall was building. Phoenix Island had its own micro climate, cut off from the rest of the world violent storms flared up out of nowhere. Emotions too … very definitely time to head back.

THE COFFIN DODGER

It was not until the intrepid researchers had moored up that Mia noticed Leela waiting anxiously in the shade. She looked odd there on the beach, in her apron and slippers.

"What's up?" Mia asked, helping Pearl from the boat.

"You've been gone hours," Leela declared.

"Big project," Pearl said, patting her bag of swag.

"This place has gone mad altogether," Leela told Mia. "First the hotel called looking for Mr Power. A leak or something, some of the rooms have been flooded."

Ross checked his pockets. "Damn, I forgot my cell phone, I'd better get back."

"Can Pearl stay while you deal with whatever it is?" Mia asked. It seemed unfair to spoil her day.

"Might be best." Ross gave Mia a grateful look. He had already started to trot ahead, taking the steps up from the beach two at a time.

"Any idea what could be wrong?" Mia asked Pearl as they walked through the garden to the house.

"There's always problems when you have a hotel," Pearl told her sagely. "Uncle Christie says Ross takes it all too personally, he needs to be more dis … dis …"

"Dispassionate?"

"Yep. It's his artistic nature, Uncle Christie says." Pearl went to wash the sand from her feet before entering the kitchen, another house rule.

"Artistic?" Mia was surprised.

"He wanted to be an artist, Uncle Christie said you can't make a career out of a hobby, and the business needs him."

Mia remembered the wonderful paintings in the hotel; maybe Ross was the artist?

"And what about your mom, will she be coming back to help with the hotel?"

Pearl was drying her feet with an old towel.

"She's in the outback researching marsupials." Pearl was matter-of-fact. "Doesn't want anything to do with the business. I heard her tell Ross she's done her duty, now he had to do his while she had a life."

"She probably didn't mean it like that." Mia remembered Ross scolding Pearl for eavesdropping, a skill she had also developed at that age.

"I'm not a kid, Mia. I know what she said." She went to the mirror, her long, golden brown hair tangled from the breeze. Taking a brush, Mia started to ease through the strands.

"I don't mind Mom not being around. She was going to send me away to school when I reached twelve, anyway."

Mia smiled at her reflection. Pearl set her mouth in a line.

"You'll help me stay, won't you?" Pearl asked as Mia finished brushing her hair.

"It's not up to me, Pearl. I'm sure your family will do what's right, Ross seems a very good uncle from what I've seen." Pearl pulled a face. "A bit scowly perhaps."

"Scowly?"

Mia had forgotten, Pearl loved new words.

"You know, frowny, grumpy." She gave an exaggerated crease of the brow.

"Oh, that's because he's been cheated in love."

"Really?" Ross seemed too sharp to be cuckolded. "I couldn't imagine anyone getting anything over on him." Fascinated as she was, Mia needed to change the subject, she hated gossip, the stock in trade of show business.

"He's very creative, sometimes he loses himself Mom always says, and that's when people take advantage. I guess trying not to lose himself makes him scowly. That and his fiancée running off with his best friend." Pearl glanced over her shoulder. "But I overheard that, might not be true."

"Like I said, he's still an excellent uncle, I'm sure he'll do what's right."

"But he's not even sure he's staying," Pearl said sulkily. Mia bit her lip. It seemed no one was sure about anything at the moment.

Leela's ample bottom stuck out of the freezer as she grumbled deep within its icy recess. Mia cast about, the usual pile of magazines tidied away, table scrubbed. Emerging with arms full, Mia gave her a quizzical look.

"Bernice is on her way back from Dublin." Mia waited, nothing unusual there. "She's bringing a guest."

"And?" Mia prompted.

"It's a man." Leela eye-balled her, giving her words full impact. "She cut me off before I could ask who, I've to get the blue room ready and here's the best of it, we're to have supper in the dining room. Three courses. Imagine, three courses and only five minutes' notice." Leela banged a couple of pots in the sink.

"I can make pizza," Pearl offered.

"Thanks, Pearl, I'm sure we'll manage," Mia said. "What do you want me to do?" Leela was pink with indignation.

"Us." Pearl came to stand beside her. "What can *we* do to help?"

The phone in the hall rang as Leela allocated tasks, piling Mia's arms with linen from the hot press.

Leela tutted. "That bloody thing's not stopped all day."

"I'll get it." Pearl was on her way.

"Some fella with a plum in his mouth keeps ringing for you," Leela told Mia.

"Rupert?" Even saying his name made her angry.

"No, that other lad, what was he called?"

"Not Courtney?"

"Yes, him. Demanding to know where you were, when you'd be back."

"Take a message, Pearl, I'll ring back," Mia called out.

"No problem, I'm trained for reception," Pearl replied, hop-scotching out to the hall.

There was still no sign of Archie. Never an early riser it was very late, even for him. Mia suggested as much, taking a basket to raid the kitchen garden for vegetables.

"Don't ask," was all Leela said, scrubbing a sink full of new potatoes. "Sometimes he goes too far, is all I'm saying." This was scathing criticism from Leela; Archie could do no wrong in her eyes, something more than Bernice's impromptu supper had the older woman riled, Mia could see that now.

Bernice was breezy, sailing into the kitchen, magnanimous with her greetings, behaving as if turning up with a male companion and demanding nothing short of a dinner party in the dining room – only ever used on high days and holidays – was the most natural thing in the world.

"You've done the blue room?" she asked in a sweet voice, something different oozing from her as she spoke.

"Mia has, sure I'm up to my eyes! Five minutes' notice for a three course meal, I ask you!" Leela said crossly.

"You'll be in better form when you see who you're feeding." Bernice tried to charm.

"I hope it's not that gormless eejit, Gordon O'Toole," Leela hissed. Bernice pretended not to hear, she was at the dresser, pulling out the silver.

"Well, this has looked better." She rubbed at the tarnish on the sugar bowl.

"Not due for a polish yet. I have my schedule, you know." Leela's schedule was a standing joke, always referred to when asked why some household task had not been performed but everyone knew it did not exist.

"Where's your guest?" Mia asked.

"Library. I'm taking him sherry, but …" Bernice was digging about for the Silvo.

"I'll do it," Pearl piped up.

Distracted, Bernice left her to it, which meant Humphrey Beaumont was both surprised and bemused when a bubbly young American delivered his aperitif. Having dropped his bag in the guestroom, he was looking forward to surprising Archie with his unannounced arrival; however, the large wooden box at the other end of the room was making him uneasy and although Pearl had introduced herself most beautifully, even her butterfly presence could not distract him.

"Oh, good, it's arrived." Pearl followed Humphrey's gaze.

"Is that what I think it is?" He could only see one end, the polished veneer and brass fittings hidden in the shadows.

"A casket," Pearl announced, running to examine it. "I hope the lining's right, we picked 'astral blue'. Archie wants to look his best."

"Of course." Humphrey drained his glass in one. "Where is he?"

"Not sure, resting or in the boathouse with Banshee."

"Banshee?"

"His boat." Pearl was examining Humphrey; he looked like something out of a movie, one of the classics her mom would leave her to watch when she went out. "I've been over to the island on her."

"Which island?"

"The island with the priests' school. The one used in the war for training spies."

Pearl liked to extol an area's virtues, something every good hotelier practised.

"Thought that place was off limits?" Humphrey said.

"I found a way in, we had a picnic there today. I found treasure too, part of my school project."

Humphrey was curious. "You found treasure? Where, in one of the caves?"

"There's caves? I didn't know that, I need to put them on my map." She went to the door.

"Where then?" Humphrey asked. Pearl gave him a distracted look. "The treasure, where did you find it?"

"In the well, the one in the middle of the courtyard." The door slammed as Pearl left.

Something crawled along Humphrey's spine; the well was still there then. He sat in the gloom, staring into his empty glass, trying not to remember what he had trained himself to forget.

It was quiet in the library, the sea calm, the wind still. Humphrey went to the window, hoping the view would distract him. He looked out to the summerhouse, the steps and the beach beyond, an ever-changing vista, season by season, month by month. Standing to the far right he could watch unhindered, Phoenix Island disappeared, the haunting hump-backed monster, out of sight, out of mind. It was not working. Another sherry would help, he was about to go in search of the bottle when he heard a noise; a faint scuffling.

He walked around the room, checking the skirting boards for rodent activity, pests thrived at Galty. His gaze rested on the coffin. Sometimes he despaired of Archie, to order a coffin ahead of his demise and have it installed in the library was insensitive to say the least. Humphrey crossed the room to examine it.

The casket stood in the corner, sleek and gleaming. The sound came again. Was it coming from the coffin? He placed his glass on the lid, leaning in to listen. He heard it again, there was definitely something in there. Taking his glass, he started to lift the lid slowly, making sure whatever was in there could not escape.

"There you are!" called Bernice.

Humphrey jumped; the lid flew open as his glass crashed to the floor. Footsteps raced towards him. The poor man stood staring open-mouthed into the casket, where Archie lay, eyes closed, arms resting across his chest. He looked so peaceful, so serene and dead, very dead indeed.

Bernice gave a cry. Humphrey turned to embrace her as she crumpled against him. There was a snuffle, this time louder. It was coming from the coffin alright. In fact it was coming from the corpse. The dead body was snoring.

"Archie!" Humphrey said sharply. The eyes opened.

"Humphrey, what a lovely surprise!" The corpse wriggled a bit. "Thought I'd give this a go, must have dropped off." Archie sat up.

"You unspeakable little shite!" Bernice yawped, landing her sibling such a blow to the chest he collapsed back onto the astral blue silk. Before he could catch his breath, the door opened again.

"I forgot you said you'd try it for size, I've been looking all over." Pearl skipped into the library clutching her map and pack of coloured pens. "Now, where are the caves?" she said, looking expectantly from her host to his guest.

SKULLDUGGERY, NO LESS

Dinner was almost over by the time Ross Power returned. Pearl had exhausted both Archie and Humphrey with questions about the island, insisting every snippet of information be added to her map. When Pearl had proudly presented her find, Archie dismissed it as something a tourist had mislaid but Humphrey left the trinket untouched; he had not touched another morsel of food either. The broken necklace lay like a question mark on the table between them.

Finally, pale with tiredness – it was long past Pearl's bedtime – Mia scooped their inquisitor up and tucked her under an eiderdown in the room next to hers. She closed the door quietly and descending the stairs, met Ross in the hallway.

"I've just put your niece to bed, she's out for the count." He looked wiped out too, exhaustion adding another layer to the worry behind his eyes. For the second time that day she saw a chink in his armour, a vein of vulnerability. "Manage to sort out the problem at the hotel?"

"Sure. Just had to rehome an entire wedding party in time for tomorrow."

"Sounds bad."

"Bad enough. Water damage to a couple of rooms. I'd to move the guests to Ashton Manor, thank goodness they'd a last-minute cancellation."

"Ouch, expensive," Mia said. "Will you have to pay compensation too?"

"We're insured." He sounded deflated. "They wanted a wedding by the sea, I'm just sorry their plans have been ruined."

"Your rooms are ruined too." Mia recalled a leak in her flat, spoiled everything including two of her favourite paintings. Leela appeared at the kitchen door, Ross's mask snapped back on, giving her a warm smile.

"Just in time," she said. "I've a lovely bowl of my award-winning chowder and a big glass of wine waiting, you look ready for it."

"Thank you, ma'am, but if you don't mind putting the wine on hold, I'm bushed, I'd hate to fall asleep in front of your guests."

"We've no guests here, friends and family only and I'm counting you in that," she beckoned him in.

"I'd no idea you were a professional cook, Leela, winning awards and all."

"It's a special system." Mia explained. "When someone declares one of Leela's dishes delicious, she asks if it would win an award. If the answer's yes, she gives herself one of Bernice's old Pony Club rosettes."

Ross burst out laughing, the mantle above the range in the kitchen was studded with ribbons. "Great idea! Think I'll introduce that at the hotel."

"You could do worse," said Leela, sniffily, pinching Mia in the arm for giving the game away.

The formal dining room was the grandest in Galty House. The Edwardian table seated twenty people comfortably, there was a large walnut cellar-board against one wall and a beautiful marble fireplace gracing another. Elegant and welcoming, the glowing chandeliers gave it a softness, blurring the faded wallpaper, worn rugs and dusty drapes.

Archie was delighted Ross had arrived, introducing him to the barrister and moving everyone round so Ross could sit between the men. Leela, who had been swathed in smiles once she realised their guest was Humphrey Beaumont, served Ross chowder while Archie, ignoring his protests, poured wine.

Bernice was also pleased to see Ross, hoping his arrival would turn the conversation in her favour. Asking about plans for the hotel might force a discussion about the future of Galty House. Eamon, taking her lead, also attempted to raise the subject but when it was obvious he was being ignored in favour of Humphrey, he ordered Driscoll to take him home.

By now Archie and Humphrey were on their favourite subject – near-death experiences on the high seas. Bernice had heard this all many times before so decided it was time to say goodnight but Mia had found her second wind; this was a rare treat, the two old seadogs who had taught her to sail, recounting some of the most exciting adventures of her life.

Ross was fascinated by the change in her. She called them pranksters and frauds and laughed till she cried. It was obvious that this Mia, this carefree, unfettered Mia, utterly adored these men and was relishing glimpses of the childhood they had given her. These were her father figures, the men who had played their part in creating her happiest times and she loved them for it.

Ross could not help but be moved by her joy. He so wanted this specialness for Pearl.

Wiping tears of laughter from his eyes, Ross explained his father had been equally calamitous where adventures were concerned, taking himself and his sister on impromptu voyages and having to be rescued on more than one occasion.

"So, we have a full crew right here," grinned Humphrey, looking around the table. "What about a sail tomorrow? I'm dying to see this new plaything, what's she called, Banshee? Must have cost a fortune, how on earth did you get that past Bernice?"

"Didn't tell her."

"Like the coffin?"

"The coffin?" Mia and Ross said together.

"Ah." Archie reached for the decanter. "*That* was a bargain. Now, who's for a nightcap?"

Humphrey declined, taking his leave, the coffin episode had upset him more than he let on.

Archie bade him goodnight. "If I don't see you in the morning, will you keep your promise?"

"'Course I'll see you in the morning, we're going sailing." Humphrey squeezed his friend's hand. "And you've my word, I'll keep my promise." He closed the door gently behind him.

Mia withdrew to check supplies, if they were taking the boat out a good breakfast was essential. It suited Archie to be left alone with Ross. He wanted to talk to him about the future, a future he would not see, yet needed to influence.

"Now, I'm all ears and the soul of discretion." Archie lit another cigar. "If I've any breath left it certainly won't be for spreading gossip!"

Ross was wary. "What do you mean?"

"I can see you're worried, son, a bigger concern than a leaky pipe, just wondered if you needed to share anything, while I'm still here."

Despite refusing a nightcap minutes before, Ross poured himself a cognac. Archie waited.

Ross lifted the brandy balloon to his lips, then put it down. "Nothing I can't handle, it'll be fine."

"Excellent! Hotel doing well. Young Pearl and the rest of the family all tickety-boo. Love life top notch. All good then."

Archie blew a smoke ring into the air.

Silence. The grandfather clock chimed the hour. Ross took a drink.

"It's not going particularly well, if I'm honest," Ross said. Archie waited. "I keep coming up against problems, new ones every day, it's hard enough keeping the hotel full but these structural problems are getting worse. I've re-examined the plans, checked the sign-off on the building regulations and it doesn't make sense."

"What do you mean, exactly?" Archie was pleased Ross was opening up.

"The structure of the building ... well." Ross lowered his voice to a rasp. "It seems unsound. Cracks appearing all over the place, almost as if it's moving."

Archie recalled the loose railing when he and Bernice were there for lunch, the day she lost her keys. "Isn't that just, what do they call it, settlement?"

"I thought so at first but now I'm not sure. I'm going to have to call in some experts to give me a worst case scenario."

"Seems the logical course of action but ..?" Archie knew there was a but.

"Time's against me, as you know the hotel's shortlisted for a major award. If we win it'll make a huge difference, international acclaim, really put us on the map." He took another drink. "But I'm not sure how long we can hold out before I call in the professionals and when I do, we'll have to close the hotel while work's underway."

"Expensive?" Archie offered.

"Expensive and disruptive and what about the award? We need the recognition but how long can we hang on, patching things up as we go?" Ross stared into his glass. Archie had seen a change in him recently. The optimism following the launch had waned, stress shimmered just below the surface and Ross was distracted, Archie had witnessed him gazing out to sea more than once, far too preoccupied to enjoy the view.

"You can handle it, you're a professional hotelier, in the blood, remember?" Archie knew about problems during construction. A tradesman sacked for stealing had blabbed how the architect was cutting corners, saying the structural engineers were abandoning the project in disgust. He had also heard about backhanders going to the planning committee and that the health and safety regulators were on the take too. Archie appreciated that most of this had occurred before Ross's arrival but wondered how much his young friend knew, because whatever had happened in the past, it was all Ross's responsibility now.

There was, however, another much bigger issue bothering Archie.

"I'm guessing if you win the award, phase two will swing into action, the phase that encompasses Galty House. That's why you want me to attend the awards in New York, so it looks as if I'm totally in support."

"I'm sorry?" Ross was confused.

"The plans for the golf course," Archie confirmed.

"Whoa, they're way off," Ross said.

The long term plans for the hotel were common knowledge, they featured in all the marketing material underlining the Power Corporation's long term commitment to the area but the scheme encompassing Galty House was supposedly under wraps. Ross swallowed, nothing remained secret around here for long.

"Would you demolish the house or refurbish it?" Archie was direct; his timeframe was tight.

"Not gotten that far."

"Well, someone's discussed it in detail with my sister, had the place valued etcetera …" Archie was no longer smiling. "We all know this house and the land is perfect for the next stage of the hotel's development but whoever is schmoozing my sister is barking up the wrong tree. That's one of the reasons I'm leaving it to Mia. Bernice would sell the lot like a shot. Mia might think about it."

"Mia's getting the house?" Ross looked uncomfortable. "Archie … I …"

Archie raised his hand. "With respect, Ross, you're being used. You're desperate to make a success of the hotel because of how much your family has invested in it and getting your hands on Galty would be relatively easy if I leave it to my sister." He stubbed out his cigar. "However, I'm leaving it to Mia. I would like the house to stay in the family, be part of the next generation. But I expect you to play nicely, nothing underhand or inappropriate, no threats, no intimidation."

"What do you mean, sir?" Ross flared. "I don't operate like that, never have!"

"Steady on. I don't mean you. I'm referring to the company, the ever *powerful* Power Corporation. Like I said, Ross, you're being used, in more ways than one, not only front man and child minder but fall guy if it all goes wrong."

"Now, come on." Ross was defensive.

"The Harbour Spa is an ambitious project but the corporation needs a return on its investment and you need an international golf course, it's the one facility you don't have that will bring in the bucks."

"You seem to know a lot about it." Ross was smarting.

"Not my line, but it *is* Humphrey's." Archie waited, watching Ross taking that in. "An investigation is already underway. A high level, undercover operation into backhanders, blackmail and all the deceit and skullduggery most of today's politicians and bankers seem particularly adept at."

Ross was really listening now.

"It's not just about the hotel, underhand dealings regarding development along this particular piece of coastline have been taking place for some time and the whistle is about to blow. If you're to make your home here, Ross, and I think deep down that's what you would like to do, you must extricate yourself from any shenanigans, because if there's one thing I know about this place, mud sticks."

Archie, quite breathless after his speech took a drink of water and wiping his eyes looked at Ross.

"You don't seem too surprised?"

He could see Ross struggling with what he was about to say.

"I'm only surprised how much you know but I'm not completely naïve, I've had my own suspicions." Ross met Archie's gaze. "I've found irregularities, evidence of payments going into certain accounts, correspondence I wasn't meant to see and the worst of it is, it looks like people I trust, trust implicitly, have been less than honest."

"Underhand practice?" Archie queried.

"Worse, bribery and corruption is what it is!" Ross's fists were clenched on the table. "If all this underhand practice, as you so politely put it, comes to light, our reputation will be shot. The whole Power Corporation brought to its knees … it doesn't bear thinking about." He picked up his glass, put it down again. "If I call in the professionals and they close us down we're out of the competition. If I patch things up until the competition is over we're in with a chance. Without it we'll never attract enough funding for the golf course and without the golf course we'll never make enough money to pay the investors back."

Archie gave this some thought.

"You could have chosen your advisors more wisely, I feel." He lit another cigar. "Eamon, for example, has never been known for subtlety. He's managed to persuade a member of your board he has power of attorney and has already taken a deposit on the sale of my estate once I'm pushing up daisies."

"What?!" Ross was genuinely shocked. "How do you know?"

"Humphrey tipped me the wink and I put a call into your uncle Christie, before I even asked him about his interest in my property, he told me how pleased he was we'd reached an agreement and that the deposit was being transferred to my lawyer's account the next day." Ross whistled through his teeth.

"Said he didn't like the idea of the Power's coming across as faceless, land grabbers and next time he was over we were to have dinner. Needless to say, I chose not to enlighten him he'd been conned. Besides we need concrete evidence if we're to nail the bastards, because those responsible are for the high jump, make no mistake." Archie's voice was faint now but his eyes were hard, glinting at the injustice of it all. He took a breath. "Sadly, Bernice is involved, naivety more than anything, so I'm leaving Humphrey to extricate her in his own way. I'm sure it'll work out, Humphrey can be *very* persuasive."

The door opened, Mia looked in. The two men were huddled together, deep in conversation.

"I'm off to bed."

She slipped an arm around Archie and kissed him.

Ross looked up. "Pearl?"

"Fast asleep, someone will drop her back tomorrow, is that okay?"

It was the first time she had looked at him directly all evening. His closeness today had unnerved her. Somehow, outside in the open air, she was fine, she could cope but here in the house she was too aware of him. She had to shield herself from those dark shining eyes, something about the pirate had been far too beguiling this evening. She turned to leave, she was tired too.

"If that someone is you, I'd be pleased to show you round, have that dinner I promised," he said, quietly.

"Thanks, but I think we're sailing tomorrow. Shall I check the weather?" she asked Archie.

"I already have, now off to bed," he ordered, not wanting to change the course of his discussion with Ross. "I'll see this young man out." She kissed him again and left. "You were saying?" Archie was exhausted, but this might be his last chance, he wanted to make the best of the opportunity.

"I'm not sure which is the lesser of the two evils, get help now or keep going until after the awards. At least if we gain some sort of recognition I'd be in a better position to face whatever else is coming."

"Faced with two evils, why on earth would you chose the lesser?" Archie asked. Ross gave him a look, Archie had a habit of throwing a side ball.

"Might the lesser be more manageable?"

"Bit pointless being evil if it's manageable and I wouldn't want the lesser of anything, myself," the older man chuckled as they walked to the hall door. "You'll know what to do when it comes to it, Ross, you seem a decent sort of fellow, the sort of guy I'd put my money on anyway." Archie was exhausted now and he still had another conversation on his agenda. Ross shook his hand.

"Well, goodnight sir, and thank you for your hospitality and your advice." Ross gazed at his host, maybe they were more alike than he thought, maybe he did not want the lesser of anything either.

"If I don't make it to the awards, remember I'm full of admiration for you in spite of everything and I'll be with you in spirit. I've enjoyed getting to know you these last few months, my friend."

"And I you, Archie. Knowing you has meant a lot to me."

Ross pulled his collar up against the coolness and looking back at the slight, smiling man in the doorway, lifted his hand; somehow it felt like goodbye. Archie blew him an extravagant kiss and closed the door against the night.

Upstairs Archie knocked and waited before letting himself in. Pearl was fast asleep in the outer chamber, the soft glow of the night-light making her hair shine like spun gold as it fell across the pillow.

"Sweet child," he whispered. "I could easily adopt that one. Her parents have no idea what they're missing."

Mia sat up. He was ghostlike before her, mouth drawn down in pain.

"You'd have liked children, wouldn't you?"

"I don't think many men think about that until they have a partner," he said. "Besides, I had you."

"You did." She took his hand. "You've been a wonderful father to me, the best."

"Not at all." Archie shrugged, but his eyes moistened. "I loved you, it was easy. You were a gift, what way we'd have ended up without you, I dread to think. You kept us together, stopped us from killing each other."

Mia looked hard at the man sitting on the bed. "I still wish I knew who my father was."

Archie glanced away. "You know I'll never say. I disagree with your mother and her vow of silence on the matter but I'd never betray her. I did what I could."

He started to cough. She passed him a tissue.

"Do you know who he is?" Mia had never been this direct.

Archie chose his words carefully. "I can't say."

She had no choice but to accept his loyalty to another.

"It will be harder with you gone and me not knowing," Mia told him, but she would not ask again.

"Sure, everything will be harder without me, amn't I a fabulous fellow altogether?" He patted her hand.

"The one and only," she said. "Subject closed." The phrase he had used when she was little.

He pressed her hand to his mouth. "Goodnight, child of my heart." And then nodding at Pearl. "We've always had a special little girl in this house, history has a habit of repeating itself, especially in this family."

He was coughing again as he left.

SEA CHANGE

"Here you are! Need a hand?" Dawn was breaking as Mia stood at the old jetty. It looked more rickety than ever, splintered wooden struts leaning out towards the sea. Archie looked up in surprise.

"I thought you'd still be in bed, it was late when I left you."

"I know, I'm sorry I put you on the spot when you came to say goodnight, I was wrong to do that, it's just ..." She climbed on board.

Archie placed his hands squarely on her shoulders; she was wearing a fleece, hair stuffed into a cap, ready for sea. She looked up into his usually bright grey eyes, today they were flat, like dull steel.

"Mia, it's time to go your own way, leave whatever you imagine the past to be, behind. Time not to give a flying fuck about anything or anyone." He lifted her chin and looked deep into her eyes. "Time to be the person I know you are. Warm and lovely, and full of piss and vinegar. Stop doing what other people want you to do, stop being who you think you should be, be you and *fuck the begrudgers!*"

They started to laugh, it had always been Archie's 'flouncing out' speech, he did a good flounce, did Archie. His deep cackle became a cough and Mia saw dark blood spot his lips as he turned away.

"Where are we headed?" she asked, going to check the fuel.

"Leave that." Archie raised a hand. "Darling one, do you mind if I make this trip alone? I need a bit of space ... you know how it is."

"Oh." She was winded. "Will you sail?" He seemed frailer

today, he might not be able to handle Banshee alone, even though the winds were light and the sun was soft.

"Thought I'd motor out a bit and see how I go. A little tack back from the island might be fun."

The fenders were in, the soothing putt, putt of the engine signaling all was ready for departure. Mia climbed back onto the jetty, freeing the stern line, she held it in both hands, not quite ready to let go. Archie took his position at the wheel, pulling up the collar of his sailing jacket, captain's hat at the obligatory angle.

"What time will you be back?" She grew anxious.

"What?" He pushed the throttle up.

"What time?"

"Later. Let go now. Time to cast off," he told her.

Reluctantly she threw the line aboard.

"Promise you won't be too long?" she said. He started to speed up as he pulled away. "*Promise*?" she shouted.

"I promise," Archie replied, looking straight ahead, as the boat pushed further and further out into the water. "Goodbye, now."

Mia bent to tie her deck shoe, then stopped. Standing up slowly she could feel her skin prickle as every hair on her body stood to attention, her pulse started to race, her heartbeat building to a thud at the base of her throat. *No, no ... NO!*

"Archie, wait!" she called. "Archie, wait for me, wait!" He *had* to turn round, he must come back. "Archie, *Archie!*" she yelled, jumping up and down on the jetty. He motored on. She leapt from the wooden platform, charging full speed along the beach.

"Archie come back, come *back*!"

Frantic, she ran into the sea, suddenly up to her waist in water, she was shouting, shouting and waving wildly. She tried to swim but her clothes, her hair, held her back, dragging her down and she was coughing, spitting out sea and sand, gasping for air.

But Archie would or could not hear, he was already halfway to the island, the low charcoal clouds blurring his eyes as he heard again the low pitiful wail, a siren call, over and over; the sound of a soul being crushed, as real as the first and the last time he had heard it.

She was standing at the shore, grey mist hovering above the water, the waves morose. Only the moon lit the scene, a shiver of silver across the sea to the island, Phoenix Island, where 'the dark one' was, where they had taken him.

She wrapped the red kimono around herself, straining her eyes in the dusk, desperate for a glimpse of him, of anything living.

"Did you hear that?" she suddenly asked. She had been inconsolable. Archie was standing a respectful distance behind.

"What?" He lit one of the French cigarettes they all seemed addicted to, a shared decadence.

"That sound, like wailing, coming from the island."

He kept staring ahead. "It could be a whale, alright."

"So close to the coast?"

"Sound travels a long way."

She heard it again. "It's so mournful, like it's lost its soul."

"They're solitary creatures, it's calling out for a mate."

"I can't bear it, how come I've never noticed it before?"

"Maybe you've never heard it before. They say you have to hear it with you heart."

"Who says that?" She turned to glare at him. He could see in the moonlight her beautiful face streaked with mascara like scars.

"Leela, she says the whales mourn those lost at sea, reminding us not to forget them." He flicked the cigarette butt into the ocean.

"We'd remember them better if they hadn't been drunk in the first place and lost the bloody boat." She swept past him, striding off along the shore.

"Fenella, come back, let's go in, it's getting cold."

But Fenella ignored him and walked on.

Archie knew she was referring to her father, lost at sea. A drinker and a gambler, he had won the boat in a poker game and lost it in the storms a month later, the reason the family had been taken in by the Fitzgeralds in the first place. He turned to follow her. The sound came again. He stopped. Sometimes whale song sounded just like a man in agony, as if his very soul was being pulled from his heart through every pore in his skin.

Archie shuddered, that weird French tobacco was giving him the horrors. He pulled up his collar, for a second the wind dropped and this time he heard a different sound, not a wail but a cry, a pitiful agonising cry. He knew what the sound was. It was the sound of a man, a man being beaten to within an inch of his life. Christ, he needed a drink, and turning on his heel went to find the whiskey he and Humphrey had hidden in the summerhouse.

"Archie, Archie! For God's sake do something!"

He woke in fright, straining to see where the voice was coming from. Jumping up, he saw Humphrey running towards the shore, a gang of youths hurling rocks at something in the water. It looked like a large fish, half-submerged, waves washing over it. A flash of red.

Archie froze.

It was not a fish. It was a body. Fenella.

Archie could not move. One thought, one despicable, hideous thought flashed across his mind. Maybe it's a good thing. Maybe Fenella and the baby dying is the best outcome of all. She loved another. The child was not his. Best they were dead.

"ARCHIE!"

It was as if a gun had gone off and grabbing a weapon he flew, flew like the wind, his feet pounding the sand, his lungs bursting for air to join Humphrey flailing like a madman at the thugs stoning Fenella at the water's edge, her blood turning the froth of the waves a pretty shade of pink as it shimmered about their feet.

"Aargh!" Archie yelled, twirling the stick with the foxes head like a shillelagh, whirling like a dervish in the midst of them, landing blows left, right and centre.

A couple of them made a half-hearted attempt at throwing a punch but once Humphrey got a good hold of one, the others scuttered off towards the town, leaving their colleague to his fate.

Humphrey pulled the sodden balaclava off his captive. He had taken a blow, his face covered in blood.

"Who put you up to this, you bastard? You'll do time, I tell you. Beating a pregnant woman, you're nothing but scum." The youth, no more than a boy was trying to pull away. Humphrey looked into his face. "Hey, don't I know you?"

A moan from the shore.

"Quick give me a hand!" Archie shouted and seizing his chance the attacker broke free, running for his life to catch up with his cohorts. Humphrey went to help Archie pull a semi-conscious Fenella out of the water and as he did he remembered who that little bastard was. His name was Dominic Driscoll. Fancied himself as the local gangster. Whatever he was up to, he was being paid for it and Humphrey had a pretty good idea

who the paymaster was.

"Let's get her into the house," Archie said, as Fenella started to cough, coming round.

"We'll have to go back to the island." Humphrey told him, lifting Fenella upright. "Once those gurriers tell Monsignor Whelan the plan didn't work he'll make mincemeat of Gregory. He seems determined someone's going to die tonight."

They were carrying her now, Mrs Fitzgerald was running towards them, arms outstretched.

"Shame it isn't him doing the dying." Archie gritted his teeth, saying a silent prayer of thanks that Fenella had been saved after all.

Archie had swung Banshee out past the rocks and around the far side of the island. He looked back, the shore no longer visible. The weather was changing rapidly, the way it did here, cloud had covered the sun, the sea mist thickening to a fog. He steered the boat closer, straining to see if the Look Out Post was still there, he wanted to remember, remember everything before it was all swept away and buried at the bottom of the sea forever more. A fitting resting place for all the sadness.

Minutes later he and Humphrey were running back down the beach.

"Start the engine." Humphrey pushed the boat into the inky water, the moon slid a sliver of light across the bay, the wind building to a howl. They sat low in the boat, driving it on, fighting against the tide beating them back. By the time they reached the island, the wailing had stopped.

"He could be dead." Archie searched for the torch, straining his ears above the gale.

"Come on, I know a short cut." Humphrey strode along the

track, breaking off to scrabble up the rocks. Archie tried to keep up, Humphrey was lean and strong, scaling the cliff like an ape. They reached a ledge just beyond the seminary wall, Humphrey hauled Archie up, jagging his knee on the stone.

"Aargh!"

"Quiet," Humphrey ordered. They could hear moaning, Humphrey flicked the light ahead; the sound was coming from a small hut on the far edge of the cliff, the old Look Out Post. They started running towards the hut. Humphrey kicked the door open as Archie flashed the light inside.

"Oh God!" He dropped the torch in fright, the bloodied mass of heaving flesh in the corner could have been a monster. "Gregory, is that you?"

The man was lying on his side, his back ripped into shards of bright pink strips, blood oozing from the gaps in his skin.

He lifted his head, one eye closed, lips split open.

"Don't try to talk," Archie said, untying the thick leather straps holding him fast.

Humphrey was at his wrists, slicing the rope with his penknife.

"He's been lashed with a birch," Humphrey whispered. "I bet I know who was beating a confession out of him."

One of the monks saw the light in the Look Out Post.

He fumbled in his habit and taking out a whistle blew hard. The Monsignor was not quite through the gate, he waved at the monk and together they raced towards the hut.

Humphrey told Archie to cover Gregory and as the priest came through the door Humphrey pounced, bringing him down.

The Monsignor kicked out, catching Humphrey on the shin, he stumbled. The older man was nimble, back on his feet he lunged at Humphrey. Archie jumped up landing a punch, the Monsignor swung round kneeing Archie in the balls as *groaning, he fell back.*

Suddenly a roar like a beast and Gregory was on his feet, he grabbed the Monsignor from behind, crushing him in his embrace until something cracked, the man in black let out a scream, his collarbone smashed. Drained, Gregory staggered back releasing the man who, clutching his shoulder pushed past, out into the night. Humphrey's long stride soon caught up. He ran ahead trapping the man between the hedge and the wall, Humphrey turned to face him, eye to eye.

"*My shoulder, it's …it's broken,*" *the Monsignor hissed, eyes blazing at his tormentor.*

"*You've been beating my friend, you evil bastard.*" *Humphrey took hold of the priest's jacket and started dragging him back. His hat fell to the ground, Humphrey kicked it away. "Now it's our turn.*"

Back at the hut, Gregory was leaning against the door, Archie propped him up.

"*Help! Help!*" *called the Monsignor. "Someone help me!*"

"*You're wasting your breath,*" *Archie told the Monsignor. "Your lackey ran off.*"

"*Now,*" *Humphrey pulled the man in front of Gregory. "Is this the man who beat you?*"

Gregory lifted his head, looked through a slitted eye and nodded.

Humphrey handed him a piece of wood. "Your turn," *he said.*

Archie stood shoulder-to-shoulder with Gregory, taking his weight.

"*Go on, man. Your turn.*" *Humphrey repeated. Gregory shook his head, dropping the piece of wood.*

"*Hey, what's going on there?*" *A shout from the wall, they looked up, the Monsignor took his chance and broke free* running as fast as he could. Humphrey caught him at the cliff edge and holding him by the scruff, glared into his face.

"You're not getting away with this, not this time," he snarled. "We're going to report you, you fucking sadist."

"Leave him," Gregory slurred, then louder. "Leave him."

"Are you mad?" Archie was shocked. "He would have left you there all night, you'd be dead."

"A confession at the very least," Humphrey said, hauling the priest to the edge. A dog bark. A flashlight. Someone was coming.

The Monsignor started to struggle, the arm beneath the smashed collarbone swinging at his side, useless.

"Confess, then I'll let you go. Go on, admit you beat him, I'll set you free."

They could hear footfall through the undergrowth.

"Confess!" roared Humphrey.

"Go to hell!" yelled the priest with such force Humphrey released him. The edge of the cliff crumbled away. He slipped, grabbing for the ledge as he fell. Humphrey saw the terror in his eyes and lunged forward, reaching for his hand. Too late, the Monsignor disappeared. Scrambling as close as they dare, Archie flashed the light below. A sheer drop. No sign, no sound ... just the wind.

The dog barked again.

"Where's the boat?" Archie asked, knowing Gregory had stolen one that very day to escape with Fenella. He pointed in the direction of a tiny bay.

"Come on," Humphrey led them downwards. A gust of wind landed something in their path, Archie's torch outlined the Monsignor's hat. He stopped and kicked it off the cliff into the sea.

Archie was about to give up on the tiller, it was pretty useless now anyway. He could feel the undercurrent dragging Banshee towards the rocks, it was time for a last drink, a final smoke. Time to let go, he had so little future left, better to spend what time he had in the past.

He heard a sound above the deep hum of the storm. A foghorn. It was a small tender, one of the coastguards' speedboats.

"Ahoy! Is that you, Archie?"

Archie grabbed the tiller, slamming Banshee into reverse.

"Aye, Jimmy, it is. Just heading back. It's getting too wild out here for a pleasure trip."

"Good man, I was just going to advise that. Need an escort?"

"No thanks. Best go and see if anyone else is in trouble." On cue the coastguards' radio gave out a call.

"Will do. Safe back now, quick as you like. And I'd put your life vest on if I were you, it's mighty squally."

"I will, of course." Archie waved him off, swinging Banshee round as best he could. He and the boat were both struggling against the tide. As soon as the coastguard was out of sight he turned everything off and went below. He had not quite finished remembering yet.

"What are you doing there?" He was back in Galty House striding along the landing, jeans covered in mud, shirt soaking wet.

Bernice jumped back, startled. "She can't go. She'll never come back, we'll lose her, the baby, everything."

"You're the one going on about the disgrace of it, the scandal it would bring on all of us."

He was high on adrenalin, amazed they had survived.

"I'd rather scandal than lose her, lose them both." Bernice was distraught.

"It's too late anyway, he's gone." Archie wiped his brow with his sleeve. He pulled the letter out of his pocket and handed it to Bernice. "Burn this."

"What is it?"

"I dunno, evidence?" He could not think straight.

"Oh God," Bernice slumped against the wall. "Do you think he'll make it?"

"I hope so, that bastard Monsignor Sylvester Whelan won't though, we saw to that alright." She turned questioning eyes on him. "You don't need to know." He looked away. "Has she tried to leave again?"

"Not yet, she's barely able to stand but she's at the window, waiting for his signal."

"Fetch the decanter, we could all do with a drink." As soon as she had gone, Archie turned the key in the lock and went to change his clothes. He saw lights and stopped to watch Leela's brother drive away having dropped her off after her day in town. Best he go and talk to her, so much of the world had gone mad in her absence.

The next thing he heard was Leela screaming. He looked down from the landing as she ran from the kitchen.

"Archie quick! Fire! The cellar!"

"Have you a key?" The cellar was always locked.

Leela tried the door. It swung open. Archie flicked a switch, tendrils of smoke drifted up from below. He made to run down the steps. "Stop! Cover your mouth," Leela shouted, taking off her headscarf and tying it around Archie's face. "I'll use this." She had a tea towel in her hand.

They looked left and right at the bottom of the stairs, the fug was building, Leela spotted the flames.

"Over there!"

He grabbed a bucket of sand from a ledge and threw it on the *flames to douse them. The smoke blackened, he started to cough.*

"Let's get out. We need a hose, there's one in the back kitchen we can hook it up there," *Archie bent to lift a tightly twisted rag from the floor, it smelled of petrol.*

"Arson," *he said. But Leela already knew that.*

Stretching to his full height to rise above the smoke something stroked the top of Archie's head. He shuddered. Probably a bat. He tried to push it away but it felt odd. Hard and smooth, moving slightly. He looked up, straining to see through the smoky atmosphere. It was a shoe, a stout brown shoe. Leela followed his gaze.

"Oh my god!" *She was digging her nails into Archie's arm, wild eyed, as she looked from him to the corpse swinging gently above them. It was hard to see who it was, but Archie recognised the shoes, he knew who it was. It was Ursula.*

The fire ignited again.

He half-pushed, half-dragged Leela to the top of the steps. Once out of the cellar, Leela came to her senses.

"Lock it." *She told him, handing over her key.* "We'll douse the flames through the grille. We'll sort the other thing out later, when I've had time to think."

Archie went to protest, Leela gripped his arm.

"I'll do what's best. Trust me, Archie. I've been doing what's best for this family for a long time." *There was steel in her eyes. He nodded.*

Leela blessed herself for protection.

"I told you not to go to that island. It's only ever meant the worst of everything, and now look where we are, in a right mess, a horrible unholy mess we're never, ever going to get away from." *And wiping her eyes with the heel of her hand she marched out with Archie, to fire fight yet again.*

Cupping his hand against the wind Archie lit one of his French cigarettes. He would make sure the box containing the manuscript was watertight. He had read it through one last time, reminding himself of what they had done all those years ago and as this was his last day, maybe ask for forgiveness, maybe not. It might transpire that at last the story would be told but this was not in his gift. He would leave that to fate, whatever. He had done his bit, his part played out. The mouth of the caves loomed up before him, reminding him of a stage.

TO THE BAT CAVE

Spluttering and wheezing, Mia dragged herself back to shore, shaking with cold or desperation, she did not know which. One thing she did know, today was the day and she was never, ever going to see Archie Fitzgerald again. Today he had broken their precious pact, today he had used their forbidden word, today Archie had said *goodbye*.

Trying to calm herself, she watched until the boat disappeared and could see Banshee no more. The blue of the sea and the sky merged as she blinked; no tears, no tears allowed and sinking to the sand, she pulled her knees to her chest and sat gazing blankly out. The sun shone, the gulls cried, a soft breeze caressed her cheek; all in all a perfect day, a perfect day to die.

Mia shook her head to clear it but the howling just grew louder. She swallowed, fighting to keep control, quash the strangest feeling and then it came … anger, a burning rage, a furious lump so livid it broiled up from the pit of her stomach, into her chest and out, out of her mouth. Unable to stay still a minute longer she jumped to her feet, pulled off her cap and threw it into the water.

"Well, fuck you, Archie Fitzgerald! You and your fucking cancer, fuck, fuck, *fuck!*" she yelled, running along the shore, kicking at the sand as hard as she could. Stubbing her toe she stumbled and fell into the waves, flailing about, spitting out water and sand and snot.

"Fuck the lot of you! Archie, Rupert, Courtney, my fucking useless father – whoever you are – fuck all of you! Who needs you? I fucking don't, so there!" She kept roaring at the sea, as it tried, tried its very best, to soothe her huge grief with its tiny waves.

Having worked through the night, Ross had decided to make the most of a clear dawn and was out for a run. Just getting into his stride, he stopped, there was a figure in the distance. He started towards it, someone was in trouble in the water, clearly distressed.

It was Mia, he would recognise that mass of red hair anywhere. He stopped again, taking in the scene of a mad woman shouting obscenities at the surf. He backed off, there were more weirdo mad women in the Power family than you could shake a stick at, besides he needed a clear head today and pushing his hands into his pockets he turned to stride quickly away.

He stopped.

Ross had spent time with Mia, she was not crazy, she was caring and funny; she was also on the edge of losing someone she adored and he remembered only too vividly what that felt like. The grim agony of watching his father clinging to life after a devastating stroke had left a sour taste. He ran towards her.

She was in the water, calling out, crying. He knew it had to be Archie. He ran into the sea and gripping her tightly dragged her back to shore. As he released her she collapsed onto the sand, coughing, gasping for breath, trying to speak between her sobs.

"Archie ... Banshee ... out there." She pointed towards the island. Ross knelt beside her.

"Hey, hey," he said gently, reaching out, taking her fingers in his. "Come on, steady now ... tell me."

He watched her chest rise and fall, her jacket and tee-shirt clinging to blue-veined skin, she looked like a small bird he had just pulled from the jaws of a slavering beast.

"Archie's …taken Banshee … out," she said between hiccups.

"Okay." He held her icy hands.

"Alone, must … find him."

Her eyes were wild and there was something else there, the worst kind of despair; hopelessness.

"Why're you so worried?" He spoke slowly, trying to calm her.

"He's not coming back."

"How do you know?"

"I just *know*."

They fell silent. She was trying to catch her breath as she wept.

He had to do something.

"I'll take the tender, he can't have gotten far, I'll find him." He hauled her upright. "You need to go back and dry out. I'll go." He started towards the jetty. Mia ran after him.

"No, I *have* to come. I saw where he went."

He looked at her; she was staring at him, chin raised, there was no way he was going without her.

"Keys, where are the keys?"

"Boathouse. But there's no **time**!" she cried.

"I'll jump start it."

Her teeth were chattering as the promised storm clouds sucked away the sun.

"Take your top off." She hesitated. "Off!" he ordered.

She did as she was told, turning away, shivering in an elderly sports bra. He dragged his hoodie over her head, still warm from his skin and passing over his cap, helped stuff her heavy hair inside.

They were at the boat.

"Have we oars, just in case?"

She nodded.

He fiddled at the engine, gave the starter a couple of tugs, it fired up.

"Hold tight."

She sat in the bow, gripping the side. He guided them out, steering past boats bobbing wildly, eager to be free.

"I'll open her up." He looked back at her. "Gonna be bouncy."

Just go, she thought. *Go as fast as you can.*

They were powering now, wash breaking in a froth of white behind them. Sailors heading for safe harbour signalled them to slow down, go back. Ross stared straight ahead; they had to find Banshee.

He slowed as they came to the island, the ripple of rocks beneath the surface coiled round the land like a string of grey pearls; the black sea between – deep, dark, fathomless.

Mia was standing at the bow, straining to catch a glimpse of Banshee. Pushing the tender back out, they circumnavigated the island as close to the rocks as they dare, still no sign of the other boat.

On the island's east side, sheer cliffs contrasted vividly with the soft, green mound visible from Galty's beach. The slab of brittle grey rose out of the sea, glinting menacingly, cold and hard. At the base of the cliff shards of stone split to form caves, dark recesses hidden behind a shark-tooth smile.

"We'll have to go in," Ross said. Mia searched in the locker for the torch. Ross slowed the tender; it was tricky, the tide was rising.

"Radio?" He looked about.

"Not on this, I have my phone though." She put her hand to her pocket, but her phone was gone.

The water sloshing against the side echoed in the darkness,

the pungency of plankton and seaweed cloyed at her throat. Mia had never been this close to the caves before, it was dangerous, boats had been wrecked, the riptide too strong. She could feel the current pulling them off course, Ross stiffened against it, using all his strength to keep control as he pushed them on. She strobed the flashlight, illuminating craggy walls running with water, stony inlets barely big enough to land a craft. Ross spotted a rock, too late they bumped against it, she lost her balance crashing to the deck, the torch fell away. Ross caught it before it rolled into the water. The light flashed upwards, revealing a colony of bats huddled together above their heads. She struggled to sit up. Ross held out his hand.

"Water's rising fast, not sure how much longer we can stay."

She turned huge eyes on him. "He can't be lost, he was only minutes ahead of us."

The tender hit another rock and as the water rose, the roof of the cave drew closer. "Mia, we'll have to …"

"Look! What's that?" She pointed. The stern of a boat was just visible, lodged in an inlet only metres away. It tilted precariously, the bowline way below the water. It was sinking fast.

"Hold on!" Ross yelled, swinging the tender round.

Mia flashed the light across the water as Ross steered. In minutes they were alongside Banshee. There was a hole in her side, water flooding in.

"Archie!" Mia yelled. "Archie, we're here!"

No response. Ross grabbed the bow rail. He looked back at the swirl of sea, an angry whirlpool building.

"I'll be quick." He leapt forward, clutching Banshee's shrouds, hauling himself aboard. He lost his footing, fell, sloshing through the water on deck. Catching a rope to stop from being washed overboard, he dragged himself onto his knees, crawling to the fly-bridge. Everything tipped at a violent angle, the galley half-submerged; charts, pictures, debris floating and it was dark ... very dark.

"Archie," Ross called, praying he would be there waiting to be rescued. "Archie, where are you?"

Ross took a deep breath and dived into the boat, swimming as fast as he could, he pulled open doors, lifted hatches but Archie was nowhere to be seen. Ross needed air. He pushed through the water and finding a small space between the surface and the salon roof, filled his lungs then disappeared, swimming down to the captain's quarters. He heaved against the door, pushing it free. The large bed was empty, although the pillows had floated away, and for a second Ross thought how inviting it looked.

The hole in the bow was large enough for a man to swim through. Ross went to the opening, looking left and right, hoping somewhere there was a patch of dry land and Archie would be there, safe. But all he saw were grey caves and black water. A loud groan. Banshee lurched. She was sinking. Ross gave one last look and spotting a newish looking box beside the bed lunged, grabbed it and powering up with one hand, swam out of the hole and up to the surface. He burst through the water, gasping for air.

He passed Mia the box as she helped him back on board.

"Anything?" she asked, wide-eyed.

"Just that." He pointed at the box. "Don't know what it is, it just looked a bit odd, so I thought ..."

Ross could not stand upright, the roof of the cave so low. "We need to go, *now!*" And bending to grasp the tiller, he steered the tender out towards the entrance of the cave. The sea was rushing in at an alarming rate, the tide and wind forcing them back. Ross pushed the engine to breaking point. A sudden wave crashed against them, Mia looked down her feet were submerged.

"Bail out! Bail out!" Ross ordered. Mia grabbed the bucket and started to bail, the torch fell from her hand, all was black. "Hang onto me," he shouted. "If we go, we go together."

Ross watched the water flooding into the cave. Instinctively he took the middle channel, hoping whichever undercurrent hit them, it would spin them round and fling them back out to sea.

He spotted a dot of light.

"Hold on," he yelled.

Mia wrapped her arms around his waist, pressing her head against his back. The boat lifted, crashed down and with one almighty surge broke free of the spin. Behind them, the waters merged into an angry wave and as the wave rolled, spewing foam, Mia saw something.

"Ross stop, it's Archie! Archie's in the water!"

Ross saw it too, there was something in the water alright but there was no hope, no life left. It might have been Archie's body but it was not Archie. Ross motored on.

She gripped his arm.

"We have to go back, it's Archie, I'm sure of it!"

He shook his head.

"Ross!" she yelled.

He stared ahead. They had to save themselves. The little boat was taking on water, they might not make it. She crumpled to the deck, head in hands, forcing herself not to look back.

They powered on, passing through an arch of rock and out into the open, choppy sea turned charcoal as the wind whipped black clouds so low they almost touched them, it was hard to see anything through the dense, grey rain. Limping towards the shore Ross pulled the throttle back, slowing the boat. Dripping wet with sea and sweat he crouched down beside her.

"Archie was gone before we got there," he said. "Too late, too dangerous, you know that."

She did know, she had been terrified, no one in their right mind would have even gone into the cave, let alone tried to bring Archie back. But she was not in her right mind and deep down she knew that too.

"I'm so sorry." Ross held out his arms, but she could not move. The next thing she felt was an embrace, two strong arms wrapped around her, holding her close, his chin on her head, tucking her face into the warmth of his throat. She breathed him in, heart thumping, his chest crushed against her; they were safe, they were alive and somewhere Archie Fitzgerald smiled … a plan was coming together.

THE LEGACY

The morning of Archie's funeral was as glorious a day as the east coast of Ireland had ever witnessed. A bleached denim sky draped cloudlessly across the bay as a shimmering, silky sun rose in the east. Mia was sitting on the shale outside the boathouse; she had been sent to lock everything away. Bernice was in security meltdown, recounting the day an entire house was cleared out while the occupants attended a family funeral only a few miles away. Bernice kept thinking of things to worry about, driving everyone mad.

Mia, glad to be outside, had not the heart to draw the doors across the front of the boathouse. She was looking at the space where Banshee had stood a few short weeks ago. So much had happened in such a short space of time; her relationship over, her career in jeopardy and her home abandoned, yet she felt strangely unmoved.

Archie, unsurprisingly, had taken destiny into his own hands. Sailing straight into the eye of a storm he no doubt knew was coming, having shut everything off, engine, sonar, radio, he had allowed the vessel to be swept away, dragged into the caves beneath the island and smashed against the rocks. The angry sea had broken Banshee into pieces and she, together with her determined-to-die captain, had floated gracefully to a watery grave on the ocean floor. Archie knew the end was near and had chosen how it would be played out. Archie was gone, Mia was going to have to get used to that.

Yet this was the hardest part, because Archie was not gone. If anything his presence was stronger than ever. She could feel him everywhere, cigar smoke drifted out from nowhere, the piano tinkled yet the lid was closed and then his laughter, the surprised, 'Ah-ha!' when he was charmed and delighted – she heard that a lot, an awful lot.

Mia could not close the doors, shut him out, prevent his return to their special place where she, the mermaid princess, fought dragons and sea monsters with Archie by her side. Even now she could hear him humming as he 'swabbed the deck', or 'spliced the main brace', terms he used for every task undertaken in the boathouse.

"There you are!"

A figure shimmered in the haze, as if emerging from the water. She shielded her eyes.

"How're you doing?" It was Ross.

They had not met since that fateful day; he had phoned, asking if he was needed but Humphrey had taken charge. He and Bernice had identified the body recovered by the coastguard the following morning, arrangements had to be made. Archie had not only organised his own demise, he had also engineered things so that Humphrey would be around to step into the breach, the best man for the job, no doubt.

"I've been sent to find you," Ross said.

"Ah." She did not move.

"You'll want to change?"

She looked down at baggy trews, sloppy top. She needed to transform herself, the funeral was in less than an hour. "I'm supposed to lock up, make sure it's all secure."

"I'll do it."

"But …"

"You go. I'll make sure we're watertight." She hesitated. "It'll be fine, believe me."

"You won't …"

"It'll be just as he left it. Locked up, that's all." He gave a smile. "Now go."

Mia walked towards the house. It would be alright, Archie trusted Ross. Bernice was making everyone paranoid, she even made Leela hide the silver, although Leela had to admit she could only find half of it.

Archie had organised two memorial services, one in Dublin and one in London, ensuring – as he put it himself – as many friends, fans and enemies as possible could attend. His funeral was meticulously planned too, a small, private affair, carried out to his exact wishes. A smattering of cousins, school friends, neighbours. The parish priest said Mass, Fenella and Humphrey handled the eulogy beautifully, while the nervous yet enthusiastic choir of the Mary Magdalene gave the *Ave Maria* their best shot.

Archie loved music and made sure his eclectic taste was well represented that sunny day. But the lone tin whistle, leading the way to the family tomb to the plaintive strains of Jimmy MacCarthy's *Ride On* was more than Mia could bear; she slipped away to stand at the highest point of the churchyard and glare with unshed tears at the sea, the sea that had taken him.

They were in the morning room for the reading of the will. By now they all knew Mia would inherit the house and estate, Bernice the property in London, Fenella most of Archie's weird and wonderful collections and Humphrey the elderly tender; for some reason Archie had singled out the boat for his old friend. Proceedings were handled decorously and on the face of it, all legacies accepted graciously.

As the barrister folded the paperwork away, Bernice announced drinks would be served in the library ahead of lunch and although Humphrey might have suspected this might not be the end of the matter, even he could not have predicted Eamon's reaction once formalities were completed.

"This is far from over," Eamon said, as Humphrey placed the file in his briefcase.

"What's that?" Humphrey asked.

"All this." Eamon opened his arms, encompassing the house. Driscoll stood up. Eamon had been drinking since early morning.

"Archie Fitzgerald's wishes have been carried out, according to his last will and testament." Humphrey looked Eamon in the eye. "Everyone he cared about has been looked after. If you have anything to say, you'd better say it to me."

"We'll be contesting the will." Eamon tried a menacing tone.

"Pointless," Humphrey said. "Who's we anyway?"

"My firm, on Bernice's behalf, of course."

Humphrey raised his eyebrows.

"You're a firm now? That's news to me. Eamon, you're a small-town country solicitor and not a very good one at that, you need to get over yourself and get on with your life, you've had all you're going to get out of this family."

Eamon lurched towards Humphrey. Driscoll stepped between them.

"You've always been a big-headed prick." Eamon glared at Humphrey.

"Take my advice, Eamon." Humphrey put his spectacles away. "Get your own house in order, you'll have plenty on your plate soon enough." By now Eamon was boiling with rage.

"We need this house, we want it back!" He spat.

"Again, the royal we? Eamon, it's nothing to do with you. The whole estate belongs to Miss Mia Flanagan. The property in London is Bernice's and all Archie's other possessions have been doled out according to his wishes. You seem dissatisfied with your bequest?"

"A pair of old shooting pistols? *Please*. After all I've done for this family." Eamon continued to glare. Humphrey shrugged.

"Any services you were commissioned to undertake were paid for. I'm handling affairs from now on."

"Bernice is my client," Eamon barked.

"No longer." Humphrey snapped his briefcase closed. "Now, I'm joining the ladies for a glass of champagne, it's probably best your friend takes you home." He nodded at Driscoll, who had Eamon by the elbow. Eamon shrugged free.

"I don't take my instructions from you, you pompous arsehole. Archie was like a brother to me, I loved him." Eamon's voice broke with emotion. "You've not heard the last of this, I'll get my dues, you see if I don't!"

"Time to go," Driscoll said, taking Eamon's arm again. "Any chance I can borrow the car?"

"You'll have to ask the new owner," Humphrey replied.

"Oh, who would that be?" Driscoll was put out, he had been left nothing.

"I'm not at liberty to say. Now, good day."

"Good day? You'll regret this day, I'm telling you." Eamon called as they left. Humphrey watched Leela show them out. She was wearing a canary yellow dress, dangling daisies at her ears, another of Archie's wishes carried out to the letter.

"Bet you're ready for a drink, love." Leela liked Humphrey, a bit of a rogue as a young man, but she knew he would turn out well, he had an aura of success about him, did Humphrey. Why Bernice had never married him, Leela could not imagine but then she didn't need to imagine, she knew.

It was that fateful summer, the summer the whole world appeared to be teetering on the edge of madness and everyone at Galty House seemed driven insane with love and lust and fear. It still made her shudder to think about it. She remembered the conversation well.

She had been in the kitchen as they all burst in.

"When will this heat ever end, it's killing me," she groaned, pulling off her already rolled down stockings."

"You never know, we might see you in for a swim yet." Archie gave her a nudge.

"Don't be audacious, Archie." Leela was irritated.

"I think you mean facetious," Fenella said, helpfully.

"It's too fecking hot, is what I meant!" Leela replied, fanning herself with a spatula.

"I can't believe he asked you to go sailing with him, you've only just met!" Bernice slammed the back door.

"We've all only just met," Fenella said pertly, clearly delighted she had been asked out.

"But I'm the one who goes to the island to paint, I've watched him working in the garden, carrying water into the lodge."

"The one who's been spying on him, you mean." Fenella was teasing.

"But I saw him first!" Bernice snapped.

"It matters not, dearest sister." Archie was at the fridge. "Once he spotted Fenella he saw nothing else."

"What nonsense!" beamed Fenella, hardly able to hide her glee. "Good-looking though isn't he?"

"Deadly," Archie agreed. "Total waste being a priest."

Fenella spun round. "He's not a priest."

"Not yet." Archie pulled the ring off a beer can and placed it on his wedding finger. "Vowed to another though, so don't be getting your hopes up, virgin child."

Fenella threw a beach towel at him. Bernice was sulking at the sink, arms folded. A clatter. They looked round. Leela was waving the blender – her waggly yoke – as she called it.

"I heard that," she said, beady eyes swivelling around the room. "There'll be no going sailing with anyone from the island, do you hear me?" She pointed with the gizmo. "That place is out of bounds, if you go again I'll tell your mother and she'll have to alert the authorities."

Archie made to protest.

Leela raised her hand.

"No! You and Humphrey know mixing with those boys is strictly forbidden, they've taken vows and anyway girls shouldn't be anywhere near them, it's wrong to encourage them to break their pledge to God." Fenella was staring at Leela in surprise, she had never seen her so incensed. "We've enough to contend with, all the tittle-tattle in the town about this and that. Don't you dare give them any more ammunition, I'm warning ye!"

And with that, she had stomped to the range, blending the pan of soup so thoroughly it nearly evaporated completely.

But they had not heeded her, and things had gone from bad to worse. The Monsignor missing, the young priest disappearing and Fenella pregnant, wanting to give the baby up and then running away because she could not bear to.

Mrs Fitzgerald stoic in the face of it all, Ursula so devastated by shame it would be the death of her and Archie, poor Archie, being blamed for everything by everyone.

She remembered the day she had gone into town, not long after Mrs Fitzgerald had told Fenella Galty House was her home and she was to stay and have her baby there.

"There's always been something about that place. All the comings and goings and wild parties during the Emergency when it was supposed to be a safe house," one woman was saying to another. "And Mr Fitzgerald, a lovely man, why did he stop coming home I wonder?"

"She'll marry anyone now, anyone who asks her, desperate to give the bastard a name." Leela recognised that voice, it was Mrs O'Grady, the parish priest's housekeeper.

"She'll get plenty of offers, she's very beautiful." The woman behind the counter said.

"Not from any decent man, anyway." Mrs O'Grady again.

"You should be ashamed, saying such terrible things." Sister Agnes spoke, the very one they were hoping to impress.

"I'm sorry sister but I don't want her anywhere near us. I've sons, good boys, one might want to be a priest." Mrs O'Grady's sons were the surge of the parish, there was nothing priestly about them.

Leela emerged from behind the shiny new stand displaying postcards extolling the area's virtues. "Are you talking about the young one up at The Seahorse Hotel, getting bigger by the day and no shame to her, walking on the beach as bold as brass." She had repeated their exact words.

"As well you know Leela Brennan, I'm no gossip." Mrs O'Grady grabbed her basket and made to push by. Leela stood her ground, the young nun beside her. Mrs O'Grady's face was puce with embarrassment.

Leela let her bag drop with a clatter and lifting her hands above her head, let out a bloodcurdling wail.

"A curse on you, you bad-minded biddy, a curse on all your kith and kin!" Mrs O'Grady screamed and ran out into the street. The nun started to laugh. Leela gave a crooked smile, picking up her bag.

"Cancel our account," she told the shopkeeper. "We'll be taking our business elsewhere from now on."

Leela let out a long sigh, closing her eyes. Humphrey placed his arm around her shoulders.

"Shall we have a quiet glass together?" he asked. "Someone amazing has left us, a little time to reflect and remember is what's needed."

She squeezed his hand.

"You're right."

But Leela was not convinced Archie had left, not entirely; not yet anyway.

Fenella, dressed in scarlet, as was decreed, stood at the still unpainted window, one of Archie's impetuous improvements, a bay of enormous proportions incongruous against the room's original features. It was so Archie – flamboyant, excessive. Yet he could be suddenly frugal, declaring only the basics were required for the perfect life.

Mia loved that side of him. The sparkly-eyed chatterbox, cooking fish they had caught on the barbecue under a starry summer sky or wrapping her in tweed, to take her on wild, winter expeditions into the mountains. Archie had given her childhood so many memories, indeed Archie had given her a childhood.

She was gazing into the fire, soft flames fluttering along the peat, as Trixie pressed a glass into her hand.

"Everything okay? Nothing to report on the Rupert front?" Trixie was pleased they had a quiet moment, the last few days had been hectic.

"Ancient history, especially with all this going on." She gave Trixie a smile, the only one who asked how *she* was now her broken heart had cracked again.

"Champagne, and not a minute too soon." Fenella crossed the room to claim her glass. "Alright, darling?" Mia was plucking distractedly at the emerald silk of her gown, her costume for the day.

"A lot to take in," Trixie said.

Fenella nestled into the couch, she raised her glass.

"Well done, Archie. Making sure your little girl is sorted."

Trixie flashed her a look.

"I will miss him," the actress said with such sadness they both turned to look at her. "No one loved me like Archie."

"And what of the inheritance, heiress?" Trixie kicked Mia's foot, playfully. Archie had planned every detail, the music, the flowers, the reading of the will, but something was puzzling Mia, there were no special instructions for her.

"I don't know. What does he want me to do with it?"

"Whatever you want. That's why he left it to you," Trixie said, laughing her throaty laugh.

"Advise the girl, Trix," Fenella prompted. "You've plenty of experience in that department."

Trixie coughed. "Me?"

Fenella crossed her legs coquettishly. "Come on, it's just us girls." She glanced around the room, cool even though the sun shone, the smell of the sea seeping in through the cracks. She imagined Archie, perched on his chair, eager to hear the gossip; the green-eyed cat sat there instead. "Go on," Fenella insisted.

Mia was about to protest, she did not care about Trixie's experience, it was her own that was troubling her, what was she to do with this huge clunking legacy?

Trixie poured more champagne, a distraction might help.

"Okay then. Way back, I had a fervent admirer," Trixie disclosed.

Mia sipped her drink. Trixie was also an actress, predisposed to character roles these days, but voluptuously attractive nonetheless, it was no surprise she was pursued in her youth.

Trixie explained. "A nice, older gentleman with a Porsche dealership in Suffolk wanted me to er … be his girlfriend and offered me things to make it worth my while."

Mia grinned, Trixie still deferred to her imagined innocence.

"Sadly, he died before we formalised the arrangement, but he did leave me something,"

"A Porsche?" Mia asked.

"Not exactly." Trixie drained the bottle. "He left me his entire estate."

Mia had never heard this story before. "What on earth did you do with it?"

"Sold it. What did I know about running a car dealership? I was a glamour model."

Mia's eyes widened. "Glamour?"

"One of the best." Fenella gave her friend an admiring glance. "A global porn star."

Mia put her glass down. *A porn star?*

"It was different then, love," Trixie told her. "Show them your tits and they were all over you, flash your fanny and most of them proposed to you on the spot, married or not."

"Stop it!" Fenella was laughing.

"But you're an actress!" Mia exclaimed.

"That came later, when I hooked up with your mother, she insisted I stopped starving myself and popping pills for the sake of my figure." Trixie grinned. "I didn't invest the money wisely but we had fun. You could have fun, Mia, lots of fun, it would do you good."

Fenella waved her drink at her daughter. "I'm sure that's what Archie would want. You do take things rather seriously darling, have a few flings, why don't you?"

"But I *am* serious, I don't want to be a 'free spirit,'" Mia replied. "You must have been serious about the man with the dealership, Trixie?"

Trixie shook her head. "Not my scene, if men became emotionally involved that was up to them. Same goes for your mother and the sheik."

Mia gave an uneasy laugh. This was a joke, surely.

"Ah, the rubies." Fenella gave Trixie a playful shove. "You've a memory like an elephant."

"Worth at least as much as the Porsche dealership." Trixie lit a small cheroot, blowing smoke up the chimney.

"Invested more wisely." Fenella gave Mia an indulgent smile.

"You slept with a sheik for rubies?" Mia was aghast.

"No, that's the best bit. She wouldn't sleep with him and he kept sending her gifts – gold, diamonds, camels," Trixie explained.

Fenella was chuckling. "He was most upset I couldn't accept the camels."

"So he sent rubies instead. Hundreds of them," Trixie confirmed.

"Not quite, but enough to buy Morleigh Lodge, a few acres and give a certain little girl a pony."

"*Ruby!*" Mia exclaimed. "No wonder we called her Ruby!"

Fenella and Trixie were roaring with laughter at this stage, their raucousness fuelled by champagne. The door opened. The green-eyed cat arched its back, taking the opportunity to exit stage right.

Bernice scowled into the room. "Ross Power is on the phone, Mia."

"How did it all go?" Ross knew the will reading had taken place that afternoon.

"He's left me Galty House, the estate, the lot, still not sure why. He made sure everyone else is okay too, you know what he's like … was like." She swallowed.

"Any plans yet?" he asked.

"My mother wants us to go to Italy for a break, says I need time to think. I feel as if I just need to get back to work." Mia's job grounded her. When everyone else in her life was flung across the globe, her career kept her on an even keel, she knew who she was when she was working. But the more she thought about it, the more she realised this ending had given her a beginning. A new start in her old home.

"You probably don't need to work quite as hard, at least for a while," he reminded her.

"Yes, of course, the money. He left money too." Somehow that did not make her feel any better.

"Maybe taking some time, is good," Ross said. "Anyway, just checking you're okay and well, keep in touch, Mia, won't you?"

"Keep in touch?" It sounded so final. "Why? What's happening?"

"I'm flying back to New York day after tomorrow. The award we entered, the hotel has been shortlisted, there's a fancy, what do you say, 'do'. I've to check out Pearl's school too, family meeting that kind of thing."

"Oh." She twisted the cord in her fingers. There was a pause. Archie had been invited to the awards ceremony as an 'ambassador', to speak on behalf of the hotel, support the project. Ross was delighted he had accepted, the endorsement of a powerful neighbour would make an impact on the judges, especially as they would all recognise the famous star.

"Found someone to take Archie's place?"

"Haven't really thought about it, guess I'll muckle through."

"I could always carry your bag."

Did she just say that?

"I'm sorry?" Ross was unfamiliar with the quip.

"Meaning if you wanted, I could come." She was embarrassed now.

"Really?" He could hardly believe it. "Yes, please, come, carry my bag, I'll carry yours, whatever," Ross boomed down the phone.

Mia found Fenella sitting on her bed, gazing at the door to Archie's rooms, as if he might breeze through any second, beg her to read with him, help him learn his lines.

"Our trip to Italy, can it wait?"

Fenella wiped her perfect nose with the back of her hand, she had been crying and tears were banned.

"Don't tell me you're going back to work?"

"No, but I *am* going to New York."

"When?"

"Day after tomorrow."

"Who with?" It sounded like work.

"Ross Power, the awards do, Archie was booked to speak, he's asked me to take Archie's place." A teeny lie.

This was staggering news.

"But you'll need a gown, jewellery, shoes, everything." Fenella lit up. She pushed her daughter eagerly towards the door, tripping over the cat. "Shoo." She flapped her hand. "Where has that bloody thing come from? Gives me the willies."

"Leela said it's been here forever," Mia told her, giving the cat's silky head a stroke before she left.

FAMILY AFFAIRS

After playing the role of dresser to the dresser and leaving Mia to pack, Fenella drifted into Archie's room. It calmed and reassured her seeing Archie's possessions strewn about the place, clothes piled on chairs, his beloved smoking jacket at the end of the bed. It was as if he might appear at any moment, quoting a line, making her laugh … breaking her heart.

Sometimes he had hurt her deliberately. Archie blamed her for banishing someone they loved. She never admitted to it and, in not admitting had never asked for forgiveness, therefore Archie considered, she should never be forgiven. She had no idea what they had done to save him, so wrapped up in her own heartache she could not see beyond it. Thank God for Mia, that's what Archie told her time and again, Mia was the only good thing to come out of the whole sorry mess, without her they would have all lost their minds completely.

The green-eyed cat watched the woman in red walk around the room, touching this and that, sighing, smiling. She knelt at the sea chest at the end of the bed, lifted the lid, it was full of pages, Archie's attempt at following his father's footsteps.

She held a handful of sheets to her nose; a scent of another time, the echo of another conversation …

"I love Archie," he said. She felt a flicker of jealousy. "He doesn't know whether to be an actor or a playwright, not too disparate a choice, wouldn't you agree?"

"Worlds apart." She was irked. "What's really annoying is he could be either, very successfully."

"Thought you had to loathe yourself to be a great actor, I

don't get that impression from Archie?"

"He's a red-head, self-loathing is ingrained."

"But you're not a red-head?" He lifted a coil of blue-black hair.

"Deep down I am." She looked at him under her eyelashes, they were in the summerhouse; she had been dared to seduce him. She needed little encouragement, ever since she had first laid eyes on him she wanted him, a weird and wonderful longing she had never felt before, or had she? Sometimes he seemed the most familiar thing in the world, as if they had always known each other, always been in love.

She slipped the straps of her sundress off her shoulders.

"Loads of red-heads in my family, mostly cocky and over-confident." He stretched out on the couch.

"Just masking their self-loathing," Fenella said, stepping out of the dress. She was wearing a pale peach camisole and French knickers; Gregory was trying desperately not to notice. "Your hair is beautiful," she said. "I wouldn't fancy you with red hair."

"You fancy me?" He picked up a battered copy of the New Musical Express; *David Bowie peering pensively out from beneath a trilby hat.*

"I said I wouldn't fancy you with red hair, I might not fancy you with blond hair either." She twirled so he could see all of her.

"I'd fancy you if you were bald," he told her, turquoise eyes glinting.

"You're going to be a priest, you'd better give up that fancying carry on or I'll shave my head to tempt you."

He rolled over to hide his body's response to all that satin and lace.

She started undoing the buttons of the camisole; he could see her nipples protruding through the fabric. He looked away, feeling hot and cold at the same time.

"I have to go," he told her.

She shrugged, reaching to reclaim the dress. He was on his feet.

"Don't go, Gregory, please I was only teasing, I went too far, I'm sorry." *She did not look particularly contrite.*

"You didn't go too far, nothing happened. What was it, a bet?" *He looked round; saw something or someone dip beneath the window.* "I get it."

"Just wanted to see if you're still a virgin." *She was unrepentant.*

"Well, you clearly are," *he bit back.*

"What do you mean?"

"Because only a silly virgin would behave like that and if I'm going to have sex with anyone, real sex, it needs to be with a real woman!" *He breathed the words into her face and dropping the magazine to the floor, left.*

"How'd it go?" *Archie asked, sliding back into the summerhouse after 'the dark one' had stormed out.*

"Couldn't have gone better." *Fenella sat, knees pulled up to her chest.*

"Did you shag him?" *Archie lit a Gauloises.*

"Senseless," *Fenella replied, and although Archie laughed out loud, she just wanted to cry.*

Fenella noticed a plastic box file on the floor and opening it took the pages out. He had been writing again. She placed the pages on top of the pile in the chest. Archie would want all his work together, in a safe place. She knew where he kept the key, well hidden. She locked the chest and put the key in her pocket, just in case.

Standing at the window, Fenella watched a young couple stroll at the water's edge and as she did a desolate sadness enveloped her. They would do what lovers always did, walk up from the shore to lie hidden in the dunes and make love, the sand soft and silky on the skin, she remembered it as if it were yesterday.

"Can love ever be evil?" she had asked, resting her head on his damp chest.

"Not real love. Love only wants the very best for the one who is loved," he replied, stroking her hair.

"Even if it meant the one who's loved can't stay? The best thing is to let them go?"

"That's sad, not evil," he told her.

"What about jealousy where does that fit?

"It's not love."

"But is it not another side of love?"

"Jealousy is all about the person feeling the jealousy, essentially selfish."

"Love of self, perhaps?" she pondered, the heat making her drowsy. "I could never feel that."

"Really? I thought you wanted to be a great actress, you have to feel everything.

She slapped his thigh. "Me wanting to be an actress isn't love of self, it's the complete opposite."

"Hate of self?" He gave an exaggerated frown.

"Even you, with your head full of bullshit theology, should know hate is not the opposite of love, it's two sides of the same coin." She rolled her eyes at him. He would dive into those eyes if he could.

"What's the complete opposite then?"

She thought. "Loathing of self. That's it. That's why I want to be an actress, so I can be lots of other people and not me, not the one I loathe."

He sat up, taking her hands in his. "Don't say that, don't you dare loathe yourself."

"But what about this, us, what we've done? Shouldn't I loathe myself for that, Mr Nearly Priest?"

He pulled her to him, crushing his lips against hers, pushing his tongue inside her mouth, fingers in her hair. She swallowed, she wanted him inside her again, she could feel the heat burning her thighs, tingling between her legs. She twisted her body, pushing the swimsuit down to free her breasts, the soft pale skin brushing his chest. His eyes turned to slits as he looked at her, she wriggled out of the suit, laying down beside him, stretching her arms above her head.

"Stop me loathing myself, Gregory, make love to me now, show me I mean more to you than anything, any vow, any god."

"You already do." His voice was barely a whisper, as he dropped his mouth to her breast and started to flick the hard pink nipple with his moist tongue.

She was crying now, unaware of her tears until Bernice sat beside her.

"I've news," Bernice said quietly.

She was wearing a floaty gown of tangerine chiffon, it spread out like petals on a lawn as she nestled conspiratorially beside Fenella crouched at the foot of Archie's bed. Fenella wiped her eyes; there was something girlish about Bernice today. "I'm going to live with Humphrey, he's asked me to marry him."

Fenella looked, uncomprehending.

"I know he's still married but Isabella has had a partner for years, they've just never divorced. Humphrey says we all need to move on."

"*You* are going marry a *divorced* man?"

This was a radical conversion to the twenty-first century for Bernice. She nodded.

"So that's why you were perfectly happy about the will in the end, why Eamon looked so furious – your plans had changed." Fenella was genuinely relieved. "What took you so long? He's been waiting for years. High time you were out of this place for good."

"Change can be difficult."

"Change is change, we can't be protected from it," Fenella told her, then suddenly a bright smile. "I couldn't be happier for you, for you both." And taking Bernice's hand, she kissed it. "We must tell everyone."

"Not today," Bernice shook her head. "Today is Archie's day, it will do tomorrow, tomorrow is the beginning of a future without him."

Fenella felt tears rise again.

THE UNDERSTUDY

The next morning Mia woke in her bright yellow bedroom strangely calm, as if a niggling worry had finally been resolved. Last night she decided to put the fact she had inherited Galty House to the back of her mind. Any decisions relating to her change in circumstance would be shelved while she flung herself across the Atlantic to one of the most exciting cities in the world and maybe have some – what was it now? That's it, fun! Trixie and her mother recounting tales of their romantic encounters had made her laugh – and think – despite yesterday's solemnity.

"Bet you're shocked!" she told the photograph on her dressing table. Archie had often accused her of being too cautious. "Me, taking your place in New York with a man I hardly know." In reality she did not know what to think of it herself.

The phone was ringing, she ran downstairs to answer it.

"Courtney? This is a surprise, what's up?"

Courtney was also surprised. Mia had just lost someone dear, she sounded almost chirpy.

"I've been trying your mobile."

"Lost it, can't say I miss it." She still had not heard from Rupert and for now that suited her.

"That explains it … but hey, so sorry, we all are, you must be devastated." Despite everything, it was good to hear Courtney's voice,

"How're you doing?"

"Okay enough," she replied.

"It was a boating accident in the end, he drowned, is that

right?" Courtney asked.

"That's right." The coroner had confirmed what they all suspected, Archie had taken a cocktail of painkillers and alcohol. It was highly likely Archie was dead before his body hit the water but this, like so many Fitzgerald myths, would remain a family secret.

They were quiet for a moment.

"I know it's early days but any idea when you might feel up to working again?"

"Not sure, things have changed, changed a lot." The past few weeks had been cataclysmic. Mia had ditched her fiancé, given up her apartment and Archie had died. Yesterday she became heiress to a country estate and today she was packing to go to New York with someone she barely knew. She tried not to think about it, it made her head reel.

Courtney sighed, a lot had changed for him too. "There's a new movie coming up, same team, Lol's doing it, we could do with you too. Leading lady's tricky and the leading man, well ..."

Mia was intrigued. She loved the pre-production process, studying the period, putting costumes together, fabrics, fittings, cataloguing the minutiae of the characters' outfits. A dresser's input could help create an icon. The costume designer may come up with the concept, but the wardrobe department made it work, she had always been proud of that.

"I honestly don't know," she told Courtney.

"Because of Rupert and Shelley?"

"Rupert? No, he's out of my life, thank goodness." Somewhere in her head an alarm went off.

"Luckier than me, then," Courtney said. Of course ... Shelley! Shelley was Courtney's wife.

"Oh my God, I've just realised. I didn't make the connection until you said her name." Mia was mortified.

"They're in total denial, saying they were rehearsing, you'd been drinking, got the wrong end of the stick, made a horrible scene. Rupert's telling anyone who'll listen that you threw him out of his home."

"His home? *My* apartment," Mia said. "What're you going to do?"

"I've done it, filed for divorce, going for custody too. I don't want my daughter growing up without her father."

Silence.

"I don't think I'll be back in London anytime soon." She had enough demons to face without reliving her spineless reaction to Rupert's infidelity every time she went through her own front door. She needed time and space, time to rebuild her self-esteem and the space to find it.

"I can't keep your slot open for long," Courtney tried. Mia was touched he wanted them to present a united front but Mia was tired of being there for everyone else.

"You'll have to count me out this time, Court," she said, replacing the receiver with a solid clunk. Hearing laughter coming from the kitchen Mia looked up at the grandfather clock; she had overslept, another first.

The tarot was spread among the breakfast things, Leela was giving Trixie a reading. Pearl wanted to know if she was going to marry a prince. Trixie said knowing her luck she would end up with a frog. Leela told them if they did not take the cards seriously, she would produce her wand and turn them both into rabbits for the pot.

"Did you hear about the Great Dame?" Pearl asked as she hopped over to greet her favourite mermaid. "Archie left Ross the car. He's going to use it for collecting guests from the airport, said it will give a classy first impression."

"It's gone to a very good home," Mia told her, taking her hand. "Are you okay?"

"About Archie being dead?"

Mia nodded.

"It's only his body that's dead, you do know that don't you?" Pearl told Mia. "It's what happens, we borrow a body from God and it wears out or breaks after a while. But we've usually finished with it by then."

"Good way of looking at it," Mia said.

"The only way. Archie explained everything. And now he's free to roam about a bit more, I can talk to him all the time. He's everywhere really. Which is what he always wanted." She gave Mia her burst of sunshine smile, then ferreted in her pocket. "Ross gave me this for you." Pearl handed her a card bearing the hotel crest. Handwritten at the bottom it read: *Please come, Ross*.

Leela was pointing to the Three of Cups. "I like this card, means a family celebration, a wedding, even a christening maybe."

"What?!" Trixie shrieked. "I hope not!"

"Not necessarily you." Leela was serious. "But someone close, whose life overlaps yours."

Mia tapped the invitation on the table. She had been turning over the decision to go to New York in her mind, not wanting the hotelier to misunderstand her motives when the door burst open, Fenella had Bernice by the hand.

"Tell them, Bernice or I'll burst, I really will." Her eyes were sparkling.

"I'm getting married," Bernice announced, hoping to shock but everyone had suspected things were developing quite rapidly with Humphrey.

Mia went to hug her, she had never seen Bernice look so

happy.

"And the lucky man?" Leela prompted, not taking her eyes off the cards.

"Why, Humphrey of course, he's always been the only one for me."

Trixie gave Fenella a look.

"About time," Leela said, gathering up the tarot and placing the deck in its special velvet pouch.

"Champagne, I think." Fenella decreed.

"Is there any left?" Bernice asked; the wine had flowed freely at the wake.

"Are you joking? Archie ordered caseloads just last week," Leela confirmed, more evidence that Archie knew exactly what was going to be required and when.

"Do I have to go back to the hotel with you?" Pearl asked. All eyes turned on Mia. "Or can I stay here?"

Mia ignored the stares. "Best I drop you back later." So dinner with Ross it was.

Mia was grateful Ross sent a car for them and once Pearl realised Mia was staying for dinner she seemed unusually keen to leave the adults alone.

They were quiet over the meal, having been through so much in so short a space of time there seemed little need to talk; it was good just being together eating, sipping wine and looking at each other, they did a lot of that. For some reason, tonight of all nights Mia felt an unfathomable draw towards him, as if he understood the ache in her heart. But it was only grief playing tricks, she told herself, the shouty stressed-out businessman was still so not her type, so very not.

However, the beguiling, black-eyed pirate with the artistic soul was. He gave her a curious look, his mouth in a half-smile, she had been gazing at his lips … wondering.

Ross watched her now, the candlelight making her hair glow like burnished copper, the pale pashmina slipping to reveal smooth shoulders dusted with freckles; thumbprints of tiredness pressed beneath her eyes.

"You doing okay?" His hand rested on the white tablecloth, fingers only millimetres from hers.

"There's a lot to take in."

"Give it time." His voice was gentle, dark eyes soft.

She looked out to sea, through the vast glass wall, the lights of vessels echoing the starry sky above. Everything felt detached and distant and she … just a tiny, insignificant, grain of sand on the shore.

"Let me show you around." He held out his hand. A late night private tour would be a distraction.

Ross escorted her through the magnificent presidential suite, cinema, kids club and luxurious tranquil spa. He took her behind the scenes via the kitchens then onto the terrace and over a bridge, twinkling with lanterns. All the time outlining this, highlighting that, explaining how a pipe dream had become his father's life's work.

She stopped when they reached the paintings she had been so taken with that first night.

"Your work?" she asked.

"I just dabble," he replied.

"I admired them when I was last here, there's real passion there."

"You have to be careful with passion, don't you think?" He slid her a look. "It can become an obsession and then where are you?" He turned away from the paintings.

"And is art your passion?" The wine had made her bold.

He gave a sad smile.

"Was. Then life kicks in and you've to bundle it away, get on with the real stuff."

"Sometimes the real stuff is the only way to stop the passion becoming obsession and obsession can be very destructive." She looked at her hand, recalling the makeshift ring she had worn for months.

"Wise words." He gave her a smile, trying to push the dull ache of loss momentarily aside. "You look done in."

"Nothing a drop of the sea air won't cure." Another of Archie's sayings.

They had reached the beach bar, an oasis built into the rock. Mia hopped onto a stool. Ross flicked a switch; music played, a trickle of water spilled from the cliff into a pool of light.

"Smooth," Mia said, then hiccupped.

"Something warming?" he asked. There was a nip in the air.

"Gaelic coffee please. You do know how to make it?"

"Ma'am, I'm a bartender first and last." He gave a grin.

She watched him work, strong arms, broad shoulders, slick dark hair bending into curls the longer he spent outside. He hummed to the music, Billie Holiday singing *Summertime*, Archie used to play it on the piano. She could smell the coffee.

"Nice here, cool little beach bar," she said.

"Will you stay?" He looked up from his task.

"Only till you throw me out." She laughed.

"Here, in Rosshaven?"

"Jury's out. What about you?"

"I've a contract."

"Just a job then?" He seemed so proud of what had been achieved, determined to make the project a success. "Someone waiting for you back home?" *Too much wine*, she thought fleetingly.

"Not now."

"Someone break your heart?" *Definitely too much wine.* Mia stifled another hiccup.

"A lucky escape. I could have ended up with someone I thought was right for all the wrong reasons." Mia was surprised, Ross struck her as the type who made a decision and stuck to it. He gave a brief smile. "Can we change the subject?"

Mia flushed. "Pearl definitely wants to go to Mary Magdalene, mind you people often want to stay when they come here on holiday."

"I'm going to need your help there at some stage, if that's okay?"

Mia was listening to the waves, letting them soothe the sadness that had seeped back in. "Poor Pearl, I can't believe she wants to go to that awful school."

"She's fascinated by it, thinks the sisters will miraculously make her a star pupil. A bit like insisting someone is a mermaid so her fear of water is cured instantly too."

Mia thought back to all the things she had been scared of, the instant cures she wanted to believe in; Leela's voodoo, her grandmother's rosary beads, Archie's legends. Her head started to throb.

"Do you mind if I skip the drink?" She slid from the stool. "I'm really tired, and we've a long journey tomorrow." Had she really agreed to go to New York?

"Not changing your mind, are you?" He looked into her eyes. "I need someone to endorse what we're doing here, and it needs to be someone outside the hotel, someone real who can validate what we've achieved."

Someone real, not dead, she thought, her throat beginning to constrict. She needed to go.

"Of course not, I'm doing this for Archie, don't forget."

He held out his hand.

"Shake on it, neighbour?"

"Okay, neighbour," she replied, turning away, tears welling up. He could not see her cry, tears were not allowed.

THE CITY THAT NEVER SLEEPS

Mia Flanagan had been to New York before, when she was at college studying costume history. She had had a ball, typical student stuff, staying in a hostel, picnicking in Central Park – the highlight, working backstage at a Broadway show – it had been a blast. Today, dressing for a major awards ceremony at the Waldorf Astoria, was a completely different experience. Her hand trembled as she fixed the drops in her ears.

A tap on the door. "How're you doing?"

"Nearly there," she called out. Funny, she dressed people for special occasions on set all the time; brides for royal weddings, officers going into battle, fantasy heroes saving the world but preparing herself to appear on stage, in what she hoped would be only a minor role, was terrifying.

She turned in the mirror, relishing the blood-red fishtail gown, scooped at the back to reveal creamy skin. Her copper hair was coiled high and twisted, loose tendrils softening the look, her only adornments crystal earrings and Archie's dress watch – a sliver of platinum – she had borrowed for luck. She sprayed perfume, gathered her notes and went to meet her host.

Walking along the sumptuously furnished corridor, she could see Ross fiddling with his tie by the elevator. He stopped to watch her.

"Need a hand with that?"

"Damn thing, should be able to tie one by now." He leaned down. She created a perfect bow in seconds. He looked at himself admiringly. "Nice to have a professional on the job."

"I doubt you'll be saying that when I make my speech." She gave a nervous smile.

"You'll be perfect." He tapped Archie's watch. "We're all rooting for you."

It had not occurred to Mia that in New York, she too was considered something of a celebrity and was totally unprepared for the warmth that emanated towards her, the daughter of a favourite actress, representing someone they all adored; Archie had been a darling of Broadway long before his movie career.

Heads turned as Ross guided her past the piano; cocktails were being served in the Silver Corridor next to the Grand Ballroom – excitement was building. People kept stopping to greet them, Ross knew all their names, effortlessly introducing her to everyone they met.

"Okay so far?" he asked, as a waiter appeared with champagne.

"You know everybody."

"They're all here, this is a big deal. But listen ..." He placed his hand on hers. "Just be yourself, they're thrilled you're doing Archie's gig, it means a lot."

"Can I just have water, please?" Her stomach was churning.

"Sure," Ross smiled. "The champagne can wait."

"And now, ladies and gentlemen, the finalists of the Best New Resort in the World Award." The list was read out. Rapturous applause. "But before we announce the winner, each resort has brought a special guest to speak on their behalf, no corporate bull." Everyone laughed.

Mia swallowed as an usher arrived to take her to the stage.

"Break a leg," Ross whispered.

Holding her gown, Mia focused on the floor, trying not to trip. Standing at the podium, she was relieved to see only lights, faces were obliterated. The notes for her speech appeared on the teleprompter – all good – then the image of herself filled the vast screen. She swayed, gripping the stand, terrified she would collapse as a wave of panic rushed up from her toes, turning her legs to jelly. *I can do this, I can do this,* she told herself.

"Ladies and gentlemen, unlike certain members of my family, centre stage is not my natural habitat." A ripple of laughter. "So please bear with me as a wobbly novice tries to represent one of the greatest actors the world has ever known." The applause was deafening. As the room hushed, she tried again.

"These are his words …"

And she read, in a calm, clear voice Archie's eloquent and heart-warming speech, recounting how the Powers had been welcomed back by the local community and how the Harbour Spa Hotel was a landmark for the east coast of Ireland and a flagship for the whole country, the homeland of so many Irish-Americans.

"…the Harbour Spa was the vision of the late Anthony Power, who never saw his dream come to fruition but believed in his heart it always would."

Mia looked into the crowd and without notes continued.

"It was something of which Archie Fitzgerald was inordinately proud, you see Archie believed in the power of dreams and I should know. When I was little I was scared of my dreams but Archie told me dreams could move mountains, change the world for the better and keep the human spirit alive even in its darkest days. So, although the Harbour Spa Hotel and the Power Corporation would be delighted and thrilled to win this award, it doesn't matter, it really doesn't matter at all … because the dream came true and that's what really counts." She gave a small bow. "Thank you."

Mia did not hear the crowd as she turned to leave the stage or see the audience standing to applaud, she kept her eyes fixed on the floor, worried she had said the wrong thing, gone off piste. Ross was at the steps waiting for her, his broad smile beamed gratitude as he squeezed her hand.

"He's *so* proud of you," he said. "And so am I."

It was a beautiful evening, a warm breeze shimmered the trees with moonlight as they approached the park.

"Do you mind not winning?" Mia asked, as Ross helped her into the carriage.

"Not in the least, the other finalists were amazing, some better, some not as good but you managed to put it all into perspective. The Harbour Spa *is* a dream come true, what more could I ask?" He gave her a slow smile as she arranged herself and her dress opposite him.

"Even though you didn't win, you definitely smile more in New York!"

"Really? But I love Ireland."

"Maybe it's the job you don't like?" He gave her a look, she had gone too far. She felt a blush rise. "I've always wanted to do this, when I see it in movies I think, that looks lovely."

The driver moved off, the feathered headdress on the horse fluttering.

"I've never taken a carriage ride around Central Park either."

"Are you serious?" She was shocked.

"Yep, we rarely came to Manhattan and this is rather er …"

"Touristy?"

"If you say so." He smiled again, a dark strand of hair fell across his forehead. She felt the urge to smooth it back. She sat on her hands, dragging her gaze from his face.

"You were the only one who got a standing ovation, that counts as first place to me," he leaned forward, she turned to face him, his lips were so close; the horse faltered and Ross almost fell into her lap. He gripped her thigh to steady himself, then quickly sat back.

"Sorry."

The spot where his hand had rested tingled. Embarrassed Mia smoothed her dress, looking away to watch the silhouettes of leaves fluttering above, moonlight playing on the lake and all around towering skyscrapers keeping the oasis safe, protecting the park, a haven for generations to come.

"I knew it would be like this," she whispered, relishing the reassuring sound of horse's hooves, the scent of roses mixed with laurel as just beyond the tranquillity, sirens wailed, traffic jarred and the city shrieked itself alive. "It's wonderful but I don't think I could live here. It's such a full-on city."

"And London isn't?"

"Doesn't seem so. And I'm not always there, work often takes me away."

"And now? Would you make Wexford your home, being the proud owner of such a fine property?"

"No idea." She had deliberately shelved any decisions for the time being for fear her head would explode.

"Might you stay, even just for a while?"

"Haven't a clue."

Ross was disappointed, he was hoping for an indication of what she was planning to do with her inheritance.

The Powers wanted to buy Galty House but if it was not for sale, if Mia decided to keep it, so be it. But Ross would rather know, decide if he was going to work through his contract or bring Pearl home and start again. Whether she realised it or not, Mia's future was now inextricably linked with his and part of him quite liked that. The more he was around her, the more he liked her around.

"Maybe you have someone in London to go back to?" He was looking at her intently.

"A rather personal question."

"Sorry, I sort of assumed …"

"I was engaged." She looked at the space on her hand where the wire ring had been. "There again, maybe I wasn't. And you?"

"I'm sure you've been told my hapless story."

His voice was gruff.

"I only know what you told me." She blinked at him. "I leave tittle-tattle to others with more vivid imaginations." Mia had been the subject of gossip ever since she could remember, it was a pastime she had come to loathe.

Ross was immediately sorry he had been curt but the memory stung, more raw because he was back in New York.

"I'm well out of it," he told her. "It wasn't to be."

She gave him a smile. "I know what you mean, I'm well out of it too."

Silence.

"Not for you then?" he asked. "Marriage, kids, all that?"

She folded her arms. "I've enough going on. I need a job, somewhere to live …"

"You *have* somewhere to live," Ross reminded her.

"But I've given up my flat, all my things are in storage …"

"Surely they'll fit into Galty? It could certainly do with some new furniture."

Mia thought for a second. "True."

"And do you *need* to work, right now? You could just take some time, see what's what as you guys say."

Mia shrugged. "What about you, will you stay?"

"Like I said, I have a contract." His turn to sound unsure. "And Pearl needs her education."

"The school's not that bad in Rosshaven, honestly." Mia felt guilty for disparaging the Good Sisters of the Mary Magdalene.

"Maybe not, but the Harbour Spa is more or less on its feet, I get hotels up and running, then I move on." He failed to mention the problems he was encountering on a daily basis, hoping in the back of his mind they could somehow be sorted out quickly, discreetly.

"Oh, so you'll move on then."

"Guess so."

The carriage came to a halt.

"Do you want to go round again, sir?" the driver asked, disappointed the attractive couple had not been more romantic, they were sitting opposite each other, more like a business meeting.

"Thanks but I'm rather tired and we're flying back tomorrow." Her eyes were sad again.

"Of course." He paid the driver.

"It was lovely though, just how I imagined."

A half-truth, she had envisaged champagne, a giggling flirtation, passionate kisses from a handsome suitor. She sighed. Ross sensed her disappointment, he felt it too, all the uncertainties of the future cluttering their evening. He had so wanted to give her a good time, put the smile back, even just for a while.

"Shall we walk, it's a lovely night …"

"How far is it?" Mia's heels were high and her dress tight.

"Only about fifteen minutes."

"With your legs maybe."

He laughed and slowing his stride, pointed out landmarks as they walked.

"Shame we're not here for longer." She was wistful, looking skywards at the buildings towering over them. He took her arm to avoid a fire hydrant. She stumbled, caught her heel, it snapped.

Ross held the neat satin court in his hand, Mia handed him the heel.

"Hmmm, don't think I can fix that here and now, Cinderella." They were leaning against a railing, Mia put her shoeless foot to the ground, he dwarfed her.

She started to giggle. "It's fine, I'll hop back."

"Well, being a mermaid if we were nearer the river, you could swim." He gave her a look. "Or I could …" He bent to pick her up. "Hear that?"

Music. The strains of a jig drifted up from below. Ross looked over the rail.

"Care to dance?" He held out his arm.

A full-on ceilidh had burst into life in the cellar of an Irish bar just a stone's throw away.

"Like this?" She looked down, bemused.

"You don't need shoes if you can really dance." He challenged.

Those gathered in the bar barely raised an eyebrow at the glamorous red-head in the evening dress, dancing barefoot with the handsome man in a dinner jacket. Soon they were clapping and swaying, swirling and smiling.

Taking her by the waist, Ross pulled her close twirling her round and round, her eyes shining as she laughed. The pair could certainly dance, anyone watching might even have thought they were a couple, more than just neighbours anyway.

Ross was pleased her smile was back, only temporarily he knew but the sadness had eased and Mia was having fun, good old fashioned fun. How long it would last, well, who could say?

SCARE TACTICS

Mia had been awake through the night, and little wonder. The awards ceremony, followed by Central Park and then wild Irish dancing till late, meant she spent the whole night tossing and turning, too disturbed for sleep. She greeted the hazy New York morning with bleary eyes and a blinding headache.

Her escort was not helping. Although Ross had been pleasant and courteous throughout the trip she could sense a bristling tension; he was on his cell phone when she arrived in the lobby of the hotel that morning. The charming companion of last night, unrecognisable as he paced the floor.

"Runner up is good, it's an international award after all." He listened. "No, too soon, anyway might not sell at all." He listened again. "No way. Strictly business." A tight laugh. "Someone's coming to assess things, may not be as bad as we think." He rubbed between his brows. "I *am* doing my best, just tell them leave me to it, eh?" He finished the call as the limousine drew up, barely acknowledging her, he looked so preoccupied.

"How did the family meeting go?" she asked, as they drove out of the city *en route* to Kennedy airport.

"We met at the school before breakfast." He looked very tired.

"And?"

"I'm sure it'll be fine," he said, unconvincingly, pulling his shades down over his eyes.

They hardly said a couple of sentences throughout the whole journey, Ross had been so engrossed in the contents of his briefcase it was a relief to find Driscoll waiting in the VIP area of Dublin airport; if they appeared strained, their ebullient driver failed to notice, yattering inanely all the way from the capital to Wexford.

Leela was sitting in the sunshine on the bench facing the sea, magazine in one hand, glass of wine in the other. The green-eyed cat was curled up on her lap, she had her stockings rolled into her slippers, daisies still in her ears; a welcome sight.

"There you are," Leela exclaimed. "God help you, flung over and back from America in a flash, you must be jaded tired."

Mia kicked off her loafers, breathing in the soft sea air. "I bet you're tired too. Anyone here?"

The driveway was empty as Driscoll pulled up, Ross having been dropped at the hotel for an urgent meeting. Fair enough, she thought, she had completed her side of the arrangement, job done. Time to get her own house in order, literally.

"All gone." Leela gave a sad smile, dazzling teeth barely visible. "Bernice is staying with Humphrey, planning a holiday, I believe. She's quite buoyed up by it, tough old time for her with Archie ill for so long, do them both good." She looked away at the mention of Archie, as if imagining him striding up from the summerhouse, hair awry, grinning mischievously. "Your mother and Trixie flew back to England yesterday, Fenella's filming next month, she could do with a rest too." She handed Mia the glass, who promptly drained it. "What can I get you?"

"I'd love one of your picnics, I'll make the coleslaw and we could open another bottle of wine, just like the old days?"

Leela blew her nose. "Lovely idea, a nice lunch together before I go."

"Go?"

"I'm having a break myself. You know, with my inheritance and all."

Archie had left Leela a few thousand euro and a provision that Galty House was her home for as long as it remained in the family. "Myself and my sister are going to Torremolinos. You know sun, sea and sangria ... not sure about the sex though," she laughed.

"Oh," Mia said.

The green-eyed cat jumped from Leela's lap, stretched and strolled off; it probably felt like a holiday too.

The following morning Mia awoke completely alone. In all her years there had always been someone else in residence: it had always been a busy, happy house. Now they had all left, one way or another. She wandered through the upstairs rooms; Fenella and Archie's adjoining suites, his extravagant bathroom, Bernice's neat bedroom with balcony looking out to sea, the four guest rooms – only one fit for guests these days, the others damp and in desperate need of renovation.

She took the back stairs, from her room on the top floor to the landing, all eyes – the formidable Fitzgerald portraits – following as she walked. She stopped to look out across the garden to the beach. The weather was turning, blue-black clouds hovered in the distance. She zipped her fleece, drawing the curtains against the draught.

Collecting a pile of post from the hall, she headed to the kitchen. Sitting at the table she trawled through bills for Archie, brochures for Bernice, cards of condolence and a letter for her, stamped with the name of Eamon's practice. She opened it.

Without prejudice – Ref: Last Will and Testament of Aloysius Fermoy Fitzgerald late of Galty House, Rosshaven, County

Wexford, Ireland.

Dear Miss Flanagan

We hereby give notice, in relation to the above, that everything contained therein, all monies, estates, properties and possessions have been formally registered as Contested. All bequests, inheritances and other legacies are herewith suspended and any that have been removed are to be returned forthwith to be held under probate by the State while investigation into the contest is undertaken and until the outcome of the contest is resolved.

The Contest of the Will is in the name of Miss Bernice Mary Fitzgerald, the late Mr Fitzgerald's sister and only living relative, in relation to Undue Influence; showing there was coercion, manipulation, deception or intimidation by another party to put pressure upon the person making the Will to influence its content to their advantage at the time the Will was made (Succession Act 1965).

You and all other persons present are to quit the property, namely Galty House and all other properties within the estate perimeter upon receipt of this letter. Under no circumstances are any contents, fixtures or fittings to be removed from any property/building/outbuilding on the estate.

Please contact this office with a forwarding address. You and any other interested parties will be informed of the results of the investigation in due course.

Yours faithfully

Messrs. Degan, Daly & Partners

She re-read it. It couldn't be true; Bernice would never do such a thing. Mia tried to recall at what stage Eamon had left, after the will reading. It was definitely before Bernice announced her engagement to Humphrey. She wondered if Eamon even knew his cousin and his arch-enemy were now betrothed. Surely this was a try-on, Archie's will was watertight.

Mia put the letter back in the envelope and took her coffee outside. Eamon no doubt was hoping the correspondence would scare her off, and being the good girl she always had been, she would just disappear, conceding that Archie, fueled with wine and awash with sentimentality had agreed to sign the whole estate over to Fenella's poor, fatherless child. With a scorch of anger burning her chest, she stomped across the lawn and back into the kitchen, slamming the door.

"Well, you can't intimidate me!" she announced, letting the cat in and closing the window. "No way! This is my house, Archie left it to me. It'll be over another dead body if they try to take it."

She swigged her coffee back. A loud banging on the door made her jump. "The bastards," she cried. "They're here already!"

Storming out to the hall, Mia grabbed the stick with the fox's head and threw open the door. Pearl stood there, face wet with tears. Mia dropped the stick and fell to her knees.

"They've … they've decided …" Pearl stuttered. "I've to go back … they're making me go."

Mia wrapped the child in her arms. "Now, now. Come and tell me all about it." Mia looked left and right, hoping Ross had brought her, so they could talk things through. "Did you get a lift?"

"No, I ran … all the way." Pearl was panting heavily. "They're sending a giant to kidnap me, I heard them talking about it, I had to come here, where it's safe." She turned huge eyes on Mia, who quickly turned the key in the door and bolted it for good measure, cursing the fact one of the gates was off its hinges at the entrance; she must make a list of repairs.

After milk and emergency fruitcake, Pearl had calmed a little.

"I'll ring Ross and see what the plan is, you could have it all wrong, especially if you've been listening in on conversations again, you know that's never a good thing," Mia told her guest.

"Caroline's leaving at the end of the month," Pearl said between mouthfuls of cake. "And Ross has been in meetings with lots of men, school governors over from the States, I heard him shouting this morning, saying lessons should have been learnt."

She swallowed. "And then he said, it's only a matter of time before the bell tolled and the game was over."

Mia scratched her head. Pearl could have overheard anything. A management meeting, Ross laying down the law to his team, Caroline leaving might be totally unconnected.

"I'll speak to him," Mia stood.

"Please don't!" Pearl cried, tears bubbling again. She was white as a sheet and had not let go of her schoolbag since she arrived. Mia knew what was in it, she had an idea.

"Tell you what, why don't we go over to Mary Magdalene and see if we can hand your project in?" she suggested, trying to distract her.

"It's not ready yet." Pearl was anxious to keep hold of her connection to the school no matter how tenuous.

"Let's find someone to discuss it with, maybe help you finish it? We can check when term starts at the same time, so we know what to talk through with Ross." Mia was clutching at straws, someone at the school might know whether Pearl was scheduled to attend come September.

Mia knew she was interfering, but the child had thrown herself on her mercy and if someone had not fought her corner all those years ago, she too would have been flung from pillar to post. Of course, she had been bullied at first, new kids with strange accents usually are, especially if the whisper of scandal comes with them but it had been *her* school, *her* choice and anyway Leela put spells on all the bullies, which of course had worked a treat at the time.

"Shocked I'm still here, young Flanagan?" The old nun lifted her glasses; poor thing, still masses of that awful red, crinkly hair. At least the coif she wore under her wimple hid what remained of her ginger mop.

"I am a bit Sister, didn't think you'd stay in the business."

Where was all this honesty coming from? Mia wondered.

Sister Agnes laughed, a deep husky sound Mia remembered well. "I don't have a problem with God, it's the guys running the administration I could do without. Besides who's going to give me a job at my time of life? Or a home? No, I'm happy to stay here and cause as much mayhem as I can opening minds ... what's not to like?" Mia gave the nun a grin, she did that alright. "I hope you've taken this delightful young lady under your wing?" She indicated Pearl, piously studying a painting of the Sacred Heart.

"Oh, she has, Sister, I'm not afraid of water or anything these days," Pearl confirmed.

"Thinks I'm a mermaid," Mia stage-whispered.

"Of course she does, isn't imagination a great thing altogether, I often thought you clamped yours down, held yourself back, on quite a few fronts."

"Really?"

Sister Agnes had never pulled her punches.

The nun nodded.

"Think big, stretch the old grey matter. Isn't that the way, Pearl?" Pearl gave the nun a beguiling smile. Mia could see she was besotted. Understandably, Agnes had an aura about her, she glowed positivity. She had always loved to turn everything upside down, making you think and rethink every single idea you ever conceived. She was so bad she was brilliant and she had frightened Mia. Correction … she had made Mia frighten herself.

"I'm sorry I couldn't make the funeral, I'm only back from holiday myself. I heard it went well, everything okay with you?" She peered at Mia over her glasses.

Mia nodded.

Sister Agnes and Archie had always been matey, a shared love of music and sport, they both liked a bit of controversy too, especially if they had instigated it.

"Well, what can I do for you?" the nun asked.

"It's about my project," Pearl explained. "It's not quite finished and I don't want to hand it in until it is, but Mia thinks you'll remember stuff."

"Give it a go," said the nun, folding her arms.

"I found this." She produced the plastic bag containing the turquoise and silver beads she had found in the well. Mia saw the nun's eyes narrow. "Could you date it?"

"Hmm, where did you find it?"

"On the island. Is it old?" Pearl was hopeful.

"Old enough, I guess. But not antique, love beads I think they called them."

Pearl was disappointed there was not a more intriguing

explanation, she changed tack. "Mia says priests were trained as spies on the island, is that true?"

"Yes, during the Second World War, a scheme set up by the Irish Army in partnership with British Intelligence. Priests were good candidates for the job; they could travel freely throughout Europe you see, serving the church as opposed to any particular government. But the beads aren't from that time, there are very few records from then."

"No movies or pictures?" Pearl was disbelieving.

"Intelligence *has* to be secret by its very nature," Sister Agnes told her.

"Can I study history if I come to school here, Sister?" Pearl almost pleaded.

"Of course, I'm hoping you *are* coming, your name is down," Sister Agnes said, warmly.

"Is there anything to give me a head start, like if Uncle Ross asked did I know anything new having been to see you, is there anything?" Pearl was determined, manipulative too it seemed.

Sister Agnes tapped her pen against her chin. "Let me see … well, I believe there was a Nazi plot to kidnap the Holy Father, Pope Pius the Twelfth. The plan was for troops to occupy the Vatican City and steal all its treasures. Hitler considered the Holy City a nest of spies, a centre for propaganda. One of the priests from the island was definitely involved in spoiling that little plan but he was betrayed and they caught him." Pearl was staring at the nun transfixed; spies and treasures, two of her favourite words. She glanced at Mia; she just *had* to go to school there.

"Did he survive?" Mia did not remember this story.

"He did, thank God. They tortured him and left him for dead but an English army doctor, also a prisoner, managed to save him and he made it home."

"Here?"

"Yep, home to the Seahorse Hotel. Never the same though, poor man."

"What about my necklace, do you think he brought it from the Vatican City?" Pearl pressed.

"No, Pearl. It's far too modern." The nun confirmed.

"Weren't they fashionable around the time the seminary closed?" Mia recalled photographs, young men lined up in the sunshine, her elderly Head Mistress declaring the world's finest priests had been trained close by, before being sent out to the missions. "I'm sure I've seen pictures."

"Before my time." Sister Agnes shrugged. "Well, if there isn't anything else, I'm in charge of the Children of Mary class tonight." She rose and swished towards the door.

"One more question sister, the guy with his chest open, Jesus, right?" Pearl said, pointing at the picture she had been studying earlier. "What's that all about?"

"Showing he died for us, giving us all eternal life." Sister Agnes was keen for them to leave now.

"Ross always says you shouldn't wear your heart on your sleeve, that's how you get hurt. I guess outside your chest counts too."

"Wise words," Sister Agnes agreed. "Jesus got hurt. Tortured and crucified. Ross talks a lot of sense. Sometimes it's worth it though, I'm hoping Jesus thought it was."

Mia guided Pearl to the door. "Thanks Sister, you've been a great help."

At last the nun smiled. "Glad to be of service."

Mia was anxious to leave too; something was beginning to niggle. Sister Agnes seemed far from keen to acknowledge the seminary's final era, as if that bit of the island's history held little glory in the retelling. She was wondering why, sure she had seen pictures of those heady days of love beads and beach parties. And if she had they would still be around, no one ever threw anything away in Galty House. Maybe she was the one who could help solve Pearl's mystery, answer a few of these fathomless, unanswered questions. Who knew what she might discover? Who indeed.

NOT ON THE GUEST LIST

Pearl was in a better frame of mind when Mia dropped her back at the hotel, amusing herself by repeating Sister Agnes's story over and over throughout the journey.

"Ross will be impressed, he didn't learn anything about treasure and the Pope being kidnapped in his boring old business school."

"I bet he didn't," Mia agreed, pulling up to the entrance.

Pearl opened the car door. "Is there a safe in Galty House?"

Mia thought for a moment. There was, Archie had one installed when he won the Oscar, although Oscar had always resided on Archie's bathroom shelf, where he could see him.

"Why?" Mia wondered what was coming.

"Can you put my project there, please?"

"Aren't there safety deposit boxes in the hotel?"

"Things seem to be breaking down a lot, what if I couldn't get it open again?" She handed her folder over. "I can trust you?"

Mia nodded gravely. Now she was going to have to locate the safe and if she could open it, heaven knows what she might find.

Ross was sealing off the elevators. He was wearing an old shirt, sleeves rolled up, jeans and trucker boots. One of the subterranean suites had sprung a leak, structural engineers were working frantically to remedy the problem but it was getting worse, Ross was beginning to despair.

"Hey!" He lifted Pearl into his arms, twirling her round. "I was about to send out a search party."

"I was at an appointment." Pearl replied, her mother's usual excuse for being AWOL.

"With whom?" He scowled.

"Personal."

Another of her mother's favourites.

"Ross!"

They looked up as Christie Power strode into reception.

"Uncle Christie! I didn't know you'd be back so soon?"

Ross quickly placed Pearl back on *terra firma*.

"Surprise visit, figured you needed a hand. Brought a few of the guys with me, see if we can help?" Three men in sharp suits appeared behind him.

Great, Ross thought, *the heavy mob.*

"You've made a report?" Christie asked, smiling at Pearl who was wearing a typical Ross scowl.

"Just about to," Ross confirmed.

"Okay, we'll check in, grab some lunch and meet you in the boardroom, say about two o'clock?" Staff magically appeared. "Now, young lady, how about you wash up and come join your old uncle for lunch? I need your take on the place, what are the facilities like for someone your age?"

"Do I get ice cream?" Pearl was no pushover.

"Of course," Christie laughed.

"Extra chocolate sauce?"

"We'll have to see about that." Christie was no pushover either.

Ross turned towards his office, reception seemed suddenly full of people.

"Mia Flanagan? Lives nearby, silly of me, lost the exact address." Cut-glass English accent, tall good-looking guy, perfectly turned out in retro tweed and a too new Barbour. Ross swung back, crossing the marble floor, hand extended.

"Good afternoon sir, checking in?"

"Not quite sure, flying visit and all that." The man gave Ross a disparaging look.

"I'm Ross Power, CEO, a hands on role today." Ross replied warmly, indicating his attire.

"Then you'll definitely know who I mean, I'm looking for Mia Flanagan, staying close by, Archie Fitzgerald's place, I believe?"

Ross considered him; high cheekbones, aquiline nose; an actor, he had to be. He felt his stomach twist.

"Friend of hers?" he asked, loathing his accent; he sounded like a cowboy.

"My fiancée, actually." The man gave a slight smile. "I'm Rupert Boniver, you may have heard of me." He handed Ross a card, mainly a photograph of himself, looking fabulous.

"Can't say I have." Ross handed him one of his own business cards. "That's me. Is Miss Flanagan expecting you?" For some reason Ross was defensive.

"Surprise visit." Rupert put a finger to his lips. "Strictly on the QT."

"I bet," Ross said, walking away. "Can someone look after this gentleman please?"

Mia looked everywhere but could not find the safe. Was it in an outbuilding? The summerhouse maybe, the old stables? She remembered it was made of metal, must have weighed a tonne … she was just about to give up, when she noticed the cellar door slightly ajar.

Pushing it open, she scrabbled for the light switch, waiting for her eyes to adjust before tackling steep steps leading down. It smelled musty and damp. *Another thing for my list*, she thought, focusing on the practical and not how much this place used to scare her.

A flickering strip light barely illuminated the shadowy space but she could see it was a total tip, piled high with battered boxes and broken furniture. Pools of water gathered in corners and the walls were covered in slime. Dismayed Mia was about to retreat when she noticed a large cupboard. She walked towards it, feet squelching and there half-hidden behind stacks of newspaper was the safe, a neat oblong of solid steel.

Crouched in front of the cabinet, black with a gold plate bearing the manufacturer's name, Mia saw a combination lock and two keyholes, one top, one bottom. She tried the handle, locked. She tried again. Waste of time. She looked around, she really did not like it here.

What was that? A rustle. Rats? She hated rats … time to go.

Starting for the steps, something shifted close by. She tried not to look. Something definitely moved again. She squawked and running for the stairs slipped and cracked her knee. She grabbed the handrail, climbing as fast as she could, trying not to fall. Nearly there, nearly at the top. She was sure she had left the door open but the door was closed and a tall dark figure stood in front of it.

Her heart leapt to her mouth.

"There you are, darling." The eloquent voice. He grinned down at her, eyes piercing the gloom.

Her skin prickled.

Something ran up the steps behind her; furry, damp, brushing her leg. She screamed and pushed past him, flying through the door into the hall, collapsing on the floor.

"*Jesus*, Rupert you scared me half to death!" she clutched her chest. "What the hell do you think you're playing at!?"

Rupert stood, glaring down at her.

"I might well ask you the same fucking question," he replied.

Something splashed her leg. She jumped. It was the cat, shaking water from its paws, water from the cellar.

"You should have called." Mia handed Rupert a mug. He was at the window, looking out across the garden, down to the beach.

"Nice spot," he said. "And you've inherited all this?"

"It's complicated."

"But it *is* yours." He strode the length of the kitchen, looking at pictures, eyeing the silver, lifting crystal off shelves.

"Do you mind!" She took a Georgian ladle from him.

"Just curious," he shrugged. "Well, you have fallen on your feet haven't you? From barely able to afford to live, to this. Nice one. Who was the old guy? I mean I know who he was, but what was he to you? Your father?"

"None of your business." She was uncomfortable.

"That's what everyone's saying."

"Everyone?"

"In the business. Saying they always thought it was the case but now he's left everything to you, proves the point." He had abandoned his coffee.

"Actually, Rupert, someone very close to me has just died, it's not just some old guy who's left me stuff." She was cross now. "What do you want anyway?"

He raised an eyebrow. This was a new Mia. He had not seen this one before; the meek-mannered, 'grateful for everything' girl he knew seemed to have disappeared. He quite liked this new feisty one; she would be good in bed. He opened the fridge, pulled out a bottle of wine and poured himself a drink.

"Help yourself, why don't you?" Mia said, putting the bottle back. "Look, I don't know why you're here. But I'm tired, so finish your wine and go, okay?"

"I came to be with my girl. Find out why she abandoned me,

why she locked me out of my apartment, threw all my worldly goods away and pissed off leaving me with absolutely, fucking nothing. That's why I'm here, you stupid bitch." He smiled at her over his glass. Mia opened the door.

"Go. I've heard enough."

"Really? Well, think again." Rupert drained his glass. "You owe me. You made a right fool of me, carrying on like some wounded Victorian virgin left at the altar. You knew where you stood, we both did. Free agents, no commitments. What's the big deal?"

"The big deal is I came home, and you were in bed with another woman."

"So?" Rupert lifted his eyebrows.

"What do you mean *so*, with another woman, in *my* bed … so?" She was not going to be riled, it was over but she could feel the heat rising from her throat.

"You totally overreacted. No reason to change the locks, throw my stuff away. What were you thinking? I'd no money, nowhere to stay, didn't even have a change of underwear for fuck's sake."

He was angry with *her*. She could not believe it.

"Rupert, we were engaged!"

"Mia, we were *not*!"

It was as if she had been slapped. She clung to the table to steady herself.

"But … you proposed, made the rings, we talked about our wedding in Tuscany?"

"Oh, *please*. Pissed-up on location, yeah of course. Grow up, Mia for God's sake." He went back to the fridge. She stood in front of it.

"I want you to go, now." She folded her arms.

"Not until you give me what you owe me, including

compensation. I know I didn't get that part because your stupid mother told the director she wouldn't work with me. You owe me big time. And now you have plenty." He indicated the house. "Well, you can put some of it my way."

"No chance." She eyeballed him, brazening it out, her heart was thumping. This was lunacy. She was alone in the house with her crazy ex-boyfriend and she was frightened. If she called for help, no one would hear her. No one would come. Her brain went into overdrive.

"Look, Rupert, I get where you're coming from but if we're going to sort something out it needs doing properly. A formal arrangement, binding, that kind of thing." She kept talking, she needed time to think, get this madman out of her house and out of her life, once and for all.

Rupert gave her a slow smile. "That's more like it, I knew you'd see sense."

She went to the sink, filled a glass with water and drank.

"It's just a bit of a shock seeing you here with all that's been going on. I need some air, do you mind?" She went to the door.

"No, not at all, a walk on the beach, good idea. We can talk things through, I can tell you how much you need to transfer from your bank account into mine." His eyes had softened a little, the way they did when he knew he was getting his own way.

As they went through the door into the garden, Mia quickly slid the key from the ledge and locked it, running to catch up with Rupert. She was not going to let him back in under any circumstances.

"All this," he kept saying. "You own all this."

Mia kept her eyes fixed ahead, the beach was grey, the sea flat.

"I don't need to stay at that expensive hotel then." Rupert

stood looking back at Galty House. "Plenty of room here, bet you have a nice big double bed too, don't you, lovely girl."

Mia pushed her hands into her pockets, desperate to hide the fact that she was trembling and scared; very scared indeed.

CHAMPIONS AWAIT

Ross was not sure why he felt the urgent need to go to Galty House but something was bothering him. Rupert Boniver was bothering him, probably none of his business but he would call by just in case.

The hire car was in the drive and the hall door was ajar. Ross called out. No response. Closing the door he went quickly through the gate to the garden. No one there. Jogging along the path he checked the summerhouse. Deserted.

At the top of the steps, he stopped. Mia was on the beach with the English guy, they were in a clinch. He had his arms around her, mouth at her throat. Ross turned away.

If he had arrived minutes earlier he might have overheard the conversation.

"So how much did you get? This lot must be worth an absolute bloody fortune." Rupert had been standing at the water's edge looking back at the house.

"Like I said, it's complicated. Nothing settled yet."

"Well, when you find a calculator big enough to add it all up, I'd be very interested, very interested indeed." Rupert's barely disguised greed made her nauseous. "You know, Mia, I'm really sorry things didn't work out between us. A stupid misunderstanding, that's all it was, you got the wrong end of the stick and now look at us." He raised his hands despairingly.

"It was a bit more than that," she told him.

"It wasn't." He stood beside her. "It was a mistake, it meant nothing and you chose to call it a day, no discussion, explanation. Not even a hint of a second chance." He gave her a soulful look. "And that's what hurts the most, Mia, you just threw what we had away."

Here we go, she thought. Mia had lived around actors all her life, she knew when they were turning it on.

"What we had was special." He took her fingers in his hands. "I've been out of my mind since you left. You never returned my calls, anything could have happened to you."

"I lost my phone."

"A second chance, surely I'm worth that, we're worth that?" He tilted her chin upwards, brushing her mouth with his lips. She stepped away. He placed his hand in the small of her back, drawing her to him.

"Rupert ... I ..."

"Don't, my darling, don't say another word. I've missed you so much, want you so much." His mouth was at her throat.

"Stop!" she cried, pushing him away.

"Not playing hard to get are you?"

He lunged at her, wrapping his arms around her, holding her tight.

"You know how that turns me on."

He pushed his tongue into her ear, nipped at her lobe. She struggled. He was hurting her. She struggled again. He was holding her so tightly, her arm was about to break.

Mia did not see where the punch came from. She just saw a fist fly through the air and land Rupert an almighty crack on the jaw. He released her. She watched wide eyed as he staggered backwards, while Ross pushed her to one side and in the same movement flung another jab at Rupert's perfect nose. It spliced. Blood spurted everywhere. Rupert gave an almighty yelp as almost in slow motion he fell into the cold, dark sea. He yelped again as he hit the water and a gentle wave washed over him and his nice new clothes.

"Now." Ross was calm. "Get up and get out."

Rupert pulled himself up and stood there swaying.

"You've broken my fucking nose," he spluttered, his now not so handsome face covered in blood and sand.

"Get out before I break your fucking neck." Ross did a perfect imitation of Rupert's accent.

"You'd better go, Rupert," Mia said, her voice trembling.

"You fucking bitch!" Rupert snarled, lurching towards her.

Ross moved swiftly to stand between them, his arms folded.

Rupert tried another lunge at Mia. Ross slapped his hands away. Rupert tried again, gagging on blood from his nose. Ross pushed him away, spinning him round.

"Now go! Get out of here, I won't tell you again."

"You've not heard the last of this," Rupert tried.

"GO!" Ross roared.

Rupert started to walk away. He turned back.

"I'll have you for this, this is grievous bodily harm." He wagged a bloodied finger. "You see if I don't, you bastard."

"Yeah, and I'll have you for breaking and entering *and* attempted rape, you see if I don't," Ross called back, watching until Rupert staggered out of sight. Finally he turned to Mia. "You okay?"

She looked totally drained but weirdly was about to laugh.

"What?" He was trying not to smile. "What's so funny?" He rubbed his throbbing hand.

"That sounded like Dick Van Dyke."

"What's wrong with that?" Ross asked. "Your American accent's hardly authentic."

"You've never heard my American accent." She laughed.

"I don't have to." He was grinning at her.

"Well, excuse me for interrupting all this beach buddiness," boomed a craggy voice. "But I haven't got all day, Irish dancing on Thursday, you should know that."

It was Sister Agnes, incongruous in slacks and her favourite *Fleadh Cheoil* festival sweatshirt.

Minutes later they were standing in the hall at Galty House.

Sister Agnes had refused a glass of whiskey, she was clearly on a mission.

"Much as I'd love to, I can't stay but something you said the other day, Maeve, has been bothering me."

"*Maeve?*" Ross mouthed, pulling a face, she tried to ignore him.

Sister Agnes dragged her saddlebag off her shoulder.

"I kept thinking about those love beads, the sort the girls used to make in Arts and Crafts, before fecking computers sucked all the creativity out of the place. Anyway, I remembered the photos. And I remembered who had them."

Mia was intrigued. "Who?"

"Archie and Humphrey. They stole them, actually. But I've a soft spot for Humphrey and Archie's family, so I said nothing. When Sister Simeon died sure, no one cared about the seminary, been closed for over thirty years." She pulled a bunch of keys from her bag, handing them to Mia. "And then I remembered these, I haven't a clue what they open, but Archie gave them to me around the time you were born, well, at your baptism actually …"

Mia stopped her. "I'm sorry?"

"That's right, my Auntie Noleen – Mrs Fitzgerald – and Archie had you baptised … in secret. That's when he gave me the keys."

Mia collapsed onto the settle.

"Baptised in *secret,* are you serious? What's that all about?"

"It had to be a secret. We all know how your mother feels

about anything to do with the church," Sister Agnes said. "And Auntie Noleen was determined you had the same rights as any child under her roof, she wasn't a great believer herself but thought a bit of help from whatever's out there wouldn't do you any harm."

"But what did Archie say, Sister, when he gave you the keys?" Ross was fascinated.

The nun scratched under her beret.

"That's the very thing kept me up all night. Could I remember? I knew the keys were with all the others, thank goodness Sister Sarah is so organised, she writes a label and attaches it to the key ring." The nun passed a piece of crumpled paper to Mia. In faded ink it read *The Seahorse Hotel*. "And then I remembered. He said, 'if my goddaughter ever wants to know, give her the keys, the keys to The Seahorse Hotel.'"

Ross stared at Mia, clutching the note.

"Archie was my godfather?" She had tears in her eyes.

"Of course. He couldn't tell you, Fenella would have lynched him. Maybe even taken you away. We couldn't have that, no way." She bent to caress Mia's cheek. "You meant the world to us, all of us." She looked up at the portraits, giving them a wink. "Now, I must away, the champions of the future await."

And pulling her bag onto her shoulder she ran down the steps to her bicycle. She stopped to look back at the couple at the door.

"Good performance down there, young man," she grinned at Ross. "Haven't seen the like of that in many a year." She gave a quick one-two, punching the air. "Love a bit of prize-fighting myself, always have." And with that, she pushed off along the gravel at a rate of knots.

"I can't stay either," Ross frowned. "The heavy mob are over from the States, I've stuff to do." He was striding towards the

Daimler, parked skew-whiff on the drive. She liked the fact he was driving it, Archie would be pleased.

"Ross, I owe you," she called out to him.

"No way, that guy's a shmuck, you're well out of that." He jumped in. "And another thing … you need to get a grip on security. Doors open, no locks on the windows, jeez, you don't even have gates up here." He pointed at the crumbling entrance.

"You're right, must do something about that." She looked down at the massive bunch of keys in her hand. Somebody must have been security conscious once upon a time. Ross left a trail of dust as he blasted away.

As Mia closed the door she was smiling. Despite a most unpleasant episode with her very ex-fiancé, she felt good. Sister Agnes's visit was a revelation and Ross Power was turning into not only a good neighbour but a true friend. Things were looking up.

Standing alone in the hall, she cast about. She had never been scared in Galty House. She had been anxious, worried and frightened half to death in lots of other places but never here. Despite its size and decrepitude, Galty was home. She glanced up at the dozens of pairs of eyes staring back down at her.

"And you lot can look sharp," she told them. "There are going to be some changes around here, make no mistake!"

First plan of attack, the silence. One of the keys fitted the grandfather clock. She opened the casement, set the correct time and wound it up, relishing the deep, soft tick.

Next, armed with a can of WD40, she started trying all the locks, following Sister Sarah's example of labelling keys, so she knew which fitted where. Mia was good at inventories, she liked things ordered.

She had been putting off going back to the cellar until she was sure no one could surprise her again. With all the external doors locked, she decided to take a torch, a deep breath and descend the steps. There were still half a dozen keys that did not fit any of the locks she tried, but two small ones looked favourite for the safe.

Bingo. They worked.

Now the combination. A four digit code. She tried the year Archie was born. No go. The year Fenella was born, stupid, Fenella was not a Fitzgerald. Bernice? She could not remember how old Bernice was. She tried her own birthday. The safe door popped open as if it had been sealed only the day before.

She swallowed, in two minds whether to lock it again; keep whatever was in there a secret. Curiosity won, she shone the flashlight into the dark recess. Well, what a surprise! She started to laugh, her laughter echoing off the dark, dank walls.

The safe held a secret alright, a neat wine rack packed tightly with bottles. She eased one out, the label read *Vosne-Romanée, Cros-Parantoux Henri Jayer,* 2001. Mia had no idea about fine wine, but Archie did and as these were under lock and key, she surmised this collection was probably very fine indeed. She made a note of the name and placing the bottle back very gently, labelled the keys and locked the safe.

Archie's room was organised chaos. On the rare occasions dusting was on Leela's schedule, she just went round everything, so Archie's room had hardly changed in all the years Mia could remember. She pushed open the door, half-expecting to see her mother, poring over his vinyl, searching for something suitable for him to wear or stretched out on the chaise longue, gazing out to Phoenix Island re-imagining their lost youth. Well, that's what Archie used to say.

Pushing the melancholy in her heart to one side, she set about her task, trying doors and drawers but none were locked, such was Archie's way, he always shared everything. She came to his desk, which belied the rest of the room. It was pristine, computer screens and keyboard just so, paperwork in folders, files neatly stacked. She opened a large drawer; a document case held insurance certificates, his passport. There was another file, it looked new, which was odd, Archie loved to recycle. She opened it.

The title on the first page read,

Harbour Spa Hotel – Phase II.

She frowned, turning to the next page.

'*Introduction:*

Five star plus requires a number of essential facilities. The only facility the Harbour Spa Hotel is without is a golf course.

Proposal:

The adjacent property Galty House and estate, a total of 250 acres is ideally located for redevelopment, creating a nine-hole links golf course. This proposal outlines the redevelopment plans, including the purchase and demolition of said property.'

As Mia lifted the document out a piece of paper fluttered to the floor. It was a photocopy of a handwritten note, it read.

'*I can now confirm the property has been willed to my client and once we are in receipt of the deposit, following valuation, the sale will proceed immediately after the demise of the current owner. By making the usual arrangements, unconditional planning permission will be granted for the redevelopment at the next appropriate planning meeting. I can also guarantee any other waivers or rights to the property will be declared null and void by the planning officer.'*

The words blurred before her. She scanned the page, no addressee, no signature. It was as if the note had been hidden in the report, passed discreetly to whoever was reading it. A done deal. The fate of Galty House sealed before Archie had even died.

Mia sifted through the file, dates of meetings, phone calls, memos, agendas. Archie had it all, all the evidence he needed. The local mayor, the planning committee, architects and builders, everyone who could have queried any element of the project was on the payroll, the payroll of a paymaster with a vested interest – The Power Corporation.

She sank slowly to the floor, clutching the file to her chest, her head spinning. What with this and the letter from Eamon demanding she vacate Galty House immediately so a legal wrangle could take place to rob her of her inheritance … she was beginning to feel very uneasy indeed. She started re-reading the paperwork slowly. No wonder the 'heavy mob' was over from the States. No wonder Ross Power was being nice to her, buttering her up.

Well, the plan was coming unstuck. The plan to demolish Galty House, build a golf course and wipe away everything that meant anything to her had hit a glitch. A great big scary glitch called Mia Flanagan.

BOARDOOM GAMES

The door burst open. Ross looked up. His expression filtered a myriad of emotions; surprise, delight, concern and sensing the ball of fury inside her, fear.

"You bastard!" she spat. "You two-faced, yellow-bellied bastard!"

The room became still. The men gathered around the boardroom table stopped talking.

"Mia, I …" He stood. "You just can't …"

"I *can* just." She walked towards him, eyes blazing, copper curls bouncing angrily as she stomped. She slapped the file down where he had been sitting, upending his coffee cup. The man beside him started mopping it up.

"Leave it," he said, barely audibly.

"You lied to me. You've been after Galty House all along. You need it, this place can't survive without it, you have to have a golf course and it's the only place you can build one. You've been trying to lull me into a false sense of security, hoping I'll sell, give up my inheritance so you can make even *more* profit. You greedy, self-serving bastard." She drew breath.

"It's not like that," he spoke sharply. No cajoling, no apology. "Now, if you don't mind, this is an important meeting. If we need to discuss anything I suggest you call my assistant and make an appointment. Good day, Miss Flanagan."

"Don't you 'good day Miss Flanagan' me," she snapped back, pointing at the file on the table, papers splayed out. "There's the evidence, emails, records of phone conversations, bribes."

He was staring at her now. A man at the far end of the room

coughed gently.

"Miss Flanagan, you seem a little overwrought. Maybe some tea in the outer office, a little time to gather your thoughts?" He came towards her. It was Christie Power, Ross's uncle, the global chairman of the hotel group. It *was* an important meeting.

"I don't need to gather my thoughts," she told him. "I've gathered my evidence and I'm taking it to the police. I just wanted to warn Mr Power here to back off. Leave me and my property alone." She glared at Ross.

He glowered back, then flicked a switch on the desk. "Security to the boardroom, security immediately please."

Mia was astounded, had he really just sent for security?

"Ross, surely ..." Christie Power began.

Ross raised a hand. "I'm in charge here."

The door crashed open and Joey Doyle's vast bulk filled the space. He scanned the room. If there was trouble here, he was hard pressed to find it.

His face sank with disappointment, it was the first time he had been called to action, he knew the big wigs were over from New York and he wanted to make a good impression.

He noticed Mia Flanagan standing in the midst of the suits. They had made their Holy Communion together, she looked gorgeous as ever, flowing copper hair, bright shiny eyes, she had never changed.

"Howaya, Mia?" he smiled, sheepishly.

"Joseph, please escort Miss Flanagan off the premises," Ross barked. Joey's smile froze. Surely they were only testing to see how long it would take him to get to the boardroom once the alarm went off. "Right now."

"Are you serious?" Joey doubted Ross was joking, Ross never joked.

"Don't worry, I'm going." Mia gathered up her file. "You've

not heard the last of this, Ross Power." Joey followed her to the door.

"Miss Flanagan is barred from these premises," Ross addressed the security man. "Make sure everyone is fully aware of that."

"Yessir," Joey replied. "Come along quietly now, Miss Flanagan."

"Ah feck off, Joey, what do you think I'm going to do, start screaming the place down?" Mia shrugged his hand from her arm. Joey had been one of the bullies, one of the cowardly sliveens who used to hide in the cloakroom and hiss, '*Sss*candal' whenever she walked past. "And you look a right eejit in that uniform, a cross between the Keystone Kops and Napoleon – doesn't even fit you!"

Joey blinked. That stung. The uniform was the best thing about the job.

Mia was storming towards the car park when she heard someone call her name. She kept going. No one in this rotten place could have anything worthwhile to say to her, she had been taken for a mug once too often. She heard steps behind her, someone running to catch up. She quickened her pace.

"Wait!" Mia was rugby tackled from behind. It was Pearl. "I tried calling but no one answered the phone. I should've guessed you'd come to get me, keep the faith, that's what Sister Agnes says."

Mia looked down at the little girl. Pearl was dressed in school uniform, hair in bunches, wheeling a suitcase.

Mia really did not have time for this now. Pearl's childish flights of fancy had no place in her stressed out world of deceitful liars, two-timing bastards and crooks.

"I came up with a plan." Pearl gazed up at her. "To stay with you until my uncle's gone back to the States."

"What? Pearl, you can't stay with me. I'm really busy. Call me next week, we'll talk then." She marched off. Wheels rattled behind her.

"Mia, please wait. I know they've come for me, I heard them talking, Uncle Christie's brought men to take me back. I'm done for." Mia gave Pearl a double take, she had obviously been reading Archie's well-thumbed copies of *Just William*. She knelt in front of the little girl.

"Pearl, listen. I'm sure it'll all turn out okay. If you've to go back to the States you'll just have to take it on the chin and do the best you can. That's what we all have to do." Pearl's lower lip trembled. "Now, I've urgent business, I have to go."

Pearl's eyes filled with tears. That's what her mom always said when she went off and left her, sometimes for days on end.

"Is it urgent mermaid business? I get that if it is. The rooms under the sea are leaking, they've been shut off. I told Ross the sea god was angry, you know, people trying to live in the ocean without the proper cred …cred…"

"Credentials?"

"S'actly. Without being mer-people. Guessing that's what the business is, huh?"

Mia sighed.

"Pearl, I'm not a mermaid. They don't exist and you're old enough to know better." Mia forced herself not to look back at the little girl in her uniform with tears in her eyes. She had enough on her plate.

Driving past the station, she spotted another case-wheeler she recognised; Leela freshly returned from Torremolinos.

"Thank God," Leela's electric smile was even brighter against her tan. "Not a taxi at the rank. Has the Driscoll fella done a bunk? Wouldn't surprise me, never stays anywhere very long, scared his past will catch up with him, if you ask me."

Mia did not answer, eyes fixed on the road.

"Did you have a good time Leela? What was the weather like? How's your sister? Did you get any sex?"

"Sorry?"

"Just talking to myself," Leela replied. "*Jesus,* slow down would you, where's the fire?"

"Brace yourself, I've bad news."

Leela put on her new Dior sunglasses. Bad news? Had Mia taken leave of her senses? There would never be bad news again, Archie was dead; that was all the bad news in the world in one fell swoop.

By the time they had finished Leela's bottle of sangria and opened the Spanish brandy, Mia had told Leela everything, even the gory details of Rupert's visit. They were sitting on the bench looking out to sea.

"I'm not surprised," Leela said, sipping her drink.

"About which bit?"

"All of it. Someone was bound to contest the will. Bernice always said she would if Archie gave her home away but we all knew that would change once Humphrey was back on the scene."

Mia tasted the brandy, winced and put the glass down; she did not need a hangover on top of everything else. "Fenella said they were engaged once. Do you know what happened?"

"Ah, Bernice can have a touch of the green eye," Leela said. Mia raised an eyebrow. "Jealousy. She accused Fenella of having a fling with Humphrey, made his life hell and then dumped him saying she was joining the convent."

That did not surprise Mia, Bernice was always a bit on the

pious side but Fenella and Humphrey? She found that hard to believe. Her mother loved the company of men but as charming as Humphrey was, he was certainly not her type.

"Bernice changed her mind about the convent, but it was too late. Humphrey had married." Leela poured another drink. Mia watched her. If anything, losing Archie had made her even more philosophical. Leela bent and kissed the snout of the green-eyed cat that had nestled on her lap. It was then Mia showed Leela the letter about the will.

"Well, that has Eamon written all over it. Thinks he's clever," Leela announced, having read it. "He was caught drinking and driving one time, actually driving the car with one hand, a bottle of whiskey in the other. Tried to bribe the Garda to let him off with shares in his apartment in Croatia."

"I didn't know he had an apartment in Croatia?" Mia said, surprised. Eamon always pleaded poverty.

"He'd have got away with it if he had. The policeman went out there with his girlfriend, they hadn't even put in the foundations. Came back and dropped Eamon right in it. Served him right." Leela poured another drink.

"And the golf course?"

"Ah, sure I knew that was part of the plan."

"Did you see it in the cards?" Mia had great faith in Leela and the tarot.

"Not at all, there's a great big poster up at the hotel, outlining future facilities – golf course, rifle range, what do they call it now? Country Pursuits centre, sure they'll have to put it somewhere. Galty's obvious but if they can't buy Galty, they'll go the other way, Jimmy Nugent must be nearing retirement and none of the family want to go into farming, he'd be the next choice."

"Oh," Mia said, quietly.

Leela looked at Mia. "You didn't know?"

"There's evidence of backhanders regarding planning, corrupt officials, all that kind of thing." Mia needed more of a reaction to her devastating news.

Leela shrugged.

"Same old, same old. It all comes out in the wash. Sure, Ross Power knows about all the planning shenanigans, Archie told me that, said there were no flies on that young fella. I'm sure he'll deal with it his own way, in his own time, seems a principled type to me. He has enough to worry about, God help him."

"Do you mean the building itself? I believe there are structural problems."

"The whole town knows about that, sure half the population work there. No, I'm talking about Pearl. You know my sister, the teaching assistant up at the Mary Magdalene? She says that child's desperate to go there, even went and bought herself the uniform, hasn't taken it off since."

Mia felt dreadful; she eyed the brandy, maybe it would make her feel better.

"I remember a little girl desperate to belong too. Begging not to be sent back to school in England," Leela said.

"I didn't go and buy myself a uniform though, did I?"

"No, but you went round talking in the broadest Rosshaven accent I ever heard and I've lived here all my life." She squeezed Mia's hand, pain flitting across her eyes as she remembered. "Are you going to get that?" The phone was ringing.

Mia blinked the memories away as she hurried into the house. Leela was packing up behind her, the sky had turned black, storm clouds rolling in.

"Is that Miss Flanagan?" A cultured English voice.

"Yes."

"Caroline Partridge, Pearl's nanny, speaking. Mr Power asked me to call. We were just wondering …" Mia could hear the tension in the woman's voice. "Pearl's not with you, is she?"

"No." Mia waited.

"Have you seen her today?"

"Is there something wrong?" Mia did not want to land Pearl in trouble, best to say as little as possible.

"We can't find her. We thought … hoped she was with you."

"I saw her earlier, had a suitcase with her. A pink one, on wheels." Mia heard the intake of breath. "You're scaring me now." Mia's heart started to race.

"I'm sorry, I'm so worried, there's been the most awful row. Pearl's convinced her uncle's here to take her back to the States, I think she overheard an argument and … and …"

"What?" Mia snapped.

"Ran away."

"Where's Ross?" Mia demanded.

"Gone to look for her, at the school, I think."

"I don't think she'll be there, term's not started yet," Mia told her. "Can you get hold of him?"

"He took his mobile."

"Tell him to meet me at the jetty, if I know Pearl she'll have gone to the island."

"But how would she get there?" Caroline was bemused.

"She'll do what she's always done, pay someone to take her." Mia replaced the receiver. Leela was standing behind her with the lifejackets.

"Take these, only one person known to have walked on water, he'll be giving you a hand though, you mark my words." She had hardly finished her sentence before Mia was running down the steps towards the beach.

The engine started first time. No sign of Ross. The tide was coming in. She had to go, she pushed the tender out. A screech of tyres, a door slammed. Ross was flying along the path by the summerhouse. He leapt from the steps, shrugging off his jacket as he landed on the sand. He jumped into the boat, rocking it violently, pulling off his tie he took hold of the tiller.

"The island?"

"Has to be," she replied.

"Mia, about earlier …"

"Another time." She zipped her life vest. "Let's find Pearl."

Ross pushed the throttle forward, they gathered pace. As they sped across the water, a strong south westerly cut across, trying to push them off course, Mia fixed on a small slice of shore still visible, the tide flooding in, half the island would be submerged soon enough.

They dumped the boat on the sand, racing along the track, calling her name. Twilight shrink-wrapped around them, turning everything into featureless shapes. By now the wind was howling, whipping their voices away. Mia fumbled along the wall to the opening, pulling Ross in behind her, they stood in the courtyard straining their ears. The ruined buildings took the strength out of the wind, at least they could hear each other speak.

"Let's split up. I'll do the church and the outbuildings," Ross said.

"I'll go along the wall, she may be asleep in a ditch." Mia tried to be upbeat. She handed Ross the torch. "Take it, the moon's coming out." She glanced up at the sliver of silver, willing it to burst into a huge glow.

Mia could see the flashlight bouncing off the walls of the buildings as she rounded the perimeter wall. She met Ross at the entrance to the church. It had started to rain. He shook his head.

"I just keep thinking about the caves." His voice was flat with despair.

"She won't be there, she's here. I know she is." Mia was racking her brain. Why would Pearl come back, what was so exciting about the island, what had really captured her imagination? The treasure, of course, *that* was it.

"The well, Ross, the well!" Mia shouted running across the courtyard, rain beating her back. She leaned over and yelled at the top of her voice. "Pearl! Pearl!"

It echoed back at her. She turned her head to listen. Nothing. Ross went to the other side, his foot bashed against something, he turned the torch on it. The pink suitcase.

"Her bag, it's here."

"Pearl!" Mia tried again, even louder, leaning dangerously over the well but all she could hear was the wind and the rain.

"I'm going in," she said.

"No way." Ross was at her side. "I'll go."

She pointed into the well. "You're too big, it narrows after the steps, you'll get stuck."

"What if you get stuck?"

"I won't. I'm a mermaid, remember?"

In a flash she hoisted herself over the wall, lowering her body onto the ledge. Ross handed her the chain with the bucket attached.

"Keep hold of this, it will guide you, tug to come up." He released her hand.

Once inside the well, the sound altered. No wind or rain, just the gentle echoing slosh of water. Mia sat on the steps, bumping down one at a time, the torch stuffed inside her life vest. She kept calling Pearl's name, but the walls deadened her voice, stopped it going anywhere.

Reaching the water, she flashed the torch bouncing light off the surface. The walls had a series of ledges; Mia was praying Pearl had managed to hold onto one of these to keep her head above water. At least the water in the well was a constant level, the depth would not change.

Mia called out again, wiping her eyes to focus. She blinked, her eyes stung. She tasted the water. Salt. There was sea water in the well. She froze. That meant the depth *would* change, the tide was coming in. Panic rising, Mia roared out the little girl's name, over and over.

Did she see something? She looked again. Rather than narrowing as she thought, the well widened, seeming to go round a bend. Holding the torch aloft, Mia pushed off the step. Ross felt the chain slacken. He tugged, calling down to Mia. Nothing. He felt panic grip his chest, the wind had built to a gale and the storm railed around him. Desperate, he scanned the sky for the coastguard, Caroline should have called them by now.

Mia was right, there was a bend. She swam through the icy water, pushing against the tide with all her might. At the far end of the tunnel she could just make out a ledge and perched there, crouched and frozen with terror was Pearl. She was wearing a mermaid outfit, clutching a large black hat. Mia fixed the torch on her, Pearl's eyes were glazed over, water lapping about her knees. Mia flashed the light at her face.

"Pearl, it's me, Mia!"

The girl let out an ear-shattering scream and leapt into the water, splashing towards the light in a desperate frenzy of relief. Mia grabbed the little body, rigid with cold and fear.

"Okay, arms around my neck. Tightly now, deep breaths, I've got you."

Ross had one leg over the entrance to the well when the chain rattled. He nearly jumped out of his skin when he spotted Mia leading Pearl up the steps, careful to keep hold of each other, using the chain as a guide rope. The first thing Pearl saw was his arms, reaching down as far as he could to clasp her hands and haul her out. Once Pearl was safe, he gripped Mia by the shoulders, pulling her up, out of the well and into the driving rain. He wrapped his arms round them both, letting out a low strangled, moan of relief. They held one another tightly for a long moment.

Blades whirred overhead. They looked up, Mia thought the moon had come out at last. It was a massive helicopter searchlight, the coastguard had arrived just in time to rescue a couple of half-drowned mermaids and one rather battered 'Superman'.

STAIRWAY TO HEAVEN

The next morning Mia felt as if she had been hit by a train, even her eyelashes hurt and as she tried to open her eyes images of the vivid nightmare that was the day before began to resurface. Yet like her childhood dreams, the night of terror started to fade as morning seeped in and softly, slowly, the comfort of knowing she was home in Galty House, soothed her fears away. It had always been the same.

Leela appeared with tea, toast and painkillers, handing Mia a mug. "I'll run you a bath, you'll need salts for those wounds."

Mia shook her head to clear it. *Ouch, that was sore.*

"Any news?"

"They kept Pearl in overnight, just for observation. Ross was here earlier, I told him you were still asleep, he'll come back later."

"Oh."

Mia was trying to remember how she had left it with Ross. She remembered making a scene at the hotel. Ross had her thrown out. Pearl in the car park, then Leela in the garden, a phone call, Pearl gone.

Gingerly she climbed out of bed. Her feet were black and blue.

"How did I get back?"

"An ambulance dropped you off after the hospital in Wexford patched you up." Leela fed her the pills. "Scared me to death, I stood on the balcony for hours, I could see a light over on the island, then the coastguard. Sure, I'd no idea what was going on." She ran her hand over her eyes. "Bloody island, death trap that place is."

Mia touched Leela's shoulder. "I'm fine, honestly." The cat jumped onto the bed, giving Mia a baleful look. "Honestly," she told the cat.

"You'll feel a lot better after a nice soak." Leela passed the robe from the back of the door. "Ross gave me this, he said, 'to add to the collection' whatever that means?"

Leela handed over a bulky envelope. Mia opened it; more keys, a small bunch, there was something else; a turquoise seahorse, a little fob with a pearl for its eye.

"Ross is very keen on security," Mia said. "Thinks I should keep everything locked up."

Leela gave a toss of her head. "Think you do that anyway."

Archie's roll top bath was filled with creamy suds, Mia let go of the sides to submerge gratefully beneath the silky surface. Up to her ears in bubbles, she admired the extravagant chandelier above her. She looked again, the chandelier was at an angle; there was a deep crack in the ceiling running towards the wall. She sat up, if it broke free and landed in the bath someone could be seriously … dead. She leapt out of the bath, pulling the plug.

Leela was in the kitchen filleting fish. "That wasn't much of a soak," she said, looking Mia up and down, her hair still wet.

"Noticed anything strange around here?" Mia asked.

Leela laughed. "This place has always been strange." She carried bones to the bin.

"I mean cracks and splits, as if it's moving?"

Leela thought for a minute.

"The summerhouse, a few panes of glass broken alright, but that's just the wind, whips up stones." She fed the cat silvery fish skin.

"And the beach, notice anything there? Has it changed at

all?"

Leela raised her eyebrows. Mia must have taken a blow to the head.

"I never go on the beach, you know that. Hate fecking sand."

Mia was through the door in a moment.

"Where are you going now?" Leela called.

Mia stood at the bottom of the steps thinking, looking out to sea for an answer. Her leg ached, the leg she had hurt when she fell through the hole in the sand, the sand that stretched for miles, smooth and safe.

Something else was bugging her. The tide was weird. When she and Ross had been in the caves, the water seemed to run in different directions. Something had altered the coast.

She looked along the sweep of bay leading to the marina and the Harbour Spa Hotel, men in high visibility jackets were out on the flats, putting up signs, barriers. It was August, the height of the season. Something was wrong, very wrong indeed.

Ross was in deep discussion with one of the men when she arrived. He gave a wave and strode towards her.

"I called earlier, Leela said you were sleeping, rough night, huh?" He stood towering over her yet looked shrunken somehow. "I came to say thank you, without you … I …"

"We did what we had to do," she said. "But having me escorted out of the hotel, now that was …"

"Hang on, I had no choice. I was on the verge of telling them I knew what was going on, you bursting in like that … could have ruined everything!"

"I realise that now. Leela told me you and Archie knew all about the bribes, the permission for Galty House to be demolished, planning for the golf course already signed and sealed."

"And paid for!" Ross said. "Thank goodness Archie had all the evidence to back me up." Taking her shoulders, he turned her to face him. "I'm sorry I had to throw you out of the hotel but I was about to confront those responsible, I couldn't have you mess things up, forewarn them so they could get their stories straight, come up with alibis, excuses."

"I'm sorry too." She meant it. "But what's going to happen now?"

"About the golf course? All on hold at the moment. I've bigger, more pressing problems needing my full and undivided attention." He indicated the beach.

"Looks serious."

"I got to thinking, these structural problems at the hotel, the weird undercurrent in the caves, sea water in the well." He pointed out to sea. "See that boat out there? A team of divers. I need to know what's going on, we all do."

"Are you closing the hotel?"

"It's closed. Some kids were playing on the beach yesterday, one of them got stuck in a hole which seemed to appear overnight." Ross pushed his hair back. "I've shipped all the guests out, nearly everywhere is full but we managed it."

"Oh, Ross." She could see the anguish in his eyes. "What about you and Pearl?"

"I'll have to send her home. This is going to be a long job, she needs to be settled. I don't want her childhood screwed too."

"Hey." She gave him a half-smile. "Can't be as bad as all that, surely?"

He looked back out to sea.

"It was a dream, Mia, maybe it should have stayed a dream."

They walked on in silence. Mia stopped.

"I have an absolutely brilliant idea!"

Ross scowled at her but she was getting used to that.

"Why don't you and Pearl come and stay at Galty? Leela and I are rattling around the place. You can manage the project from there and Pearl can go to Mary Magdalene, just as I did."

"Won't that look a bit odd? You know how people love to talk."

"Let them, they've always talked about the scandalous goings on up at The Seahorse Hotel. And anyway, I'm just being neighbourly." She was serious.

"Hey, that's really kind but no way. I mean you're not even sure you're staying yet." He gave her a look. "*Are* you staying?"

She pulled a face. "Nowhere else to go. Besides I've started making lists and schedules." She gave him a broad grin.

He laughed. "It's *that* serious then?"

"You betcha!" she said, trying out her awful American accent.

Later that evening, after putting a very excited Pearl to bed, Mia and Ross were sitting at the kitchen table, replete from Leela's delicious fish pie and exhausted by recent events.

"A nightcap," Mia offered; she longed for sleep but Ross was a guest.

"If you're having one?"

She fetched the decanter filled with Archie's favourite cognac, it was only then she remembered the wine.

"By the way, the keys opened the safe," she said as she poured. "The ones Sister Agnes gave me, locked doors too, very helpful."

"Did you look in the safe?" Ross was curious.

Mia took a sip of the smooth, warming drink, at last some of the anxiety of the past few days beginning to ease. "Yep, full of wine, seemed Archie kept the best stuff under lock and key."

"Wise man," Ross confirmed. "A few of his acquaintances are proving to be less than honest."

"Anyone I know?" As if she could not guess.

"Eamon Degan, lawyer and Dominic Driscoll, my erstwhile driver. Looks like Eamon banked a large sum of money as a deposit on the sale of this place."

"How did he manage that?" Mia was intrigued. "Sounds ambitious even for Eamon."

"Forged a copy of Archie's will, sent it to my uncle Christie. States he and Bernice inherit the estate, fifty-fifty split. He asked for a deposit to secure the land for the hotel, Christie had half a million dollars transferred to his account."

"Wow!" Mia was grudgingly impressed. "What happened to the money?"

"It's disappeared and surprise, surprise, so have the dastardly duo." Ross took a drink.

Mia was shocked, so much had been going on behind the scenes. "Eamon did write, trying to scare me off."

Ross looked at her. "The bastard." Then smiling wryly. "Good luck with that."

"What?"

"Trying to scare you off … you're terrifying." He laughed. "And the other keys?"

"The ones you dropped off? I forgot about those, where did they come from?" Mia went to retrieve them.

"The hotel, I came across them in Lost Property. When I saw the seahorse, I thought they were worth a try here. No go?" He took the bunch from her, looking at them thoughtfully.

"Haven't tried, although you know that weird door in the library, the one that looks like it's plonked in the middle of the bookcase?"

Ross nodded, it stuck out like a sore thumb.

"It's never opened as far as I can remember … do you think?"

They raced to the library, Mia was so excited she could hardly hold the keys. Ross took them, trying one at a time. No luck.

"Wait," Mia fetched the WD40. "This time turn the other way."

Ross tried again. Nothing.

"Aargh!" Mia cried, kicking the base of the door in frustration. It opened, just a crack. They looked at each other, she pulled on the handle, the door swung wide.

They stood open-mouthed before a steep, wooden staircase.

"This place is full of surprises," she said. "Come on!"

He followed her up the creaking steps, cobwebs in corners and one single light bulb hanging halfway down. There was a door at the top, Mia pushed it open. They found themselves in the boiler room on the second floor, it had not been used for years.

"Well, I never," Mia folded her arms satisfactorily.

The clock chimed the hour, it could be heard quite clearly from the top of the stairs. Ross stifled a yawn.

"You'll have hours of fun getting to know this place but I'm afraid I've had enough excitement for one evening." He made a slight bow. "If you don't mind, I'll head to bed."

"Of course, goodnight," she said, remembering her manners, a disused staircase in an old house was hardly Tutankhamen's Tomb, she was probably boring Ross rigid.

He took his leave and as he did she nestled down on the top step to ponder her find and consider the various questions fluttering through her mind, thoughts and images that just would not go away. She must have slept because that's precisely where the green-eyed cat found her as dawn broke the following morning. She could hardly walk, she ached so. The cat stretched and followed her to bed, let some other early bird catch the worm for a change.

THE RED KIMONO

"Are you getting up?" It was Pearl, she was wearing her Irish dancing costume and a large black hat. Mia opened her eyes the merest slice. She tried to move; she was even stiffer today. Pearl pirouetted into the room.

"You look nice, is it Thursday?" Mia whispered over the duvet.

"Yes, I'm ready for my lesson." She gave a quick high kick at the foot of the bed.

"Humphrey and Bernice are having coffee with Leela, we've been packing boxes all morning, Bernice is going to live with him, happily ever after, that's what Leela says."

Mia struggled to her feet and dressing as quickly as she could followed Pearl downstairs. Pearl stopped when she reached the mirror.

"I'll lose the hat." She threw it onto the hall table. "Take care of that please. It's to go with my project." She did a little jig as she left.

"Have you made your decision?" Humphrey stirred his coffee. "I'd understand if you thought it was too much to take on and you've your career, of course."

Mia was leaning against the sink; she had been turning things over in her mind.

"I've time to think things through?"

"All the time in the world." He gave a warm smile. "There are funds invested for when you need them, you might want to put money into the house, do it up, sell it, whatever."

"How does Bernice feel? It's her home after all."

"Not any more. We're buying an apartment in Dalkey, turning one of the bedrooms into a studio so she can paint."

Humphrey laid down his spoon. "She's in the morning room, she wants to talk to you. She still feels guilty about all that carry on with the will and Eamon. Although he's gone too far as usual, ended up in a right mess, the eejit. No one's seen sight nor sound of him or Driscoll, and the latest I heard is the practice is being investigated for embezzlement and not just regarding the Harbour Spa Hotel either."

Standing by the window Bernice looked younger somehow, in her new jeans and sailing top.

"I'm delighted by your news," Mia said, giving her a smile.

Bernice's expression was serious as she turned to face her.

"Mia, I've something to say. Well, really something to ask." Mia waited. "I've come to ask you to forgive me for being a silly, stupid girl all those years ago." She was using Humphrey's words, words they agreed she would say to release them, free them to get on with their lives.

"Really?" Mia was intrigued.

"It's to do with your father."

"Archie?"

"No, love." Bernice took her hand. "Archie was not your father. It was a long time ago and times have changed but please don't think badly of us, we were so very young – just teenagers really."

Mia stared at Bernice. She knew this day would come, she had hardly dared to imagine it but when she did it was always Fenella who told her what she wanted to know, her mother who finally told her the truth. But now, in reality, it was Bernice.

"When it all blew up and the boy, only a boy really, was sent away, your mother asked for a letter to be taken to him, telling him she was pregnant and that she wanted to be with him, she wanted them to be together no matter what." Bernice took a deep breath.

"You discussed what was in the letter?" Mia was hardly able to speak, trying to imagine Bernice and Fenella ever being that close.

"No. But I read it and after I read it, I'm afraid I destroyed it. He never received it and that was my fault."

"But why?" Mia's voice was rising.

"I wish I knew. It's hard for you to understand but it was such a desperate time and I was scared, we all were, scared of losing everything, it was like the world had gone mad."

Mia watched the older woman and briefly she did look frightened, as if just remembering was terrifying too. Bernice gathered herself. "That doesn't matter, not now. All that matters is you know I'm ashamed of what I did and I'm sorry. Your mother did try to tell him. Why he never got in touch again, I don't know. We could speculate forever …"

"But," Mia stopped her. "You know who he is, you've always known and still you, my mother, Archie – *all of you* – chose not to tell me. Why? What was so awful I couldn't know?"

"I'm sorry Mia, it just wasn't – isn't – our secret to tell. We made a vow, Fenella would have lost her mind completely if any of us had let her down," Bernice had tears in her eyes. "The way she felt *he* had."

Mia despaired, things would never change, whatever hold Fenella had over them, it would never be broken, the secret never told.

She looked at Bernice. Bernice had been in her life as long as she could remember, teaching her to sew, arrange flowers, kindling her passion in art. Bernice made sure her homework was done, her school uniform immaculate. Bernice had been there, sometimes misguided but there, a constant. Bernice had always loved her.

"It's not for me to forgive you, I wasn't even around when you destroyed that letter." Mia looked into her eyes. "You've always done your best for me, Bernice and I love you for that."

A cough. Humphrey at the door.

"All done here?" he asked gently. "We need to be getting back, there's a lot to do before we head off tomorrow." Italy, of course. It was all falling into place, Bernice was exorcising her demons ahead of settling down to her new life with Humphrey.

"Will you see Isabella?" Mia asked Bernice.

"We're having dinner with herself and Giovanni while we're there, I'm looking forward to seeing them." She gave Mia a nervous smile. "What about you love, what are your plans?"

"I've a mind to stay," Mia announced. "With Ross and Pearl needing a home and me letting the flat go, I think I'll give it a few months, especially if I don't have to rush into anything."

"That *is* a relief," Leela had overheard. "At least I'm not being slung out on the scrapheap just yet."

Mia rolled her eyes. "Surely the cards told you all *you* need to know."

Bernice laughed and excused herself, she still had bags in her room. Mia followed Humphrey into the hall.

"Humphrey, do you remember the staircase in the library?"

"Sorry?" Humphrey was dragging on his jacket.

"The staircase, behind that odd-looking door."

"Can't say I do. Mind you, I wasn't often allowed in the house. Archie's mother thought I was a bad influence, I've had a hard time getting this family to love me, I can tell you." He glanced up at the portraits, seemingly still unsure if he was accepted. "One last thing. Bernice wondered if there was a set of keys anywhere, seahorse charm on the key ring?"

Mia thought for a moment, technically the keys were hers, they belonged to Galty house. "Not seen them."

As Humphrey looked around hopefully, he spotted the battered black hat on the hall table. Mia saw a flicker of recognition.

"Where did that come from?"

"Pearl found it, it's for her project," was all Mia was prepared to say.

"For the journey." Leela appeared, handing Humphrey hastily wrapped cake. "I was telling Humphrey all about the other night while you were upstairs, you and Ross over on the island, rescuing the little one from the well."

"Awful business," Humphrey agreed, he had picked up the hat. No distinguishing marks as far as he could tell, could have belonged to anyone.

Bernice arrived with her bags, the tears had started again, time to go.

"Don't be a stranger," Mia called to her as she climbed into the car, she knew Bernice felt closer to Archie at Galty; they all did.

"I'll wait to be invited. It's your home now," Bernice said, then thinking better of her words, wound down the window. "When we're back from Italy, we could come then."

Humphrey followed his fiancée. Mia stood at the door, watching him, thinking.

"Humphrey, wait!" She ran out, catching him up.

"What happened to the photos?"

"Photos?" Humphrey was puzzled.

"The ones you and Archie took from the school. The pictures of the student priests."

He gave her an odd look.

"Sister Agnes said you had them."

"God knows, we often had a bonfire though, Mrs Fitzgerald insisted Archie burn all his seedy magazines and awful scripts. Doubtless ended up in one of them. Why do you want them?"

"Just Pearl's project." she replied, waving them off.

The Range Rover scorched down the drive. Humphrey Beaumont seemed in an awful hurry to escape.

Leela was looking for Mia, with everyone gone the house was suddenly very empty. She found her in the library looking at one of the many photographs on the piano – Archie and Humphrey playing guitars – she was trying to decipher where it had been taken, there were buildings in the background, it could be the seminary on Phoenix Island. But no priests. The pictures Sister Agnes said Archie and Humphrey had stolen had probably been destroyed after all.

"I thought that place was out of bounds," she said when Leela appeared brandishing a duster on the pretext of attending to her 'schedule'.

"Not then, the general public weren't permitted but they had a friend – a trainee priest, they used to go over and see him."

"Who took the photo?"

"Bernice, I'd say. She got the camera for her birthday that year. The latest, a Polaroid, very expensive."

That explained why the pictures suddenly changed from grainy black and white to technicolour. Not the realistic colours of today's imagery but garish yellow, tangerine, bright red.

"They look a bit orange," Mia said.

"It was a very hot summer." Leela took it from her, gazing at them pictured there in the sunshine. She gave the frame a cursory flick and put it back.

"Who gave Bernice the camera?" Mia asked.

"My father."

Startled, they turned round. They hadn't heard Bernice enter the room.

"I forgot something."

"I've never really looked at this before, was it taken on the island?" Mia said.

"It was." Bernice confirmed. "Our own private paradise, music, dancing, barbecues … heavenly."

"Shouldn't have been there at all," Leela muttered under her breath.

Bernice put the photo back. "I had permission to go whenever I wished, special dispensation if you like."

"Because you were an artist?"

"Because of my father."

She picked up another frame. A black and white photo of a group, formally dressed, a reception of some kind.

"Here he is."

She passed the picture to Mia, who was fully expecting to see the elegant features of Mr Fitzgerald, an image rarely displayed in the house. But Bernice was pointing at another man. A broad handsome man, dressed in black, standing next to Mrs Fitzgerald, laughing.

"Monsignor Sylvester Whelan. My father."

Leela gave a loud harrumph. Mia was stunned to silence.

"He and my mother were in love. When she found she was pregnant, to avoid a scandal she asked Mr Fitzgerald to say the child was his. They had an agreement. She would leave him to his life in Dublin and we would live here, the official explanation being I was the result of a brief reconciliation that didn't work out."

"Wow," Mia said when she finally found her voice. She had been so preoccupied with her own back story, she had never considered anyone else might have an equally dark secret hidden in the closet, least of all Bernice.

"I'm sure it happened a lot." Bernice could see she was shocked. "No one free to say they'd made a mistake, the wrong choice. Everyone supposed to just get on with things, some people desperately unhappy and others living a lie, a miserable state of affairs." Bernice gave the photograph a sad glance.

"But what happened to your father, did you know him well?" Mia pressed.

"He could never acknowledge me officially of course, but he was always kind to me. Disappeared the night of a terrible storm." Bernice was standing by the window now, gazing out to sea. "That was the worst night of our lives, wasn't it Leela? How any of us survived I will never know."

A car horn sounded. Bernice sighed heavily. "I have to go. I'll call when we get back." The door closed.

"What on earth was she talking about?" Mia looked askance. "The worst night of your lives?"

"Not for me to say." Leela replied, glaring after Bernice. "Not my place, I'm just the hired help around here. I've never been allowed to forget that." And taking the unemployed duster from the desk she left the room.

But Mia was rattled. Bernice's confession was one thing, her way of clearing the decks ready for her new life but now with 'the letter' and the 'worst night of their lives' mentioned on the same day, almost in the same breath, surely more clues would come to the surface. The story was definitely emerging and she felt that if she just held her nerve, Galty House would tell her all she needed to know.

Fired up, Mia started striding around the room, books everywhere; pictures too, on walls, in frames, standing on every surface. Where would she look when she did not even know what she was looking for?

She stood at the desk by the window and finding a tissue started cleaning the picture frames. She stopped, holding in her hand a colour photograph, a row of men. Had it always been there? She looked again. Some of them wore dog collars. Of course, trainee priests. She looked closer; the one in the middle stood out, tall and dark, no dog-collar. His striped shirt was open at the neck and he was wearing beads. Choker-style love beads, silver and blue against his tanned skin.

She nearly dropped the picture and catching it just in time, caught her nail on the clasp as the back came away. Turning it face down to put it back together she saw there was handwriting on the reverse. It read – G*regory, centre stage, The Red Kimono* – in Archie's mad scrawl.

Gregory, whoever he was, was wearing Pearl's necklace.

Mia felt a shiver crawl along her spine, why had Archie saved this one photograph and hidden it so cleverly, on full display? She had never noticed it before and why would she? It was unremarkable and then she spotted another picture, one taken in the library, Archie at the piano, Fenella close by, probably singing. There was something odd about it, where the door now stood there was no door but a bookcase. The staircase had been hidden behind the bookcase, a *secret* staircase. Mia was bemused, the longer she was here the more the house seemed to want to reveal. So what was *The Red Kimono*, a code, a message?

"I'm back!" Leela called from the hall. Mia had not realised she had left

"In the library."

Leela lumbered in waving a celebrity magazine.

"Look at this." She pointed at the cover. The headline screamed, '*Silver Star Strikes Out!*' above a picture of a beautiful woman, cropped silver hair, draped in a sheath of metallic silk. It was Fenella. The story read:

> *Irish actress Fenella Flanagan revealed her fabulous new look at a star-studded premiere in London last night. Fenella, famous not only for her award-winning performances but her trademark blue-black hair, declared it was time to reveal 'the real me'. In an exclusive interview with Outre! Fenella said: "I'm a woman of a certain age being offered more roles than I know what to do with, it's a great time to be in this business as it at last recognises one of our greatest gifts is age and wisdom. I applaud my age, I salute silver, bring it on.'*

Mia re-read the article and started to laugh. Something else now made sense too, it was time to make a call.

"Where are you?" Trixie shouted, the line was crackly.

"Galty House, think I'm staying. Is my mother there?"

"Excellent news. Is it urgent? She's giving an interview."

Mia would not normally interrupt.

"It's desperately urgent!" Mia insisted.

"Sweetheart, what is it? What on earth is wrong?" Fenella cried into the phone.

"I've seen the picture." Silence. "You know, the picture. I've seen it."

"Really?" Fenella's voice barely a whisper.

"Yes, in one of Leela's magazines."

"Oh." Relief. "*That* picture! What do you think?"

"I wondered why you were wearing all those bandana things with a pile of curls on top. A wig, right?"

"Yes, been growing it out for ages, sick and tired of dying it,

I was beginning to look like a witch."

"But why the wigs?"

"Archie, really. He was so old-fashioned.'Don't change it, Fenella, your fans will hate it.' Meaning he would hate it, trying to hold on to his lost youth. He could be a real control freak if you let him!"

Mia silently agreed, Archie controlled Fenella that was for sure. "Well, I love it, you look amazing."

"Thank you, sweetheart, it's so liberating, I can't tell you!" It was the happiest she had sounded in a long time. "Must dash, darling, I'm giving another interview."

"One thing before you go, does *The Red Kimono* mean anything to you?" Did Mia notice a slight halt, just half a beat?

"What was that?"

"*Red Kimono*?"

"I had one once darling, why?"

"Anything to do with Archie?"

Fenella was thinking. "Now you mention it yes, one of his bloody awful plays, imagine naming a play after a dressing gown, I ask you?"

"Did you read it?"

Fenella laughed. "Not at all, never read any of his plays, far too depressing." The actress rang off.

Mia frowned. If she never read any of the plays, how did she know they were awful? Poor Archie. One thing Mia did know, was where Archie kept his scripts, an old sea chest at the foot of his bed. Taking the photograph with her, she was unsurprised one of Bernice's keys opened the chest and there right on top was a fresh sheaf of paper, *The Red Kimono* by *Aloysius Fermoy Fitzgerald*.

Opening the first page, she saw that Archie had written an

outline of the story set in the nineteen seventies. It was so melodramatic, so Archie, but could it be true? Mia had studied the era – another world, another time. She knew this by the costumes she worked with, clothes reflected history. Today, of course, not everything was perfect but so many things had changed for the better. The past was indeed another country.

Mia settled back and in the fading light started to read Archie's dramatic and desperately sad play. By the time she had finished her face was wet, the desperation of the separated, unrequited lovers making her cry and once she allowed herself tears, she wept and wept, the relief painful and exquisite at the same time.

Eventually wiping her eyes, she lifted the photograph for a better look. Now she knew who the characters in the play were based on. The young man wearing the love beads was Gregory, the trainee priest. The novice actress, Fenella and the jealous friend, probably Bernice. The cruel, sadistic Monsignor, inspired by the man she now knew was Bernice's father and the brave rescuers, Archie and Humphrey, who else? And of course, the actress's unborn child, herself, Mia.

Emotionally drained, Mia curled up on the window seat and dragging a throw over her shoulders, laid her head on the script and was soon asleep. As she slept – a strangely deep and dreamless sleep – she could feel, somewhere in her subconscious a sweet release, the endless tossing and turning of many years easing away, no more anxious worrying, no more empty answers and no more questions, at least for now.

Such a soothing, blessed release … at last.

SHOWTIME

Mia was in the kitchen, fabric swatches splayed across the table. Leela had overslept, there was little evidence of breakfast and not even a pot of coffee on the range.

"Leela?" Mia tried.

No reply.

"You okay?"

Leela was far from okay, she had been awake all night, not even a lavender bath or rum cocoa could soothe her. Mia had started clearing rooms, Galty House was opening for business next spring and there was much to do.

In deference to the housekeeper Mia had decreed Archie's suite Leela's domain, leaving her to shift through his eclectic collections, deciding what to keep and what to skip. She had spent the week holed-up there with the green-eyed cat and apart from moving things from one side of the room to the other, not a lot else seemed to be happening.

"Leela, what's wrong?"

"I'm sorry, love." She turned to face her, Mia was shocked, Leela was in public without lipstick.

"It's the day that's in it." She stifled a sob.

Mia thought for a second. "Of course, Archie's birthday. Oh, Leela." She put her arms around the older woman, who collapsed gratefully into her embrace. "What shall we do, the occasion needs marking we can't let the old traditions slip."

"It was always a party on the beach, whatever the weather." Leela sniffed.

"So be it!" Mia gave a watery smile. "Maybe Pearl and Ross will join us?"

"Taxi picked Ross up early, he's taken the train to Dublin. Important meeting, Department of the Environment, I believe."

Mia remembered Ross said there would be a hearing, the results of the report he commissioned had been revelatory. The dredging and construction work carried out during the Harbour Spa Hotel's build programme was dangerously substandard. Geological tests and subsequent findings had been ignored in favour of a quick fix, an entire stretch of coastline destabilised as a result. It appeared Ross had decided to take the blame, resolve the situation as best he could, he did not want the family name besmirched in anyway. Typical Ross.

Mia fetched her new mobile. If she was to get to Dublin, fly to Manchester and back in time to be there for Ross she needed to get a wiggle on.

Twenty minutes later she reappeared in the library where Leela was arranging lilies in a crystal vase. Mia had changed into a fabulous cream linen suit, soft against her golden skin. Leela thought she looked lovely, she also thought there was something very different about Mia today, she could do with the cards giving her a steer, any more changes she was sure she would implode.

"I'm heading up to town, I'll meet Ross there, give him a bit of support."

"Shall we save the birthday till this evening? Pearl and I can get everything ready for youse coming back." Leela placed the flowers on the piano, she had been crying again.

"Do you know what happened to him?" Mia asked, calmly.

Leela followed her gaze, giving no indication she was surprised Mia was asking about the dark, handsome man in the photograph.

This had been coming for some time, she had seen that much.

"He got away alright. Convalescence in a convent in Kildare and then off to the missions in Africa."

"For his sins?"

"For his vocation. But you're right it's tough enough out there."

"Did my mother know?"

"No. She was so fragile with it all, and then losing her mother at the same time. Dr Morrissey thought it best she knew as little as possible, I'm sure she can't remember half of what happened anyway."

"Or doesn't want to." Mia looked directly at her. "Anyone know where he is now?"

"Maybe." Leela touched her shoulder. "But that's not for now, maybe when the time is right, love."

Mia looked into her shrewd eyes, brimming with tears.

She knew what she meant, everything was still raw after Archie, in flux, off kilter. The world needed to settle back on its axis, a new course set and steered towards.

"You're right." Mia agreed. The green-eyed cat jumped off the sofa, giving his tail a languid flick. "You're both right," she said, not quite as convinced as she sounded.

It was not long before Mia was zipping along the coast road towards the harbour, humming along to Elvis Costello's *Watching the Detectives* and remembering Archie's hilarious 'one size fits all' dance routine, when she was jarred back to the present by the siren and flashing lights of a squad car bearing down on her.

The police car nipped out from behind. A camper van careering towards them blared its horn, wheels screeched as the three vehicles struggled to avoid each other. Both the Daimler and the camper van stopped nose to nose. The Gardai had somehow managed to squeeze through, going like a bat out of hell *en route* to the ferry port. The driver of the camper van stuck his head out.

"Flippin' heck that was close." English accent, nice looking man about Archie's age. "Phew! I'd rather have hit the police car than that." He gave the Daimler an admiring glance. "Who do you reckon they're after, gun-runners, drug-dealers, illegal immigrants?"

"Probably just late for lunch!" Mia laughed, putting the car into reverse.

Motoring on, Mia was pleased there was no roadblock at the roundabout as she turned onto the main Dublin road. She had a plane to catch. Yet if she had been forced to follow the gardai down to the harbour she would have witnessed a rather arresting scene.

"Well, well, well if it isn't me old sparring partner." Sergeant O'Brien sauntered over to the solicitor.

Eamon Degan pulled nervously at the collar of his new jacket.

"Brendan, there you are!"

"Haven't seen you in a long time." The policeman leaned against the railing. "When was it?" Eamon fidgeted. "I remember, I'd just arrived back from your non-existent apartment in Croatia."

"Ah, Brendan, water under the bridge."

Eamon surreptitiously kicked his travel bag to one side, casting about as if waiting for someone to arrive off the ferry.

"Really? My wife was waiting for me with divorce papers when I got back. She didn't know about the girlfriend until someone told her you were having a great laugh about a certain

Garda headed to your 'not quite finished' apartment over there. The girlfriend wasn't too impressed either."

Eamon started to sweat. The ferry was ready to leave.

"I need to go," he said. The policeman barred his way. Another Guard appeared at his side.

"You do, in fact we all do. We all need to go to the station right now, you're under arrest." Sergeant O'Brien swung a pair of handcuffs in front of Eamon's face. People queuing stopped to watch. "Will I be needing these?"

"How dare you!" Eamon tried, but he was beaten. He knew he should never have listened to that eejit Driscoll, telling him to board at the harbour, act natural, no one will suspect anything. And where was *he*, the snidey, two-faced, slippery sliveen? Long gone, changed his name and on a cruise ship, half way to the Caribbean by now, jammy bastard.

Mia was at the studio. Normally she would have found security intimidating, but nothing would stand in her way today.

"I'm Fenella Flanagan's daughter. I need to see her urgently, a private family matter."

The security man gave the attractive young woman the once over.

"It's a closed set today, I'm afraid."

"Well, I'm afraid you'll have to open it. I have to see her, now!"

"I'm sorry."

She spotted a rail of costumes being wheeled through a door. "Hello, wardrobe!" She shouted on the off chance.

A spikey head popped up. "Bloody hell, about time too!" It was Lol. "Jeez look at you, look like a bleedin' movie star yourself, what's going on?"

Mia glanced at the security man.

"It's alright Mick, she's with me, wardrobe mistress," Lol said.

"She ain't got no badge."

"She don't need no fucking badge, her mother's the lead, her ex-fiancé's the baddy and I'm her best mate, got it?"

"Alright, keep your hair on."

He handed Mia a visitor's pass.

Lol took her arm. "I can see by the outfit you're not joining us then?"

"I thought you were filming with Courtney?" Mia fell into step, helping Lol wheel the costumes away.

"Haven't your heard? He's left the business. His granny in St Kitts is getting too old to run the restaurant, so he took his little girl and moved back. Far less stress and lots of sunshine, what's not to like?"

Mia smiled, pleased for him. It seems things were changing all round.

"And Rupert's here?" She glanced around, he was one person she did not want to run into.

"Yeah, just a small role but he's good in it. Not mended his ways mind but not as attractive as he was. He's been in an accident or something, bashed his nose in. He told me he was going to get it fixed but since it's happened he's been offered more roles, so reckons he'll keep it. Thinks it suits him, always was a vain bastard though." They were walking through the back lot now, Lol needed a cigarette, some things had not changed.

"Where's my mother?"

"Due on set anytime now."

"Her trailer?"

Lol pointed. "Just there. What's up?"

"I've something to tell her."

"Oh, what's that?"

"I know who my father is."

"Archie! He told you!" Fenella had been expecting this, she waved the makeup boy away.

"No, he didn't tell me and how I know is not the point. But what I *do* want to know is, why haven't you told me, ever?"

Mia watched her mother fanning her face in the mirror, taking tight little breaths.

"But darling you know why, he rejected us. Didn't even acknowledge we existed. What would be the point?"

"The point is, Mother what if he didn't know about us? Maybe he had no idea."

"But he did know, I wrote to him, told him everything." Fenella took a sip of water. "Darling this is not the time or the place, I'm due on set any second."

"But if he never received the letter?" Mia kept her voice calm. "What if the person sent to deliver it, destroyed it and he never knew. And what if he did try to get in touch and his efforts there were thwarted too."

Silence.

"I've always suspected that might be the case. Archie always said not, but jealousy can manifest itself so wickedly." Fenella looked at Mia in the mirror. "It was Bernice who destroyed the letter, wasn't it?" she asked quietly.

Mia did not really need to answer. Fenella had always known, her anger and despair had dissipated over the years but what she did not know was that it was Archie who had told Bernice to burn it – they were in it together.

"He still rejected us though." Fenella was remembering how Humphrey had tried to comfort her, telling her to prepare for the worst, to imagine she might never see Gregory again, because after finding him half-dead, who knew if he even survived.

"How do you know that?" Mia pressed.

A young female director opened the door. "In five please, Miss Flanagan."

"Of course, I'll be right with you." She looked at Mia through the mirror. "I never heard from him again …" Her voice broke in a sob. "I felt betrayed, abandoned. I was going to give you up, but I couldn't, so I ran away with you instead. I was so desperate."

Fenella remembered only too well when the baby arrived she had loved it and hated it at the same time. Adoring its pale, squishy flesh, the scent of freshly washed skin and gripe water. Then despairing at its inconsolable cries, even though she rocked and rocked the shuddering bundle through the night.

Arrangements were made, a new home for the infant, a better start in life. But she ran away, taking the baby with her, the child she did not want yet could not give up, the wailing alien, sent to chain her to their sin forever. Oh, the shame of it, the scandal she had wreaked.

Archie had found her, in a miserable bedsit in Liverpool and begged her to come home. 'Let he who is without sin cast the first stone', he told her and besides, it would be good to have a child in the house. 'She belongs to us all', he had insisted, smiling adoringly at the little auburn-haired dote.

"And?" Mia pressed.

Fenella gave one of her tremulous sighs. "Thank God Archie found me."

Although she hated having to come back to Galty House to throw herself on the mercy of those she imagined despised her.

"You should have read more of his plays," Mia told her. "Most enlightening."

Having devoured *The Red Kimono* is one sitting, she had read it again more slowly and it was good, very good. It also told of how the young priest had written repeatedly, his correspondence either intercepted or destroyed, an unspoken conspiracy to repress the truth, eradicate her father's identity because the shame of it would have been too much to bear. It had certainly been too much for Ursula.

Fenella was being called, camera waiting.

"Darling, now is not the time. I'll come back soon and explain everything, we can talk, you'll understand, I had no choice."

Mia steeled herself.

"No, Mother, don't come back. You're right, now is not the time." No drama, no histrionics, not in Galty House, not in her home. She lightened her tone. "You know I'm turning Galty into a guesthouse?"

"Yes, Trixie mentioned it." Fenella was agitated now, keen to be gone.

"So I'm afraid I need your old room, don't worry though, I'll pack everything up and ship it over to you but just so you know, that's what I'm doing."

Fenella gasped.

"But … my things …"

"It'll be fine, I'll make an inventory, do it properly."

Mia bent and kissed her mother's pretty silver head. "Once we're open for business, come and stay then."

Fenella turned to look at her, gazing into her child's beautiful turquoise eyes, her father's eyes, clear and deep and pure.

"The shame was never about you, Mia, you made everything alright, made the whole thing worthwhile. Never forget that."

"I'll never forget that you've all lied to me, one way or the other all my life," Mia said, softly.

"We never lied … we just couldn't tell the truth."

"A conspiracy of silence, whichever way you look at it."

"It wasn't unkindly meant, we all loved you, will always love you."

"I know." Mia opened the door.

"Where are you going?" Fenella was not used to being dismissed.

"I've a plane to catch, Mother. I'm going home."

Sitting on a rug by the crackling bonfire on the beach Mia was gazing absent-mindedly at Ross stretched out in the sand, the waves creeping closer to where he lay dozing in the evening sun. Archie's birthday barbecue had been a great success, Pearl and Leela had even made a cake.

Mia went to kneel beside him.

"You'll be swept out to sea if you're not careful."

He slid open an eye. "Party over?"

Leela and Pearl had retreated some time ago, Mia was surprised Leela had stayed as long as she did, wearing wellingtons to protect against the tiniest grain of sand the entire time.

"Last orders," Mia said, handing him a beer.

He chinked the bottle against hers.

"Thanks for today, it was great to see a familiar face. Really meant a lot."

Mia had arrived at the hearing as Ross was giving his statement.

"I'm just relieved by the outcome. The Power Corporation had to be fined, we knew that, but you offering to fund the reinstatement of the damaged coastline helped mitigate what could have been a far more serious charge, isn't that what the minister said?"

Ross nodded.

"Didn't harm having Humphrey on my side either."

Mia laughed. "I know, by the end of his summing up the minister even suggested looking into a grant to help. A win, win. Probably didn't harm today being Archie's birthday either."

"That too." He looked at her. "I feel very lucky." She smiled back, pleased to see the worry-worn look of the last few weeks smoothed away from his handsome face. "Anyway, enough about me, how's the mass clear out going? Find any more treasure?"

Mia thought for a moment. "Well, I have found something."

"Really? What?"

"I've found out who my father is."

After explaining the revelation of her find and her earlier confrontation with Fenella, Ross sat quietly, listening as she went over her childhood years; being banned from knowing her father's identity, bullied at school for bringing scandal and shame to the family and the nightmares, her terrifying mermaid nightmares, the ones where she swam away from the monster who would eat her because she had no one to protect her.

"You've been very brave, you know. This must have been hard on top of everything else." Ross was watching her intently. "But enough has festered over the years, it is what it is, the time has come to face it and accept it. No more secrets and lies, do things your way from now on, Mia. Your choices, your life." She looked down, he was holding her hands gently in his. "If Archie's death has given you anything, it's given you the power to set yourself free from the past. I believe that, Mia and deep down, I think you do too."

FINALE

By the time this most remarkable summer had melded into the mellowness of autumn, Ross Power the hotelier had become a formidable project manager, skilfully balancing work on Galty House and the Harbour Spa Hotel, fulfilling the dream, his way.

Mia was in charge of finance and budgets; with lists and inventories coming out of her ears and she absolutely loved it.

Galty House was being transformed into an elegant, period guesthouse and The Harbour Spa Hotel – once foundations had been reconstructed – into a scheme of exclusive luxury apartments.

Leela kept busy ensuring everyone was fed and watered, even managing to address her errant household duties given Pearl's audacious assistance but only when the youngster took a break from being the world's greatest Irish dancer or the second best mermaid on Ireland's sunny east coast.

Of course, Leela and Pearl had another project, something they worked on with spells and prayers and candles, calling on all the powers of the universe to make the two people they each loved most in the world realise they were destined to be together forever. Everyone commented they were perfect for each other, they were already a loving, hardworking family unit.

But Mia and Ross could not, or would not see it. Pearl and Leela were beginning to despair, it looked like the two they hoped would be one, were only ever going to remain friends.

Ross had agreed to help reinstate the false bookcase at the

entrance to the secret staircase. Chisel in hand, he was lifting out a section, while Mia checked for woodworm.

"Hey! Look what I've found," he called. She poked her head out. It was a flash of crimson, looked like silk. He held it up, a kimono, a red one, tired and tattered now, it would have been exquisitely glamorous once upon a time. She took it from him, wrapping it round herself.

"Do you recognise it?" he asked.

"No, but I think I'm familiar with it, somehow." She lifted the soft fabric to her cheek. "I think I'll keep it."

"No way, finders' keepers," he laughed. "Besides might have another girl to give it to."

"Go away," she grinned as he chased her up the stairs, grabbing at the silk. It fell from her shoulders as she turned, something brushed against her leg making her jump, losing her balance. He caught her as they tumbled down the stairs, landing flat out, nose to nose. She breathed him in.

Suddenly all was still, the world had stopped.

"Ross Power, are you scowling at me?"

His eyes were half-closed. "This, I'll have you know, is a smoulder."

"That's a smoulder?" She started to laugh.

Seriously, all this time, is that what he thought he was doing?

He moved in.

"It's supposed to be alluring."

She could almost taste him, sea, sweat, heat.

She swallowed.

"I'm allured," she whispered. "So, what're you going to do about it?"

"Up to you to make the first move," he said. She flashed him a look. "You're the lady of the house, the owner of The Seahorse Hotel."

"I see." She took a deep breath and wrapping the silk around his neck, pulled him even closer, she could feel his muscles through his shirt. Looking deep into his black, black eyes she thought she might melt. She moved a fraction of an inch, almost touching his lips with hers, he held back, she tried again.

"I'm making the first move," she murmured against his mouth. "You can try now if you like."

She felt his arms encircle her, crushing her against him, he took her head in his hands.

"About time," he said, a smile curling those longed-for lips, as she relaxed into his embrace, the exquisite softness of his mouth seeping warmth right through her as he kissed her, really kissed her, a long, dark, delicious kiss, that went on and on until every inch of her tingled.

Finally, hardly able to breathe she gazed into his eyes.

"How do I know you just don't want me for my inheritance? You could still build a golf course, you know."

She felt his body tense.

"Mia Flanagan, after I've made love to you, every single inch of you, you'll be completely assured of what I want you for."

"Whoa, cowboy, wait a minute." She tried a crooked smile. He gave her that look again.

"Mia." His voice was hoarse. "I think I've waited long enough, don't you?"

And before she could answer he pressed her mouth in another deep, delicious kiss and as he kissed her, she knew she had never felt so warm, so calm and so completely and utterly home in her entire life. Ross Power had his answer, she had waited long enough too.

The library door opened.

"Your stuff has arrived from England." Leela tried not to raise her eyebrows at them wrapped around each other at the foot of the stairs. "You'd better come and supervise, it's all over the drive."

The green-eyed cat slipped out between their legs.

Mia struggled to her feet. "What's that you have?" She pointed to the box Leela was holding.

"Just some old clothes," Leela replied truthfully, having recognised the box in among Mia's recently delivered possessions. She pulled the door closed quickly and hurried to take the turquoise oblong, containing the antique wedding dress to her lair.

Safe in the back kitchen, she poured the green-eyed cat a saucer of milk.

"Might be needing that sooner than we think," she said, smiling at the feline with her bright, white teeth and then tapping the box.

"Welcome home."

THE END

REFERENCES

Unpicking a finished novel to uncover where elements of the story originated is always fascinating and *That Summer at The Seahorse Hotel* is a prime example of this author's ability to absorb lots of influences and then discover she has no clue where at least half of them came from. However, of those I remember these following certainly deserve recognition and my grateful thanks.

I'm particularly grateful to Dr Michael Kennedy, the executive editor of the Royal Irish Academy's Documents on Irish Foreign Policy Series and his book *Guarding Neutral Ireland – the Coast Watching Service and Military Intelligence 1939 – 1945 –* (Published by Four Courts Press, Dublin) a fascinating and enlightening resource for this work.

Also to blog *Irish Central* for Daniel Rosehill's piece about Nazi plans to invade Ireland, stating: '*Dublin was earmarked by the Nazis as one of six regional administrative centres for Britain and Ireland right after Dunkirk when an Allied collapse seemed imminent. Had the occupation taken place, the Germans thought it crucial that their advancing units reach Ireland as soon as possible after the initial invasion.*'

I'm happy to acknowledge that brilliant 21st century resource, *Google* who informed me that SS officer General Karl Wolff claimed while testifying at the Nuremberg Trials that he had disobeyed an order from Hitler to kidnap the Pope and instead

sneaked into the Vatican to warn the Pontiff. Other allegations of a plot to kidnap Pius XII are based on a claimed 1972 document written by Wolff, maintaining Hitler summoned him on September 13, 1943 and stated: '*The Vatican is already a nest of spies and a centre of anti-National Socialist propaganda.*'
This then became one of Sister Agnes's favourite stories.

Leela's Tarot was guided by the brilliant tarot teacher and interpreter Josephine Ellershaw, whose book *Easy Tarot Handbook* (published by Llewellyn Worldwide) and beautiful gilded Tarot deck illustrated by Ciro Marchetti were not only simple and delightful but truly inspirational; thank you.

Judith B Herman's brilliant blog *Strange Movie Job Titles - Explained* for Mental Floss UK was also invaluable.

GLOSSARY OF TERMS & QUOTATIONS

PROLOGUE

Tiny Dancer by Elton John and Bernie Taupin, from the album *Madman Across the Water* (1971) DJM Records.

Polaroid SX-70 Land Camera (1972), combined camera and instant printed pictures.

SENDING SIGNALS

Boboli Gardens, a park in Florence, Italy.

'Our revels now are ended. These our actors, as I foretold you, were all spirits, and are melted into air, into thin air.'
Prospero, *The Tempest*, Act 4. Scene I by William Shakespeare.

STATION TO STATION

Station to Station, an album by David Bowie, released in 1976, RCA records.

The Three Musketeers: historical novel by Alexandre Dumas, published 1844.

'True is it that we have seen better days'
Duke Senior: *As You Like It*, Act 2 Scene 7 by William Shakespeare.

LAZARUS

Lazarus was the man Jesus brought back from the dead four days after his death.

Wexford People: Local weekly newspaper for county of Wexford.

The Quiet Man, (1952) classic Irish movie directed by John Ford, starring Maureen O'Hara and John Wayne.

Banshee, (in Irish legend) a female spirit, whose wailing warns of death.

The Last Supper – painting of the last supper of Jesus with his apostles by Leonardo da Vinci (circa 1495-96).

A LONG LUNCH

'The missions': the name for outposts where religious orders undertook work in education/health in places usually considered 'third world' countries.

HER MAIDEN VOYAGE

The Rolling Stones – legendary British rock band.

TOTAL RECALL

Sophie's Choice (1982): movie directed by Alan J. Pakula based on the novel of the same name by William Styron. Meryl Streep played Sophie, Kevin Kline her tempestuous lover, Nathan.

It was Kevin's feature film debut.

CASE CLOSED

Couturiere, robes de mariée et robes de bal, - Seamstress/Dressmaker, wedding dresses and ball gowns.

THE KISS OF JUDAS

Judas Iscariot one of the twelve disciples of Jesus Christ. He betrayed Jesus with a kiss.

'Let he who is without sin cast the first stone.'
Paraphrase of the Gospel according to St John 8:7.

The Hellfire Club was a society of aristocratic rakes in the 18th century. The ruins of the Irish club are in the Dublin mountains, where legend has it, a gambler dropped a card on the floor and when they bent to pick it up, the man opposite had a cloven hoof (the sign of the devil) instead of a foot. (So our dad, Harry, told us).

Far From the Madding Crowd; Thomas Hardy's fourth novel, first published in 1874.

MEMORY MAKING

Hogwarts, the fantastical gothic school in the *Harry Potter* novels created by J K Rowling.

WELL, WELL, WELL

'All the world's a stage'
As You Like It, Act II, Scene VII, William Shakespeare.

An Cumann Gaelach – The Irish Language Society.

ARCHIE'S FAVOURITE

Theobald Wolftone, a leading Irish revolutionary and one of the founding members of the United Irishmen, regarded as the father or Irish republicanism.

Pan's People, female dance group who featured on the BBC TV show Top of the Pops 1968-1976.

UNDRESSED REHEARSAL

From 'not a dry eye in the house' idiom meaning the performance was so moving everyone was in tears.

HONESTY IS THE BEST POLICY

'Is this a dagger which I see before me?'
Macbeth, Act II, Scene 1, William Shakespeare.
'A little sincerity is a dangerous thing, and a great deal of it is absolutely fatal'
Oscar Wilde, *The Critic as Artist* (Published 1891).

Jaws is a novel by American author/screenwriter Peter Benchley, published in 1974. Based on the novel, the movie by Steven Spielberg was released in 1975.

NEEDS MUST

Clarice Cliff (1899-1972) was an English ceramic artist, her work is collected, valued and admired all over the world.

Novena; a form of worship consisting of special prayers said on successive days.

The Rockefeller family made one of the world's largest fortunes. In 1965 Laurence S. Rockefeller built the most expensive hotel in the world, on an Hawaiian beach. It was named one of the 'three greatest hotels in the world' and it had a golf course.

TREASURE ISLAND

The Knights Templar was a medieval Catholic order who were among the most skilled fighting units of the Crusades.

THE LEGACY

Ave Maria: Musical interpretation of Latin prayer to the Virgin Mary original music composed by Johann Sebastian Bach improvised by Charles Gounod, with the popular version known today attributed to Franz Schubert.

Ride On written by Jimmy McCarthy and recorded by Christie Moore 1984.

FAMILY AFFAIRS

New Musical Express, British music magazine first published in 1949 and considered the 'oracle' for rock, alternative and indie music.

David Bowie (David Robert Jones – January 1947 – January 2016) English singer, songwriter, actor and artist. (Thanks for everything, main man).

THE UNDERSTUDY

Gaelic Coffee – classic Irish drink of fresh coffee, Irish whiskey and cream.

THE CITY THAT NEVER SLEEPS

Waldorf Astoria: legendary Manhattan hotel built in 1893 by millionaire developer William Waldorf Astor.

CHAMPIONS AWAIT

Dick Van Dyke: American actor, comedian, writer – his cockney accent in the movie Mary Poppins (1964) was, er interesting!

Fleadh Cheoil (na hÉireann) is Ireland's most important traditional music festival.

Wine maker Henri Jayer's Vosne-Romanée, Cros-Parantoux (2001) is worth around $8,300 for a single bottle.

BOARDROOM GAMES

The *Just William* books were written by the English author Richmal Crompton and first published in 1922.

STAIRWAY TO HEAVEN

WD40 is the trade name of a popular lubricant used to combat rust and corrosion.

SHOWTIME

Elvis Costello, born Declan Patrick MacManus: English musician, singer-songwriter. *Watching the Detectives*, top 20 hit 1977.

ALSO BY ADRIENNE VAUGHAN

The Hollow Heart

A Change of Heart

Secrets of the Heart

Fur Coat & No Knickers
– A collection of short stories and poems

All available from Amazon

PRAISE FOR ADRIENNE VAUGHAN

'This novel will tug at every heartstring, evoke every emotion and fill your thoughts.'
Sharon Booth

'Beautifully written, gripping yet with great warmth between the pages. I loved it.'
June Tate

'This is the best yet, great story, great characters, feel good ending – hope there's another novel from this wonderful author on its way soon!'
Alice Neville

'A brilliant storyteller, another five star read, prepare to be swept away!'
Lady Rochford

'Completely compelling from start to finish. Thoroughly enjoyed this novel, so many different depths and very unpredictable. Not your average romantic story, twists and turns throughout which leave you surprised until the very last page.'
Amazon Customer

Printed in Great
Britain
by Amazon